To

Rosie with all my love

and in affection for the people of Oman

ALSO BY J E HALL

Flashbacks (2016)

IStanbul (2017)

Harry's England (2017)

"If we ever forget that we're one nation under God,
then we will be one nation gone under."

Ronald Reagan, Former President, USA
Ecumenical Prayer Breakfast, Dallas, 23 August 1984

"An education is the basic pillar
of progress and development"

Qaboos, Sultan of Oman
Council of Oman, 31 October 2011

"Even if you drive me from your door,
I swear again that we will never be separated
because you are alive in my heart."

Rabi'a al-Basri, Sufi poet
Quote n° 3292, (CE717-801)

Main Characters

Raqiyah Nahari (Abdul Aziz's daughter)
Adam Taylor (British foreign correspondent)
Abdul Aziz Nahari (Raqiyah's father)
Walood Nahari (Abdul Aziz's brother)
Maryam Nahari (Abdul Aziz's wife)
Abdul and Mira Zayed (Abdul Aziz's sister and brother in law)
Aiesha al Nami (Abdul Aziz's intended bride)
Brian Merryweather (British Embassy official)
Mohammed Mansoor (Eastern Diplomatic Services partner)
Hassim Nahari (Raqiyah's brother)

Other Characters

Hamad bin Saif (Sultan)
Ted Heath (British Prime Minister)
Asad and Jasmine (Nahari family driver and maid)
Tim Landon and Spike Powell (British Army officers)
Omar Hassan (Maryam's father)
Khimji (Marriage lawyer)
Dr Michael Campbell (Nahari family's physician)
Abbadi Nahari (Raqiyah's brother)
Tariq Nahari (Raqiyah's brother)
Emma Styles (Raqiyah's governess)
Dilwar Patel (Security Forces Training Contractor)
Karen (British Embassy receptionist)
Rodney Smyth (British Embassy official)
Ali and Sunita (Muscat corner shop proprietors)
General Sadique bin Mahmut (Sultan Armed Forces)
Tanvi Nahari (Hassim's wife)
Walood, Dana and Faheem (Hassim and Tanvi's children)
Said and Jassim (Hassim's friends)
Hanif (Hassim's father in law)
Said Dibashi (Imamate Armed Forces major general)
Imams Azzan and Faisal (Imamate leadership candidates)

Oman

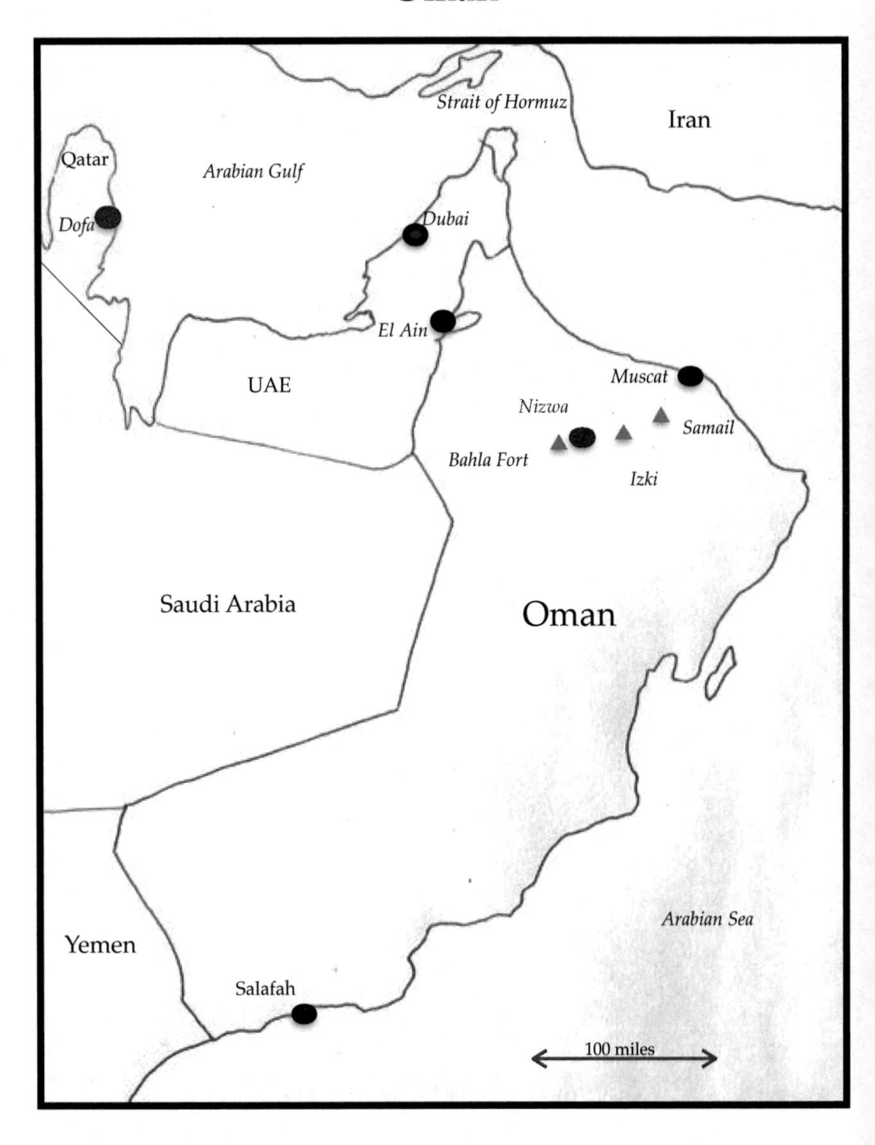

Strait of Hormuz
Iran
Qatar
Arabian Gulf
Dofa
Dubai
El Ain
UAE
Muscat
Nizwa
Samail
Bahla Fort
Izki
Saudi Arabia
Oman
Arabian Sea
Yemen
Salafah
100 miles

1

Dying changes life. It had come in the night, now it was early morning. The Oman Air Airbus A330 overnight flight from London landed smoothly at Muscat's modern International Airport. Another busy day was already under way.

Raqiyah and Adam peered out of the plane's oval windows to glimpse the Omani capital, seeing a flat, spread out, low rise cityscape rushing past below. Buildings were hemmed in by dry desert earth against a distant backdrop of mountains. Where the rising sun caught anything it looked as if it was in flames. A slight shudder and they'd landed followed by a roar from the jet engines as they quickly slowed to a crawl.

A searing blast of hot Gulf air hit them as the aircraft doors opened to disgorge a full load of bleary-eyed passengers. Even so, Raqiyah's spirits lifted as the two moved down the steps. Then they were inside the airport bus waiting to take them the short distance to Arrivals. They observed fluorescent-jacketed airport personnel, those having to go outside, doing their best to avoid the already sapping heat of the Arabian Gulf. Noticeably, people walked in the shadows, darting into air-conditioned buildings or vehicles as quickly as they could. Raqiyah smiled, this was home.

It was August, a full month since the two had been awarded their degrees in Arab and Islamic Studies at Exeter University. Student life was already slipping into the memory bank as other realities beckoned.

They'd delayed leaving England as Adam had a job interview in London for a position as a junior foreign correspondent covering the Middle East. His commitment and reputation had swung it for him. Everyone seemed to know who Adam Taylor was – the young man whose spontaneous act of self preservation nearly three years earlier had led to the death of a British Prime Minister. Whether it was his celebrity or his notoriety that clinched the job Adam couldn't tell, he was just on cloud nine for having landed it.

There was further delay in leaving England as he'd had to send off paperwork – evidence of the journalism module he'd completed and copies of the pieces he'd had published during his final year as a student. Then there had been an interminable wait to get a visa. During all this time they'd been staying at Adam's parents' home in Muswell Hill, north London, until finally, cases packed, Adam's Father had dropped them at a grey and rainy Heathrow the previous afternoon. August in England was in his view predictably cool and wet. In the fierce burst of heat Adam mused on the the thought, wondering when next he'd see rain.

Raqiyah's father, Abdul Aziz, had promised to be at Muscat airport to collect them. He'd supported her throughout her education and she was so excited at seeing him and enjoying a family reunion. These days her father used a driver rather than get behind the wheel himself, a sure sign he was one of Oman's elite, or as he insisted "one of the nearly elite".

Once through passport control and cases reclaimed from the baggage hall, Adam and Raqiyah were already both perspiring heavily as they edged slowly forward, shuffling outside with the crowds, out into the glaringly bright exit from the Arrivals area.

Then they saw him, the tall figure of Abdul Aziz, in his long white robes and turban, waving cheerfully as he too had also spotted them. He waited as they made their way across to him dragging two cases each. Warm greetings exchanged, they moved as he did, slowly in the heat, the remaining short distance to his latest white Mercedes. At the last minute, his driver stepped out of the vehicle to open the doors and assist, loading their luggage into the car's cavernous boot.

Father and daughter sat in the back. Meantime, Adam made the classic mistake of making to climb into the driver's side before remembering driving was on the right hand side in Oman. He quickly made good his error, waving his arm in a gesture of self-deprecation, to re-enter the cool sanctuary of the luxury car's interior, dropping into the front passenger seat where he was expected to sit.

'So good to have you home, my daughter,' began Abdul Aziz, a warm open smile upon his face. 'Your Mama will be so pleased to see you and have you back. And Adam, we are delighted to welcome you as part of our household again. You look just the same as last summer. Congratulations on your new job. So very exciting. You must tell me more about it. When do you start?'

'Yes, well, that's the thing. The job seems to be up to me. In theory I'm available right now to chase any story down 24/7. I might be asking you for some leads! The world press wants war and threats of war stories – and while it waits, readers need amusing with captivating human tales of extremism, or sex and suffering. Oman might just give an exotic Arabian gloss to what I end up writing.'

'That sounds cynical to me,' said Abdul Aziz thoughtfully. 'I'm not sure we can deliver what your looking for. This is the safest place to be, Oman, nothing ever happens here, not a terrorist incident, not a public scandal. Beside it's the height of summer – too hot for anyone to get up to anything!' He laughed.

'It sounds both a bit cynical and a bit dangerous to me,' added Raqiyah, speaking up.

'That's how it is – otherwise no-one's interested,' said Adam. 'I feel sure something of interest will come up. I just have to wait and keep my eyes open, you'll see.'

Adam's mind returned to his first visit to Oman the previous summer. It had been a shock. Raqiyah had tried to prepare him, to soften the blow, but even so he hadn't expected what had happened.

Whereas in London, his parents had totally accepted the two were an item, Oman had been like stepping back into the dark ages. It hadn't been possible so much for the two to hold hands, let alone be allowed to be in the same space without a chaperone. Raqiyah had tried to explain, best she could, that their relationship had to be their secret, but Adam had never really accepted this until he'd come to Oman and seen for himself just how conservative a place it really was. This time he knew better what to expect. He didn't exactly welcome it, but understood it, and had prepared himself for it. Thankfully Abdul Aziz was a generously minded man, and had accepted Adam and like most Omanis was quite prepared not to say anything, and turn a blind eye, if Adam's inadvertent indiscretions crossed an unseen culturally determined boundary line. Adam liked the man.

After a couple of roundabouts, their car picked up speed, riding swiftly and comfortably down the immaculate new dual carriageway toward Muscat.

New buildings were being constructed everywhere they looked, cranes piercing the blue sky. It was little more than a thirty minutes drive to the Nahari family house – the only place Raqiyah had known to call home. This place held all her memories from the earliest squabbles with her brothers to her departure to study abroad in England on an Omani Sultanate Scholarship, three years ago.

They were slowing. Traffic was building all the time, then, rather unexpectedly, they came to an abrupt stop. When they hadn't moved in two or three minutes and everyone was looking up ahead, Raqiyah spoke up.

'Is it always like this these days Daddy?'

'No. Something must have happened. In the past it was goats on the dusty roads, now it's road traffic accidents – people here drive so badly. I expect it'll clear in a few minutes.'

But it didn't and it wasn't ambulances or roadside assistance vehicles that drove past, but military vehicles, and more than one truck full of soldiers. Something about it sent a shiver up Adam's spine.

'Something's happened that's more than a road traffic incident – we've got army manoeuvres – and I sense tension in the air. It isn't normal,' added Abdul Aziz, his smile now gone. At just that moment his mobile rang and he took the call. He listened intently, his face a picture of concern. The call was brief and as soon as it was over, Raqiyah was the first to speak.

'Something's up isn't it. I can tell.'

'The Sultan's dead. Adam, I think you've just got something to write to your paper about.'

'Might need some help from you there. I've hardly put my foot on Omani soil,' he replied, wondering where to make a start. 'How does my knowledge of Oman, as a long-time centre of peace and stability in the region, square with the feeling of menace and unease I'm getting seeing these hard-faced soldiers on the streets?'

'The Sultan's been ill for a while, for years – we've all kind of expected this to happen at some point – ah, it's just been announced on the TV. Apparently there are soldiers on the move everywhere – control points going up at every road junction. There'll be a curfew tonight they say – all precautionary no doubt. We should be home soon, it's less than a mile. We should be OK.'

At the makeshift road block, every driver and passenger was being scrutinised by soldiers before being allowed to continue on their way. Sometimes the military could be seen making phone calls, holding things up still further. Eventually, nearly an hour later, and with much relief all round, they were able to pull into the small, gated estate, where the Nahari family's smart looking home was situated.

'As they arrived, both Abdul Aziz and Adam had been making mobile calls. Then in the same instance, both stopped speaking and looked at each other.

'My line's dead, your's too?' said a serious Abdul Aziz as Adam nodded in agreement, staring down at his phone with a long face as if it were a dead thing.

'Let's get inside. And double lock the gate,' he shouted as an instruction before his driver was out of earshot. The front door was half open. They were about to go in with their cases.

In unison they turned as one, as shouts and noises reached them from the street. Soldiers began pouring into the front yard, leaving their hapless driver standing to one side holding the gate open to let them in.

'Abdul Aziz. Are you Abdul Aziz?' yelled the man in charge. Abdul Aziz turned in his doorway and nodded.

'You're under house arrest. No-one is to come in or go out of this house without my say so. My soldiers have orders to shoot any miscreants. Inside, all of you,' he ordered crisply, waving his arm toward the door to underline the point.

Before a reply could be made the officer was striding out of the yard. He passed through the gate and disappeared from sight. Most of the soldiers followed.

However, two soldiers remained. They brandished their weapons without a word, dropped the butts of their weapons in synchrony to the ground and took up station, one each side of the front door. They looked dispassionately on the party with suitcases. It was enough to ensure everyone scurried quickly inside.

The family group pulled the door firmly shut behind them. It was as if the door separated two worlds, one of cool and calm inside, one of heat and menace out.

To Adam and Raqiyah, it felt like something had gone strangely awry with the homely, warm welcome they had been so long anticipating. The past half hour had been profoundly unsettling.

2

It was early morning, Thursday 23 July 1970. There was silence in the world of men – three bachelors were contemplating the day before them. Each of them hoped the coming hours would turn out well, but was this too much to expect?

*****

For the young man, Abdul Aziz Nahari, love was in the searingly hot, Omani, air. A summer day of sweet happiness was promised. Aged twenty two, tall, elegant, accomplished, and most of all eligible – he was getting married. He stood perfectly still, mindful of both the shimmering heat and his impending situation. Introspective by nature, he tried to analyse his feelings, concluding that everything was subsumed by his growing apprehension and anxiety.

His brow furrowed. He'd had weeks to come to terms with it, but he was still struggling with the very idea of taking a wife, and being in charge of a family of his own.

At this precise moment he was trying to get a handle on what was about to happen to him and find some inner peace. His efforts weren't proving to be successful. It was one thing to recognise his feelings but quite another to change them.

In his head and his heart, he asked himself time and again, 'Am I ready?' A pause, before he muttered for the umpteenth time, 'Inshallah' – God willing. He held the word like a mantra under his breath. But was he obediently ready and waiting to do Allah's will? – Well, maybe he wasn't ready so much, for his parents had sprung this on him sooner than he'd anticipated; but waiting, yes, every minute seemed to hang as heavy as the scorching summer air. It was custom and expected. Now, where was that brother of his? He leaned forward to peer into the distant glare – nothing but glaring light.

His apprehensive thoughts turned to his bride to be, about whom he knew next to nothing. He'd been told she was younger than him by six years. With no Omani education system for girls, unlike himself, she almost certainly couldn't read or write. He despaired at what they could talk about, what else except the home, and her family's goats?

She had almost certainly not travelled beyond her immediate locality and spent most of her life securely enclosed within the walls of her family home. Yes, her family owned much land to the West of Nizwa, and their huge herd of goats was a measure of their status and wealth – most would say that counted for a lot. Their herds ranged over the foothills and wadis of northern Oman's Western Hajar mountains, and his family had emphasised the family's good credentials time and again.

His father had described the Al Namis as a good respectable family, known through generations in Nizwa for their piety and support of their community. Their religious Ibadi Muslim credentials were equally impeccable. His father was convinced it was as near perfection an arrangement as any family could wish for.

The dowry, marriage contract and all other details for today had been most amicably agreed and now all Abdul Aziz had to do was to turn up for the ceremony. It was all stitched up as tight as an unripe, date palm pod.

But who truly was his intended bride? What was she like, how did she look, and most importantly how compatible were they? – to these and all his other questions he had absolutely no way of knowing and it frightened him.

His glanced again into the bright morning glare knowing his older brother Walood would arrive in his own good time to take him in the family's old Land Rover to his new bride's family home. He shuffled his feet in the dust. Still no sight or sound of him.

The ancient city of Nizwa where they were headed was half a day's drive away. It would be there, in his new bride's family home the simple marriage ceremony would take place that afternoon. His parents had arranged everything.

He knew they would have been thorough, dutiful about such things, and the marriage contract drawn up strictly between the two families just as custom dictated. The finality and legality of it all had been settled without him and certainly without his bride having any say. Waves of fear and uncertainty kept washing over him, or was it the humidity as well as the heat making him sweat so? He kicked at the ground again and watched the dust rise.

All he had to do, he reminded himself, was go along with what had been fixed by his family and submit himself to Allah. Believing himself to be a faithful Muslim, a good man, he tried to tell himself all would be well, but he couldn't be certain. Everyone's role was laid down for these occasions, it was too late for change or doubt.

Though the idea of taking charge, being responsible for a bride he didn't know was overwhelming him, he pictured everyone else being happy for them both, ready to support the new couple – well wouldn't they?

The image of a man drowning in quicksand came to mind and he took a deep breath to reassure himself he was still alive. Trust Walood to be late today of all days, where was that brother of his? He noticed how dusty his sandals had become.

*****

In London, July 1970 had been cooler and wetter than usual. The new Prime Minister, Ted Heath, pushed the crisp white linen sheets and blankets away from under his chin. Sitting up in bed on the top floor of 10 Downing Street, he looked down at his new striped pyjamas, a 54th birthday present from a party admirer, given him just two weeks ago. Lifting his heavy eyelids, his blue eyes gazed out of the bedroom window as his thoughts turned to the day ahead.

He'd been only a month in office since his surprise victory over Harold Wilson in the June General Election, and his first thoughts were, what to tell his Cabinet, meeting downstairs later that morning. He'd got a demanding set of ministers, all nipping at his heels, impatient to see Conservative policy enacted as if there was no tomorrow. Picturing them in his mind's eye, he immediately thought of Reg Maudling, his Home Secretary, Keith Joseph at Health, and the blessed Margaret Thatcher in Education. 'Humph!' he caught himself saying aloud, as he shrugged his shoulders and tried to make himself more comfortable – a formidable lot!

Foreign affairs appealed to him more than domestic policy. The far away agenda always looked easier to deal with than the troublesome economic and labour issues nearer home. Needing to find comfort, his mind turned to Britain and her role overseas. Contrary to what some people thought, ideas of Empire had not yet entirely disappeared into the history books. Britain, he believed, still had and needed to have an influence in the world.

His eye fell on the daily papers he'd been reading the previous night lying scattered on the floor beside his bed and he dropped one arm down from the bed to reach down and retrieve them. He glanced at them for inspiration.

'Oil and the sheiks. Humph!' The country needed to forget the set back at Suez, and move on. Surely Britain still had friends in the Gulf? If not, she needed some, he surmised.

Then he had an idea. A phrase came across his stream of consciousness along the lines of, 'encouraging and assisting local leaders in the Gulf to shoulder their responsibilities.' He played it over again in his mind and decided he liked anything that was in the guise of being benignly helpful, using the power in relationship to gain policy outcomes. Yes, the sentence seemed to fit the bill perfectly.

Not trusting himself to remember its precise wording, he pushed his silvery, lank hair back from his forehead in one slick movement, and grabbed the silver fountain pen and paper he kept beside him. The words were duly jotted down – Cabinet Meeting sorted.

Then, pleased with himself, and momentarily forgetting what he was doing, he clipped the pen into his striped pyjama jacket pocket. He pushed the newspapers back on the floor and rolled back his bedclothes. He'd taken control, was still in charge, and now ready to start his day.

*****

A third man, Hamad bin Saif, the only son of the ruling Sultan of Oman was, in July 1970, rather to many people's surprise, being held as a political prisoner in his own land.

Educated in England, then employed in local government, he finally graduated in the British Army whilst at Sandhurst. Hamad had returned home to Oman after ten years away, only to be locked up by his unpredictable father, the Sultan, and placed under house arrest. This intolerable situation had gone on for an insufferable four long years – far too long for an ambitious and determined young man!

In order to cope with the powerlessness he felt, he tried to put his military training to good effect and live a self-disciplined life. Today, the end of another week, he'd begun to feel for the first time a renewed sense of hopefulness. His British friend who had, much to his surprise, recently come to advise and support him, had enabled him to set in place some escape plans and these were now running.

Hamad had to use all his military discipline to retain personal control of the welling anxiety he was feeling. Twenty-nine years old, he made himself stand proudly erect and then stroked his short, dark, smart beard with as much dignity as he could muster, hoping the day's events he had in mind wouldn't lead to his early exile or even more likely – his death. Why, he asked himself, had his Father allowed his military friend to visit, was there a trap?

He told himself he had nothing to lose. Not being married, having no brothers, he had to become a self-made man in a hostile world. The uncertainty of his position was unbearable – it was so hard waiting for news and the intense humid heat of the day didn't help. He tried to guess which one of the many possibilities the day offered would actually materialise.

He loved his country, his people and his British friends, but just how, he wondered, would the day work out? Powerless, he longed for power. Could he trust those mounting his coup d'etat? Failure was not an option he could bear thinking about. Treason in Muscat and Oman could only result in one thing. The stakes couldn't be any higher.

*****

Life is about love, politics and death. On Thursday 23 July 1970 three men pensively waited for the day's events to unfold. They were men standing alone, carrying the weight of their apprehension, political fights and fears.

In the silence of waiting, one thing was certain, the day was one of promise; these men hoped it would deliver much. It could though, as easily bring intense disappointment as success, costly failure in the face of high expectations, even death.

3

Being under house arrest, Abdul Aziz recalled a distant though familiar feeling – that of being a state suspect. It had happened once before in his life. Like a rusty, serrated edge catching on his white robe, something nasty was now holding him back, restraining him, leaving a mark, a tear running through.

He was a prisoner in his own home. There were five of them beside himself – his wife Maryam, his daughter Raqiyah, his house guest Adam Taylor, and two resident domestic employees – his Bangladeshi driver Asad, and their Filipino house help, Jasmine. Adam was a complication.

Sharply painful memories of his previous incarceration flooded back. Back in 1994 the threat of a coup had led the Sultan to arrest and detain many including himself. Of the hundreds of people rounded up in the security trawl, he'd eventually ended up being one of the luckier ones, however not before the terrorising trauma of the experience had taken its toll.

Though free since then, to official eyes there had remained a non-specific, tainting cloud of uncertainty hanging over him personally. In the short term this had resulted in an unsought for change in career direction and in the long term kept him at a distance, as a man always on the fringes of Oman's privileged elite. It was as if he carried around an invisible bad odour everywhere he went. Every now and then key people avoided him.

Back then in 1994 he was thought to be too close to Israel and the US. After release, he'd been forced to report to the local police station for a while, his diplomatic career then having to be rebuilt in a new direction, outside the ministry. It was a time he'd prefer to forget and thought he had largely succeeded. Today, a couple of decades on, the feeling of unease and foreboding at being enclosed in his own home was an unwelcome reminder of these things long past. For him to be caught up a second time, when he was already seen as suspect by some, well, maybe he wouldn't be so lucky again.

Abdul Aziz's anxiety led him to retreat to his home study, his den, where his immediate concern was to double check his most recent work contacts and contracts just to ensure he'd not left himself inadvertently exposed to criticism or worse. It was his extensive list of overseas contacts and many diplomatic forays outside the country that especially worried him. Things until now had felt very relaxed, and perhaps he'd been too relaxed? His recent delight at seeing Raqiyah again and bringing her back home had in a moment been turned on its head. He now felt fearful, and preoccupied with his own troubles. He began to feel terrified at what might happen next.

His thoughts turned to Adam. Adam's very presence in his home felt awkward. Would they think he was once again too close to the West? What was it Adam was doing? He knew Adam had just secured a job, working as a foreign correspondent, but for which company? One pro-West? He didn't know.

That kind of work was often the disguise of spies, wasn't it? Surely not? Not Adam, but then hadn't Adam had contact with secret services in the past? And if he wasn't a spy, they might surely see him as one and then what was to become of the family harbouring him? He tried tell himself he was being needlessly anxious, his mind running away with things, but however much he tried, Abdul Aziz found his growing sense of apprehension just wouldn't go away.

The internet was down and stayed down. His mobile unusable, he could only access what he'd downloaded earlier on his laptop. He hurriedly examined his most recent emails, both sent and received. He opened files that he wasn't sure about, and being cautious deleted some.

After five minutes he realised he was working in a flat panic and missing things. He told himself to calm down, that he really had nothing to fear, and that in a short while, possibly by the morning, everything would return to normal. Conscious he was neglecting his family, who must also be worried, he knew he should join them, but couldn't yet do so – he was rooted to his desk.

Abdul Aziz's diplomatic skills got him thinking forensically – he racked his mind to think what possible incriminating information might be held against him? Then he realised he didn't know, he'd no idea. His lack of knowledge as to his present circumstances and as to what was happening just outside his Muscat front door, let alone what was taking place in the Omani corridors of power down the road, sent a deep cold chill through him. It was the lack of knowledge, the uncertainty, the powerlessness – taken together it knocked all the self-confidence out of him. He needed to know more. Then he had an idea and went and opened his study door.

'Maryam, Maryam. Come. I need you to do something for me,' he called, with as much calm in his voice as he could muster. He heard his wife in the kitchen, holding a muffled conversation with the others. Then her soft footsteps approaching – she was coming to him. She had a pale face and right now dark, unfathomable eyes.

'Maryam, I need to talk to the men, the soldiers outside. You understand me. Come with me, ask them if they would like a little refreshment – don't take "no" for an answer. Then when it's prepared, let me take it to them. We're all in the dark and we need to know what's happening. I can't think of any other way.'

'Yes, OK, I'll do that right now. I want to know if our sons and their families are safe – we've heard nothing,' Maryam replied, her concern mirroring his. He could see his own fear reflected in the circles round her eyes.

'I'm sure they'll be fine. They'll be locked down in their homes like us. Perhaps if you go onto the flat roof area you'll be able to see over to Hassim's house. You might just be able to see if there's any sign of life – see if their car's outside, you know. But drinks…'

'Yes, yes – right. I'll see to the lemonade first.'

She went over to the front door and after adjusting her veil, opened it cautiously, Abdul Aziz keeping out of sight. The heat outside was as oppressive as ever and she anticipated it would make her offer of iced lemonade to the two soldiers irresistible. And so it proved. She spoke. They softened, smiled, and nodded in appreciation. They had mother's too. Then, closing the front door as she returned inside, she went straight to the kitchen. Their Filipino maid, Jasmine, was told what to do and five minutes later, when all was ready, the jug prepared, Maryam called across to Abdul Aziz.

'Drinks are ready.'

As Maryam approached the front door, carrying the tray, Abdul Aziz noticed she was clutching her prayer beads tightly in her right hand – always the first sign of stress. The cold ice cubes clinked and tinkled against the sides of the glass jug.

Maryam handed him the tray and opened the door to let him outside. Tray in hand, the iced lemonade and glasses carefully balanced, Abdul Aziz looked up to see the two soldiers standing some paces off, leaning against his wall, calmly talking to each other. They immediately fell silent when they heard him approaching.

Abdul Aziz took control, his hand taking the jug and holding it still while he eyed the men. With no commanding officer nearby they appeared more relaxed than earlier and he took this as a good sign.

'Salaam Alekum. You guys had a long day?' Abdul Aziz offered in a friendly voice. He noticed the shorter soldier had a military radio.

'Salaam, yes, but that's fine,' answered the shorter one. 'We're following orders, doing what has to be done,' he said almost apologetically, his taller colleague offering a disapproving scowl.

'Well, let me know if you need anything we can provide from the house, to make your duty here more agreeable,' Abdul Aziz said, in an offhand remark. He waited as they drank thirstily.

Wanting to give the soldiers the impression he was about to leave them to it, he then added, 'We'll be having lamb and rice later. If you'd like some… I'm sure there'll be more than enough. When I did my time in the army, like we all have to, I was always glad of good home cooking.'

The remark seemed to further break the ice, the two soldiers glancing at each other and then offering him something of a smile.

Abdul Aziz then spent the next few minutes reminiscing on his own army days. Like everyone else in Oman, he'd done his stint in the forces and the experience, though long ago, now stood him in good stead.

The camaraderie banter got the two guards even more at ease and soon the three were laughing and jesting together. In the pauses, Abdul Aziz noticed how still the afternoon was. With all the traffic prohibited, the neighbourhood normally busy, was unnaturally quiet. We could be in any time in history, he reflected, all Oman's recent progress and semblance of modernity presently suspended by the interruption of this silent Arabian day – broken only by their hushed conversation in the shade of the white wall surrounding his home.

'I hate it when things get unsettled within the country,' he volunteered, 'so much easier when we're all united defending ourselves against foreign forces. I remember back in '94 when my daughter was born, I think it was Israel up to her tricks then,' he said, laughing conspiratorially, and shrugging his shoulders as if to say, what else would they be doing?

'Well, that was all before my time,' returned the shorter, wiry man, offering his glass for the jug's remaining lemonade. 'This is different, but then whose to say? What do we know? Reckon one of the old Sultan's many relatives has found friends somewhere to give him a leg up – that's why we've be called up, to keep the peace while he handles the succession. But then, there's other talk that another of the Sultan's relatives is listening to Iranian or is it Saudi friends? No-one seems too sure what will happen next – the fear is, the planned for smooth succession could go belly up. Might even see one of our foreign neighbours come marching in.'

'So our dear Sultan is dead and a relative's stepped in? Can't say I'm surprised. Poor guy has had cancer for years. We've all been wondering what would happen. Everyone's been expecting the new man taking charge to be his cousin, Sayyid Zawani? That so? I've been abroad, out of touch – has Sayyid taken the reins? I've just got back from a business trip, come back to all this, bit of a shock…' his voice trailed. Abdul Aziz could see the skinny soldier was the talkative type, but his companion was now rocking from foot to foot indicating his discomfort at the direction of the developing conversation.

'Yes, Sayyid Zawani's been named, but there's a counter-claim,' continued the guy.

'From one of his other cousins?…' enquired Abdul Aziz.

'Think enough's been said,' interrupted the taller more wary soldier, stepping in and using his elbow to non-too-discretely nudge his verbose colleague.

'We've got our duty to do. Thank you for the lemonade. Now I'd be grateful if you'd return inside, Sir. Just following orders, you'll understand, being an old soldier, Sir.'

The man looked round just in case someone else was listening, watching and with a face, fearful he might be caught out as if he had been fraternising with the enemy, moved in close and started pushing Abdul Aziz away from him, in the direction of the front door. Gripping the drinks tray firmly, Abdul Aziz took the hint, nodded, and quickly made a step toward it.

He just had time to make one final parting comment. 'That's alright. I'll leave you two to it. But just knock the door if you need anything,' he added trying to keep on friendly terms, making light of the physicality. The tall soldier removed his hand.

Abdul Aziz placed one hand to the door handle, the other holding and balancing the drinks tray. He could not resist one more final, parting comment before going in for the night. Thinking from their accents the two soldiers were from the Nizwa area, he paused, standing in the threshold, and pursued a different line.

'Once Ibadi Islam held authority in this land, Oh that it would be so again,' he ventured, appealing to the strongly held Omani tradition of Nizwa and the Interior, with its proud tradition of standing full square against Shia Iran and Sunni Saudi.

'Yes indeed,' replied the shorter man, 'but with new voices raised from outside it will be hard to hold the ring, to keep the tradition of a middle path of toleration. Everyone needs to remember to do what is expected of them. Take my advice and keep the curfew.'

At that the taller soldier stepped forward again and ensured with an arm to Abdul Aziz's elbow and one foot inside the house, that the conversation was well and truly over as he levered him back inside, pulling the door firmly shut after him before returning to his post.

Abdul Aziz took a deep breath. In a few minutes he had learned much, and what he'd heard deeply troubled him. The army clearly feared a collapse into chaos following the Sultan's long anticipated demise. The lock down wouldn't have been ordered unless it was a likely possibility. If he was right and this was what was actually happening, then no-one would be safe.

He was drawn from his thoughts by a movement nearby. He was somewhat startled to find Adam had been standing just inside the door. He'd been eavesdropping. Abdul Aziz felt a mixture of both concern and admiration simultaneously arise within him.

'I… I didn't expect you to be there,' he ventured.

'Sorry, forgive me. I just wanted to know what was going on. I suppose my investigative journalist instincts are already tuning in. Doesn't sound good does it?' Adam surmised.

'You understood what was said I presume?' Abdul Aziz asked. He was warming towards Adam.

'Yes, and I know a man with diplomatic skills when I meet one,' Adam added smiling, the smile then quickly disappearing from his face.

'I never got to ask the question I really wanted to and Maryam won't forgive me for it. Give me a moment. I need to pop into the kitchen. I'll be right back,' and Abdul Aziz was gone, pulling the kitchen door firmly shut after him.

Adam heard their voices. He knew Maryam was asking after the safety of the rest of her family. Raqiyah's three brothers all lived nearby in Muscat, but Abdul Aziz had gained no news. He hadn't had chance to ask the question, but would Maryam accept that?

As good as his word, once the volume of the muffled conversation taking place in the kitchen had subsided, Abdul Aziz was back in the entrance hall. He looked straight at Adam, the look on his face saying he wanted a serious conversation. A wave of the arm and Adam was ushered into his study. As the two men moved the short distance across the hallway, Adam caught sight in the corner of his eye of Raqiyah making for the kitchen. She gave him a half smile and then the fleeting moment of connection had gone.

'Adam, you've arrived at a time all of us in Oman hoped would never come. Our adored Sultan has died from his illness and we've now entered the period of uncertainty we've all dreaded.'

'It must be nearly half a century since he came to power. There must have been plans laid for this eventuality?' said Adam.

'Yes. For years we've been fed snippets of information in the newspapers – The Oman Observer and The Times of Oman. More recently there have been various new regulations passing power from the Prime Minister's Office to the Deputy PM's Office from time to time. Though nothing was ever said directly about succession whilst the Sultan was still alive, it was all rather implied that there would be a planned for transition of power into the hands of Sayyid Zawani, the Sultan's younger cousin, his Deputy. A year ago the Sultan began passing some responsibilities over to him. There were signs given as to what was intended, but nothing clearer than hints.'

'And no-one really pushed the question "What next?"' Adam said, 'or "please clarify", because here in Oman your press is under the Sultan's control – true?'

'Yes. I'm afraid, scratch the surface Adam and you'll soon find we're not like your Western democracies. The Sultan is our ruler by divine right, rather like one of your early English Kings – he's been much loved and as I said earlier adored. But you're right, he's also an absolute ruler – what he says, goes. There's no truck with opposition voices or actions. And what goes into the press is under his say so.'

'But looking at this as an outsider, the Sultan's a despot, albeit you think of him… sorry, you thought of him, as a benevolent one?'

'Yes, and maybe that doesn't help us have the robust succession plans you'd have back in the UK as one of your Prime Minister's politely steps aside for the next. It's not like that here, you understand. It's all… well… less democratic… rather more, rule by might.'

'From your conversation with our soldier friends outside, I gather that the actual situation remains somewhat unclear. Succession might not yet be the done deal everyone thought?'

'Soldiers, like all soldiers, they know nothing except the orders they've been given and what's doing the rounds in the rumour mill. We'll need to see what comes to light in the morning – it seems all communication's been shut down in the interests of security. My guess is that we'll all be kept in the dark for the next three days whilst the Sultan Family Council deliberate, and if they can't agree on a successor name, that's when they start looking inside the sealed envelopes the Sultan left behind. These contain the letters in which he states his personal choice of successor – maybe you're right, the more I think about it, the more I think this could play out badly – but don't tell the family I said that!' Abdul Aziz added quietly.

'As we've got a bit of time, would you mind filling me in on background. I need to better understand all things Omani if I'm to write and send accurate reports of what is happening. Will that be alright?'

'Yes, but first, let's all have a meal, then you and I can retreat back here and I'll tell you what I can. Will you be comfortable enough in our guest room, Adam? Same as last summer? Oh, and feel free to use my study when I'm not around – I insist you feel at home here.'

'Thanks, I really appreciate that – yes, I could do with something to eat,' said Adam, thinking he'd have been even more comfortable if Raqyiah had been able to join him, but that was an arrangement in Oman about which there was absolutely no discussion. Raqiyah was to stay firmly in the women's side of the house, their past life in Exeter a secret between them.

Adam reflected on the cultural shock he'd experienced on his first visit to the country a year ago – the discovery he'd made as to Oman's strict Victorian-style morality and the reality of enforced separation from Raqiyah didn't come any more easily the second time around. Having a political succession to report on might prove a welcome distraction from his personal and domestic issues, he mused.

Abdul Aziz led the way as they walked across the hallway toward the kitchen in silence. Adam could hear no sounds coming from outside. All was ominously and eerily quiet. He didn't like it and it was making him feel on edge. He thought Abdul Aziz looked remarkably calm considering he'd just been told they were under house arrest. For his own part, he was already feeling vulnerable, and having to work hard to keep his anxiety levels manageable.

4

The waiting was turning out much longer than he'd anticipated. The young Abdul Aziz Nahari told himself once more, he was prepared for his wedding day, though as he'd done the very same thing several times already in as many minutes, he knew that in reality he wasn't ready at all!

He reflected on what lay ahead whilst standing just outside his white-washed Omani family home – a typical Arabic looking flat-roofed building with a matching wall surrounding it. Though still early morning, the sun's burning glare already made it hard to look down the dusty road. He shuffled backwards to make the most of what little shade the porch offered him.

He cut a fine figure, trying to look confident, hiding his fears. Wearing his finest and newest, white dishdasha, what his British colleague at the office dismissively described as a nightgown, he considered himself to be a proud Ibadi man, in his flowing full-length robe. He was fortunate in being tall, had found it advantageous in life and considered himself handsome without being vain.

Looking back, he felt his life so far had been kind to him. Coming from a good Muscat family, his parents had believed in the importance of giving him a broad education and with only three schools in the country he had had a place with the best. He'd done well.

This had been followed by a short time in the army and a Western university education in London. Considered one of the country's educated elite, he'd quietly and privately held on to the Ibadi Islamic tradition passed down to him. He'd found it wasn't easy for him to live openly as a practising Muslim in the West, though privately he'd always unquestionably considered himself to be one. Now, as his wedding approached, he tried to convince himself his faith would help him through the day ahead – it would not.

Hanging from the neck of his white dishdasha was the distinctive short, cord-like tassel, serving to waft its impregnated sandalwood smoke incense beneath his nose. His sister Mira had steamed and pressed the garment before leaving with the rest of his family for Nizwa the previous day.

On his head he wore an expensive white-coloured turban, meticulously hand-embroidered with hundreds of small stars and flowers. It was the most extravagant thing he'd ever worn, fabricated by a master tailor his family knew in the Muscat Souk. Made specially for him from the softest, finest, purest wool, it perfectly matched the sash tied neatly around his slim waist. He liked the image.

Abdul Aziz shuffled anxiously thinking of the day ahead, tucking the ends of the shahtoosh headwear inside, against his luxuriant dark hair, until it was tight, firmly fastened against his skull as local custom required.

Beginning to feel more confident about the day, he reminded himself he was an Omani man of education, someone from the capital – Muscat, from a successful family and embarking on a career in the diplomatic service, provided he made the right friends and greased the right palms. His bride's family should know what kind of an excellent deal they'd be getting. Adjusting his turban yet again, he told himself a Muscat man had to be like his turban – proud, smart, tidy and held tightly together.

Hearing a vehicle, he turned his head, and in the dust of the graded road he recognised the sound of the family's beaten up Land Rover approaching at speed. He could see his beaming older brother, Walood, leaning across to wind down the passenger window. Returning from Nizwa where he had already driven the previous day to drop the rest of the family off, he was now back for his final passenger – the groom himself. Abdul Aziz stepped the few paces from the house to the road.

'Salaam alekum, Walood. Don't make so much dust, I need to look my best for this.' He chided his brother as the vehicle squeaked to a grinding halt, the vehicle's khaki canvas roof, whose matching canvas sides were rolled and supported by a metal fretwork frame. The canvas offered the promise of some protection from the heat of the day.

'Jump in my brother, all the others are safely delivered and getting everything ready. Mira is so excited. I've never seen our sister like it. I left her helping prepare the food. Only the best goats still need to be chosen and killed. It'll be such a feast. Inshallah we shall be there before Dhuhr – midday prayers,' he said. 'C'mon, jump in. Let's go! No time to waste!'

There were hardly any vehicles in the country, and the family had acquired theirs from a British businessman working for BP Oil who had had to make a sudden return to the UK. Battered and at least ten years old, the vehicle was perfect for the terrain. Their route lay on a poor, graded road to Nizwa that wound up from the coast through the high Western Hajars mountain range.

Walood put his foot down. In the whole of Oman, a country the size of France, there were still only ten miles of asphalt surface; dirt desert trails and graded roads like this were the norm. Abdul Aziz couldn't understand why proper roads weren't being laid as in neighbouring Saudi and the Emirates, concluding the Sultan down at Salafah just hadn't got his act together. Come the day, thought Abdul Aziz, holding on tightly as Walood pressed the Land Rover on.

'Take it easy, give me time to enjoy my last ride as a bachelor,' Abdul Aziz cried, gripping the ledge below the Land Rover's tilted open front windscreen.

'We need the breeze,' he yelled, 'besides, we want to get you off our hands! It's one hundred and twenty miles, mainly uphill and whilst this old heap is still running we need to keep going. If you behave yourself I might stop for coffee and dates at Samail. I know a place.' There was always brotherly banter. Abdul Aziz envied Walood's carefree character. He seemed able to enjoy life more, not a care in the world.

'Sounds good to me.'

Abdul Aziz glanced back at their now tiny family home clouded and increasingly hidden in the swirling yellow brown dust from the vehicle's tyres. He could visualise his past disappearing just as swiftly as the view of his house seemed to. As he once again contemplated the coming weeks, beginning his married life living with his new wife in her Nizwa family home, he anticipated an issue – he would soon have to leave her there to return to his pressing work in Muscat, seeing her only at weekends.

In time he imagined they would have a home in the capital, but all that was as yet unplanned. The future seemed as impenetrable as trying to see the way in a desert sandstorm – just about impossible!

Never having seen her, he was again full of apprehension at the prospect of meeting his bride. He told himself he had to trust his family in this and trust Allah. They'd told him her name was Aiesha, but nothing more. His fate was settled by other hands and there was nothing he could do about it. It comforted him little to think she might well be as uncertain of things as himself.

As the bumps in the dusty road jolted him and the building heat in the day's sun burned through his dishdasha, his brother took upon himself the task of chatting endlessly, knowing it was the older brother's responsibility to keep Abdul Aziz's spirits up for his big day. Abdul Aziz could not criticise his devotion to the task, but it did little to change his despondent mood. He put on a smile and tried to appear cheerful.

On the outskirts of Samail his brother called out above the engine's roar, 'Hey look there, up ahead. Looks like some kind of road block – it'll be your new in-laws, decided against you!' he jested, playfully punching Abdul Aziz on the arm.

In fact they quickly saw it was some kind of army unit out on patrol. One of the squad had seen them approaching and had stepped into the road to wave them down. He was European looking, wearing a military uniform, a makeshift turban of sorts on his head, not local. His weapon, a rifle, until now pointing down to the ground was slowly raised toward them and firmly gripped. Unlike Omani soldiers, the man looked hard, a no-nonsense professional and he meant business.

Once they'd stopped, with the engine turned off at the soldier's request, the man glanced quickly in the back of their Land Rover. He said nothing. Now it was clear he was British, probably one of the many so called advisers the Sultan had allowed in to help his own troops. Only a month earlier the National Democratic Front revolutionaries had been defeated in Nizwa and nearby Izki and things were still unsettled, no-one sure whether the so-called final victory over insurrectionists in the area really meant the complete end of conflict in the region. Inland, away from Muscat, the interior was tense and edgy which was one reason why the planned wedding had been put back twice in as many months.

Abdul Aziz interrupted the officer's thoughts and in perfect English boldly asked, 'What's happening? Is there a problem up ahead?'

Surprise written on his face at the English words, the soldier looked him straight in the eye and replied. 'Routine stop and search, Sir. Please step outside the vehicle for a moment.'

Both Walood and Abdul Aziz obliged and stood out in the sun whilst the officer signalled to two of the waiting Omani troops to do his bidding and look over the Land Rover. It took no more than a glimpse and the opening of a couple of lockers before they stepped back and nodded their satisfaction to the British CO, who was still not ready to let them be on their way.

'Where are you from?' he quizzed.

'Muscat, where we live,' said Walood.

'And where are you headed?'

'Nizwa.'

'Then what brings you here to the mountains, away from the safety of the coast?'

'It's my wedding day,' said Abdul Aziz thinking the explanation would help.

'Wondered why you looked so miserable,' smiled the soldier, waving them back into the vehicle with a now cheerful, 'on your way.'

Needing no second bidding, they climbed in and moved off. Abdul Aziz felt the soldier had read his heart.

'Did you have any of that yesterday,' asked Abdul Aziz, his brother gazing over the steering wheel at the road ahead.

'Yes, just the same, we were nearer Nizwa, different faces. Though the communist led insurgency came to an end here in the north of Oman just a month ago, I hear things are still very tense. Many of those who took part in June's attack on Nizwa fled to the mountains and villages, taking their weapons with them and are yet to come back. People are still being routinely rounded up and questioned. I think those guys were with the Sultan's Muscat Infantry. It's all part of the mopping up operation. Personally, I don't think it's all over yet, there'll be guerrilla attacks next, just you wait. All those fighters who fled up into the Hajar mountains won't just disappear. No worries where we're going, we're safe enough here, this main road is regularly patrolled.'

'It's supposed to be settled enough for a wedding though, isn't it? So everyone, including Sultan Said tells us.'

'Of course. Doubt if we'll see anymore military activity now. Relax, you look like your going to a funeral not a wedding!' he jested.

'As I understood it, I thought the only rebels still fighting were those in the far south, in Dhofar,' asked Abdul Aziz. 'I thought it's all but over with round here.'

Walood nodded in agreement.

'Yep, this country's in a mess, one war finishing, another one still going. What a time for me to get married!' added Abdul Aziz.

'There's never a right time to get married, brother. Forget all that, today's not for politics, it's for family,' Walood reminded him.

'Isn't that the place where politics is the trickiest of all!' replied Abdul Aziz, giving his older brother his first smile of the day.

Walood's teeth flashed white as he beamed back. At last his brother seemed to be relaxing, he thought, but in reality he couldn't see behind the mask.

5

Under leaden skies, Ted Heath climbed into the back of his chauffeur driven, immaculately polished, dark blue ministerial car, a Rover P5. He was heading off for Parliamentary business scheduled for the end of the morning.

As he shuffled down into the leather seat, he reflected on his Downing Street Cabinet meeting. Yes, indeed, it had gone pretty well all things considered. Ministers must have felt, by the end of it, reassured that Britain's vestiges of imperial power and political hold on the Arabian Gulf were still substantially in place.

Inevitably economic realities meant there would be budgetary cuts so far as Britain's future operations in the Gulf were concerned, but as he'd told them, local rulers in the region would just have to respond by stepping up to the mark. That had gone without saying and there had been little comment in return, though he knew they would have to be local leaders the UK could trust, men with whom he could do business.

He'd been able to provide his Cabinet colleagues with some reassuring examples of neat diplomatic footwork – the Shah of Iran had been persuaded to drop his claim to Bahrain in return for acceptance of Iran's right to occupy islands in the Persian Gulf and there were sound plans for the creation of a future United Arab Emirates, but would Bahrain and Qatar be part of it? Yes, he'd said. In sum the picture he'd painted for them made it all look pretty good out there – plain sailing! There was just one big nagging doubt. What, he wondered, was currently going on in Oman?

As an often overlooked Middle Eastern country, second in size only to Saudi Arabia and as big as France, it had oil, was strategically placed guarding the vital tanker route – the Straits of Hormuz and faced toward the Indian sub-continent, with which England had had a long love affair.

Oman had been a consistent friend of Britain for years, but would it stay that way? The country, if one could call the gathered tribes of the region that, was unstable, backward and it's political leadership fragile, with internal wars in both the north and south. Yet earlier he'd had promising, if unexpected news.

Soon after the Cabinet's discussion on the Gulf had finished, he'd been about to walk out of his Downing Street front door when Sir Alec Douglas-Home, his thin-lipped Foreign Secretary, had beckoned him over for a private word and whispered in his ear, 'watch this space – watch for breaking news from Oman.' It was a tease of a comment, the trace of a smirk on Alec's face as he'd said it.

Ted Heath had immediately wondered what Alec had meant and had turned to request of him that he be told as a matter of urgency of any developments in Oman, but by then Alec had gone. Being PM meant he daren't risk not knowing what was happening on his watch. Maybe something promising was afoot that would make things that bit better for Britain in the Gulf – Alec's interruption sounded more positive than negative – his instinct told him so.

As the car turned right out of Downing Street and into Whitehall, he asked himself again – what on earth was Alec up to this time? There, he thought, was a man with deep political ambition if ever there was one. Another Brutus to watch.

Opening his Prime Ministerial document case, he reached for the next set of briefing papers, the one's titled, *Prime Minister's Questions,* quickly setting aside the troubles of distant Oman for the pressing domestic issues on which he would be questioned shortly.

6

Being confined to a palace under house arrest might not be considered too great an imposition for some people. However, for Hamad bin Saif, the Sultan of Oman's only son, enough was enough. His situation was intolerable and he could see the signs – it was making him bitter and angry.

Even his visitors were strictly controlled, it felt like his world was being shut down. Maybe it was a security oversight somewhere, but when one day he was unexpectedly given the opportunity to meet up with the British Army Brigadier Tim Landon, his old friend from military training at Sandhurst days his eyes lit up in expectation, and his mind turned to matters of liberation.

With Tim's advice and encouragement, he took the opportunity to turn a, 'hello, how are you doing?' conversation into a 'come on my old army chum, let's explore ways to turn my fortunes round and get me the hell out of here.'

After warm handshakes and several coffees in the Arab style, the two began talking in earnest. It's easy to reconnect with old friends and very soon the idea of a coup d'etat was the primary topic of conversation.

Deep in conversation and keeping their voices low, they immediately saw eye to eye and quickly came up with a workable plan. It's tricky to conceive of something you've never envisaged before and the risks looked huge, if not insurmountable. But, Hamad knew how the Sultan's palace worked and Tim had the sharp military mind to draw up a campaign with a realistic chance of success. Both knew it would take loyal men, a good dose of courage and lady luck on their side.

Success depended on getting a small armed force past palace guards, who at a number of points could stop them in their tracks and sound the alarm. The one thing Hamad hadn't got was any real military muscle to call on and Tim felt diplomatically constrained and had next to no military resources to offer of his own. Their single strategic aim if they were to succeed, was to gain rapid access to the Sultan, make him their prisoner, obtain his resignation and elicit a transfer of power to Hamad. Calls for wider loyalty and key support would then have to be quickly put in place.

It was Hamad, unable to tolerate his house arrest any longer, who was desperate to act. Initially, he pushed Landon hard to get him to help. To his immense relief Landon turned out to be a more than willing accomplice. Maybe he was an adrenaline junkie? Both knew the stakes they were playing – high treason carried a high price.

Fearful of interruption or discovery, they went over their plans carefully in whispers one final time, both deciding the huge risks were still worth the taking. Once just friends, they'd now become co-conspirators in a dangerous plot to overthrow Hamad's father, the Sultan.

In his heart of hearts, Hamad desperately wanted a peaceful coup. He dreaded having patricide staining his legacy, though any squeamishness at what lay ahead was suppressed in the methodical professionalism, in the planning and in his personal determination to do what was required.

Hamad knew that only with Landon's friendship, his military advice and significant, covert British help could the plans put in place for the coup d'etat stand a real chance of success.

So it was but a short while later, whilst the action began to roll, Hamad himself had to stay put in one of the palace houses. He was kept company by a loyal friend as he waited news from Langdon. Only then, would he emerge – to power, exclusion or death.

Conducted under a blazing sun, as coup's went, this one turned out to be simplicity itself – involving a minimum number of people and a few strategic placed, very affordable bribes, to encourage key guards to turn a blind eye. Today, the plan to put aside Hamad's father began as a slow army lorry with twelve tense men in it finally set out for the Sultan's palace at Salafah – the date, 23 July 1970. What could go wrong?

At that precise moment Ted Heath was planning his own campaign, a tricky Cabinet meeting later that morning in London. Unknown to him, but known to Sir Alec Douglas-Home, Hamad's coup d'etat was already under way in the early Omani afternoon.

Hamad himself waited anxiously, his hands wet with sweat. He knew little of what was happening. A British Army officer, Major Spike Powell, was included in the small armed force of a dozen Omanis now entering the Sultan's palace. Guard by guard, sentry box by sentry box, they steadily negotiated their way to the palace's interior and their target. Finally, confidence building, they confronted the Sultan in person in the palace's north tower.

In no uncertain terms the startled Sultan was told to relinquish his office. The man, unpredictable at the best of times, naturally felt affronted at the turn of events and drew his pistol from under his robe. Waving it carelessly as one not used to handling such things, the weapon was discharged and it marked the real moment he fell from power.

The Sultan had accidentally shot himself in the foot. With that, his ineffective rule characteristically came to a rather messy, inglorious, painful and ignominious end. He yelled out for medical help.

The British, ever ready to help in the cause of Empire and influence, were prepared to fly the deposed Sultan with his injured foot right out of Oman, as an involuntary tourist to where else, but a friendly power – the UK. He really couldn't argue otherwise.

Within days he was airlifted out, by military plane initially, to RAF Brize Norton in Oxfordshire. His wound tended, he was later made as comfortable as an exiled loser can be, occupying a suite in the Dorchester Hotel, London, where he would spend the rest of his days.

In the luxury of his hotel suite, the former Sultan forever rued the day he'd let Landon into the palace to see his son, later declaring his greatest regret in life was, 'not having Landon shot.'

But it was all way too late, his son Hamad, with the help of the conniving British, who could barely contain their absolute delight, had ousted him and there was no going back. In terms of coup d'etats, this one, with the only casualty having a shot foot, was as the army mess room banter rowdily acknowledged, by common consent, as good as it got!

By late afternoon on the 23 July 1970, when Hamad himself was told the excellent news, he could hardly believe his good fortune. He would become Sultan! He was free!

The transition to power paperwork was hurriedly prepared, all to hand and ready to be signed off within the coming three days, and his accession to the Sultanate gained in the easiest possible fashion.

A determined and capable man, Hamad then moved quickly to further secure his position – there was still much to be done, but the most hazardous part was over. He still had a hearts and minds job to do both at home and abroad and he had no doubt of the many challenges that lay ahead.

As the latest Sultan in a dynasty, one of a family who had ruled the locality since 1749, Sultan Hamad bin Saif, as he now liked to be known, could finally allow himself to begin to feel safe.

Now was a most opportune time to come to power. In recent years, oil wealth had already begun to flow in Oman and he could use the petrodollars increasingly to his advantage, to win friends and modernise and secure his country's future.

However, in the coming days he would need to turn his early attention to the serious matter of the Dhofar rebellion to the south and mopping up the remaining insurgents in the areas around Nizwa and the Hajar mountains to the north. Then hopefully he could begin to both unite and secure his country as a modern functioning state, a place which had hitherto been little more than a gathering of disparate and independent tribes.

For his amazing loyalty, Hamad decided he would keep his friend Tim Landon, later called the 'White Sultan of Oman', at his side and he would see he was generously rewarded. Soon Landon would receive a £1 million pound cheque in his Christmas card as a thank you! He would also amass a £200 million personal fortune by the time he finally left Oman for a quieter life in Hampshire, England.

But that was in the future, and for now Landon had a number of urgent good news intelligence messages to send to London.

The direct line call to Sir Alec Douglas-Home at the Foreign Office had clearly made the man's day. Landon could imagine he heard champagne corks popping even as he spoke!

Political masters more than satisfied for now, he then turned his mind to the profitable business of arranging arms contracts, his particular specialist area of interest. Of course the primary reason for doing this was to ensure his friend Sultan Hamad had the militarily wherewithal to stay in power, but the promising sound of cash rolling into his personal coffers was a huge distraction. He thought he would allow himself a double whisky before making the first of many business calls.

In a life of otherwise barely significant military exercises, Landon knew he had just landed himself a once in a hundred lifetimes success – and with it, the most enviable military reputation and unlimited spoils! In Hamad he also had a friend for life.

7

Nizwa's Al Nami family were getting ready for a wedding.

Aiesha, at sixteen, was now considered old enough to be married off and the family were delighted that a suitable arrangement had been made with a successful Ibadi family from the capital, Muscat. Though tradition tended to favour marriage contracts with local families and cousins from the same tribe, this time they had been persuaded it stood to the family's advantage to bring Abdul Aziz Nahari into their own family and so strengthen their links with the capital in these uncertain times.

On Wednesday 22 July 1970, the temperature was unusually hot, even by Omani standards. The Nahari family had begun to arrive for the climax of the celebrations. Many local extras had been drafted in to help with the festive preparations.

Having seen everything was in hand, Aiesha's father thought it would be a useful distraction to take Aiesha and her remaining younger sister at home out to the goat herd. He liked to check them daily and then they needed to choose one of the best to bring in to slaughter ready for the wedding feast. He thought one goat sacrificed would be enough.

The three took a stout cane each together with a coiled length of rope and began the half hour walk. In the heat, they walked slowly out across the dry, scrubby, gravelly terrain toward where they knew some of the goats would be grazing. Where the deep wadis cut into the arid mountains there was enough ground water to feed some sparse vegetation. It was there where they'd most likely be found. Even so, nothing besides the occasional, hard and thorny, low spiky shrubs grew there – and goats and camels it seemed, were the only creatures able to thrive on such a brutal diet. It was an unforgiving landscape. Aiesha was accustomed to it. It was her world. She'd never travelled.

Aiesha's mind turned again to her wedding day. In a family of eight, she had seen her older sisters married off one by one and now it was her turn. It was what was expected. Would she be happy? Would Abdul Aziz be a good and kind husband, gentle and maybe loving? Would she be able to please him? She was lost in her thoughts and in anticipation of what lay ahead.

After a further hour's walking, they were taking one of the many tracks away from the city now lying in a dusty haze far behind them. They made their way largely in silence, only the two girls exchanging quiet conversation as they slowly walked in the shimmering heat, their heads and faces partially hidden by their veils. Their father was scanning the approaching wadi for any sign of his goats. It was exceptionally hot and even their father's gentle pace led them to complain to him.

His response was to raise his arm, and using his wooden cane pointed out a large herd of dun coloured goats but a short way off. Different shades and sizes, some with horns others without. Thankfully, the goats were grazing quietly on the lower slopes of the mountainside. They would not need to climb. He wanted to get the job done and get back rather than spend too long out under the burning sun, which was climbing ever higher in a cobalt blue clear sky.

In a well accustomed drill, the three began to silently separate and spread out making a line, the girls using their sticks in their outstretched hands, the many yards of uncoiled rope held horizontally between them – it made them a human fence.

Moving off to their right, their father had taken the steeper side, Aiesha's sister in the centre of the arc, Aiesha herself keeping to the path on the left flank. The goats seemed unconcerned. They stealthily and steadily approached, all conversation ended.

All their attention was focussed on the task ahead. It was too hot for any endless chasing and they wanted to go straight in and take their chosen animal. Their father had his own rope with a loop for the task.

Another five minutes and they were close. Fortunately, today, the goats were easy going, familiar with their herders and it being too hot for unnecessary movement, appeared quite happy to continue grazing peacefully. A brown, dusty bird flew up from the ground and made off in alarm, but the goats were unbothered. Still the three moved forward, ever closer. Aiesha's father had got his rope ready. It would be easy.

Aiesha looked and saw the goat her father had set his eyes on – tall, handsome, dark brown with a tuft of white hair on top of its horned head. It looked down at them, turning his head from one to the other and waited. Did it know the future, she wondered?

The grey gravel-like rough-edged stones of the path under Aiesha's feet gave way to an orange sandy stretch. She didn't need to think where to place her feet and she could now look the goat in the eye. It stared back unblinking, gazing down on her, as if superior, even knowingly.

She never saw the flash or heard the blast that took her away. A mine laid by retreating insurgents on the path to the mountains had claimed another victim. Rock and metal shrapnel ripped away her flesh and cut life from her body, leaving her bloodied remains shrouded in her torn clothing scattered across the sand. Her sister, deafened and herself pierced by flying shards, fell sideways to the ground. The girl's father blinded by the brightness of the blast was thrown down, unable to keep his feet on the slope a little way off.

Their father, his brown eyes opened unnaturally wide at the bright flash, was rolling sideways. Over and over he went, dust, sky, dust – turning and bumping on the ground until he came to a stop. He lifted his ringing head and turned in the direction of his daughters.

He realised what had happened and lifted his hands to his head in pain and despair. Cautiously he moved toward his girls, pulling to raise one, whilst trying not to look at the lifeless mangled form of the other, ignoring the goats now running every which way and disappearing into the safety of the mountains.

8

Over coffee and dates at Samail, Abdul Aziz and Walood joked and relaxed in the shade, their journey half done. The air smelled stale, a competing mix of sweat and spices.

When those in the Samail Souk discovered a marriage was happening, they were brought Arabian desserts too. The inviting aroma of strong sweet coffee scented the air. As custom dictated, the small handleless coffee mugs were refilled time and again. Finally, Abdul Aziz flipped his upside down, signalling he'd had enough. The two needed to press on.

The watching men smiled and their small talk was brought to a close, Abdul Aziz also having shared what news he thought might be of interest from Muscat. Passing on news by word of mouth was a time honoured tradition. Time was pressing and the men in the souk, for whom time seemed not to be an issue, had to be left to put the world to rights without them. The two walked back to their vehicle and continued on their way.

By midday they were on the outskirts of Nizwa itself and the sun burned and created a stillness, a hardness in the air, as it glowered directly overhead. It was nearly time for prayers and Walood pointed out a mosque a little way off. He thought they would go there, its white minaret clearly visible beside the dusty road up ahead. A minute later and they pulled over and parked up.

Before getting out of the vehicle, Walood tugged at Abdul Aziz's sleeve to gain his attention.

'Before we go to mosque, I just wanted to give you something, a small gift to celebrate! Here brother, from me!'

He handed him a blue handkerchief pulled from his pocket. Abdul Aziz carefully unfolded it. Inside was an ancient piece of Omani silverware, a rectangular shape, a few inches long, dangling silver Hamza decorations below. It was a fine piece, and costly – a prayer box. Inside he spied a piece of old parchment. He'd have spent a lot on this thought Abdul Aziz. He was moved. Time was tight, Walood knew this, and was urging them both to swiftly get inside the mosque, his way of avoiding any embarrassing exchange of thanks. Abdul Aziz pushed the small precious item carefully in his pocket.

Local men were already strolling to gather and perform Wadu – their ablutions, their ritual washing, before entering the main worship hall for prayers. Abdul Aziz's hand felt Walood's gift deep inside his dishdasha pocket, then once in the prayer hall, he hardly heard a word the Imam chanted for thinking about what lay ahead. He was once again a man lost in an inner world of questions and uncertainties and found no spiritual comfort.

Twenty minutes later they were back on the street. He noticed a small group of men eyeing them from a little way off. They continued to look their way and Adbul Aziz nudged Walood with his elbow to draw his attention to them. They continued walking the few remaining paces to the Land Rover. The men were still gazing in their direction.

'More well wishers I think,' Walood opined.

'I don't think so,' replied Abdul Aziz, having noticed the seriousness in their intent.

'Not more trouble, another search and going over to come?' speculated Walood.

The men got nearer, one of them, the oldest in the group, was seemingly being pushed to the front to act as an unwilling spokesperson.

'Salaam alekum… Is one of you Abdul Aziz?' the guy asked.

'That's me,' said Abdul Aziz, growing increasingly apprehensive, then alarmed and much puzzled at hearing his name.

'Then there's sad news to tell.' The man hesitated, taking in a deep breath. Abdul Aziz immediately knew something bad must had occurred.

'Your betrothed, Aiesha Al Nami, died earlier today. They were out choosing a goat for your feast when she stepped on a land mine. Allah was merciful… It was quick. I am sorry my friend. It is the will of Allah,' he added raising his hands in the air. 'My… our condolences. I don't know what else to say.' A stunned silence followed.

'What? What happened?' asked Abdul Aziz not believing what he was hearing.

'She died instantly, where she took the blast. It was on a goat track up into the mountains. It's happened before, on the paths to the mountains. Her sister was slightly injured and has been taken to hospital. I think the funeral for Aiesha will be later this afternoon, before sunset. You need to go to the house,' he said, pointing in the direction they were headed.

'Sorry, I don't know any more. The local fighters planted mines as they retreated to the mountains, to stop the Sultan's troops chasing them. Nobody's done anything about clearing them. Many goats have died too.'

His friends nudged him at the inappropriateness of his remark and he fell quiet. He waved his arms as if to say it was only to be expected something bad would happen.

Then the guys parted as the two brothers, presently lost for words, got back into their vehicle and moved off slowly. They both knew they had to get to the house, but neither really wanted to make the journey.

'I hope this isn't true,' said Walood, trying, as he always did, to ease things. 'It could be someone else.'

'No, I think it's as they say,' Abdul Aziz replied quietly. He reached for the bottle of water in the car door and took a great gulp before passing it to his brother. Their remaining journey passed mainly in silence.

'There's the house,' whispered Walood, 'and there's father… I don't like it.'

They pulled up in front of the low building. There was no-one else in sight and they could tell from his serious expression, he had sad news to share. The Land Rover slowly drew to a halt and the two stepped out.

Before he opened his mouth, Walood raised his hands to stop him and said, 'we know. We were told outside the mosque.' Abdul Aziz could see the redness in the father's eyes. It was not something he'd seen before and it unnerved him.

'Son, this has turned into a day of sorrow. What was to have been a wedding is now a burial. Happiness has turned to dust. I don't know what to say to you. Your mother is trying her best to console Mira – your little sister is quite distraught.'

I'm OK Father, really I am,' and he was, for he never knew his intended. Aeisha had been but a name and young woman of his imagination, not yet a person to him. He could not share how unready he'd felt to be married or the guilty relief he was now feeling that there was no longer a wedding to face. In the privacy of his own turmoil, he had to masquerade his feelings to show the expected grief and he resolved to do what was expected of him over the coming hours.

His father, taking his son's loss for words as genuine sadness, put his arm over his shoulder and began to lead him toward the house and the waiting Al Nami family. It was a meeting Abdul Aziz didn't want to have. He steeled himself. Family and friends were already assembling and preparing to process to the nearby burial ground before late afternoon prayers. Muslim tradition thankfully dealt with the practicalities very quickly, but the sudden and devastating emotional loss of the bereaved would take much longer to be processed.

To the mourners, Abdul Aziz found himself an object of untouchable curiosity and through the events of the afternoon, he was allowed to be a solitary figure, often found standing alone on the edge of the group, supposedly cocooned in his own grief, whilst others took the lead in the funeral proceedings.

From time to time, curious glances were shot in his direction, the still burning sun beating down on the sixty or seventy people hastily gathered round him. He realised he represented a Janus character. Those stealing glances in his direction, saw at one moment what might have been – a happy bridegroom, but in the next, what he was now – a cursed man, whose life had been turned on its head, a man looking death in the face. A man who didn't belong.

The cruelty of Aiesha's death by a land mine meant that she had been denied the chance to say the shahada prayer declaring her faith in Allah alone. It made the occasion all the more bitter.

The gathering of her broken body and scattered remains meant the shroud hastily wrapped round her looked all wrong and disfigured. As prayers were said and assurances given of eternal life, Abdul Aziz for the first time in his life began to really wonder whether he could go along with what he was being told.

There was no escaping the pain in the tears, the wails and the cries of the Al Nami family and friends. It tore into everyone present, him too. He knew it would always stay with him, as if he had also been blasted by the mine, a piece of its shrapnel piercing and lodging in his heart for him to carry with him everywhere.

Did he still believe after what had happened? He felt shocked he was actually thinking this way. He realised he was asking a heretical question and initially he explained this to himself by putting it down to the traumatic circumstances in which he now found himself.

But the thoughts wouldn't go away and he found in the privacy of his own mind that he was arguing with Allah – God and wanting some explanation for the tragedy before his eyes. What kind of god was responsible for the loss of such an innocent life and for inflicting such grief? 'Where, Oh Allah do you live?' His very soul was screaming for an answer – but none came.

He knew in that moment something fundamental had shifted in him and life would never be the same again. Death had not only claimed a young woman's life, that of his betrothed, but he also knew part of himself, that he had hitherto been so assured about, had also died with her – his religious conviction as a devout Muslim.

He steeled himself to the three days of mourning ahead. The world now seemed to him a foreign land he was beginning to gaze upon with fresh eyes.

When his time came to leave, he determined he would return to Muscat, push ideas of marriage far away and make something of himself as a prosperous, free-thinking man.

9

Adam and Abdul Aziz retreated to the study after the afternoon meal. By now it was around sunset. At no point in his visit the previous summer had Adam been invited in this room; he felt a sense of inclusion, being allowed into his host's private world.

The room had, to Adam's eye, the unmistakeable marks of an educated man – it was unusual for an Arabic home. There was the collection of small Western paintings he'd mounted on the walls, images of people enjoying themselves – one in a Western city, possibly Paris; another a painting of people on a beach, modern, blurred, the subjects nonetheless distinctly under-dressed. Against one wall was a book case with a range of novels betraying a widely read and eclectic taste – mainly English texts, some political, some biographical, and amongst them many classics. This was Abdul Aziz's private zone, his sanctuary, the space providing Adam with further insight to the man.

Clutching a glass of mint tea each, the two men in the study, a generation between them, sat facing one another across the corner of the luxury, marquetry finished, wood top desk.

Both were acutely aware of the two soldiers' nearby presence. The soldiers on duty outside had yet to take up the earlier offer of lamb and rice. They hadn't knocked or made other sounds, from the other side of the front door. Abdul Aziz decided to leave them undisturbed for now. He looked up at Adam.

'Well, where do you want to start?' he asked.

'Suppose I'm left wondering what it's like living in an undemocratic country at a time like this. Tell me, do the Sultan's family operate like our British royal family, the hereditary line passing on, down through the generations?'

'They do. The late Sultan's dynasty have held power for more than a dozen generations, but that wouldn't be giving you a true picture. The last Sultan's father proved to be mentally unfit, paranoid, incompetently ruling a divided country – or believing he was. Everyone knew things were run badly from the top.'

'You get what you're given,' said Adam.

'He was eventually deposed in a British supported coup back in 1970, a coup led by his son, the Sultan who's just died. Ted Heath was the British PM at the time at the time of the coup. Today though, there's no son and heir as such, so the Ruling Family Council, made up from some of his eighty-odd strong family, need to come up with a successor and announce a name. If my memory serves me right, I think they've three days to do it. Everyone will be waiting pensively for a declaration, except unlike in England we don't have democracy and we don't have Returning Officers!'

'So it's open season – there's actually no clear heir? Then what happens, white smoke rises from a palace chimney, to say they've decided on someone, like a new Pope at the Vatican?'

'No theatrical dramatics – just a public announcement.'

'Do you think they'll agree? And if they do, do you think all the likely contenders will accept their verdict?'

'I don't know. This is new territory for us,' Abdul Aziz offered hesitatingly. 'I'm pretty well clued up on knowing how politics works here since I've been circulating with diplomats all my life in my work, but right now, I just don't know what's going to happen – uncharted territory.'

He paused before continuing, 'Now look, in Oman we have a tradition, what is said and done in the home stays private. If you're happy with that principle I'll share my thoughts with you further.'

'Yes, fine, of course. I won't attribute anything to you anyway,' Adam assured him. 'Do continue.'

'Well, as you overheard earlier, I think there could be a problem with finding a name. There are at least three people who think they are in the frame for the top position. All are son's of the late Sultan's uncle. For each of the three cousins the result matters hugely. All have massive business interests here in Oman and stand to consolidate their hold and personal wealth if they can take power. This is all public domain information – please understand I'm not telling you something you can't read elsewhere. You can draw down more from the net once we're connected again – check it out for yourself.'

'These were the names you mentioned to the soldiers outside, right – yes?'

'Yes. I was trying to find out what was happening and one of them rather implied we're actually in a stand off between rival cousins. I hesitate to say this but my instinct is this could be very bad for Oman.'

'How's that?' said Adam, busily scribbling notes as he listened.

'Oman's in a key strategic position in the Arabian Gulf. Over 20% of the world's oil passes through the Gulf of Hormuz, and neighbouring Iran and Saudi Arabia have greedy eyes and barely veiled foreign policy aspirations to take control of our waters. The two see themselves as rivals – you know, Shia Iran versus Sunni Saudi. Other smaller neighbours will line up behind these two, Qatar with Iran, the Emirates with Saudi, and so on and so forth. If what's been happening in Yemen is anything to go by our neighbours are not ones for sticking by Western ideas of human rights or just war.'

'I see. There's big stakes to play for here. Other countries see a chance, if not to seize some real estate, to curry favour and win influence.'

'Whilst Oman remains strong and secure, it can play the role of a little Switzerland in these parts. Against the odds it has done so for many years. As a small, yet surprisingly stable and powerful neutral figure holding the ring, it has so far kept hostile predators at bay. The world looks on as Iranian-Saudi aggression is currently being played out in a nasty civil war just over Oman's southern border in Yemen. If Oman is seen as weak and divided, the chickens will come home to roost here. We'll be corn in the feeding trough.'

'Yes, I see that.'

'And that's not all. Don't for one minute think Britain and the US have any less interest in what happens here. When your Prince Charles came over, he brought his head of MI6 friend along with him. I was there – now what do you think they talked about? It certainly wasn't the market price of fresh dates!'

'No – maybe succession handling, maybe shared intelligence, maybe British support at a covert level, who knows?' mused Adam.

'All those things and more! While the Royal Council are busy having a three day chin wag to sort out the name of a successor, in my view the reality is, it's the security services and head of the armed forces that will currently be running this country – just look outside our door! Believe what your eyes tell you – the army are running Oman!'

'Do you really think the West is as involved as you say?'

'Absolutely. I've spent a lifetime doing the diplomatic rounds here and overseas. Why do you think Britain has ensured our deep water naval port of Dqum remains capable of taking the largest of Britain's and the US's aircraft carriers? Look here, the West doesn't have many, if any, other friendly state port options for naval moorings – Oman's Dqum is of huge strategic importance to Britain. More to the point, the last Sultan was joined to Britain at the hip – he's as much a product of the UK as the Land Rover. The UK might no longer be the colonial power it was, but in these parts it still thinks and acts the part.'

'Is there any other hat in the ring? I mean other than the three cousins. Where else might a bid for power come from?'

'A young pretender perhaps. Many people would like to see a dynamic young Sultan in his 30s. That's a distinct possibility, just look at our neighbours, Qatar and Saudi –

they've gone for the younger man. People like that. That's not all.'

'No?'

'One of the tribal sheiks could fancy his chance at seizing power – it's only a few decades since we had a civil war here – you heard me mention Nizwa to the soldiers – one of the sheiks at the heart of Omani Ibadism might find enough backing in the interior to mount a serious bid for an Imamate style Muslim state resurgence. The interior and capital have always been divided – conservatively religious interior versus a liberal and modern capital. Then there's the business interests – they might have their own ideas and agendas too, but I'm just speculating on that one.'

'All in all then, plenty to worry about. Maybe there's a few days of uncertainty ahead of us before things settle again. Beside the three front runners, you're saying there are at least three other possible challengers.'

'Afraid so. But please remember, all that I've said to you is pure conjecture on my part, guesswork, just between ourselves. I don't even know what's really happening, even outside my own front door!'

The two fell silent as Adam completed his scribbling and Abdul Aziz sipped the last of his mint tea.

Their reverie whilst Adam scribbled on, was eventually interrupted by a loud knock on the front door. Abdul Aziz leapt to his feet. There was a second, louder, more insistent knocking before he could get to open it. Abdul Aziz heard the kitchen door open as he stepped out into the hall and got there first.

'What can anyone want at this hour? It's getting late,' he said muttering anxiously under his breath as he released the lock and cautiously peered out.

The taller soldier blocked the door, his colleague a few paces behind him.

'We've taken a call. You're to come with us Abdul Aziz.'

'Can I get a few things? Where are we going?'

'No. We'll provide what you need. You're to come with us, right away. Don't make things more difficult. Just come out into the road. Shut the door, you'll be picked up presently.'

Abdul Aziz was yanked outside by the arm, the door forcefully slammed shut after him, leaving all in the house alarmed and afraid at the sudden turn of events. Those inside made for the windows, levering open a shutter to peer out.

A moment later and a vehicle was heard approaching. It was what some called a snatch Land Rover with different soldiers in charge. Once their prisoner was handed over, the two guards made their way back to their station by the front door. Those watching could see Abdul Aziz being bundled unceremoniously in the back, the rear door firmly and loudly shut after him.

Abdul Aziz now began to feel afraid, very afraid, for the first time in many years. He pulled his robes tight around him.

Back inside the house there was consternation, not least because no-one quite knew how to react. Adam felt that he ought to step up and offer some kind of leadership, but he wasn't sure of local custom. He decided nonetheless that he would get Maryam and Raqiyah to hold a council of war with him right now. They all needed to talk together urgently, formulate some plan of action – consider if there was anything they could possibly do.

'Raqiyah, Maryam, since they've taken Abdul Aziz, I'm going to ask the solders outside what they know, at least to tell us where he's gone.'

He felt Raqiyah's restraining hand on his arm, 'No, stay inside, its safer. They won't know anything and even if they did it wouldn't help; only expose us and you, in particular, to more danger.'

Adam stopped in his tracks, he knew she was right.

'Let's gather in the kitchen,' he offered quietly. The others followed his lead. The two house staff were nowhere to be seen. They had kept their heads down elsewhere in the house and the three decided not to include them at this point.

'Is there any reason you can think of why Abdul Aziz has been picked up?' asked Adam of the others.

'He's never been trusted by the ruling elite, ever since the early 1990s. Around 1994 I think, well before you were born my dear,' stuttered Maryam, her eyes darting anxiously from face to face, before finally fixing her glance on Raqiyah.

'I remember that time well. Hassim was about a year old. The government thought Abdul Aziz to be "unsound," yes, that was the word he once used to tell me about it. He was on the fringes of diplomatic discussions that involved Israel and America. They picked him up in a general sweep back then. He had to report to the police for ages afterwards. It ended his career aspirations. It's like it's happening all over again. This time he might not be so lucky.' She began to weep quietly, reaching for some kitchen roll to dab the corner of her eyes.

Raqiyah put a comforting arm around her shoulder. Then Maryam was clutching her prayer beads again, working them hard through her fingers. She seemed to need to do it, finding the religious ritual a place of solace, a comfort in a time of trouble. Adam interrupted her.

'That was all a very long time ago. I think the army are simply doing what an army does, acting on orders from on high, rounding up anyone and everyone who might be considered a risk. It's all about now, not something so long ago in the past, 1990 whenever it was. My guess is they'll hold him for a few days and then he'll be released, you'll see,' he said, trying to sound confident.

'You're probably right, Adam. Did Daddy... did he say anything further whilst the two of you were together in his study?' asked Raqiyah.

'No, he just described politics in general and how things get played out in Oman,' Adam replied airily, 'nothing that might suggest what's just happened to him. You could see in his face, he was as surprised and shocked as any of us. I think the only call he was anticipating was the soldiers wanting to take up his offer of something to eat.'

'So what shall we do?' asked Raqiyah.

'I think we have to wait until morning and then see what we can do in the cool light of day – sorry that was an Englishman speaking...'

'We know what you meant,' smiled Raqiyah, briefly.

'Is there anything I can help with?' offered Adam plaintively.

'No,' said Maryam, 'I don't think so.'

'Let's try and get some rest tonight. Let's see you to your room. I'll speak to the servants after – tell them what's happening. Mama, try and calm yourself, please,' Raqiyah said gently, taking her mother's arm and leading her away as another burst of her sobs and tears could no longer be restrained.

Each went about their own business, eventually all making their way to their own rooms. It would be a long night. No-one could resist checking from time to time for a phone or internet signal – a media shutdown was all they found. There were no calls, no messages, no news – only silence and a blue screen.

They were isolated, under house arrest, restricted, but that was nothing like the incarceration and future uncertainty that faced Abdul Aziz.

10

Hamad's fist crashed down on the table, with a shouted, 'Yes!'

He could not believe his good fortune as news of the coup's success reached him from the Salafah Palace. Not only was he incredulous, but he could barely contain the euphoria he now felt, giving his feelings of delight and excitement expression as he moved to put on his best shirt and a clean turban.

Then he quickly left his quarters to taste and take up his new gained freedom. His first priority was to consolidate his power and establish control of the whole country in the uncertain hours and days ahead.

Messages were immediately sent to London. He knew, through Landon, that in Britain, he could count on the support and backing of one major international power. Others, he was certain, would soon follow.

At home, releasing news of what was happening was more tricky. He set to work to plan how he could set in motion and provide the necessary assurances that his would be a benevolent and stable government. His deposed father had been surrounded by such internal disasters, wars to the north and south, Hamad knew he needn't worry unduly about the loyalty of influential countrymen. They had long said in loud whispers that anyone would be better than the leadership they had had before!

Hamad also had to sow the seeds of social, economic and political development quickly and methodically. His ambition was to see huge changes take place in the country in a short time. With Britain's help he'd bring back the exiled, very able, former Prime Minister from Dubai. With his experienced help and diplomatic efforts the two of them would see that Oman's place in the world would be internationally recognised and safeguarded.

There was a ruthlessly pragmatic, zealous side to him and in his long and ever lengthening to-do list, Hamad knew he needed to swiftly tighten the country's grip on its precious oil industry, with him personally taking decisive control of it. He'd also need to draw together the many disparate tribes that defined the present Muscat and Oman, and redefine them with a new identity into one new national state for the very first time. The old Muscat and Oman would have to go and from henceforth they would be one Oman, a single people and one nation. There was so much to do, but he soon found he was pushing on an open door and at every stage, good fortune continued to smile on his every move.

As Hamad reflected on the day's events, he knew 23 July 1970 would be a date forever to be commemorated – where else had there ever been an almost bloodless coup? His right hand man directly effecting the removal of his father was Omani army Colonel, Said. In him he saw the man he now needed to help him run his armed forces, and so a hasty promotion was arranged. Everything was coming together around him, but he knew he would still need to watch his back.

The good fortune the Almighty had bestowed upon him was extraordinary and it was now up to him to show his worth and gratitude. There was much to do and he was determined to be up to the task and transform his country.

Hamad thought of the ways the Jews had looked across the Jordan to a promised land, though he'd never tell anyone else Israel bore any comparison with Oman. As he looked out his palace window, for the first time in years a free man, he smiled to himself, knowing he had just received his own promised land.

He could do with Oman whatever he wanted. Perhaps he'd start by moving house; somewhere in Muscat would suit him perfectly.

11

On 26 July 1970, as news filtered through to Nizwa by that remarkably effective media carrier, word of mouth, the mourners learned that the Sultan's son Hamad, had ousted his father and taken charge. 'More instability,' was the only comment that was heard. Abdul Aziz and the two gathered families were otherwise too preoccupied, bringing the initial time of mourning for Aiesha to a close. The far off political news simply passed them by.

Abdul Aziz had learned more about his intended in the three days since her unexpected death, than ever he knew of her in the months before their planned wedding.

People spoke kindly of an innocent and good daughter, whose pleasures were centred around her home and family. She could make a rare humus from chickpeas and oil and loved spending time in the family kitchen.

The grief shown by his intended in-laws was palpable and he could only begin to wonder at the greatness of their loss. He recognised the trauma, numbness and looks of shock too; those expressions that came with an unexpected and sudden death.

Beyond this, Abdul Aziz registered nothing. To his mind, the Al Nami family appeared as though they lived on the other side of a deep wadi from himself. Their raw grief characterised a foreign country, one he could not enter. He felt drawn in on himself, his own mind in a whirl, indeed a turmoil.

Everyone put his reticence and reserve down to the trauma of his own loss of his betrothed, but truth be told, the loss of someone he never knew, was not very great. The bigger and more fundamental loss was that to the moorings that had hitherto anchored his life.

The very foundations of his being, built so securely to date, had been shaken to their very core and he didn't yet know whether there was anything solid left to support his future life. It was as if he who had always lived on land had slipped offshore and was now adrift on an uncertain sea.

Abdul Aziz turned inward on himself. It wasn't that he couldn't face the world, rather he needed the chance to look at, understand and prevent further unexplained wreckage that he knew was occurring deep inside himself. His inward place was like a butcher's slab at the day's end; it needed to be scraped clean of everything that had marked and stained it so that it could be of use again.

In the three days of mourning, he'd felt totally alone and couldn't find anyone or anything to help him. He hardly ate. Inside himself he could find no inner strength of character upon which he could draw – ultimately, employing another metaphor, he thought of himself as shipwrecked, much like one of the old unwanted wooden dhows beached near Muttrah – of no use or value to anyone.

He spent a lot of time gazing without focus, his attention only suddenly drawn to the sound of a tile crashing to the ground – was that him – so easily fragile and broken?

His thoughts went round and round in his mind and he dared not let them out for fear of the damage they might do. The anger he had first felt toward Allah upon hearing the news was still as strong as it was three days prior. The questions he was demanding answers to were waiting to be answered. His accusation that the Almighty was busy elsewhere, was only met with by a resounding silence from on high.

As each day passed so the resentment and anger continued to build inside until Abdul Aziz felt himself to be unsafe to be with, certain he too might cause an explosion of his own. He feared what he might be capable of doing if he let his rage break out.

So it was, with immense relief that when the time came to say goodbye and his brother drove the Land Rover round to the front of the house to take him back to the city, he was more than ready to make his escape, to find some semblance of normality in the comfort of familiar routines.

His parents, uncles and aunts, brother and sisters would make their own way back to the capital, Muscat, over the coming days. For his part he wanted more than anything to be simply left alone. Life in the Al Nami family would return to some kind of equilibrium, he told himself, they'd be absorbing their loss into an adjusted and lesser life. He didn't want to be near them whilst they made their journey through loss and grief.

The political news, set to one side earlier without a second thought, suddenly seemed significant. Abdul Aziz had already said he intended to return to work immediately and the news from the far south of a coup d'etat in the palace at Salalah made him think he'd be needed. He'd told the family he'd be expected back and could stay away no longer. This was partly true, in that being a career diplomat, the sudden governmental change would indeed require his presence, but more of an incentive to be on his way was the unbearable situation in Nizwa he was so desperate to escape.

As he'd made his solemn farewells to the traumatised family he knew he would never again include them in his own life. The certainty he would never come back to this place was firmly set in his mind. Walood understood this much too, and that his duty was to get his brother away, and soon. He could see the changes in him, things others who knew him less well may not have noticed, and he was worried at the transformation he was seeing take place. To his eyes, Abdul Aziz looked not only traumatised but dangerously inward looking.

It was only after almost an hour on the graded dusty road that Walood dared to break the silence between them. He spoke whilst looking straight at the road ahead.

'I'm so sorry for you, brother. But you'll get over it, you'll see,' he said, attempting to be positive, trying to be supportive.

'You mean well, Walood, but no, I don't think getting over it is how I see it at all. My world's changed and I don't yet know how. I feel scared for the future and the life I have now, I have to face alone.'

'Give it time, the family will soon arrange someone else for you. Give it six months, maybe a year – inshallah. It wasn't meant to be. Things will work out.'

'I don't mean alone in that sense. And, no, I don't think I can ever face going through another marriage, not after all this.'

There was a pause as Walood registered Abdul Aziz's reply.

'You aren't alone. We're all behind you. You'll get over it, you really will. Give yourself time. We all belong to Allah and to him we all return. You need a change of scene and a few days to put things behind you.'

'Don't you ever ask why a good and compassionate merciful Allah inflicts such suffering upon his creatures?'

'That's too hard for me to answer brother. All I know is that it's Allah's way.'

'I used to think that too, but now…' Abdul Aziz's voice drifted away on the wind, his thoughts, his words not yet ready to be said out loud. It wasn't done in Oman to voice heretical thoughts, and he didn't want to start now. It wasn't fair to burden Walood with his worries. He closed the matter and looked out at the passing desert.

'What do you want to do when you get back today? I could drop you at your office as you wish, but why not come home? You know they'd understand if you took a few days off, why not?'

'No, no – take me straight there, please.'

With silence between the two again, they focussed on the bone-shaking, half day's drive – so hot and dusty. They passed through a barren landscape of fractured rock, empty, dry, soaring mountains, searingly hot dusty pebble plains and hills where getting lost was far easier than finding a way through.

'What's your take on the coup?' asked Walood thinking a change of subject would help.

'Can't make things any worse than they are. The last Sultan had thirty-eight years to pull this country together. What's there to show for it? – not ten miles of asphalt road, no schools,' he corrected himself, 'sorry three schools! No education, no nation, nowhere we could wish to belong to! Hamad can only be an improvement. He's young, had a good education. He should have learned a thing or two from the West, don't you think? Things have got to get better in this god-forsaken place.'

'Suppose so. Can't think anyone will be rushing in to mount a counter-coup, can you?'

'No. I think we're looking at a settled future for now. I'm just a bit worried that Hamad will purge anyone who worked for his father – that might mean me.'

'But, pardon me, you're a small cog in the diplomatic wheel. My take is the top people might change and if there is a clear out to bring in new blood, you're just the kind of well-placed person, to progress himself. Well, that's my reading. He won't get rid of you.'

'I aim to ensure I keep in step with the new regime. Maybe you're right and I'll get a good diplomatic posting if I'm lucky. I need to get talking to people and do it today.' He turned to his brother looking intently in his eyes for the first time in a while, 'Any chance you can drop me at the office in Muttrah? Better still, leave the Land Rover with me after we get home, and I'll make my own way.'

'Fine. I've not got any plans for today. Go for it, that's what I say,' said Walood, relieved to think his brother was now in a better place – at least with something positive to occupy his mind.

The dusty track in an empty terrain, except for scrubby ground hugging trees, began to give way to buildings and they were once more approaching the villages on the outskirts of Samail, their half way point to Muscat.

'Time for a stop soon, to let the engine cool down. It'll be time for prayers when we get there,' suggested Walood.

'I'll take the break, drink some coffee, but I'll give the prayers a miss.'

Walood looked at his brother quizzically, thought of saying something, but let it pass. Today was not the time to ask for explanations.

'Whenever I come to the mosque here, it means something extra special. Did you know this is the site of the first mosque in our country? Mazin ben Ghadooba, the first Omani Muslim – he built it,' said Walood, trying to spark some interest.

'Nice try, but I'm still not coming to prayers,' answered Abdul Aziz resolutely.

Walood fell silent. It concerned him to see his brother like this. Just how well did he really know his brother? He started looking for somewhere to park.

Abdul Aziz looked around him as the buildings drew closer. Samail had precious water. Between the houses, date palms now filled every available place that could be reached by the irrigation channels. They'd left the mountains behind them and were in the foothills, ground water and springs were feeding what green there was. The Samail wadi provided life, and an ancient Fallaj stone channel, sent fresh, crystal clear, life-giving mountain water cascading in a fast flowing hewn stone slot hundreds of miles on to the east.

Walood decided it was time to swing off the road and parked in the shade of a date palm. The two stepped from the vehicle in search of a cool spot for coffee, passing a table with locally produced mangoes and bananas for sale. The scruffily dressed boy minder wafted a palm frond unsuccessfully, vainly attempting to sweep away the cloud of swirling flies.

As they stepped into the shadows between the buildings, all that Abdul Aziz was thinking was that the world he once knew was unravelling like a reel of cotton and there was no way he could see of rewinding it.

Coffee downed, Walood raised his hand, pointing where he was headed, setting off for the mosque, leaving Abdul Aziz alone to his thoughts.

In the shade of a tired looking date palm, Abdul Aziz considered the mosque here. However ancient and venerable Allah's domain was considered to be, before he ever went inside there was unfinished business to be settled first.

As things stood now, there was no way he was going inside this or any other mosque. He would sort things out with Allah on his terms and in a place of his own choosing. He'd come to a decision – it was no good leaving things to the Almighty. From now on he had to take control of his own destiny. He had work to do and he was itching to get to it.

12

It was both a long and a short night for Maryam, Raqiyah and Adam. Long, because as they waited patiently in the darkness, but no news came from Abdul Aziz. Short, because the daunting new day arrived before they felt ready to face it. Next morning, the troubled household, eyes tired from lack of sleep were all up early. As they gathered in the kitchen after the women's early morning prayers, no-one wanted to go back to bed.

Soon the first rays of sun began to pierce the brief dawn, promising yet another fiery furnace day – the weather mercilessly unchanging. Maryam quietly boiled some water in a pan for hot drinks, then reached into the cupboard to retrieve three plain white china mugs. They hunched over their drinks wondering what next.

There shortly followed a sharp rat-a-tat on the front door; it was unlike the one the previous night. No-one dared to move, not knowing who it might be at this early hour. The knock came again and Adam moved first to get up and open it, waving the women back into the kitchen as he did so.

He immediately recognised the distressed looking man. It was Walood, Abdul Aziz's older brother. They'd met the previous summer, but unlike last time, there were no big smiles. Glancing around him, Adam could see no sight of the two soldiers and beckoned the stooping Walood inside. A hasty greeting and Walood's scared eyes quickly scanned the lobby. Hearing his familiar voice the two women soon reappeared from the kitchen and his face began to relax.

‘I’m glad to see you, but I came over as soon as I could, to see if it was true,’ said Walood, ‘that Abdul Aziz has been taken?’

‘Yes. Late last night. They came and took him away. We’ve no idea where and we’ve heard nothing since. I half hoped when you knocked it might be some news,’ explained Adam.

‘What’s happening out there, uncle? All we know is that the Sultan has died and the army seem to be in charge until a new Sultan is proclaimed,’ asked Raqiyah.

‘This morning, Oman TV re-started broadcasting. They’re not saying anything much – all sombre stuff. In between broadcasting recitations of the Qur’an a solemn newsreader makes periodic appeals for calm telling us that the Ruling Family Council are in session to decide on the country’s future leader.’

Adam wondered why he himself hadn’t thought to put on the TV.

‘I also tuned into the BBC World Service overnight,’ Walood continued. ‘Their Arabic service is still reaching here. They were saying they can’t get news from inside the country. Statements are being made by our Middle East neighbours – banal messages of polite concern, but really they are just biding their time waiting in the wings, like vultures watching an injured goat. It’s a total lockdown across the country as I read it. In the meantime the army’s keeping everyone quiet and not worrying about how heavy handed they are in going about it. A couple of my neighbours were also swept up yesterday. It’s probable they’re all being detained in the new army barracks on the Western edge of Muscat. I only got here by walking from house to house when I thought the coast was clear. The last part of my journey was easier than I imagined; the guards outside happy enough to allow me entry.'

'Who do you think they're picking up?' asked Adam.

'It's all very random. Anyone who's ever been outspoken. Anyone who's popped above the radar on police records. That's why Abdul Aziz got taken I'm sure. They were going through their records at police HQ, and eventually came to an AA Nahari, saw he'd been under suspicion for treasonable activity in the 1990s and sent the heavy mob round. I think, all being well, they'll hold him until things are settled and then begin a phased release when he'll be freed. It may take a little while yet. The last Sultan was liked because he was keen to remit sentences and release prisoners – let's hope the new one does the same. We should know something by tomorrow,' he said in something approaching the usual cheerful manner, Adam remembered from first meeting him a year ago.

Adam detected the mood lifting; the women spotting the cheer leader side, that so characterised Walood's personality, but Adam himself was not feeling so easily reassured. Walood was ushered into the kitchen to join everyone for breakfast. Adam was pleased the family were including him, relying on him even, and he wondered if he might be of more use. He'd had an idea.

'Walood, I think I'm going to try and get to the British Consulate. I'll get Asad, the family driver to take me, if that's OK. It's only a short distance, a couple of minutes away. It's a chance worth taking. I might be able to be of more help there. The soldiers aren't likely to stop a foreign national. What do you think?'

'Only risk are the road blocks. Though from what I could see, they're mainly targeted at blocking off the main thoroughfares. You'd just need to mind out for passing patrols on the local roads – there are plenty of those about, military and police. Oh, and there's bound to be a military presence outside the Embassy building itself. The last few years there's been a permanent military detail there for fear of terrorism. You'll have to take your chances on that one. You may be OK, being a British Citizen. It really must be your call, Adam. Oh, I forgot to say, but congratulations to Raqiyah and yourself on achieving your excellent degrees. We're so proud. And Adam, to have a job as a correspondent too – though I think you'll need to sit quiet on that one for now – could be the wrong profession to have,' he quipped, somehow another smile coming as he did so.

'I think I'll do that, there's no love of journalists in times like this. I think I'll head off to the Embassy. My parents in London will want to know I'm safe and I'll come back as soon as it seems prudent to do so. I like the idea. Might even find out a thing or two.' He went to the back of the house to summon Asad.

Asad agreed to take the risk. As a Bangladeshi driver he seemed less phased by what he saw as an internal Omani matter. He believed he could talk his way out of any situation – no-one would want to hold him. He was an invisible nobody, he told them. 'Some Omanis would like to see us all sent back to Asia,' he said. 'That's the worst that can happen to me. I've never had a stake in this place anyway.'

Adam thought it best if he took with him one small rucksack with a few things, mainly clothes, and leave behind anything that was possibly incriminating – his laptop and correspondence, these he'd leave at the house in Raqiyah's care.

With Asad at the wheel and Adam beside him, they set off in the white Mercedes and all went well until they were almost at the British Embassy. The Embassy, like many others was situated on an excellent ocean-facing site, fine balconies and luxury rooms overlooking the beach, the shimmering blue sea and the broad sky of the Gulf. To be posted here must be a holiday dream come true, thought Adam.

They were at the approach roundabout, about to enter the long driveway to the Embassy entrance when they saw a group of six soldiers, four of whom were standing idly a little way off on an irrigated patch of green lawn, guns pointing down to the ground. The remaining two were making the vehicle checks. Their car, the only one around, was given a casual wave down and they drew to a halt just yards from the Embassy door.

'Leave the talking to me,' instructed Adam who was taking his passport from his pocket.

'Identification please,' ordered the soldier, his palm extended. Asad showed his first and it was waved away as of no consequence. Adam gave his next.

'I need to report to the British Embassy. My parents back home will be worried about me,' he offered.

The soldier looked at him cooly, not giving anything away. 'Wait,' he ordered.

He then turned and walked across to the larger group of soldiers, carrying Adam's passport with him, obviously needing to discuss the situation. Then a second vehicle pulled up behind the Mercedes, a British flag perched on the bonnet. It was an Embassy car. Seeing an opportunity, Adam leapt out and walked to the driver's window. A window was wound down.

'Hi there. Name's Adam Taylor. Just wanting to report in to the Embassy,' he said to the elderly couple sitting quietly in the back not knowing what to make of him.

The soldier holding Adam's passport turned back. He looked on at the conversation taking place. He clearly didn't want any trouble, handed Adam back his passport and used his thumb to indicate he was letting him through. Breathing more easily, Adam said goodbye to the bemused couple before climbing back in the car, moments later to be dropped off at the Embassy entrance. He waved off Asad and the Mercedes and watched as it disappeared, then with considerable relief he was let inside.

He found himself in a room full of other people, shortly joined by the elderly couple. All were waiting to be seen in turn. It wasn't until mid-morning his name was eventually called and he was ushered into a side room to be interviewed by a smartly dressed woman in a dark green suit. She was friendly enough and listened to his story. After requesting that a message be sent to his parents in London, as to his well-being, Adam then asked her for information as to what was happening in the country.

'I think your guess is as good as mine,' she said. 'There's a period of transition taking place following the Sultan's death. It may take a few days for services here to fully return to normal, but we have been assured by the head of the army and London that there is nothing for our citizens to be unduly concerned about. There is no report of any trouble. There's just a degree of understandable apprehension as people await news of the succession.'

'But people are being picked up by the army,' interrupted Adam.

'I wouldn't know about that. We've no reports to that effect.'

'Well, can I be the first to make a report. Abdul Aziz Nahari, whose house I am staying in here in Muscat, was taken away by soldiers last night and we have heard nothing more. I have heard reports from a local man that this has also happened to others.'

'I'm sorry, but to our knowledge no British nationals have been picked up and internal country matters are beyond our jurisdiction.'

Adam realised he was getting nowhere and tried a different line. 'And what about communication? Did you know internet and mobile communication are impossible?'

'Yes, we've had reports to that effect. We have our own means of communication from within the Embassy, but outside there have been reports of some problems here in the capital. If you like I can make an enquiry about the area where you are staying if that would make you feel more secure?' she offered trying to be helpful.

'Thank you. We're within a mile and a half of here. I think the family I am staying with and myself would feel more comfortable if we can make calls.'

She stood up.

'Please wait here a minute Mr Taylor, I won't be long.'

It was nearly fifteen minutes later when she reappeared and Adam's patience was wearing thin.

'Yes, you were quite right. There is an extensive shut down of communication. Our contact at the Ministry tells us it is in the interests of security and stability, a temporary measure and as soon as things are normalised, all services in the capital will be restored.'

'Then I think I would like to return to where I am staying. The question is, how am I to tell them I need picking up?'

'We're running an Embassy courtesy car service for people like yourself. Diplomatic plates and a Union flag on the bonnet guarantee hassle free travel. I'll arrange a lift for you,' she said with a smile in what was becoming an irritating monotone tone, her voice sounding like she'd be equally suited to working in a call centre.

'But how will you know from day to day I'm safe and haven't been picked up if I can't call you and you can't call me? As an international journalist I also need to get my stories out and work closely with you,' he added in amount of inspiration. Her eyes lit briefly.

'A journalist you say. Hold on a moment Mr. Taylor. I need to fetch someone else.' She got up and once again left Adam alone in the rather sterile interview room with a smiling picture of the Queen facing an equally smiling picture of the late Sultan; looking down on him from matching gold picture frames. That picture has to go, thought Adam, wondering just how well they can handle change here. He'd just about had enough and was impatient to get back.

This time a middle-aged man with thinning ginger hair, in an immaculately ironed white shirt entered the room and sat down facing him. He was clutching a laptop in his hand. He had the kind of skin that should never be let into hot countries – papery white with lots of brown freckles. Adam thought he was probably the type of person who never ever risked anything, least of all exposure to sunlight.

'The name's Brian Merryweather,' he said, 'Embassy media services,' he explained, offering a hand. 'You're a journalist from London, I'm told. It's important we work together.'

Adam himself hadn't said anything about 'London.' He made a mental note and let it pass.

'Who are you with?' he followed up.

'CNPI, that's Central News Publishing International. I'm their on the spot foreign correspondent and covering what's going on here,' Adam said, boldly not overstating his brief, but neatly summarising his current role.

'OK, I get the picture. You and I need to have an understanding. At this delicate time, you need to be aware of the sensibilities and sensitivities – follow?'

Adam wasn't sure what Brian's angle was, but he instinctively knew he was on the receiving end of a blunt political message, so he replied in kind.

'You mean I need to make sure my copy agrees with your copy and London's copy, so that Britain's interests here in Oman are best served and no-one gets hurt?'

'Nicely put. I think we understand one another.'

'But I'm new to all this and need to know how this will work. When I've written my story and need to send copy out, I'll need to do it through the Embassy communication lines – it's the only route out. Does this mean I pass it through you?'

'You're a fast learner, Mr Taylor. You've been taught well. Yes, through me.'

'I'll have something to send each evening. Can you lay on a car to collect it?'

'Hmm. If what you write serves British interests, then that will be entirely possible.'

'Thank you. I'm sure we can work together Brian, and do call me Adam,' he offered, though inwardly having already decided he was only going to be working with this man, so far as it suited his own purposes. At the very least he'd found a way to play politics to keep himself safe and in the loop. He couldn't see any further value to be had from Brian Merryweather, but couldn't resist a parting shot.

'I need to get back to where I'm staying shortly. I'll have something written for despatch before curfew, shall we say, you'll collect the piece around five pm? But tell me, do you have anything you can tell me, you know, as to what is going on, what *we* think,' he said, touching the side of his nose.

'Let's not rush ahead of ourselves Mr Taylor. You see what you can send me and I'll have a nosey around to see what I can find out. That will have to suffice for now. We'll try our best to oblige you, though everyone here is running around at nineteen to the dozen. Good day, Mr Taylor.'

Back in reception there was a short wait until a car was free and then he was on his way. When Adam was dropped back at the house at around twelve, the soldiers were right outside the front door where there was a little shade. He saw the taller one speak into his radio as the two had watched the flagged British Embassy car approach, dropping Adam off. By the time he had come off his radio, Adam had pushed by him and was safely back inside, his transport already heading off.

Maryam, Raqiyah and Walood were hungry for news and he told them all, well most of what there was to tell. The politics he kept to himself. Somehow his now extended presence in the house, offering a link with the free world outside lifted all their spirits a little, and this pleased him.

However, there was no getting round the pain of not knowing what was happening to Abdul Aziz. After a humus and stale bread meal, Adam excused himself saying he had to write his first piece for London and that it was important to keep his route to the Embassy open. He grabbed a bottle of cold water from the fridge.

They left him alone and he retreated into Abdul Aziz's study, laptop and bottle in hand. He found it hard to concentrate. Some of his old anxieties had been provoked by all the tension and he took a few moments to breathe quietly whilst he had time to himself. It took a while before he felt a measure of calm and control return. His mind wandered, as he gazed about him he could feel the presence of Abdul Aziz in all the things in the room. Item by item they spoke to him.

He came to a conclusion. Here was a someone who might easily upset traditional views. He was liberal, open minded, tolerant and had spent years living and working in the West.

No wonder he was suspect. Abdul Aziz was an anomaly, he didn't belong in this place, neither politically nor in his family.

13

It was late afternoon when Abdul Aziz finally arrived at work. Relieved to be back from Nizwa and the wedding that never was, it felt comforting to be back in a familiar zone that brought no threats. He drove slowly into the vacant parking space under the projecting first floor balcony of the white plastered two story office block. He pulled up slowly, as he always did, so as not to send swirling clouds of dust up into the air.

It always was a tricky parking space, care had to be taken to miss the single metal pole supporting the overhanging structure of the building above – very Omani! He reckoned that one day someone, maybe himself, would inevitably drive into it and the whole edifice above would come tumbling down, along with any poor souls who happened to be in the first-floor office at the time. His own office was downstairs, on the ground floor – it contained just an old cane chair and a rudimentary desk to work at, but he felt that was just fine.

Mohammed Mansoor, his boss always worked late, and today was no exception. On entering, the receptionist, rather than give his usual knowing nod, looked quizzically at Abdul Aziz before raising his eyes to signal that the boss was in residence upstairs.

Without hesitation Abdul Aziz began ascending the stairs. It felt good to have something to do again. Pausing on the small landing, he politely knocked on Mohammed's door, seeing the familiar outline of his head and shoulders behind his desk through the opaque glass window.

'In,' he heard him call.

'Sit,' he was instructed, Mohammed neither raising his head in greeting nor his hand from his notepad. Abdul Aziz was aware of the humming pedestal fan that served only to push the hot, humid air around. Totally ineffective at keeping one cool, it was, in reality, little more than an office status symbol. He could smell Mohammed's cigarette smoke, neither the open window nor the humming fan moving the air sufficiently to take it away.

Abdul Aziz noticed his boss was starting to put on weight and he wondered if he too, in time, would become like him. He'd always thought Mohammed was born in the wrong country. Every time he saw him, Abdul Aziz thought him every bit the stereotypical Turkish businessman – thin moustache, greased hair, shaved chin and the endless chain smoking.

After a few minutes, when Mohammed had remembered he had company, he stopped writing, put down his fountain pen and looked up. At heart he was no Turk, rather he was every bit the urbane modern Omani, and the contrast he represented between the Muscat business life community of the capital and far away Nizwa he'd so recently left behind struck Abdul Aziz forcibly. Mohammed wore a loose light suit, a collar and tie, his traditional white robe hanging on a hook on the wall, rarely worn, but ready to be called into service if ever required.

'You've had some terrible bad luck I hear. I must say I'm surprised to see you in. My condolences.' Mohammed had one of those voices that sounded like it was ultra-smooth, taken from the movies.

'Thank you.' Once again, Abdul Aziz was aware how efficiently the word of mouth news flow worked.

'In your absence we've had rather a time of it here and your colleague Suleman's not in. The new Sultan's men have been rounding up anyone they're not sure about and because his brother works in the palace of the old Sultan, I guess he needed to be checked out. I heard he'd been told to stay at home where they can find him. His family are worried sick. That I think is the sum of it. They've quizzed me twice in as many days, but that said, they seemed happy enough with the firm and I think this could turn out well for us in the end. To my mind the new man, Hamad, seems to be playing a good hand, already lining up political and diplomatic support as fast as a thirsty camel heads for water – which is pretty damned fast.'

'I thought I'd check in, try and finalise that contract with the Indian Consulate. Their building is fifteen years old, and either they'll refurbish it or require a new embassy. My guess is the latter, but it will be a good deal for us. With the Indians we might even get both, a refurb deal now and the new Embassy contract later. The worrying thing is, the change of regime here might have unsettled things, frighten business off. How do you read it?'

'It's all good. Hamad is already sending messages that he wants our friends abroad to be on side. He's not stupid. From what I heard this afternoon, the Palace want us to start developing on-the-ground diplomatic missions here as fast as we can and I think he's pushing some of the oil money our way to help lubricate the wheels. It's all about putting Oman on the map, giving us a position in the world, and a place at the table. That's what I was working on just now,' he waved his hand at the papers on his desk. 'I want to offer them your services. You're our best man Abdul Aziz. I think you could do with a step up, a fresh challenge. Something to take your mind off the last few days. I'm offering you a partnership in the business and the chance to pick up and run with all the new government business I see coming our way. What do you say?'

Abdul Aziz was stunned. He'd worked for Eastern Diplomatic Services since returning from university in London. Barely a year had passed. He couldn't believe he'd proved himself, yet Mohammed seemed to be making him a genuine offer. He was being offered a serious advancement, how could he refuse?

'What would it mean? How would it all pan out?'

'To start with you'd take Suleman's office next to mine. I can't risk having Suleman back here. If he shows up I'm sending him straight back home – his work here is over, done, end of. His very presence could threaten the business. Don't worry about him. His family will sort something out for him. He's only ever been a pen-pusher anyway. You on the other hand, you work like the British, you get things done! We're going to need people like you. You'll take the office next to mine – all the business, decisions, profits, all shared 50:50 between us. I'll be forty next year. I need a younger partner, this is our time, your time. What do you say?'

Abdul Aziz could not believe his good fortune. Then he had a doubt.

'Is this because my bride to be died. Are you just saying this to be kind?'

'Bloody hell! I'm sorry of course for what's happened, but I'm a business man. While you were away it gave me the chance to think. If the Palace can have a revolution and introduce a few changes, well so can Eastern Diplomatic Services. I missed you. I'm glad you're back. We need you. I want the phone in Suleman's office, I mean your new office, to get red hot with the calls you make to grease a few palms and win a few friends. Tell them Hamad supports us – when they hear that they'll fall over backwards for our business! This is an opportune time of us – come on!'

'OK. OK. I'll do it,' said Abdul Aziz offering his hand. Mohammed grabbed it, shaking it hard, the ash falling from the cigarette hanging from the corner of his mouth.

'You've made my day. Now all you've got to do is make me a million Omani Rials! How long do you reckon it will take you?'

Abdul Aziz smiled. 'If we get this Indian contract, there's your first thousand. Reckon the countries of the world will need our services in the days to come. It may take less time than you think.' At this upbeat assessment, Mohammed smiled in return.

To his surprise, Abdul Aziz had been given all he wanted. The promise, the dream of building good business, the opportunity that he now had, though tied to a personal stake; these were all enough to take the edge off what he had been through in Nizwa. Fate had been turned on its head. He knew it was time to start moving on and to put the past behind him.

14

It was late, nearly midnight when Sir Alec put a call through to Number 10. Ted Heath was thinking about turning in, but hadn't got round to it.

He was trying to do two things at once – enjoy a glass of Taylor's 55 Old Port whilst playing Mozart sonatas on his piano. It was just as he had his right hand reaching for the glass and his left hovering over the bass notes, the phone rang. It was at moments like this his default grumpiness slipped out and he 'hurrumphed' quietly as he rose to his feet to walk the few paces to the ringing black telephone.

'PPS here Sir, a private call. Alec Douglas-Home on the line. Do you want to take it? He said, you should be the first to know, but told me no more.'

'Put him through.'

'Alec here. Wanted to brighten up your evening Ted. We've had some success in the Arabian Gulf. Since your little piece at Cabinet last Thursday things have perked up. Nice touch that, 'encouraging and assisting local leaders.' You'll be pleased to hear we've done just that.'

'Come on. It's late. Get to the point Alec. Stop playing games.'

'Well, Muscat and Oman have swung our way and without, I hasten to say, Her Majesty's Government having to put its head above the parapet. Our man, Hamad, has mounted a successful coup all of his own making. That's the benefit of going to Sandhurst I think Prime Minister. He knew precisely what to do – it's been a master class in how to carry out a coup d'etat. We had a couple of our guys with him of course, covertly showing our support, protecting his back as it were, but it all turned out just so, well, picture perfect for us. The extra forces we had all primed and ready weren't needed. Every PM needs a foreign policy success. I'm ringing to tell you of yours! You need some good news. You've got it!'

'And what will this mean, Alec, tell me, what will all this mean – economics, Alec, influence? What?'

'In a nutshell, oil, armaments and a friendly port of call for the British Navy. That's just for starters. Oman's in the bag, Ted. The coup last Thursday marks the beginning of a new chapter. The place faces both the Arab world and the Indian sub-continent for goodness sake. But…'

'I was waiting for the "but", Alec. Spit it out. What's the "but"?'

'Nothing really. Just… discretion's the word.'

'You mean we enjoy Hamad's success, but we don't say anything that shows we were implicated in any way.'

'Exactly right. I knew you'd understand. I wouldn't have called you myself, but at the FCO they worry about how these things look and wanted me to check you were on message. I'm off to my estate in the Highlands in a few days. Just wanted to be sure to catch you personally, to explain. Job done, see you after the weekend.'

'No worries Alec. Thank you.'

'But...'

'Surely not another "but" Alec?'

'No. I just think a personal private message sent to Hamad from you Ted, is what's needed right now. It would do a lot of good. Settle him, keep us in the frame. Would that be all right? Maybe drop him a line?'

'Of course.'

'We've drafted something for you at the FCO. I'm sending it to your PPS – a letter of congratulation and support. Would you mind terribly if you sign it off before you turn in. Time is of the essence. Hamad will appreciate it, really appreciate it. It'll pay us dividends, handsomely.'

'No problem.' Ted turned and looked longingly at his glass of port, but from the hesitation he knew Alec hadn't quite finished.

'And...'

'Yes... We'll be bringing out the deposed Sultan, Hamad's father. He needs to be right out of it, so he can't pose a threat.'

'And where will you put him? In the Tower?' replied Ted, laughing out loud.

'Nearly – The Dorchester!'

'What? What on earth were you thinking? How will that work? You sure that won't back fire on us?'

'He's enough money. He'll take a suite. Oh, he'll needs some medical attention, something to do with his foot, so he'll be preoccupied for a while. We'll take care of him. We'll tell him how it is – we'll tell him we can't interfere in his country.'

'He won't' believe you!'

'He won't have any choice. That's how it is. Important you know. Glad to have caught you. Good night Ted.'

'Night and thank you,' he said, placing the handset back in its receiver, tucking the curling cord to the side. Then he reached for his unfinished port, with its warm inviting red glow.

Foreign policy always lifted his spirits. The more so when it worked well. Picking up his sparkling, crystal port glass, he downed it in one gulp, and decided to make one final attempt at Piano Concerto 21, the second movement, the Andante, before finally hitting the sack.

Imagining the lead of strings and woodwind, he was poised over the keys and then took it away, the cares of the day washed away by the glories of this piece in C Major.

As the ivory tinkled and the port worked its magic, he allowed himself to think what a great end to his day he was enjoying. Being a PM when good news came, well it didn't get any better than this.

15

Suleman was one of the more fortunate ones. He merely lost his job and would soon find other things to do. His family were into luxury carpets and rugs.

Over the coming days the new Sultan Hamad's men went everywhere, and if they didn't, everyone imagined they were all seeing. Following a coup d'etat, no-one dared step out of line, gossiped fears set the public mood – these were thought to be dangerous times, but in reality it was a peaceful transition.

Hamad meanwhile had already got a secure grip on power. First things first, he had secured his position as Sultan – the key power brokers – the armed services, the tribal sheiks and the merchant classes – all were saying the right things in his ear and in return were able to secure their positions in the new regime.

An early reassuring call from the new British Consul-General, who headed up the UK's Diplomatic Mission in Oman was particularly pleasing to receive. Donald Hawley had much experience in the Middle East and had only just been appointed by the Foreign Office two months earlier, in the May. Hawley had been told he'd be the country's first Ambassador, but the new title had to await Hamad's rubber stamp of approval; something Hamad would attend to in his own good time.

Hawley made favourable noises about the new leader and when Hamad got to hear and was told Hawley had done much to improve governance and offer invaluable business advice in neighbouring Dubai, he decided to trust the man.

Hamad knew a good ally when he found one. An affirming letter from Ted Heath in London had just arrived and he felt it politic to respond with a reciprocal kindly gesture.

One big problem in Hamad's mind was, how to set about uniting his warring country? Rumblings inland away from the coast following the Imamate rebellion against his father had been largely defeated, but he needed to be certain things wouldn't flare up again.

Old conflicts between coast and interior, between Sultanate and Imamate, could not be allowed to derail him. Further, the communist inspired and supported insurgency in Dhofar to the south needed to be overcome and soon. Like a bleeding wound it needed to be cauterised before draining the nations coffers and morale dry. On this matter he'd already got a favourable indication from Hawley of active British military support to help. To this final campaign he now applied his mind with characteristic military precision and vigour – he didn't go to Sandhurst for nothing!

Almost immediately he decided to move from the Sultan's Palace at Salafah in the south of Oman and make Muscat to the north, his new capital – a new unambiguous beginning. He set about appointing people to his administration. Some of the more senior appointments were easy to make, but he would need to rely on others when it came to finding good and loyal people to fill the lower ranks.

To improve his public profile he started to prepare an urgent programme of visits to key towns and villages up and down the land where he'd seek big audiences to cement his rule and gain pledges of allegiance from the all-important local leaders. A week after the coup, on 30 July, he began planning his accession ceremony – recognising the symbolic importance of public rituals and rites of passage. This needed to happen quickly – he settled on Sunday 2nd August.

Another early decision was to get his trusted uncle back from exile and make him his Prime Minister. Naturally he agreed and as Hamad gazed around him to survey the scene, he saw, like King Midas, everything he touched turning to gold; all falling nicely into place.

A new Sultan would mean a new name would be given to the nation – the Sultanate of Oman. From henceforth Oman would have a single identity in which he foresaw all its people would soon come to belong. Building a sense of pride in a national identity was right there at the top on his agenda.

In Muscat, in these still early days of his reign, and despite the sapping heat and humidity of high summer, there was much new energy, buzz, and excitement. Apart from the underlying sense of uncertainty caused by the chaotic, rapid and sweeping changes, after years of nothing happening, it seemed Rome really was about to be built in a day! The effects would soon be felt far and near.

In just a few days, Abdul Aziz and Mohammed received a call from the recently established Ministry of Foreign Affairs which instantly catapulted their lowly business into the diplomatic limelight. Hamad was desperate to begin securing diplomatic support from other nations, for without it he would remain vulnerable. Any promising ally in business development, however humble, and Eastern Diplomatic Services was certainly that, was called upon to up their game to an unprecedented level and support the cause. Failure was not an option with the new Ministry figureheads desperate to show their Sultan they could deliver exactly what he required of them.

Within days, the contract with India was favourably and finally signed off. Then Abdul Aziz found himself required, as part of a Ministry team, to make a whistle stop tour of neighbouring Gulf nations. There was no choice. It was more of a summons – not that he minded, in fact he was glad of it, and the financial rewards were good, very good.

Mohammed meantime opted for minding the office whilst Abdul Aziz did the running around. The arrangement suited both men.

Increasingly Abdul Aziz travelled as the sole companion of a senior ministry official whose task it was to take with him the Sultan's personal mandate. Abdul Aziz served as the Personal Assistant ready to deal with whatever eventualities were directed his way. In this he had to be very versatile. The truth was the ministry official knew less than he did. It was therefore up to him to arrange the transport, find the contacts, identify the places to stay, set the agendas, draw up and sign off the contracts – and then to produce the notes that would go back to the Sultan's office in Muscat. The notes were the tricky bit, but at least they went in under his senior colleague's name and not his own.

Over the next few months Abdul Aziz discovered he had a natural flair for diplomacy and he found himself increasingly relied upon to find the right words and grease the correct palms with what was required to achieve the Sultan's foreign and economic policy purposes. His quiet, urbane manner went down well and as a result he was rewarded, and the money, initially a trickle, started to flow like a river into

Eastern Diplomatic Services' coffers, which Mohammed back at the office watched with wide eyes.

By the Spring of 1971 Mohammed treated himself to a second hand American Ford. For his part, Abdul Aziz began saving and was astonished at the fortune building in his bank account. International oil prices kept rising and the Sultan was fortuitously riding on the crest of an economic boom; he spread the largesse around and the feel-good factor in Muscat was palpable, not just in the Eastern Diplomatic Service's Office.

All the while, Abdul Aziz tried to forget what had happened to him in Nizwa and his overseas travels meant he rarely had time to face his family and be reminded of that time. On those few occasions when he did call home, he disliked it, seeing the legacy of pain still written in their faces. Consequently, when he was at home, he quickly retreated to his room clutching papers to read, whether they were actually important or not. However, they saw him sufficiently often to feel pleased at his new-found success, but inwardly all wondered as to his true state of mind.

Just as Abdul Aziz had not seen Allah at work in Aiesha's death, reasoning that if Allah did not prevent such a thing happening then he was not the Allah he wanted to believe in, so he did not see Allah's hand in granting him his new-found material blessing.

When once, Allah was his taken for granted companion on life's road, now he was ruled out, exiled – he reassessed everything and increasingly found he could explain everything rationally without Allah having a hand in any of it. If there was such a thing as a Humanist Muslim faith, perhaps that now best described him.

Allah had failed him and caused such pain. He believed himself to be much better placed to taken control of his own life, applying his own reason to do so. This was not a process he could openly show or express. He kept it all hidden, buried deep inside, but was pleased that his travel opportunities gave him the chance to enter more liberal spheres and to further feed his questioning mind and intellectual appetite.

Once, whilst in Turkey, the three days he spent in Istanbul allowed him to go to bookshops and coffee shops on his own, where he could freely argue with strangers and put the world to rights through an intellectual questioning disallowed at home. Best of all he was able to see his Sister Mira in their Istanbul apartment and enjoy her cooking. He always loved seeing her and her husband, now working at the university.

There was a freedom to talk openly and debate ideas in Turkey, and it recalled for him his student time in England. He realised how much he missed those days, but also how little use he'd made of it whilst he had the chance. Maybe if he hadn't gone into diplomatic work and business contracts, he'd have liked the life of working in a university. His brother in law, Mira's husband Abdul, had such a relaxed take on Islam, urbane, light-hearted, inclusive – it made him wonder why he himself was so reserved when talking about these things in Oman – what had he been frightened of? Perhaps he was a coward at heart. He believed there was still a part of him, as yet unformed, something not ready to be exposed.

Perhaps he was also reticent out of a young man's loyalty to his parents – after all they'd sent him to a Western university at great expense to themselves. How could he criticise their views? As a younger man, he thought he probably needed the clear framework of dogmatic Islamic faith and practice to help him along. Presently, what he believed back then, didn't help him. It wasn't that he didn't believe, but rather he didn't know what he still believed, and he was hungry to find out what could be salvaged from the wreckage. This was difficult territory and meantime he deemed it prudent to hide his world of inner uncertainty from public gaze and scrutiny.

Dealing with politics and diplomacy was proving more straightforward. The new Sultan was using Muslim loyalty as a political instrument to bring local leaders on side in the continuing Dhofar conflict, dividing them off from the Marxist insurgent elements backed by their atheistic communist overlords. This political strategy was a further reminder to Abdul Aziz that being publicly questioning or anti-Muslim was not a practical route to take. To do so simply spelled trouble for him.

One particular journey was oft-times repeated. The Sultan was keen to build his friendship with neighbouring Iran and he was sent there time and again. The two countries shared a common interest in oversight of the critical ocean highway – the Straits of Hormuz, through which much of the world's supply of oil passed.

Then in 1971, as nearby Iran celebrated the 2,500th anniversary of the Persian Empire, Oman's new Sultan secured a precious invite to Iran's magnificent party to mark the occasion. His attendance at such an event would finally properly affirm his legitimacy as the country's leader, it meant he would now be recognised on the international stage.

When the day came, Hamad sat proudly alongside the heads of neighbouring Gulf states as an equal. No longer seen as an insurrectionist behind a coup, he was now a legitimate Head of State. His newly endorsed public profile validated the new nation itself and thereby attracted further support for his efforts to defeat the Dhofar insurgents to the south once and for all.

Two months after all the celebrations were over, Hamad made a return trip back to Tehran and secured a security arrangement which would allow Iranian troops to join and strengthen his own force in Dhofar. This, together with similar help he secured from Jordan marked the beginning of the end for the insurgents. The future security of Oman was all but sewn up.

In all this vital politicking, Abdul Aziz was a backroom messenger, a lowly diplomat who carried and typed letters whenever he was called upon, and that was often. Words tied up the actions required and he'd been fortunate to be brought in from the beginning.

Message and note making was only the start of it. More and more formal agreements and contracts needed to be drawn up and Eastern Diplomatic Services took the big step of employing a Western lawyer as well as a room full of extra clerical hands to spread the ever expanding workload around. Newly purchased typewriters clattered and the money kept rolling into the partners' bank accounts.

It was exactly two years on from the coup of July 1970 that Mohammed and Abdul Aziz decided they needed to hold their first proper business meeting to appraise their good fortune and decide the future direction of the company.

It was the end of a long hot day and Abdul Aziz had arranged for coffee and dates to be delivered into his partner's first floor office. The rest of the building was now quiet, the other staff having finished and gone home. Mohammed poured out the first round of coffees in the small ceramic mugs and the two slumped into the only comfy seats there were. For sentimental reasons Mohammed had kept his old upright fan, which these days spun with a noticeable metallic rasp, whilst remaining as ineffective as it ever was.

'Keeping your head above water?' asked Mohammed smoothly.

'Just. Can't complain. Work's coming in so fast it's hard to turn it around to meet the deadlines, but I see we've taken on some good guys. It'll be fine.'

'I was checking the books again today. The return on our efforts is more than I can believe. The money I've now put into your bank could buy you a fine house here in the capital, and still leave you with a sack full of money to spare.'

'I'm thinking of investing in a small house building project here in the capital. I've enough put by to buy the land and set a builder to work – call it putting something aside for what the English call, a rainy day!' answered Abdul Aziz cheerily. He noticed Mohammed fingering an envelope on his desk, swivelling it round and round under his index finger. He knew a sign that something significant was pending when he saw one. He waited.

'I've got a problem, the kind of problem that comes with success. You see, your efforts have not gone unnoticed in the lofty circles in which you move, and they want you to work for them. That will leave me without my right hand. As my partner I need to cut a deal with you.'

'You're sounding very mysterious. Is that envelope something to do with all this?'

'Open it! It came addressed to you this afternoon. A personal courier from the Ministry delivered it. My guess is they're making you an offer you won't be able to refuse. Come on, open it,' he pleaded, offering the white envelope with outstretched hand, waiting for Abdul Aziz to take it.

Curious and more than a little apprehensive, Abdul Aziz ran his finger under the embossed heraldry of the ministry's envelope. He flicked it open, extracted and unfolded the crisply folded letter. He quickly scanned its contents before raising his head.

'They want me to head up the Ministry's mission to the European Union – starting immediately. It's a stunning pay rise,' he said, casting his eye to the final paragraph to ensure he'd read it right the first time. And, a permanent desk with my own back up team in the Ministry here in Oman. It looks like they really want me to build Oman's links with Europe, a kind of diplomatic travelling salesman role – political, economic, social and cultural. It's a big brief, not sure I could do all they seem to be asking.'

'Nonsense, and let's face it. They don't give you any choice in the matter, now do they? All I want to say is, may I be the first to offer my congratulations – you make us all here so proud. Your family will be pleased for you too.'

'Thank you,' said Abdul Aziz warmly shaking the offered hand.

'And I've an offer of my own to make. I want to propose that, notwithstanding your new post, your partnership here remains in place and on the same terms.'

Abdul Aziz raised his hand in protest, but Mohammed waved it away.

'Your meteoric rise to the heart of things will be very good for us here. You know what we do, how we can help and you will have discretion to put business into your own company – it'll be good for you and good for us. I shouldn't say too much, you'll be wanting more than your 50% cut,' he jested.

'No, no – I need to think what this means. It's rather a lot to take in all at once. You're right, I have to take it – immediately, they said. Have you got time now to go through the cases on my desk – I need to hand them over? Shouldn't be too difficult. Won't take long.'

'No problem, I've already sent a message home to say I'll be working late.'

The two drank more coffee. Abdul Aziz made a quick phone call through to the Ministry to say he'd be in in the morning. It was settled.

The two partners began going through the papers on Abdul Aziz's desk. By midnight they were done and both set off for home. Both were happy. Success and prosperity looked to be going hand in hand.

Abdul Aziz, still in his mid-twenties, could hardly believe the career path that had opened up for him. Some might have attributed it to Allah's blessing, but Abdul Aziz was quite clear it was entirely predictable. He was the right person in the right place, at the right time.

16

Working in Europe and with Europeans was like working with a cool, constant, fresh wind blowing and Abdul Aziz quickly felt himself at home.

It suited him to spend most of his time away. As the years passed the trauma of his nearly-marriage slipped further and further from the front of his mind. Once or twice his brother Walood dared resurrect the subject of marriage, but he wouldn't stand for it and stopped his brother in his tracks each time he tried. It was well intentioned, but Abdul Aziz was not prepared to go there. Gradually, the ever cheerful Walood got the message.

Whilst in Rome, Paris, Berlin and Brussels, and as a frequent traveller between these and other European capitals, Abdul Aziz opted for wearing a suit, saving his Omani robes for more formal occasions and use back home.

A short while later, in 1973 Britain, as a new European member, was added to his travelling itinerary, even though, a public referendum wouldn't be held until 1975 to confirm the public's backing for the idea.

Although he occasionally tried a drink, he never saw the pleasure in it, and in the end refrained from taking alcohol. Over time he found himself adopting ways that Muslims back home would have called haram – forbidden. He became less discriminating in what he ate and he rarely visited a mosque. Since that fateful day in Nizwa he had ceased offering the obligatory five rounds of daily prayer. He now saw himself as still loosely belonging to a Muslim community, but not sharing in its believing.

It was slightly different when back in Oman. Whilst there he'd go along with normal religious practice, though in reality his heart was far from what he put his body through.

Each time he went back, he noticed how he was increasingly being treated differently – as one of the country's elite. He worked for the Ministry, he was one of the Sultan's men. People gave him respect, often kept their distance, which suited him, or rubbed up to get close when they wanted something, which didn't. People also treated him deferentially, wanting to help him, open doors for him, give him gifts – all things that repulsed him.

His new-found income had given him an unexpected hobby. Now, with a plot of land to his name, he was creating a small, gated housing estate; building a house a year on it. He had plans for thirty houses in all – there was still a long way to go.

But by the beginning of 1990, the twentieth house was almost complete. The nineteen others were all occupied, every last one lived in by foreign migrants. The communal swimming pool he'd built in one of the particularly prosperous years early on, was proving a winning attraction. In addition, the house sales were filling his coffers faster than he could decide how to spend his ever-accruing wealth.

As Abdul Aziz reflected on his good fortune, he thought he modelled the ideal capitalist; everything he'd turned his hand to had prospered.

His twentieth house, slightly bigger than the others, he decided to reserve for himself. He had long thought by then that it was time to sever the final tenuous link with his parents' home, the family home, by moving out. If he gradually moved into the new place by degrees, took occupation of it over a long period, his parents then wouldn't be able to say when he'd actually moved out. He'd decided to still keep his room at theirs – that way it would all go smoothly and he wouldn't have to engage in unpleasant conversations.

It could be tricky, but he consoled himself with the thought that like other successful Omanis he was also a man who enjoyed the privacy and freedom that came with living away from family – something that was only really possible for those with independent means and top jobs in Muscat. Elitism lifted one above criticism – it definitely had its advantages.

Walood had got wind of what his brother was planning with the new house and took him to task when he arrived home from Brussels for a few days holiday. Abdul Aziz knew something was up when his brother met him off the plane at Muscat Airport. It wasn't something he usually did. His first thought was that something must have happened to his parents, but then he quickly realised that wasn't the case and Walood had a different agenda.

'Good to see you back,' his brother said. He pointed in the direction of his new taxi, a brand new top of the range Toyota and smiled, 'Yes, it's mine!'

'Nice! Good to see you too, but this is a surprise. Something must be up,' said Abdul Aziz wanting to quell his rising sense of anxiety.

'You're not working in diplomacy without a good instinct for when people want to talk about something,' he laughed, his open hands showing he felt found out.

'Well, come on, a Rial for your thoughts. What's on your mind, Walood?'

'Two things. You've probably got an answer for both but hear me out. First, your builder says you intend to move into the estate your building, house 20's apparently got your name on it. Problem – our parents have wind of it and they aren't happy. They're worried what people will say? They've got a point – it's not customary. They feel embarrassed, people will think bad of them, you know how it is. I don't have to tell you, what people think of each other counts for a lot round here.'

'And the second?'

'It's been a long time, but they want you to meet someone.'

'You mean… someone to marry?'

'Yes. They're worried for you. You're over forty, well into marriageable age, and it's been a long time since, you know, since what happened in 1970,' he shrugged, knowing Abdul Aziz never liked to go there.

'Well thanks for the heads up. The first one is practical… I'll make sure I don't stay there all the time and they can still think of me being at home. I've already decided to keep my room at home – I'll be there often enough for them to feel OK about it. Tell them not to worry on that score. Reassure them. It's all nonsense. I'm hardly at home as it is.'

'Well, you need to tell that builder of yours to keep his mouth shut if he wants to keep getting work from you! He's the one who's saying you're moving in there, stirring it. He's even said, you'll be in by the end of the year.'

Abdul Aziz was shaking his head in agreement.

'OK, I hear you brother – it's not a problem. I get it. But I'm your brother and I'm watching your back. You're not the only one trying to handle diplomacy, and believe me, family politics can be the hardest to deal with!' He laughed, in part with relief at having got a load off his chest.

'Tell me more about what's happening about a bride? That's the big issue. What have they been arranging for me behind my back?'

'It's not like that. It's their duty, their obligation to you. Between you and me, they've talked to a lot of people to try and find someone suitable and until now they've said "no" to every one of them.'

'I'm glad to hear it!'

'They're not pressurising you on this, giving you loads of time, but I really think you need to come and talk to them. They're understandably concerned to make sure you're happy. I think they've been very circumspect in arranging this one, and they've said to me they'd like to talk to you more about it before taking it further. As I say, there's no pressure! That's fair enough isn't it? They've often said that they were far too close when they arranged things last time. They hadn't included you enough beforehand and as a result you never really knew what you were getting into or indeed who you would have married.'

Walood fell silent and for a moment both were thinking back to that dreadful few days back in July 1970.

It was then that Abdul Aziz realised this was the first time he was thinking of those events as having taken place a long time ago. Initially, wanting to avoid any conversation on the subject of marriage he now found, to his own surprise, he was finding himself curious.

'Hmm. Look, I'll come back home with you now. I've got three days leave due to me and I'll come and stay. It sounds like I have a few fences to mend with them anyway. I need to give them more time. They're getting on a bit too. I'm really grateful for the heads up on all this and thanks for coming to pick me up. The two of us could do with a bit of time catching up anyway. How about taking tomorrow off and spending a day in the mountains?' Abdul Aziz sat back in the comfy leather seat, realising he was enjoying this time with his brother.

'Could do,' his brother hesitatingly replied.

'How's the taxi business going? Business good enough to take time out or have you got to earn something to pay for this motor?' A thought came to him, 'Let's give my old Land Rover a run, twenty-three years old and still the best vehicle I've ever had!'

'It's the only one you've ever had! You're a sentimentalist at heart, I always said you were.' Walood grinned again. His good mood was infectious. Nothing seemed to dampen his spirits. Privately, Abdul Aziz wondered what it would it be to be like him.

'Since we're talking about sentiment, what can you tell me about this prospective bride of mine? You must know something? Come on Walood, you smug git, spill the beans. What do you know?'

But Walood merely grinned mischievously at him, then turned his attention to the road and the short journey home. He wasn't saying anything more and Abdul Aziz began to reflect quietly, wondering if there was indeed a big change in his life pending, and what it might mean. He was surprised how well he'd taken the news in his stride. Maybe, he said to himself, just maybe, this might be a good thing.

Then his hand happened on something sharp and rectangular in his pocket. It was the old silver prayer box Walood had given him just before the last time he was about to marry.

He didn't know why, but he always carried it with him in his dishdasha pocket. He told himself he didn't believe in superstition and good luck charms, but often his fingers would caress the box, a habit he hadn't ever managed to stop. After all others believed in what it could do even if he didn't.

17

As the new taxi with the two brothers inside arrived at the Nahari family home in Muscat, it was suddenly dusk.

Darkness comes very quickly in Oman, the dusty, hazy, half-light lasts just minutes before all is transformed by night. The August heat didn't disappear with the sun as in Europe, but continued to radiate from every surface, and the heat coupled with the unbearably high humidity created by the nearby presence of the Arabian Sea, made conditions much of the time barely tolerable for human existence.

It was this hot, saturating heat that nearly floored Abdul Aziz as he stepped from his brother's air-conditioned taxi to take the short walk from the parked car to the sanctuary of home. The front door opened as he approached, his Father, stooping now, gave him a smile and a blessing as he came in. Walood hung back to mess with his new taxi, or pretended to. He noticed his brother had the same stoop only less so.

Abdul Aziz saw his mother, then other members of the extended family. Sweet dates piled high and chilled fruit drinks were brought out, along with a chilled fragrant flannel, which was passed for him to wipe his brow and hands. He was home and the warm familiarity of it almost overwhelmed him.

In walked Walood, still in taxi driver role, cheerfully carrying his brother's suitcase and briefcase, propping them against Abdul Aziz's bedroom door. Smells of roasting lamb and fresh bread wafted in on the air from the kitchen and soon there'd be a feast. Abdul Aziz read all the signs – this was laid on as much to soften him up as well as to welcome him home. They wanted to win him over.

After refreshments, the men in the house, took Walood's taxi over to the nearby mosque for evening prayer. Abdul Aziz fitted in as if he never missed. Now, he decided, was not the time to take issue with religious custom and practice. He worked hard, to suppress his rising sense of hypocrisy and guilt.

On return they were all hungry. Abdul Aziz knew it wouldn't be long before the inevitable conversation about marriage would be broached. He bided the time quietly.

For the next hour and a half, as food was brought and eaten, nothing of consequence was said beyond an exchange of news – where Abdul Aziz had been and how his work had gone for him, how the family date palms had fared and how the sale of garden produce had worked out this year through the family shop in the souk, and finally how his father's brother with cancer was faring in the hospital. There was no news of substance in all this – it was but polite family conversation, and Abdul Aziz wondered how long the charade, however socially necessary, would continue. He saw Walood cast a knowing look in his father's direction. It was a sign the moment of truth had finally come. His father looked over to him.

'Son, I have something to tell you. As a parent and head of our house, it is my duty to look to the future of our family.'

'Yes, Father.'

'So, the time has come, probably long overdue, for me to arrange a marriage for you as custom requires. This has not been an easy thing. I don't want to talk about the events of 1970 again, they've weighed heavily on us all over the years.' Then he paused, as if in reflection, before turning his gaze back to Abdul Aziz and continuing. For his part Abdul Aziz listened quietly, feeling somewhat uncomfortable at this mention of the past. Sensing his his son's feelings he quickly added, 'but we've moved on, happier times have once again returned to our family. You yourself have prospered and been greatly blessed. In fact, with the passage of time and much searching I have to say, I think it has been possible to find for you a woman who will be very suitable to be your wife.' He looked carefully at Abdul Aziz, as if trying to read his response before pressing on.

'Like yourself she has been educated. She can read and write, something women are only just beginning to do in this country, and where this will lead is not for me to judge, though some will.'

'You say she is educated, clever even, Father?'

'Yes, she's from a well respected family living here in Muscat. When Sultan Hamad came to power only boys went to school. In fact in our country I think there were less than a thousand school pupils in sum at that time. But things have changed rapidly, many girls took to schooling and even surprised some of us. This girl did very well and left with excellent grades. Her parents have been working abroad in Saudi Arabia for years in the oil industry, but have now returned home to Muscat where they have a successful business with an office in the city. They are well travelled, something else you share in common. Other factors affect the suitability of a bride of course and she has met all the criteria we have been looking for. Reports are that she is very beautiful, reliable reports – in fact your Mother has seen her and spent time with her.'

'I don't know what to say, but thank you for doing this. I had not been thinking about marriage. My work has preoccupied my attention – first in Europe and the West, then working for the Ministry during the difficult time of the Iranian Revolution. Recently I've had my work cut out dealing with Americans and the Iraq invasion of Kuwait and its aftermath – but now, there is something of a lull in my diplomatic duties. Well, a relative lull that is. It must be time to think about marriage.' He smiled at his Father.

His parents smiled back. Abdul Aziz knew how much this meant to them and he didn't want to make the conversation any more difficult than it was.

'I'm glad you see it like that, Son. All I can say is that her family have been very agreeable in every respect and we have reached an understanding. It will be good in that she is one of our own tribe too. All I need to ask of you is whether you feel ready for us to take it further and begin to bring matters to a conclusion?'

Then too his own surprise, he found himself saying, 'yes, it seems very good to me. How old is she? When are you thinking this might result in a wedding? Have you had any discussion with the family about the kind of dowry I might need to agree?'

'She's not as young as most brides, she's twenty-one. Her brothers and sisters have all married and she's the youngest. Oh, and I forgot to mention, she's an excellent cook too. I learned that from her family – thought you'd like to know!'

'And when?'

'I'd like to think you could talk to her Father yourself about that. It would need to be agreed to fit around your business and his. He still travels and stays in Saudi pretty frequently.'

'Thank you for that. And the dowry? What are the expectations do you think? I'm kind of out of touch with these things.'

'Talk to the family. Families still like to be given gold – something they can put in the bank. I get the impression they are more concerned to see that their daughter will be happy than they are about a dowry. Talk to them. I feel quite relaxed about the practicalities. They seem reasonable people.'

'Ok.' Abdul Aziz was pleased to think his intended's family had prioritised happiness.

'Look!' his Father said, as he reached across to the side table. He grabbed a piece of white paper he'd obviously written on earlier; his weather-worn brown hand, the aged skin and the hard fingernails suddenly very apparent to Abdul Aziz. He couldn't think why he hadn't noticed his father was getting older before. As the paper was offered, he took it. He cast his eyes down the sheet and skim read the lines here and there. His father had written down everything he could think of that might be useful information for Abdul Aziz to have.

'I'll call them tomorrow, arrange to see them. I've got three clear days.'

'But you said we were going to the mountains tomorrow,' jested Walood, pretending to be hurt.

'Things change,' he simply replied.

All three knew a potentially difficult conversation had moved to a most satisfactory conclusion.

18

For twenty years, Abdul Aziz had handled diplomatic conversations, they were his stock in trade. He was rarely nervous or anxious, but practical and reasoned, stoical even. Rarely did anything ruffle his inner calm. Outwardly he was an able and confident man with a suave and engaging manner. Not so, the next morning.

His early morning phone call to the home of his intended had resulted in an invitation to visit – not in a month's time, but later that very day. It was early Spring 1990, but being unusually hot, it felt like the longest day of the summer. He noticed his index finger was stroking the old silver prayer box deep in his pocket.

His brother Walood offered to drive him. After all, they were no longer going on an outing to the mountains, what else could he do?

Arriving at the Hassan's house at the agreed time of 4pm, Walood did the discreet thing and parked round the corner, choosing to sit outside and wait ready to take his brother back, though in reality he was eager to be the first to hear how things had gone.

On the journey Walood had noticed the more bashful side of his brother and their were long silences as they drove the ten minutes to the house. Walood also noticed the extra detail Abdul Aziz had put into his appearance – his white dishdasha and colourful turban, both were his best and freshly laundered. The leather sandals on his feet were his finest pair, and he carried a bag, some gift no doubt inside – he didn't like to ask what it was.

The house they pulled up at was substantial, one of the older Muscat homes, probably formerly owned by British or Portuguese merchants. One didn't need to look any further to know who ever lived there was doing very well. It was centrally located, wearing a faded white glory and the accumulated desert dust lent it a timeless air.

The front door had an old-fashioned brass bell-pull and he heard the metallic jangle inside when he pulled its lever hard. As he waited, Abdul Aziz was momentarily unnerved as he noticed a rather incongruously out of place security camera pointing down at him from above the porch.

He waited patiently, the historic front door before him, beautifully carved, possibly of teak – another mark of status. Then with barely a sound, the door suddenly swung open and a smiling Omani man, with a trim modern beard, dressed in a matching outfit to his own, held a hand across his chest and greeted him warmly. Abdul Aziz guessed him to be in his late 50s.

'Abdul Aziz. I am Omar Hassan. You are most welcome. Do come inside.'

Unlike his own father, this man was younger and fitter, and moved with the grace of an antelope.

The house's interior was dark and refreshingly cool – a cultivated sanctuary. It took a few moments for his eyes to adjust from the brightness outside as he followed his host. The quiet hiss of the air conditioning system again alerted him to the owner's prosperity as he was guided into a reception room.

It appeared as if this was to be a private audience, a meeting just between the two of them – but in this he was about to be proved wrong. After pleasantries were exchanged, and mint tea brought in by what Abdul Aziz took to be a Filipino maid, his host, Omar Hassan, began getting straight to the business in hand. Interrupting politely, Abdul Aziz offered his host the gift he'd brought.

'The best chocolate truffles in Belgium! I brought them back from Brussels yesterday.' His host took them with a smile and placed them to one side, his mind on other matters.

'I trust you are comfortable Abdul Aziz, and everything is to your satisfaction.'

Abdul Aziz nodded in agreement. He could not fault the hospitality he had received.

'I have two other people in the house I would like you to meet. First, providing you are happy we are not proceeding too quickly I want you to meet my daughter. Then I will bring in the marriage lawyer.'

'If your daughter is happy to see me now, then I will be happy to meet her,' he replied. 'Perhaps the lawyer can wait until the meeting has taken place? Yes?'

'Absolutely, please excuse me for a moment and enjoy your tea,' he said, rising from his chair and exiting the room.

This gave Abdul Aziz a moment to appraise the situation. He'd not expected to be able to meet his intended so quickly and he had no words prepared or indeed any he could call to mind. The moment of first encounter seemed momentous, he ought to think of something, but for once in his life words failed him. He tried to reassure himself that small talk would be fine.

The room and the house indicated that this was a most successful Omani family. Going by the usual protocols this gave every prospect of being a most advantageous marriage, but the dowry, how much was this going to cost him? Before he could think any further, he heard people approaching and stood to his feet.

Omar entered the room first, followed by a veiled tall and slim young woman, who was introduced to him as Maryam. She wore a traditional Omani abaya, partly hiding her lower face, but it took little imagination to see she was an elegant and beautiful woman.

'Please sit Abdul Aziz, please,' said Omar, being the perfect host.

Abdul Aziz resumed his seat whilst Omar took his and Maryam remained a few paces off, sitting in a chair near the door.

'I'm pleased to meet you Maryam. Our families have been talking to each other and here we are,' he said as warmly as he could, his words nonetheless sounding rather more lame than he'd have liked.

'Yes. I'm very happy to meet you and have learned a lot about you,' she replied.

'I hope you heard the good bits,' he joked and smiled. And then she laughed, nervously at first, but genuinely. He liked what he was discovering, and he'd already decided he liked the sound of her voice.

'I know you had a tragic loss when you were about to marry many years ago. It was a happiness denied. That made me sad. But I also heard that since then you've worked tirelessly and gained an enviable reputation for what you have achieved for the country, as well as for your family. They're obviously very proud of you and I like that.' Then she fell silent, Abdul Aziz wondering if she felt she had said too much or something out of place, but he felt reassured she knew something of his past – he himself didn't need to say anything further about the matter.

'I can see you too will get on,' her father interrupted, smiling. 'I wonder if some of those honey pastries you were making earlier will be ready. Would you mind?'

Abdul Aziz knew a prearranged plan when he saw one and he watched as one enchanted, as Maryam elegantly rose from her chair and retreated briefly to the kitchen, Abdul Aziz following her every move.

'She's been a wonderful daughter, faithful and caring, and so very talented. But I'm her father and father's tend to be biased,' he laughed.

'I can see she is a lovely person,' said Abdul Aziz thinking he ought to say something affirming.

'Well then, whilst she goes and see if those pastries are ready, may I be presumptuous and bring the lawyer in?'

'Why not?' Abdul Aziz found himself saying, allowing himself to be happily swept along by events. Again, Omar slipped out of the room and he heard him call out to someone.

Abdul Aziz was left reflecting on two minutes of encounter. He would not see Maryam again on this visit. He thought himself fortunate to have been given the opportunity he'd had and in the briefest of encounters had been favourably impressed. He heard the sound of approaching male voices. Omar arrived with a little wizened man in a plain brown dishdasha, holding a roll of papers gathered under one arm, a pen in his free hand.

'This is Khimji. He's the expert in these things. And these are the honey pastries.' He lowered the tray and put them beside Abdul Aziz, the hot scent of fresh sweet baking proving irresistible. He took one.

'Delicious,' he said, as the lawyer began pulling one paper out from his bundle.

'Abdul Aziz Nahari, isn't it?' he enquired, his pen poised.

'Yes.'

'I will draw up a draft marriage contract which will then be agreed between your two families. You follow?'

'Yes.'

'But before I do this I need to know if the two of you have agreed the dowry. Yes?'

'No, well we haven't discussed it yet,' said Abdul Aziz looking at Omar Hassan. 'I'm not experienced in these things, Mr Hassan, I'm only aware of local custom and practice.'

'I've always said as each of my other five daughters were married, I am only interested in their future happiness. I am happy to settle on a token dowry. Your real dowry will be your gift of lifelong love to my daughter – do we understand one another?' he asked quietly with a new look of seriousness.

'I can assure you of that, but I would still want to do what is right,' said Abdul Aziz.

'Then let us settle on a gold necklace and a diamond bracelet of your choosing. I plan on trusting you with my precious daughter, so I will have no problem trusting you with a little thing like providing an appropriate necklace and bracelet. Are you happy with that arrangement, shall we shake on it in front of Khimji here?'

'That is absolutely fine by me. I will see something suitable is brought round to your home,' said Abdul Aziz, extending his hand, recognising that behind the smiles there were clear and formal expectations in their exchanges.

'Then, Khimji, it is over to you to draw up the marriage contract. I have sent a message out to Walood to come in and act as a second witness. He must be very hot waiting outside,' he said, with a knowing smile.

Moments later Walood was standing in the room, his required presence having been explained to him.

'Abdul Aziz, I have already asked my daughter, the intended bride, if she is happy with the proposed arrangement and she has indicated she is. I now have to formally ask you if you are also happy – to marry Maryam Hassan?'

‘I am,’ said Abdul Aziz calmly, smiling as he saw his brother Walood’s look of amazement.

‘Then it’s settled,’ said Khimji.

Upon this declaration, and as custom demanded, Omar and Abdul Aziz then faced one another and grasped each other’s hands. The marriage would be made official and a day would now be set for the malka – the public reading of the contract to take place sometime later in both family homes. There would also now need to be a visit to the mosque to tie things up there too. Preliminary discussion of practical arrangements would be held, and a decision made as to when the wedding day should fall.

As neither groom nor bride were young, it was agreed it would happen sooner rather than later. Families, though, would need a little while, a few weeks at least, to make preparations for the big day.

Two hours later, as Walood and Abdul Aziz made their exit, they heard excited squeals of delight, high-pitched women’s voices coming from somewhere else in the far reaches of the house – the home’s hidden household were celebrating some good news. It was infectious.

Though Abdul Aziz was apprehensive, he had a good feeling about it all, and he responded in kind to Walood’s usual bonhomie as they made their return journey.

19

An Omani wedding in the capital was quite different to one held in the interior of the country – in somewhere like Nizwa. Abdul Aziz had come to realise from his travels that in Oman, weddings were generally rather less ostentatious and unremarkable compared with elsewhere in the Middle East. For a start, the numbers of those attending were usually much smaller, even in the capital, Muscat.

Abdul Aziz thought the events twenty years previously in Nizwa were securely boxed up in a compartment of his mind he'd labelled, "remote history" and he'd rarely find cause to remember the events of that day. Even so, once or twice as the wedding day in June 1990 approached, he felt the dark cloud of the past, like a hostile sandstorm, brush across his consciousness, awakening dark shadows – but these he summarily banished back to the place he felt they belonged. In sum, he generally didn't find it at all difficult to be upbeat about his present life.

Abdul Aziz was counting on a typically quiet wedding day, separate events in both family homes to start things, then after all the feasting and greeting, the leaving with his new bride to live in House Twenty, as he now called it. That was how it would go in his mind's eye, but he knew things in life don't always go as one imagined they might.

In Muscat things tended to have a more celebratory upbeat air and on the wedding day, word and invitations had been spread far and wide and in fact many hundreds of people turned up to share in their day. That was the first surprise for Abdul Aziz. He found himself the popular centre of attention and it was as if everyone else found some happiness of their own in his good fortune.

Both families were evidently very happy too, and the day included much music and dancing; men with men and women with women, just as custom dictated. When finally, the time came for Maryam and Abdul Aziz to leave, Abdul Aziz surprised everyone when Walood drove round to the front of the house in a brand new white Mercedes saloon 190E. His brother leapt out and handed him the keys.

'Nice motor you've bought for yourself brother,' he said, with just a trace of envy in his voice.

The couple drove off, just a short distance to their new home in Abdul Aziz's gated estate; finally leaving the celebratory crowds behind them. From the little they knew of each other so far, they both thought they'd find a happy future together. Indeed, they were both full of optimism, smiles and excitement.

However, the wider context, relationships in the Gulf were not looking so good.

Tensions across the Middle East were once again increasing. Abdul Aziz had more than half an eye on the increasing acrimony coming from Iraq, raising the prospect of imminent conflict.

It was little more than a month after their wedding, the Gulf War began, Iraq invading Kuwait in July 1990 to declare it as its 13th province. Following worldwide condemnation, the US responded in leading a military coalition attack for the Liberation of Kuwait. Two years of fighting followed until Saddam Hussein's Iraq was taken to the brink of total defeat.

Throughout this period Oman was backing the American coalition and Abdul Aziz was called upon to ease the wheels of diplomacy, not least because the US wanted to make use of the conveniently located Omani soil to host its attacking forces.

Abdul Aziz realised that the old Arab League, which was supposed to be the guarantor of peace in the region, had failed and the diplomatic future was looking uncertain. So, he helped Oman work behind the scenes, to make the Gulf Cooperative Council its more effective successor and future guarantor of security in the region.

Consequently, his attention and his time were taken up with diplomatic business and he was frequently called away from his new wife and home, as he endlessly shuffled from nation to nation in the company of senior Ministry officials. Abdul Aziz found himself increasingly talking to US diplomats, as Oman sought to position its own security through agreement and military cooperation with the US. It was then, he thought, he first detected in Maryam the harbouring of some anti-American sentiment. It was usually expressed in personal comments directed at him and her fear, as she put it, that he might be corrupted.

Then in the summer of 1993, when the still new president of the USA, Bill Clinton, ordered a cruise missile attack on the Iraqi Intelligence HQ in Baghdad, Abdul Aziz found himself called upon to visit New York and Washington for the first time.

His experience in the USA opened his eyes to Western ways of seeing and thinking, and he found himself enjoying a freedom of expression and belief quite new to him, all eased by the wealth he now enjoyed. There was the slight discomfort he carried with him, that Maryam would not understand this part of him. He felt that in enjoying these new experiences, he had negotiated an uncrossable divide lurking beneath the surface; like quicksand waiting to swallow them both up without mercy. What had begun as marital bliss began to feel less so with both beginning to see the other's domain as questionable, even then as unbridgeable.

Even so, visits home were largely happy times and Maryam proved to be an excellent manager of the household that they'd created. He also discovered she had an ever-widening circle of women friends. The two had found a compatibility and friendship, that some would call love, and almost everything – work, wealth and marriage, gave Abdul Aziz a glow of self-satisfaction. Life, he told himself had, on the whole, turned out well – really well.

Despite their differences of opinion, he found much contentment in that Maryam was evidently very happy, her smiles and laughter filled their home as did the sweet smells of her cooking, but that was all to change after their first child was born in October 1993.

20

Even before Abdul Aziz boarded the Lockheed Tristar from the United States for the first leg of his journey to Oman at the end of October 1993, he knew something untoward was afoot. A brief final telephone call home, made in Washington before leaving his hotel, had felt all wrong.

It was the best part of a day's bumpy flying before he finally arrived back in the Middle East and then, as his plane was reaching home, he was nearly re-routed. Muscat airport was so shrouded in a dust storm there was uncertainty whether, on the last leg of an interminably long journey, they would be able to land.

The gale-force wind made a few last attempts to make susceptible passengers sick, as the jet rolled in on the turbulent air, before it finally relented and let them make their final descent into Muscat. By then Abdul Aziz was very tired. In spite of the benefit of travelling first class, the time change on such long flights always got to him. It had been a hard tour and he was all in.

Leaving his baggage to be collected and brought to his home by willing hands later, he walked smartly through Arrivals, then paused after Customs to make a phone call. He then moved quickly to the exit to look for his waiting car. As he did so he glanced up, noticing the upbeat publicity boards – the national airline, Oman Air, announcing the introduction of its inaugural international passenger services, a measure of the country's ever growing economic progress. He hardly slowed his pace, he was needing to get home.

Then, despite his darkened glasses, he had to squint through glass doors to accommodate the sun's harsh glare. He saw his lift – his white Mercedes was there, his personal driver looking out for him. Contact made, the car instantly pulled across in front of the other traffic. He pushed his way outside and in seconds they were on their way.

Back in the phone kiosk, in his brief telephone call made at Muscat airport, he'd called to say he'd landed and was on his way home. Once again, he detected a mood change in Maryam – something he couldn't quite put his finger on and it alarmed him. He gave an involuntary shudder. He worried it might be her health or maybe that of their baby son Hassim – until he was home there was no way of knowing.

His unease wouldn't go away for the whole duration of the thirty minute ride. He was very tired yes, his eyes gritty and dry, but he was now also a worried man and he was alarmed when he saw in the car's interior mirror how strained he looked. He told his driver, rather more brusquely than he intended, to step on it and the car silently picked up speed moving between outside and inside lanes to get past traffic on the last leg.

The Bangladeshi man on the gate to their estate, whose name Abdul Aziz didn't yet know, saw them coming and opened up to let the car through. Then, finally, he was home at House Twenty. Reassuringly, the house itself looked no different to before, though the new landscaped trees and crimson flowered Bourgainvillea were now well-established, hiding the stark white contours of the modern build. Dropped outside the dark wood front door, he left his driver to put the car away under the car port.

Once inside, he announced his arrival to what he thought was an unusually quiet house. Not even baby Hassim could be heard crying. He made straight for the kitchen where he expected to find Maryam, but she wasn't there. Their Filipino maid was at the sink preparing some salad; washing and chopping with her head down, concentrating on what she was doing, a sharp knife in her hand.

'Where is Maryam?' he asked quietly.

'In her bedroom,' he was told. He feared she was ill.

'Maryam, Maryam,' he called softly as he walked upstairs. There was no reply. His worry built with every step.

'Maryam,' he said quietly, unable to hold back the concern in his voice as he pushed open the bedroom door. He saw her before he heard her, lying on the bed, her head turned away from him.

'Hello. You're back,' she replied in a flat tone, turning her head slowly toward him, a faraway expression on her face.

'What's up? How are you? Hassim?' he blurted out anxiously.

'Hassim's fine. He's with Jasmine. She's looking after him in his nursery.

'Then what is it? You can tell me,' he added, moving to sit by her on the bed.

'The doctor says I'm feeling low after the birth of my baby. That's all. He's given me a prescription. It happens sometimes, he said.'

Abdul Aziz felt some relief on this. The more upsetting possibilities that hitherto had seized his imagination began to recede, and he felt waves of compassion for Maryam, reading sadness, as well as a mysterious distance in her dark eyes.

This was the first occasion his home had seemed gloomy, as if some of the life in it had been drained. He couldn't put his finger on what exactly had changed. The world outside still so full of sunshine and colour; the interior world painted in altogether contrasting dark and lack-lustre hues. Abdul Aziz floundered, lost for words, not knowing how to respond, so he sat silently and reached for her hand. It felt cool, damp and unresponsive in his – he gave an involuntary shudder, as it felt like the touch of death, when both of them were meant to be alive. He immediately let go and stood up.

'Shall I organise a drink or something?' he said. Even as he spoke he felt his effort at trying to be helpful was clumsy and misplaced. He watched her withdraw into herself and dismiss him.

'I'll come back later,' he said, observing the distance between them grow. It seemed to his eyes like a deep impassible wadi; like a cleft in the Hajar mountains, which had come to separate each from the other.

That night, tired as he was, Abdul Aziz stayed up, sitting in a chair. His mind repeatedly played over a myriad of negative thoughts – of things that had gone wrong. He sat with one hand on his brow, his other subconsciously clutching the silver rectangular prayer box in his pocket.

Was he himself to blame? Should he speak to the doctor? How should he behave now his wife was, well, how was she

– sick? His parents would talk about jinns – mischievous spirits who would cause trouble, but he had long since stopped believing in such things. In the dark, sitting alone, glancing into the shadows, it would be easy for some to believe in these things once again. He went and lay down to restless night in the spare room. In his dreams he was walking in the desert ever so slowly, fearful lest his step would trigger an explosion. Every now and then it would happen. Bang, he'd be flipped up in the air, spin round and land in the sand. He'd struggle weakly to his feet and try to press on.

At the first hint of the new day, and as the sudden shafts of sunlight outlined the closed metal shuttered windows, he realised that he needed to marshal his thoughts before the house came to life.

He decided for the first time in his life to take a day off from the Ministry and spend it at home. Once he'd made his phone call to the Ministry, he turned his attention to the day ahead. As yet, there was no sound of Maryam or Hassim, only Jasmine busying herself in the kitchen. He decided to begin by talking to her. He felt certain she would tell him how things really were. Heavy with tiredness, he wearily lifted himself from his chair and went first to the bathroom to freshen up. Then, after changing, he walked into the kitchen.

'Good morning Jasmine, how are you today?' he said. Then realising he'd startled her, added, 'Oh, sorry, I didn't mean to surprise you.'

'I didn't hear you, that's all. I'm fine, Sir, I'll just pop out to get the bread, I'll be back to fix breakfast. Tell me, what would you like today? Coffee to start?'

'That will be fine, thank you,' he said, watching her prepare the coffee. 'Are things all right here, Jasmine? Is Maryam all right?' he asked, knowing that to put it like this gave her the chance to say just how she saw things.

'Well, she's not been herself for the last month. I didn't think it was anything but an off day to start with, but… then she would cry lots. I mean lots, Sir… most days, every day. I couldn't understand it, could see no reason for it. She has everything she needs, doesn't she? It's been very troubling. I didn't know what to do.'

'I had no idea,' Abdul Aziz said plaintively.

'I told her to call the doctor in the end and that seemed to help. Apparently, some mothers, after their baby, find it hard to get back to being themselves, and the doctor said, she was one of them. He gave her some medicine. It's stopped her crying, but she still doesn't seem right yet, Sir. You may have noticed. Guess it will take a little time. I'm so glad you've come back.'

'Yes, I see. And how does she find looking after Hassim when she's like this? Can she? Is Hassim OK? Do I need to get in some more help?'

'She's already organised that. The nursery nurse, Rosa, she comes in each day. She'll be here any minute. I usually wait until she arrives before I go out to get the bread. That's so Maryam is never on her own. The doctor said we should make sure she wasn't left on her own.' Abdul Aziz noticed that Jasmine then went quiet, perhaps thinking she had said too much. For his own part he was horrified just how little he knew of what had been happening at home.

'Well done, Jasmine. I'm really grateful for what you've done. We must make sure she recovers quickly, is well again soon. Thank you for the coffee. I think I'll take it into my room.'

With that he walked across the house, listening to the clattering at the windows as Jasmine began opening the shutters. He entered his office and pulled the door shut behind him. He looked around at all the artefacts that he'd brought home to make the space feel his and realised something. He'd never known Maryam come in his study, but perhaps she did when he was away. They'd never talked about any of the beloved possessions that he had so carefully collected in his travels and displayed in his working space. Perhaps he should go to Maryam again now, but first he needed to gather his thoughts and come up with a strategy. He decided he'd start by calling their doctor, believing professional advice would help.

Doctor Michael Campbell was one of the best. Edinburgh trained, he was the senior man at a private medical practice nearby. When Abdul Aziz called at 8am he was put straight through.

'Postpartum Depression – a classic case,' the doctor said with a marked Scottish accent.

'What's that then?' he asked.

'Well, typically, symptoms include sadness, lack of energy, anxiety, not sleeping well, crying, mood changes – no-one's quite certain what the causes are, but usually they arise in the weeks following childbirth. I've given her a course of anti-depressants to help her in the short term, but I've suggested she might like some counselling as well, though

I'm not sure she's keen on that – I think she thinks it's a bit of Western hocus-pocus. In my experience, the combination of medication and some counselling usually works best. Perhaps you can try and help her see the sense in talking with someone. Believe me I've tried Mr Nahari, but she won't hear of it from me.'

'And, how long will she be ill?'

'Och, difficult to say. Maybe six months, with some returning episodes. She might be one of the lucky ones and bounce back sooner. Would you like me to see her again? Are you concerned about her condition? Has it changed?'

'No, no. It's just I got back from abroad yesterday and she's, well, different, yes, different. Remote even. I'm a bit at a loss as to what to do for the best.'

'I can understand that. She'll need more support over the weeks ahead. That always helps. Give her some space. Try not to make demands on her. Allow her time to come through it. That kind of thing – you follow me?'

'Yes, that's really helpful. And I'll get her to see you again soon – best if we both closely monitor this thing while it lasts.'

'I'm afraid it is likely to last. Never easy, PPD.'

'What's that?'

'Sorry, doctors are always doing that, I mean, Postpartum Depression.'

With that he had gone, and Abdul Aziz was left once more to his own thoughts, alone in his study. He heard a far-off voice. It was Jasmine, back already, calling everyone.

'Breakfast's ready.'

He got up and made his way to the kitchen, only to find when he got to there, he was sitting on his own.

21

On the one day he was absent from work, an important call came through to Abdul Aziz's office at the Ministry, but of course he wasn't there to receive it.

Two days later a fax followed. This was a dinner invitation, personally addressed to him – the event arranged to mark the coming into force of the Treaty of Maastricht and the formal start of the new European Union on 1 November 1993.

As a diplomat, this was something Abdul Aziz had been watching progress over recent years, and as an outside friendly sympathiser, he was now being invited to the formal celebration. Such invitations carried with them an expectation of attendance.

The invitation had first been copied into Sultan Hamad's office some days earlier, but not being sure who might be attending on behalf of Oman's Sultan, they'd delayed replying to Holland. Having finally come to a decision, a last minute, urgent, three line whip was sent by fax, one to ensure Abdul Aziz was in the visiting party. In consequence he was required to join the already booked-in group, including one other senior ministry official, to meet them at the airport and fly immediately to Holland.

A phone call from his office to his home alerted him and they successfully arranged a last minute ticket change to get him there. Some hapless businessman found himself taken out of the queue and told to await a later flight.

Abdul Aziz was torn – he realised he would have to leave his home in the hands of fate and whatever extra care he could lay on at short notice. There was only time for a quick call to brief his brother Walood and his wife. They understood and promised to visit Maryam in his absence. He told them he thought he'd only be away three days.

Hastily, he grabbed his overnight case, some paperwork from his desk, and dropped them by the front door in readiness. Then he sent an urgent call to his driver to come round and have the car ready to take him to the airport in an hour's time. He'd just enough time to try and talk to Maryam one more time before leaving. He found her sitting up in bed.

'Maryam, I've had a call from the Ministry. I'm to go to the airport in an hour. Europe this time. Three days I think. I really don't have any choice in this.'

'That's all right. You go. I'll be fine,' she replied in a flat voice with a dead pan, blank expression on her face.

'I'm torn – I know you need me at the moment. I've just called Walood. Asked him if they'd pop round while I'm away – give you some company, spend some time with you.'

'Thank you. I'll be fine. I've got some of the ladies from the mosque visiting later. They've been round before. I like them, they understand me.'

The comment unsettled Abdul Aziz. He didn't know what to say. Since when had Maryam found friends at the mosque to be helpful? Who were they? Looking around the bedroom he knew why the room had struck him as different to before. Here and there there were calligraphic words he recognised from the Qur'an, all in silver frames, cold metal dogmatics that chilled his heart.

'Did your friends bring you these?' he asked pointing to them.

'Yes. They've told me Allah will help me. The women come and recite prayers with me at home.'

Abdul Aziz began to feel more concern. Whether true or not, he didn't know, but the pictures symbolised a heavy cloud of conservative religious practice reaching into the very heart of his own home like a suffocating fog. As the holy words had come in, the first things to have gone out, were spontaneity and lightness, brightness and laughter. Where were conversation and love? What was worse was that Maryam in her illness was at a distance from him, held afar by new forces, new unknown friends at work, and he felt a pain, as if he was losing something, even a part of himself.

'I'll be home soon, very soon' he offered trying to bridge the gulf.

She reached for a book of prayers at the side of the bed. He recognised the green leather binding. 'I'll be fine. I'm learning new things to help me,' she said, as she turned away from him and began thumbing the pages. She was looking for something, he thought, but he couldn't quite see what.

It was time, and he had to leave her to her thoughts. He turned and felt a strange coldness in the air. He hoped she would soon be well again, but was so concerned, though time was tight, he decided to make a second call to Walood.

He had no-one else to turn to. In the seclusion of his study, he dialled up his brother.

'Hi Walood.'

'You again! This is a surprise. I hear nothing from my brother for days and then two calls in twenty minutes! Everything all right?' he enquired.

'Not exactly. It's Maryam. It's more than just the illness. She's changed. Do you know her friends from the mosque?'

'I've heard mention of them. They're mainly older women, known for supporting women going through difficulties, that kind of thing. Come on, not a group I'd know, except by reputation, brother.'

'What kind of reputation?'

'Oh, they're respected. Good, kind, say prayers regularly, trust in Allah; they're well thought of for what they do say the men of the mosque. No worries there.'

'The trouble is, I don't feel comfortable about it. Something's not right.'

'You've been overseas too much brother, lost touch with how we do things,' said Walood, suddenly thinking he'd overstepped the mark as there was a pause on the end of the line.

'I guess you're right. You two keep an eye on things for me, will you, until I'm back, OK?' he pleaded.

'No worries. We'll call in this afternoon. Safe journey – inshallah.'

With that his brother had gone and Abdul Aziz knew for certain that he himself had also become someone different. He had changed and so had Maryam. His fear was that two different people might find it difficult to make a happy home for their baby son Hassim to grow up in.

As he thought on, he realised that he knew other couples where husband and wife seemed to see the world through different lenses, yet they somehow made things work for them. The thought lifted his low mood. As head of his household, he knew he had to create a safe space for his son to grow up in, and he knew instinctively the importance of a happy home.

Hopefully, he told himself, Maryam would find herself again. The Postpartum Depression might go as quickly as it had appeared. As she got over her illness, things would return to how they once were, but just in case, he had to think how things were to be organised for the best.

He resolved there and then that just as he'd made a success for himself in work, he would ensure his home would be rebuilt from the sad place it had fallen into. It didn't do to dwell on the guilt his own neglect provoked. Little did he realise what a challenge he had taken on.

He was disturbed in his reverie by persistent calling from his front door. It was his driver, ready, impatient to take him to the airport. He looked at his expensive Rolex watch. It would be a close run thing if he caught his flight.

22

Maryam's second and later pregnancies had been well prepared for with Doctor Campbell's help and counsel, and the depths of severe Postpartum Depression were not repeated. Her dark days of 1993 did not return. Life in the home became full.

In 1995, 1996 and once more in 1998, Maryam and Abdul Aziz again became parents – two more boys, Abbadi and Tariq, and then finally, a girl. They called her Raqiyah.

Raqiyah was a name Abdul Aziz chose himself because he had great ambitions for her. The Arabic meaning was – progressing.

Somehow when he first saw his beautiful baby daughter, he thought he glimpsed something of himself in those early signs of personality. It little mattered that he might have imagined it – she became the vessel for his future hopes. He saw her as a sign of optimism, as bearing the flag of progress. He couldn't explain it, but from the beginning there was a special father-daughter bond.

As one who had seen girls in Europe going to school and taking jobs, he saw in Raqiyah someone he hoped would break the mould and similarly climb great heights. He had no doubt his sons would be fine. Life was much more straightforward for them – no worries there. But for Raqiyah, he saw in her an adventure beginning. In naming her thus, he hoped he was setting her on her way and he wanted her to put an end to a culture built on restrictions – to become a truly independent, self-confident and modern female Omani. He had begun to see other leading men in the country thinking like this, freeing their daughters – giving them an education, opening up possibilities for them that had never existed before. He wanted to be one of them.

It was as if the children themselves had also been a medicine and in the weeks after Raqiyah's birth, though Maryam was not the same person as she was before she had her four children, she was certainly in a better place than five years previously. Only in one respect had things not improved and Abdul Aziz feared they never would.

Maryam's embrace of religion, with all the new found enthusiasm of a convert, had stayed with her. As she had taken steps in one direction, so Abdul Aziz had reacted by going in another, allowing his rational and liberal tendencies to further flower. The world of opposites they created made for a heady and sometimes explosive cocktail in the home, though Abdul Aziz determinedly kept his earlier resolution to, first and foremost, build a safe and happy home for his family.

Fierce as the sudden storms were between the couple, they always blew over and a harmony, of a kind, returned. Both parents found fulfilment in the progress of their four children. Their young family were loved and sheltered as far as possible from the tempests that beset their own relationship, and though they didn't know it then, their family of four children was now complete.

Since the birth of their first child Hassim in 1993, Abdul Aziz had been through a more difficult time at work. It had all come to a crisis in 1994, a time when the Sultan had been developing friendly relations with Israel. It was a policy that proved unpopular with neighbouring countries and increasingly with many Omanis at home. Many pointed the finger and saw Abdul Aziz as, along with his Ministry seniors, serving an American agenda of building dialogue and agreement with Israel and they claimed the pace of modernisation in Oman had somehow, somewhere, taken a wrong turn.

His attendance at a Water Resources Working Group international meeting in Muscat in April 1994, where there was an Israeli delegation present, might well have been, with the benefit of hindsight, the final straw that broke the camel's back. Like the deluge of water down a dry wadi after rain washed out everything in its path, so was the Sultan's retribution on those who he believed, or was told, had betrayed him.

It was only after the delegates had headed for home, all hell broke loose. Suddenly, having no truck with the threat of personal criticism and wanting to head off threats to his rule, Sultan Hamad promptly ordered mass arrests, panicking and unsettling many, but effectively bringing things back in line and restoring his grip on power at home and overseas.

More than 400 people were swept up by the Sultan's security services in the following month. Fear descended on Ministry top officials and those in their wake, including Abdul Aziz. He was right to be afraid.

Though he was spared the indignity of an arrest, he was summoned without notice to report to Police Headquarters in Muscat to give a full account of himself. The experience shook him and by the end of the process, when he was finally allowed to return home, he knew he would forevermore be viewed as tainted and, so far as any future advancement in his hitherto successful diplomatic career went, well, he knew that was now out of the question – it was never going to happen. It was time for a fundamental re-think.

For a year after that first call from the security services, he'd had to report weekly to Police HQ to explain what he was doing, where he had been to, and with whom he had held conversations. He was a marked man – his phone lines were certainly tapped and his every movement tracked. He now had to be very careful indeed. This was no country for an individual to fall out with its Sultan. He had to use all the diplomatic skills at his disposal to rehabilitate himself and it took time. It was stressful and in the process he felt himself age.

At the same time he knew he had only ever acted under Ministry orders, never once allowed himself to be exposed out on a limb. Though he could end up being the scapegoat, the fall guy for his masters, he was increasingly confident that as the weeks passed, and with care taken, he could avoid any catastrophic fallout in his direction. With his work options in the Ministry closing down by the day, he had just one plan in mind, one piece of action to help himself out of his predicament.

To forestall future employment difficulties, he resolved to talk to his old colleague, Mohammed Mansoor, at Eastern Diplomatic Services. He still had leverage there and the firm had, so far as he knew, avoided any Ministry surveillance, their recent work having focussed much more on lucrative business contracts than foreign policy.

Mohammed had done very well out of his former partner and Abdul Aziz knew that he could probably cash in on this now at his time of need. So it proved. Mohammed was only too glad to welcome him back, a warm handshake sealing the deal. His old upstairs office was once again at his disposal, the junior member of staff then occupying it bumped off down stairs.

Thus, in the summer of 1994 Abdul Aziz took a career step down and returned to his old firm. His world was smaller, but for the sake of his family he accepted this, choosing to keep his head down, and his presence out of the limelight. He was back, but in a backwater, where the air conditioning in Mohammed's office was still only an ineffective ancient electric fan, now held together with black electrician's tape.

There was some relief a year after the arrests, when in November 1995, on Oman National Day, Sultan Hamad's birthday, everyone arrested, all those who'd been imprisoned or otherwise rounded up, were suddenly pardoned by Hamad himself, and the world returned almost to normal once more. Abdul Aziz knew a shrewd politician when he saw one.

As things settled down again, Hamad took the lead on an economic programme of liberalisation and diversification in Oman; and ironically, this very soon ensured Abdul Aziz's ability to turn a tidy income, through managing business contracts, could begin to show itself again – much to Mohammed's delight. Clouds did indeed seem to have silver linings! In particular, Oman's new interest in the Asian Rim Association for Regional Cooperation opened several new doors for business expansion.

Though the building of the thirty houses on the gated estate where the Nahari family lived had long since been complete, Abdul Aziz was now able to make plans for another more ambitious, fifty house complex that he wished to build on the outskirts of nearby Muttrah.

All this meant that as his young family were growing up, Abdul Aziz was around for them much more than if he'd stayed at the Ministry. He found he was able to do things with them, including giving time to his youngest child, his daughter, Raqiyah.

He'd silently promised on the day she was born that from that day forward, in 1998, he would not only be alongside his five, three and two year old boys, but he would also be there for her, and he would ensure she lived up to her name and with the same opportunities as her brothers.

Abdul Aziz was a man who believed he always kept his promises.

23

It was late evening. Abdul Aziz was at home. He felt tired after a busy day of endless contract negotiations. He was so weary he simply wanted to flop down in a chair.

Moving slowly, he took some fresh mint and lime iced juice, in a glass from the kitchen, then put the TV on in his study. The tiredness fell from him instantly. Immediately, he was shocked at the images of what he saw.

It was 11th September 2001 – the TV pictures, scarily compulsive. He wondered how many incidents were taking place, then realised the TV were playing endless repeats of the same shots – a plane being deliberately flown into a skyscraper. The skilled diplomat part of Abdul Aziz knew in that instant the world had changed. He wouldn't need to wait too long find out how.

Eleven days later, President George W. Bush told the world there would be a "war on terror" and in the same address to a joint session of Congress, he told everyone, "you are either with us, or you are with the terrorists."

Abdul Aziz knew Oman was close to America and anticipated many in the Middle East, and some in Oman would see the West as attacking Islam. This was the moment the world divided between the West and Islamist poles. He feared how things would play out in the Gulf – ever the battlefield for the proxy wars of others.

In the Nahari household this same division and polarity was undeniably present. Abdul Aziz spoke as the voice of solidarity with the West, Maryam saw America as a symbol of all that was morally corrupt. Soon he could hear her standard responses before she gave them – usually expressed as – "what is happening is an attack on Islam."

The new tension left Abdul Aziz worried for his children. Yet, so far as his household was concerned, the differences between Maryam and himself, even when they expressed strongly held opposing views were still aired politely, their debates, for the most part, generally conducted in a moderate tone, emotions tightly restrained. They developed a pattern – any difficult conversations were routinely, but not always, held after the children were asleep in bed.

Abdul Aziz felt some relief in that Maryam and he shared a prior loyalty to the welfare and happiness of their family; this taking precedence over any political or religious views either might hold. Even so, on occasion, this line was crossed and the children picked up the tension between their parents.

Even Raqiyah, now a little girl of three, would toddle off into her room when the arguments arose, only to reappear when she felt it was safe to do so. Attempts to mask differences failed, as did efforts not to betray emotion. Raqiyah was a sensitive child and her barometer recording the tensions between her parents was well-attuned. She learned early the survival skills necessary to manage her own emotional life.

One of her earliest memories was of her father, Abdul Aziz, coming to seek her out, pretending to play hide and seek with her. He'd call, "Are you hiding under the bed? – No! Are you behind the dolls house? – No! Are you under the bedclothes? – No!" Then she knew he would find her, and with a big smile, scoop her up in his arms, throwing her up and catching her as she squealed in delight. He always made sure things ended well, and as a youngster home life was settled and routinised, and she never knew what insecurity was.

In time, Raqiyah found her father to be ever playful and open, even though he would disappear off to work for long periods. Always he would melt when he saw her. Often he would bring some treat home for her, sometimes a soft toy he'd found in the souk. Her Mother was altogether more serious and dogmatic, she seemed to smile less and less, appearing to carry the worries of the world on her slight shoulders.

With help around the home provided by Filipino maids, Maryam could also give time to her children. The boys, now at school and pre-school, allowed her to have time to delight in her daughter's company, getting her to play along with household activities and entertain the many female visitors and other children coming to their home.

The four Nahari children learned, as they grew older, to play one parent off against the other, to show allegiance to one to gain small privileges from the other. Both parents knew this was happening but were powerless to combat it or work together when it occurred. It frustrated Abdul Aziz.

When Raqiyah was four years old, Abdul Aziz took the unusual step of employing a non-resident governess. She was called Emma Styles, the grown up daughter of an English lawyer, a man whom Abdul Aziz trusted and with whom he had often done business in Muscat. He expected Emma to teach his daughter English and Raqiyah in turn proved to be a keen and able pupil.

The education of girls in Oman was still seen as a novel experiment by many. Raqiyah, for her part, having had Emma's tutoring, was more than ready to go to school when she was five. The transition was not easy.

Maryam wanted Raqiyah to attend a nearby state school where she knew many of her friends had sent their children. There was a solid Ibadi base and a sound teacher the nearby mosque had full confidence in. However, Abdul Aziz had his mind set on sending her to a fee-paying school. What really annoyed Maryam was not the high fees, which he knew they could easily afford, but the fact it was one where many American children attended and she was deeply suspicious of the teaching.

For Abdul Aziz, only the best was good enough for Raqiyah and he did something he rarely did, pulled rank as head of his household to settle the matter. It was his trump card and Maryam had no answer to it. She insisted that Emma's services would no longer be required, and Abdul Aziz recognised a concession worth making and agreed. Raqiyah was bought her uniform, all the peripherals in bags, books and pens she would need, and duly sent to the Muscat International Private School for Girls.

Only when Abdul Aziz pointed out to Maryam that Arabic and Islam were an important part of the school curriculum did her worries ease somewhat. He did not feel it prudent to show her the brochure emphasising the school's strong English teaching programme, which had first caught his eye when choosing a school.

Abdul Aziz was very glad his daughter was not growing up with the restricted opportunities that had still been in place when Sultan Hamad had come to power in 1970, and the education of girls was an unheard of novelty. He for one was going to see his daughter got the very best from the new system – the world was changing quickly and to his mind he knew she would need every good educational resource at her disposal to make the most of what lay ahead.

To be fair, Raqiyah wasn't favoured over her siblings, the boys also attended good schools and Abdul Aziz found he had to slow his second house building project slightly to ensure he covered all his children's school fees. This was no hardship.

As he stroked the silver prayer box in his pocket, now worn smooth on the one side by its constant caressing and though not truly religious, he reflected on his many blessings, attributing his family's comfortable standard of life to his own Western education and vocational training, that and of course, a large slice of good fortune!

24

As dawn surely follows the crowing of a cockerel so, after all the noise in the media, pictures of the military build-up, political murmurings and counter-protests had given prior warning; a new day of Middle East hostilities dawned.

News of the US-led coalition attack on Saddam Hussein's Iraq came early in the morning on Thursday 20 March 2003. Abdul Aziz once again felt the shock waves personally, just as when he had when watching 9/11 on his TV back in 2001.

Abdul Aziz knew that Oman, being friends with the US, would be caught up – in the thick of things, lending airfields and other support. After all Oman and the US were long-standing friends. Saudi Arabia, their bigger and powerful neighbour, would be even more screwed up by what was happening – long held ideas of not letting American infidels on sacred Muslim sand would have to be set to one side, notwithstanding local religious sensitivities. No-one he thought, was going to come out of this well. It was unsettling him and it was bad for business. Today, he thought, has begun badly.

The news of the attack brought to mind the thought that there was also a noticeable cold war going on at home. Seeing the footage had made him realise that Maryam had been gradually withdrawing from him. Their paths had not been crossing and it alarmed him he'd been too preoccupied to have noticed. Things had slipped, rather like Saddam Hussein had gradually stopped complying with expected norms and understandings, so she too had for some time been withdrawing cooperation and isolating herself from him. Maybe he also had been more remote, disconnected, over-working himself – it took two, he mused. He resolved that when he got home that evening he would address the matter, do something about it.

During the day he kept thinking about what he would say to Maryam when he got home. He worked hard to clear his desk to get away early. First, he reflected on the children – all fine in that department. Yet, even there some issues had started to arise.

Hassim, nearly ten years old had suddenly shot up in height and was already showing signs of premature adolescent rebellion. Nothing to be overly concerned about, he concluded, but Abdul Aziz wondered how long it would be before he would have to put his foot down firmly. Hassim was increasingly testing the limits as to what he could get away with. Soon he would be a young man. As the oldest son he'd need to be made aware of his responsibilities. It was never easy being a parent, he concluded, whatever age the children were.

Maryam for her part indulged all three boys and never, to his knowledge, shared his concern for parental discipline. That was another ongoing point of contention between them, but he knew inside that was never going to change. Thankfully the boys' school provided all the necessary structure for education, discipline and learning, which he'd hoped for and, on that front, all were progressing well.

Abbadi, the middle boy, was now seven, and showing an aptitude for music. This was rather surprising given Abdul Aziz could think of no-one in the family who had ever done likewise. The school provided an after school music tuition class – who knew where it would lead? His favourite pastime was playing with his electronic "LeapPad", a kind of talking book. Like all the boys, Abbadi was a quick learner. He was for ever asking for accessories and add-ons for his "LeapPad" which Abdul Aziz got Jasmine or one of the other Filipino maids to purchase for him. He realised how much his country was changing – you could buy anything from anywhere in the world these days.

Abbadi liked to be given affection and reassurance, he enjoyed a cuddle. Never quite sure of himself, being in the shadow of his more extrovert older brother Hassim, he was quieter than the other boys. More often than not he'd be found playing with his younger sister Raqiyah, quite happy to play the games she enjoyed with her.

Then there was Tariq – all rough and tumble. Strongly built and well-coordinated, he excelled at sport. Although still six years old he was almost as tall as Abbadi and able to stand his ground. Football was his first joy and when there were cards to collect of his favourite players, he would spare no effort in seeking out the ones he needed to populate his album. Of the boys, maybe Hassim was the one most likely to come off the tracks at some point, thought Abdul Aziz – he resolved he'd better keep a closer eye on him.

He could see Raqiyah enjoyed being the only girl in the family. She felt special and being a girl, she had a trump card to call if her bigger brothers got to be a nuisance. Most of the time things were fine, she was no threat to them and the four siblings got by happily enough. Though only Abbadi showed a real interest in her and what she was doing.

It was then, as he thought about his children, that Abdul Aziz had a moment of insight. Watching his daughter grow up, Raqiyah was proving to be exceptionally good at reading people's feelings – she instinctively knew whether they were happy or sad, with her or against her. That was a great gift to have. She always seemed to have bundles of affection and invariably wanted to be helpful. He had no doubt then that she'd learned early on to observe her parents varying moods and respond as the situation required. He knew that if he asked her, she couldn't have explained any of this, but he saw she had the foundations of character in place to build an independent, knowing and socially confident personality. The thought pleased him immensely and he felt himself flush with pride.

No, he concluded, the children are fine. He was being drawn back time and again to the same issue – the problem at home wasn't the children, it was the cold war raging between Maryam and himself.

But how to understand it and what if anything was to be done? It was time to go home and face things. Things couldn't be left unattended any longer, not if the children were to flourish.

25

At home, after the children had gone to bed that evening, tensions seemed to ease – at least on the surface. Maryam was watching TV, the Qatari based Al Jazeera channel. It had produced the most graphic coverage of the US bombing of Iraq as it had done of the Afghan war.

The news story currently showing was a debate on life for ordinary people in Baghdad. It was entirely speculative, since all the remaining Al Jazeera reporters there had been pulled out. This was subsequent to a US bombing which had killed some of their journalists. Abdul Aziz could see the coverage feeding anti-Western sentiment. He sighed out loud as he stood silently, watching his wife sitting on the white leather sofa, her eyes glued to the TV screen, her hand occasionally reaching across for some red grapes on the coffee table beside her.

The programme presenter started winding up, and Abdul Aziz thought it was as good a moment as any for the two of them to talk. The moment the presenter said, "Goodnight" he was ready.

'I thought we might discuss the children,' he offered.

'Oh, nothing bothering you is there?' she asked, turning her head toward him. He went and sat down next to her, wondering when he'd last done that – something he couldn't recall.

'Not really. They're all doing well, I think. They make us proud, they really do, don't you agree?' he said.

'Then what is it? What's on your mind? I don't follow.'

A silence fell between them. She turned away and reached for more grapes.

'You and I, well, we see the world through different lenses. Where does that leave the children. Are they confused by us, having parents with alternate takes on the world?'

'As you say, they seem fine. Sometimes I wish they'd take their Qur'an studies more seriously. Like all children, they're so easily distracted. But no, parents often have different perspectives. It's pretty usual.'

'You know boys – they're young. They'll learn, as they grow, how to fit in, do the right thing. They're Omani and proud of it,' he added, keen to keep the conversation going.

'Mmm. I'm not so sure about that,' she retorted with a flash of dismissive contempt in her eyes. 'They mix with too many kuffar – non-Muslim boys, in that school you sent them to. They pick up too many bad ideas and I'm worried as they get older, they'll be disrespectful, or worse. Have you ever thought of moving them to a good Muslim school?'

Abdul Aziz was shocked to hear her use the word, kuffar. It was so disparaging, and he wondered where this had come from. She'd never said that word before in his hearing. Did she really despise the other, Western children, so much? He didn't want to fight with Maryam, but neither did he just want her comment to pass without challenge.

'I'm happy they're mixing with other boys, having to think things through for themselves. Their education will stand them in good stead for the future.' Abdul Aziz looked intently at Maryam, feeling the unbridgeable gulf between them. 'I want them to get to university, and get good jobs. I don't think it would be good to move them right now, do you? They love their school – you know that.'

'So long as you, as their Father are fulfilling your duty, making sure they grow up to be good Muslims, then I'm happy.'

He wasn't convinced by this. He felt as if he were being reprimanded.

'What do you think of me, Maryam? Am I a good enough Muslim in your eyes?' It was a provocative question, but he had to know, it's what they needed to talk about.

'You lost your way a long time ago Abdul Aziz. Your eyes are full of questions, your head full of foreign ideas. Your Muslim practice has long been… well we both know, I'll say it… it's been a sham.'

The comment was as brutal as it was unprecedented. It stung him. He realised he must be so transparent, certainly in her eyes. It surprised him that she could see right through him.

She hadn't quite finished and raised a finger at him, before adding, 'I was always second best, the replacement wife for the one you lost, but I've found solace in Allah and I pray for you and our children. Don't worry yourself, I know I am blessed living here. I shan't make waves and I'll do everything I can for our children's happiness. We still share that much, if not much else. Your first love is your work Abdul Aziz, always has been – you love your freedom.'

Abdul Aziz's head spun. This was not how their conversation should be going.

'Those are harsh words. I'm sorry you think so little of me, what I think and believe. Certainly, there's much I question and it's true I cannot find comfort in religious platitudes, however well intentioned. I can't help that. But believe me when I say I never married you as a replacement or as second best. I wanted to marry you. When Hassim was born, after...'

'No!' she interrupted, 'Don't blame me, don't tell me I was ill, that it was my fault. It was, as I think back to then, the time when I realised you were somewhere else, adrift in your own world, preoccupied by business in Europe and the United States of America – it's you I blame.' Her voice was getting so loud, he wondered whether others in the house might hear.

Abdul Aziz began to wish he'd never started the conversation and wondered, with all the diplomatic skills at his disposal, just how he was going to enable things to end more amicably. For the sake of his children the two needed to remain friends, at least. He had an idea.

'Do you think we might go away together? A holiday? In the summer, when the days are too hot here to do anything and the children have finished their school year. Why don't we go and visit my sister Mira? Her husband Abdul has just landed a good job at Istanbul University. They've always wanted us to go. What do you say?'

'I can't win, can I? Abdul's just like you. That man questions the very ground he walks on.'

'But you get on with Mira and you like him too really. Abdul's a gentle, amiable, kind academic. You like them both don't you?'

'Yes,' she conceded, 'and I think it would be a good idea to take the children to see the Blue Mosque. It's a better idea than going to London or any other of your usual, decadent Western destinations. A holiday… all right, we'll tell the children in the morning. Who's going to make the arrangements, you or I?'

Abdul Aziz felt a small reconciliation had been won and to acknowledge it, he briefly put an affectionate hand on Maryam's shoulder to show – love? Well, if not love, perhaps some friendship. Surprisingly, there was a reciprocal response – he felt her hand placed on top of his.

'You arrange it, Maryam. I'll see that Mohammed covers the office while we're away.'

He rose and walked to his study, closing the door behind him. Increasingly it had become his den, his place of retreat.

As the study door closed he realised they had never talked about Raqiyah, and wondered why that was. Maryam no doubt had her own ideas as to Raqiyah's future, a betrothal when she was ten or eleven maybe, a wedding before she was twenty. 'Not if I have anything to do with it,' he muttered under his breath.

And where had their conversation left him. Was he any the wiser, any further forward? The holiday offered promise, a respite in their cold war, a summer truce if they were lucky. But he found little comfort in the thought.

He pictured them to be like two ships passing at night in opposite directions on the busy Bosphorus Straits. In the distance, he could hear the Al Jazeera channel was on again in the other room.

26

Sultan Hamad had a problem – how to keep two friends of Oman, the US and Iran, from falling out with each other. The bone of contention was Iran's developing nuclear programme and America's stated concern it might not be put solely to peaceful use. Would Iran end up being able to enrich Uranium for its military? – The Americans thought so. More tension filled the diplomatic airspace.

Abdul Aziz saw the Middle East continuing to be a fiercely contested place well into the future, whether focussed on Iran's nuclear potential or another on-going problem. Once again Oman was lined up in someone else's cross hairs – whose side was Oman on? Iran's or the USA's?

Sultan Hamad was working overtime to maintain a Switzerland-like neutrality, but the Middle East wasn't Europe, the gloves were off, and Abdul Aziz felt like anything could happen, the lid could blow off any time with more overt conflict and start another proxy war.

As the rumbling between the two main protagonists rolled on, with Saudi Arabia fretting to the West, Abdul Aziz who always had a close eye on what was happening on the diplomatic front took a bold decision.

Notwithstanding all the current diplomatic tension and its negative effect on business he was going to drop all work and spend a month on holiday with his family in Istanbul. Tickets were booked by Maryam and just days later, off they all flew. He justified this to himself, saying there was certain to be yet another diplomatic crisis ready to engage with when he returned. He had his own personal peace mission to attend to.

The day came. The family were at Muscat's airport. It was the first time Maryam and the children had flown and Abdul Aziz was aware of the excitement and apprehension his family were feeling. He realised, as they passed through the airport's routines, just how unlike the rest of his family he himself was, being so very used to it all.

He took charge, guided and instructed, as they had to produce passports and boarding passes. They all dutifully followed his lead, the children, aware of adult expectations of proper behaviour, were barely able to contain their excitement. He detected their pride in their father and their genuine trust in him as he led the way.

Travelling with his family made Abdul Aziz feel proud and he felt reassured he'd made a good decision. Surprisingly quickly he forgot about the foreign conflict and the general international situation and slipped into the role of family man. The children would remember this, he told himself.

Looking at Maryam, pulling a large case, he was surprised she had chosen one of her more formal conservative garments, a dark formless abaya, not the colourful ones of the past. Perhaps she had misjudged the Turkish culture, being something outside her experience, or maybe she was wanting to make a statement of her own. He had noticed she had been doing more of the latter recently.

The flight took most of the day. On landing and passing through airport formalities relatively quickly, they moved into the airy Arrivals hall. Abdul Aziz immediately spotted his brother in law, Abdul Zayed. He looked delighted to see them, and a warm open smile spread across his face, enough to melt any heart. Maryam's eyes betrayed her surprise to see him in a Western white shirt and trousers. Abdul Aziz could read her disapproval – his brother in law had slipped below an acceptable threshold, he'd fallen short. Then she eased up, perhaps having noticed most men in Istanbul seemed to be dressed in a similar Western style – this was no Arabia. She became less sure of herself and simply smiled back.

'Good flight everyone?' he enquired cheerfully, embracing Abdul Aziz warmly. 'I've borrowed a minibus from the university – it's the vacation. It's over there.' He waved his arm airily. 'Here, let me help you with those,' he ordered, taking two of the cases from them. 'You look like you've come for a long stay,' he jested, as he sized up their baggage.

Abdul Aziz had been all set to hire one of the many Ataturk Airport porters, but he let Abdul Zayed have his way and pull the cases to their waiting vehicle. He thought his brother in law would not appreciate him flaunting his affluence, tipping people to do this and that. Life as a lowly lecturer meant there was little money to spare.

Soon they were all inside the white minibus, the air con cutting in to take the edge off the summer heat, though it was nowhere near as hot as Muscat.

'We're so pleased you've finally made it to see us. First, we'll have a meal. Mira has been busy in the kitchen all day – she's so looking forward to seeing you.' Good humour positively oozed from under the man's skin.

It took the best part of an hour to get from the airport to the Zayed's flat. As they entered in turn through the front door with their suitcases, they found themselves squeezing awkwardly through a door into a side room.

The place felt tiny, but then all the apartments looked small to the visitors. Abdul Aziz realised just how used they were, as a family in Muscat, owning a large house with its luxurious spaciousness and walled enclosure.

Small as it was, the flat felt cosy and homely and the welcome was heartfelt. His brother in law hadn't stopped talking the whole journey and didn't let up now home. He was tireless in his suggestions of all the things for them to do whilst on holiday in Istanbul.

Soon they all began to tuck into a meal together. Maryam responded with warmth when Abdul Zayed explained they'd absolutely got to include the Blue Mosque in their itinerary.

Not only the first week but also the whole of the month turned out much better than Abdul Aziz could ever have imagined. The city had more than enough destinations to keep everyone happy.

Whilst inside the flat, Maryam and Mira found a point of mutual accommodation, each very happy to be busy in the kitchen. The two also took frequent trips by themselves to the numerous markets and bazaars, followed by seemingly endless food preparation, which both appeared to greatly enjoy. Maryam realised that she had a buying power that Mira lacked and she used the fistfuls of Turkish Lira, Abdul Aziz had given her, to be a generous visitor. The earlier fears Mira had had as to how to afford to cater for all her visitors quickly dissipated.

The children for their part enjoyed themselves too – the change of scene, was a refreshment in itself. Though Abdul Zayed and Mira didn't yet have children of their own, their friends made good the shortfall and the playful sound of groups of children enjoying themselves was often heard.

As the days passed, Abdul Aziz began to feel some of the heaviness he'd been carrying when he'd left Muscat lift. Now as the practicalities of travelling home loomed, the end of the month's visit seemed to have come far too quickly. In the final days he found his mind returning to the issues he'd soon have to face once they were back.

The parting was sad, the children clearly finding it difficult to say goodbye. Abdul Zayed and Mira had been the perfect uncle and aunt and a bond of affection had been created that would ensure many future times together, sometimes in Istanbul, other times in Muscat.

A month to the day, they all returned home after an uneventful return flight. Almost as soon as they unlocked the front door, Abdul Aziz knew things had quickly returned to the old pattern – Maryam becoming distant, retreating to the kitchen, while the children, not taking too much notice of the adults, took their new things and toys from Istanbul to their own rooms.

At least Abdul Aziz knew that a regular family holiday with his sister's family would be one positive tactic he could use to sustain his own struggling relationship with Maryam. He resolved the very evening they returned home that he'd ensure such trips would happen regularly.

The first thing he did when entering his own study was to send a long email of thanks to Abdul Zayed and Mira, concluding with an invitation that didn't allow 'No' for an answer, for them to make a reciprocal visit to Oman before the end of the year.

Meanwhile, a quick glance at the Oman Times newspaper headlines and he saw relations between the United States and Iran had become even more strained than when they'd left. Now the two nations were set on a collision course – worryingly, Oman looked like ending up caught in the middle.

Just before they'd gone on holiday, Iran had, in a provocative move, opened the seals the International Atomic Energy Authority had placed on its uranium centrifuges and now they'd restarted building work to operationalise them. Very possibly Oman's near neighbour intended to enrich their uranium for atomic weapon use. Soon Israel will be getting anxious, he surmised, and the pot would then really begin to boil.

He decided he needed to get back to his office at Eastern Diplomatic Services as a matter of urgency, to chat with his trusted colleague, Mohammed. This was an uncertain time for business and he needed to be back at his desk.

Within hours, Abdul Aziz and Maryam returned to their modus operandi, two ships of the desert passing one another silently in the night.

Abdul Aziz was drawn quickly back into the world of work, brokering tricky deals with overseas contractors whilst placating concerns in the Ministry at the friends he was keeping. Maryam took to managing her house with a zeal for care and efficiency, which whilst it sometimes lacked warmth, delivered the stable fabric within which their four children continued to thrive.

When Abdul Aziz was at home he found Maryam had taken to leaving Muslim Dawa literature, strategically placed on tables and surfaces so that he couldn't miss them. In a rare expression of anger, he angrily swept up the evangelical Islamic tracts nearest him, screwed them in his hand and threw them in the nearest waste paper basket. If she was going to change anything about him, he vowed, his soul was the last place she'd reach.

Increasingly, he found her presence a critical one, and a constant irritation. She wanted to see him giving more attention to the mosque and the men running it. 'Why couldn't he join them? Was he too busy to be doing good, supporting jihad?' she asked, never short of a prodding question or cutting gibe.

One comfort he took from all this was that his children didn't unquestioningly swallow what she fed them on. Raqiyah, as their only daughter and the one who might naturally be thought to grow up closest to her Mother, had a quiet self-assured independence, a definite mind of her own, and she used, what he took to be the diplomatic skills she had inherited from himself, to find her way through. Yet, he told himself, she was still very young and vulnerable to these constant pressures.

He was more concerned for Hassim. Rebellious at heart, he could so easily be impulsive and easily led. Tall for his age, Hassim was drawn to mixing with older boys, and his last school report had shown some worrying signs. He'd need to keep a close eye on Hassim. No such worries with Abbadi and Tariq. Though quite a bit younger, they nevertheless showed every sign of turning out well.

Not really wanting to, but thinking it was better to grasp the thorn and pull it out sooner rather than later, Abdul Aziz marched into the kitchen and found Maryam working alone preparing vegetables.

'Maryam, as head of the house,' a phrase he instantly realised was like a stick to a camel, 'I am concerned that you are taking it upon yourself to be the sole arbiter of the spiritual well-being of our children. That is an imbalance that needs correcting don't you think. I'm concerned the children might be fed too stern a religious line, something out of step with the tolerant open traditions of Ibadism.'

'If you acted as the head of the house there wouldn't be a problem,' was her sharp retort, 'but most of the time you're not here, and when you are, the children are picking up all kinds of Western and liberal ideas that are, are haram – forbidden. I try and do my best by them.' Now she was the one wondering if she had gone too far.

'There is no compulsion in religion, wouldn't you agree?' he offered.

'Of course, dear. But that doesn't mean we all agree on what religion teaches us,' she immediately quipped.

After a pause, Abdul Aziz decided to drive his point home. 'One of the great tenets of our Ibadi Muslim tradition is that unlike most of our fellow Muslims, we highly value human freedom in seeking to understand the will of Allah. We use our own minds to understand and shape what we believe. This is where we stand quite separate from our Sunni brethren in Saudi. This is where we Omanis stand, and where I stand.'

'You're too free thinking, you put yourself outside what is customarily understood. I wonder what you really do still believe Abdul Aziz,' she countered, facing him, 'you can't claim to be an observant Ibadi - that's rich coming from you, the man who rarely goes to mosque.'

'As I see it, our children must be free to think and work things out for themselves. They must be free. These tracts, imports from across the Saudi border, these things you've been leaving around the house, well… they demean Allah, make him out to "will" everything. If we follow that kind of thinking, then we reduce our understanding of Allah's greatest creation – we his creatures. He gave us minds to use.'

'Yes, but the human mind is fickle and we need the help of our religious teachers to guide us. You set yourself above them, you really do.'

'This is where we so fundamentally disagree with each other, Maryam. You believe – all is given, all set in stone. For me, it's not so easy. Forgive me for bringing this up, but who killed my first betrothed? Was it Allah who predestined me never to marry her, or was it man who willed that a land mine be laid where she walked? You tell me?' he asked earnestly.

'I knew we'd come back to this. I'm second best. It's all about your own emotional baggage from those days. From what I heard, you were a decent, observing Muslim until then. I feel sorry for you, lost in a sea of uncertainty. At least I know what I believe and, yes, I will continue to teach the faith to my children. I look after the home and our children – that is what a good Muslim woman does!'

'It's not about my emotional baggage. That was unfair. I once heard Dr Muhammed Abdul Rauf speak. He's one of our greatest contemporary Ibadi Muslim scholars. He says there is a large area of human freedom within the Qadr – the divine determinism. I for one am with Rauf. I do try and listen to our leaders, not ones from Saudi, and I will help our children to use their freedom to think for themselves in order to work out their own understanding of Islam.'

The discussion was over and as if to symbolise their polarised views, each retreated once more to their own domains.

Maryan grabbed some onions and began to skin and slice them, Abdul Aziz took his thoughts with him back to his study across the foyer. He didn't like the way Maryam was so determinedly using the knife. She had been so fiery and combative, he couldn't recall ever having had such a contested and bitter conversation with her before. Things were definitely getting worse.

27

Early 2011, when the air temperatures were at their coolest of the year, around 30ºC, hotheads were raising the temperature on Arabian streets. The Arab Spring had arrived!

Oman watched as Tunisian President, Zine ben Ali, fled in January to Saudi Arabia, and then Egypt's President, Hosni Mubarak was overthrown in February. Where was this leading?

Each leaders' departure was followed just a few days later, by demonstrations in Oman. Small by comparison, some 200 people nonetheless took to the streets to protest at rising prices, corruption and to campaign for higher wages. Then teachers staged a protest against their employment conditions, following the pattern of similar earlier unrest in the nearby town of Ruwi, on the edge of Muscat, the previous year.

These unsettling rumblings were not something Omanis were used to – no-one knew where it would all end – only in tears, Abdul Aziz concluded.

That Islamist sympathisers in nearby Saudi, the Emirates and Qatar were strengthening their grip and internationalising these protests, told Abdul Aziz that tectonic plates in the Muslim world were shifting, and a new religious fundamentalism was also flexing its muscles, itching for political power. He feared the direction things were taking and watched each news bulletin come in with a growing apprehension.

Social media – text messaging and the internet, became the primary means of spreading discontent and planning – setting forth what revolutionary action should happen next. So-called Green Marches were organised in Oman and these were backed by a petition of demands which was delivered for the Sultan's attention.

Then, to the south, in Dhofar, and in the north, in Sohar, further Omani protests erupted. When a governor's office and a police station were occupied, violence and criminality broke out. Enough was enough, and upon this latest outrage, a robust response from the government followed. Abdul Aziz heard the army firing live rounds into the air. While the tense atmosphere lasted, he hid himself and the family indoors.

Everywhere in the Arab Spring world things looked to be in melt down, but in Oman things were turning out nowhere near as bad. Abdul Aziz saw some of the local sit-in protests, and there were other similar ones held across the sultanate – people wanting welfare reform, railing noisily against the high levels of unemployment and against corruption in high places. But by and large these were proving to be peaceful and manageable.

In response to these, some of Abdul Aziz's wealthy Omani friends made the point they were loyal subjects and organised their own pro-Sultan demonstrations. Abdul Aziz steered clear.

The early months of 2011 left Abdul Aziz increasingly worried as one overseas government after another began to look vulnerable. Even visitors from abroad, who had come to do business with him, were finding the Muscat hotels, where visitors usually stayed, inhospitable as staff withdrew services protesting for greater wages.

An increasing number of arrests were being made, and a clamp down by the Omani authorities eventually got under way, Abdul Aziz wondering if this, by international standards, gentle response, would be sufficient to calm things. He'd observed for some while the numbers of the unemployed had been increasing, especially among young people, their paths to careers closed, and the promised land with its material benefits and associated freedoms, all fuelled by oil wealth, just hadn't materialised for them. The resultant deep disillusionment these economic factors created made for a persistent toxic and potentially volatile mix. Going soft was a risky option.

However, much to his surprise, a few weeks later, things began to quieten down and by May 2011 the Omani version of the Arab Spring appeared to have entirely run out of steam. Meanwhile, a growing long list of demands, petitioning for reform, now rested on Sultan Hamad's desk. Nonetheless Abdul Aziz was reassured at the sense of order in this, as throughout the long Spring, the government took proactive measures to address these complaints, and see them off. As Spring moved into summer, Oman gradually returned to its normal settled state, the traumas of elsewhere passing it by.

At this Abdul Aziz breathed a huge sigh of relief. This time he'd kept well clear of any protests. The last thing he'd wanted was to find himself swept up by security arrests as he had been back in 1994. There was just one moment in April that truly unnerved him, that was when a police-man called at his home.

Two of his business contacts from Egypt had apparently fled events in Cairo and the officer simply required assurances from Abdul Aziz that Eastern Diplomatic Services were not going to proceed to sign contracts with the two. Abdul Aziz was only to happy to oblige – besides he had no intention of making new deals with Egypt until he was quite sure things were stable in that country. With the issue settled to the policeman's satisfaction, Abdul Aziz turned his attention to other contracts. Business generally remained good and it was no problem.

In this time of demonstrations, protests and security responses, Abdul Aziz made a particular point of ensuring his four children were kept safe – thankfully their school was a haven of stability, probably because it was one of the leading fee-paying schools. As it was attended by the children of Oman's wealthy elite there was always a strong security presence outside the school gates.

As summer time and Ramadan approached, the school year came to an end. Late on the final morning of term, he received the children's school reports. They were handed to him by Tariq, now entering his teens.

He'd been charged by the school secretary with safely delivering the three boys' reports home to his parents. Abdul Aziz took the three sealed white envelopes from Tariq's hand and carried them into his study to read them without being disturbed. On his way, he swept up the remaining one on the hallway table in his hand, the one he'd received earlier from Raqiyah's school.

He read them all, then leant back in his chair. Three reports were fine, if not really good. One was not.

Hassim, the eldest, now eighteen years old and leaving school that summer, had evidently been giving his teachers cause for concern. Across the board, teachers reported his attention hadn't been on his academic study as it should have been. He was described as mixing with the wrong kind of boys. As this was his final school report it did not paint an encouraging picture. It both surprised and unsettled Abdul Aziz.

He took Hassim's report in his hand again. Upon rereading it, he saw further down the page unexplained absences when he had failed to attend school. Abdul Aziz made an unwelcome connection – he'd noticed these were the days of the demonstrations and Green Marches. Hassim had said nothing about this. Relieved his son hadn't been picked up and arrested, he was nonetheless alarmed at the implications of Hassim's actions for the safety of the family. Even now his photo would be in security service files and at any time there could be an unwelcome knock on the door.

He decided he needed to talk to Hassim as a matter of urgency, but where was he? He called for Maryam.

'Maryam, Have you seen Hassim?' he said, his raised voice loud enough to be heard everywhere in the house.

'He went out, to the mosque, I think he said,' she called back sounding quite unperturbed.

'When's he back?' Abdul Aziz enquired.

'He didn't say. He doesn't always come straight back after prayers.'

'I'll bet he didn't say,' he muttered under his breath, clutching and involuntary scrunching the damning report in his hand as he spoke. He sat silently for a moment and then began pressing it flat again. Then he had a thought.

'Which mosque?' he yelled.

'The one directly the other side of 23 July Street. The one he's been going to with his new friends.'

This was news to Abdul Aziz. He felt marginal to his family, caught out again, convinced the rest of the family knew more about what Hassim was up to than he did.

He marched straight from his study to the kitchen where he was pleased to find Maryam on her own. He calmed himself before speaking.

'We've just received the children's school reports. All's well… except for Hassim's. His report really is most worrying.' He saw the flash of alarm cross Maryam's face.

'He seemed to be doing all right to me. I'm surprised. Is it really as bad as you say? I'm the one who'd have noticed anything amiss, and I can't say I have… You've been working so hard recently you wouldn't know what our eldest has been doing,' she said, unable to hold back the opportunity for making another reprimanding comment.

Abdul Aziz felt as though cut with a knife. He knew this to be true and saw in that moment that Maryam was party to knowing more than she was letting on. He followed up.

'Do tell me what I've missed. I want to know.' He saw he had wrong footed her, but his concern for his family's safety in the aftermath of this troubled Arab Spring dominated his thoughts and he was determined the wellbeing of his family came first now. Hassim was in a perilous position.

He pulled a chair over and sat himself down ready to listen. He was staying put and Maryam had nowhere to hide. He knew she had no interest in politics and guessed the seriousness of their situation had probably passed her by.

'Well, actually, I've been encouraged by his, by his growing maturity,' she offered hesitatingly. 'He's been giving time to his prayers and to becoming more… devout.'

'What, Hassim?'

'Yes, and that shows how little you know. The small mosque he goes to have been getting him on track, filling in the gaps he never had filled by you – the Father who's always so very busy and neglects his obligations as a Muslim.' She felt a certain pleasure, a sense of one-upmanship on Abdul Aziz. Right now she knew Hassim better than he did and felt a certain pride in Hassim's religious enthusiasm.

'Maryam, thank goodness Allah is the merciful one!' he offered ironically, pulling a doleful face, before adding 'Have you any idea of the danger he's put our family in?'

He saw a flash of alarm cross her face. He could see her mind making connections and a look of fear replace the one of recrimination.

'I'm sorry Abdul Aziz, I spoke out of turn and overstepped the mark. For the sake of our family forgive me. Tell me more.' When the crunch came, any squabbles between the two of them were invariably laid aside – it was family first. Abdul Aziz had her full attention.

'Hassim's school report describes a son I barely know. He's been dropping out of class on days when public demonstrations have been happening. He's been out on the streets instead of attending lessons at school. He's been mixing with pupils the school calls "bad influences", and now you tell me he has been taking religion over-seriously. I know we differ on the latter, but take it from me, I've learned enough about Hassim in the past ten minutes to ring every alarm bell in my head. The boy's in trouble, I sense it – he's in peril, and threatening to bring us all down with him. Now do you understand?' he said with a passionate concern. He knew that what he said had hit home, judging from Maryam's contrite reaction, maybe he'd put it too strongly. She nodded meekly.

'I need to find him… talk to him. I'm just concerned he'll have anticipated this report, and my reaction to it, and chosen to put in a no show at home. Call our driver, it's nearly time for prayers. There's a mosque I need to attend. As you'll be attending your prayers here, might I, for the first time in our marriage, ask you to pray to the Almighty for us all. I'm getting ready.'

With that he disappeared out of the kitchen and within a minute out of the front door. As he got into the car he heard the local muezzin already calling the faithful.

He was going to find his wayward son and try as hard as he could to bring him in line before it was too late.

28

He was almost late for Jummah prayers, completing his Wadu – ritual washing hastily. He slid himself into the back of the mosque with the last of the worshippers. All standing in lines, shoulder to shoulder, facing Mecca.

A few moments later, he spotted Hassim, near the front, to the right. Hassim had no reason to turn round and he could watch him unobserved. It struck him that Hassim had grown his young beard a little longer. As he glanced left, then right again, he thought something wasn't right. It didn't feel normal, but he couldn't put his finger on it.

Then after the second set of prostrations, he looked again and realised what it was. Unusually, here he was in a mosque of mainly younger men and boys. There were relatively few older men or middle-aged men like himself, and for some inexplicable reason this made him feel increasingly nervous.

Prayers followed their familiar routine and the Friday sermon, issued centrally by the Sultan's office, was dutifully read out.

Prayers over, people began filing out to reclaim their shoes and chat with friends. He didn't follow the crowd but moved against the human tide to try and intercept Hassim. However, Hassim was not coming his way. He and most of the younger men were heading off into a side room, presumably for some form of instruction or meeting.

Abdul Aziz didn't know what he should do. He didn't want to act as though spying on Hassim, though his curiosity made him inquisitive. As Hassim disappeared from view he decided to follow after him.

As soon as he got to the doorway he was accosted by a man acting as a guardian doorkeeper, the man clearly intent on not letting him pass. This again felt quite irregular. Mosques in his experience weren't like this. They were open and relaxed.

'Can I help you?' the man asked bluntly. He was blind in one eye, his other one full of suspicion upon seeing someone new.

'Oh, I just wanted to join my son,' Abdul Aziz added, trying to sound relaxed and continuing to push forward.

The man didn't know what to do and looked round, possibly to seek a second opinion. That split second gave Abdul Aziz the opportunity he needed to slip in and sit down at the back. No one was going to remove him from a prayer hall.

So far Hassim hadn't noticed him, but now he'd got to within a few metres of his son he decided he wanted to be open and declare his presence.

'Hassim,' he called out, just loud enough to be sure the lad heard. Half a dozen quizzical heads turned in his direction, Hassim's startled face among them. Hassim then looked to his friends, first to one side and then the other. He whispered to one of them, excused himself and then made his way over to his father. With an unreadable expression on his face, he waited for his father to speak.

'We need to chat,' whispered Abdul Aziz, not wanting to say too much as some kind of talk was about to be given from a man at the front – he looked Saudi. Abdul Aziz was confused. The mosque felt Omani but simultaneously strangely Saudi and Sunni too. He couldn't quite put his finger on it, perhaps it was the accents, perhaps what some of those present were wearing, he wasn't sure – but it was definitely different. He heard Hassim speaking to him and tried to focus.

'OK, Dad, but can't it wait until I'm home. Not like you to come here? Has anything happened?' he asked.

Abdul Aziz, detecting something unpleasantly disingenuous in his tone, wondered how Hassim could not know what had come home in his school report. It was also as if he were saying 'I know you're spying on me, but prove that you're not!' Abdul Aziz felt the gulf opening wider between them. Where had he gone wrong? This was painful.

'It can wait until you're home,' he answered flatly. 'When will that be?'

'Instruction is usually around an hour, so about an hour and a half.'

'Fine, I'll see you then. You'll excuse me if I won't wait for the instruction.'

Abdul Aziz had spotted two men, he assumed to be mosque trustees, making their way slowly toward him, accompanied by the zealous doorkeeper. Why, he wondered were they so suspicious about him or secretive about what they were doing? His instinct told him this was not a good place to be and without looking any longer in their direction he walked straight outside, grabbing his sandals and making for the exit.

Sandals on, he strode briskly over to his waiting, air-conditioned car. His driver had kept the engine running the whole while and the car was refreshingly cool. Abdul Aziz said nothing. After all, the waste of petrol wasn't a worry, he had bigger issues to think about, fuel these days cost a lot less than water. Besides, he needed to cool down. 'Home,' he said and the Mercedes pulled smoothly away. Five minutes later he was back at House Twenty and made once again for the sanctuary of his study.

He needed to chew things over. Not only was there a chasm between husband and wife, now his oldest son stood afar – again he saw it all visually. He was on the other side of a raging wadi in full spate, now there were two people, their backs to him standing on the far side.

Maryam had clearly had some inkling as to what Hassim was up to and more than that, a degree of sympathy for his new-found religion. However, when he'd alerted her to the danger that Hassim had put himself and the family in he could see that this was news to her ears and it had frightened her. Her fear might offer him room for manoeuvre, a bargaining chip.

In retrospect, the visit to the mosque had shown him that Hassim had picked up with people who were opposed to the Sultan and dangerously aligned himself with the political and religious opposition – those traditional Muslim voices making increasingly strong noises about the need for a greater Islamification of Oman.

Inside the mosque, there had been no warm welcome for him – he'd had the distinct feeling he'd been perceived as a spy, some kind of threat to what was going on there. There could be no other reason for their watchfulness of him and then their wanting to see him off the way they did. Upon reflection, the missing older generation of men was a sure sign of the mosque's radicalism.

But what should he do? Maybe he could use the external threat to the family's safety as a means to keep Maryam on his side – could he count on that, use her to help lean on Hassim?

As for Hassim, he feared driving him further into danger. Somehow he needed to talk to him – at least alert him to the risks he faced. After all he was their oldest son and at eighteen he needed to be taking responsibility for himself. In the future he'd be the head of the family. Right now he needed to think about what career he might pursue. Perhaps hearing him out and offering him some support might help win him round. He wished he'd given his oldest son more time. He feared it could all be too little, too late.

It was a full two hours before Hassim reappeared. As soon as Abdul Aziz heard him enter, his study door open to hear him arrive, he called out to summon him.

'Hassim. Hassim.'

Hassim quietly entered, sitting himself down, the look on his face indicating he was expecting a grilling or worse from his father. However, Abdul Aziz spoke kindly to his son.

'I might not be the best Father in the world, but I do care about my family, and this evening I'm very aware you and I have some long overdue catching up to do.' His voice was calm, measured and the conversational tone was not what Hassim had expected. He looked up at his father's face.

'I wondered whether we might talk over a few things.'

'Like what?'

'Three matters in particular. First, your school report and where you go from here. Second, your views and involvement with the current political protests, and third your religious take on things, given your new-found commitment to the mosque. There might be more to talk about, but that should get us started, don't you think?'

'This could take some time,' said Hassim resignedly.

'These things are so important, as is your own future, that I've got all the time we need. Where would you like to start?'

Hassim hesitated and shuffled in his chair, he was more used to his father taking the lead, telling him things. He composed himself. He was ready, he'd been expecting the coming conversation and for weeks had been rehearsing what to tell his father over and again in his head. The time had come.

'Most of my friends are pretty disillusioned with all the promises we've been fed by the government, all the lies and corruption. We can't see a future and we want something better. It's not the Sultan we blame, but some of his ministers and officials. Something's got to be done before things get out of hand. Don't you agree? Or are you just another person taking their cut, doing well out of how things are?'

Abdul Aziz let the gibe pass. 'These are difficult times, I know. Unemployment's high, people feel let down, especially young people. Some things need to change. I admit I'm fortunate, in a good job and we live well. You live well. Our family is well provided for.'

'But think about it,' interrupted Hassim. 'I have two sets of friends, those whose Fathers are so privileged by the status quo, the kids of the elite, they don't need to worry. Then there are the others, like me, leaving school, and what are we to do? The best professional jobs go to the British and the Asians. The ordinary Omanis, like me, get left with nothing, nothing at all. Look around you. There are too many young Omanis without a job or the prospect of one. What's the point of education, training? To what end do we do it – why bother? Something's got to change.'

'Which is why you've been taking yourself off to the protests and marches…'

'You know about that?'

'Well, not exactly, but your school report doesn't need a detective to tie the absence from class days with what's been happening this year,' said Abdul Aziz tapping his finger on the open report.

'Suppose.'

'It's your school report that first alerted me. It's no game getting involved in protests – though I hadn't done anything wrong, I once got swept up by the Royal Oman Police when they thought I'd been too closely allied with Israelis and Americans. It wasn't true, but after letting me go, it shut career path doors once and for all. It could have been worse, much worse. Fortunately, after it had all died down, I still had an education and a business to fall back on. Things worked out. But you, you can't take the risk, you could get swept up in today's Arab Spring arrests, then you'll never get a job, or worse. It'll be bad for the family, don't you see this? As our eldest son, what example are you setting the others, your younger brothers? Please think about it.'

'Yes, but if no-one says how it is, nothing will change. It's not like in the West, we can't go running to opposition MPs – there are none! We have to take on the Sultan himself, risks and all. I want a future. How things are right now, I don't see I have a future,' he said with more than a hint of desperation entering his voice.

'Look, if that was all it was, I would feel easier about things. I know a just cause when I see one, but you know it isn't just about protest. Across the board, subject area by subject area, your teachers say your school effort has been dropping. You find yourself an alternative to school, somewhere you no doubt feel sympathetic to the cause, through the mosque you are now going to. Isn't that right?'

'OK, school performance isn't good. It's true, I've kind of lost interest, it's so unrelated to the real world, and yes, I've found a new place of learning. We all need ideals to inspire us and live up to.'

'Let's talk about school for a minute. Getting a good education and leaving with qualifications is really important, don't you think?'

'As I said, I've lost interest in their education, all the boxes they want me to tick for them. The point of education is to help us to live a good life isn't it? Well, I just don't see it anymore. They just want mild, unthinking, unquestioning pupils who will be a credit to their school. If they were really interested in an education for life, they would include a proper programme of Islamic instruction. They haven't, they don't, they won't. They've swallowed Western curricular programmes and that's it. When I tell them, they don't like it and call me disrespectful, a troublemaker, being insubordinate – that kind of thing. Nearly all the staff have written me off. That makes me a square peg in a round hole and I'm glad to be able to shake the dust off my feet and leave this summer. Good riddance to them. I wouldn't want them to have the smug satisfaction of saying all their pupils excel. This one doesn't!'

'So where does this education for life come from if it can't be found in one of the best schools in the country?' Abdul Aziz fired back, his voice raised, and now finding it hard to keep his temper under control.

'You saw, you were there – the mosque and their school. I've found people there who understand how things are. I'm learning lots of new things there. They're really interested in me and my ideas and they're not afraid to confront the government where things need to change. This isn't about my willingness to work hard or my attitude, this is about putting in the effort where it matters, where it counts.'

'I have to say it was no ordinary mosque. There was something different about it. What was it?' Abdul Aziz asked, as much to himself as to his son.

'They teach the Qur'an as relevant to life. They don't compromise and then they try, through jihad, to help us all bring faith alive for each one of us personally, as well as for society. What's more I've been offered an opportunity to work there as an intern. In fact, that's what I'll be doing now I've left school.'

'Doing what exactly? And when were you going to discuss this with me?' asked Abdul Aziz once again finding it hard to restrain his irritation at being by-passed.

'Soon,' he said, evasively.

'Let's try now, this minute. What have you in mind?'

'I'd be working as the administrative officer for the new mosque teacher. Oh, and I'd be living away. There's a room in his house by the mosque.'

Abdul Aziz could again feel his son slipping away from him by the minute, like the water in a puddle after a summer shower – disappearing in an instant. He felt he wanted to offer a hand to pull him back in reach, but something told him that it was too late for that. It would be a futile gesture. For once in his life, despite all his diplomatic skills, he didn't know what to say and he knew he didn't want the conversation to end badly.

'Hassim, I'd really like you to think about this further. I'm sure we could set something up for you at Eastern Diplomatic Services.'

'No Dad, that's not what I want.' Abdul Aziz knew not to make the offer again. 'I was late home because I said I'd be ready to start now… now school has finished. They asked, "is tomorrow OK?" and I said, "yes".'

'Come, let's go into the kitchen and talk to your Mama,' suggested Abdul Aziz. He saw Hassim's face wince, but that didn't stop him making for the kitchen as they left the study together.

A difficult conversation followed. Maryam didn't want to see her son leave home like this and, though she was pleased for his new found Muslim zeal, she was inwardly worried that it was driven by all the naivety of youth and she was now as worried for him, as was Abdul Aziz.

Nothing the two could say made Hassim think twice. His mind had been made up and he asked to be excused to pack a few things. Within twenty minutes he had left, leaving his stunned parents standing silently alongside one another in the kitchen.

Before he finally disappeared, Abdul Aziz at least got Hassim to agree to come home at the weekend, 'for the sake of your brothers and sister.'

In the doorway Abdul Aziz took the reluctant Hassim in a tight embrace, urging him to think carefully at every stage and remember his home would always be there for him. The least he could do now things were so fraught between them was try to keep a door open.

29

Back inside the Nahari family house, having been dropped off by the British Embassy, Adam realised he was in reality a prisoner in all but name. He had no freedom to go where he wanted, it was too dangerous outside.

Whilst confined to the house, he knew he ought to use the time to write something, well two pieces actually, and he settled down to the task. The first piece, to his new employer in London, CNPI or Central News Publishing International, the second to Mr Brian Merryweather, the so-called Media Services man at the British Embassy.

To Adam's mind, Media Services personnel were like Cultural Attachés, both were shorthand for intelligence officers and spies. The trick was going to be how to keep both his news hungry employer and the Embassy spy happy. He opened up his laptop and began typing.

To begin with he felt he didn't have a lot to go on, but then a few minutes later discovered he had rather more than he initially thought. Though he hadn't any real knowledge of what the overall picture was, he was nevertheless able to write a piece giving his personal story. As an observer, dropped in on the unfolding Omani drama, he was able to give a current personal impression of life in the capital, Muscat, now that Sultan Hamad was dead. He described what it felt like to be in a power vacuum where fear and tension hung in the air. The image that came to mind was like being under a very dark cloud, a climactic thunderstorm just about to break.

He typed away some more. He outlined, as he saw it, the political process during the three day purdah period, whilst the Ruling Family Council were in session. He also commented on the two envelopes Sultan Hamad had left containing his personal wishes as to his successor. As Adam wrote he felt he held an advantage, for he doubted whether there were many, if any, other media outlets that could claim to have their man on the spot.

He thought hard and long about whether to include the sweep up into custody of anyone thought to be a risk, the guards outside his house, and wondered how much to include of Abdul Aziz's own story.

Writing always got harder to manage when it became personal, but the human interest element was something readers always liked – there was a risk, but he decided it would all go in. He hit away at the keys furiously.

As he wrote he paused and thought of Abdul Aziz, probably in a cell at the Royal Oman Police HQ or a nearby barracks, maybe only a short distance way from his home though it could be a million miles as far as Abdul Aziz was concerned. He recalled his own time in confinement a few years previously. He was young then, but Abdul Aziz was his parent's age and looked older, he could be finding it much tougher.

And as he typed, not for the first time Adam's own memories, so often suppressed, came to mind, his period of incarceration at the hands of IS immediately prior to university. Back then his food had been brought to him irregularly, pushed at him on a battered tray. Whatever came, he'd had to eat it – even the dry, hard bread. The memory made him shudder – he didn't want to go there. Though two or three years had since passed, the experience still haunted him – the isolation, powerlessness, fear, the foul smell of his body and the trauma. Thankfully, the past year had seen the flashbacks, the post-traumatic stress with the debilitating and embarrassing anxiety attacks, diminish both in number and severity. Some welcome kind of normality had returned to his mental health. He really hoped Abdul Aziz was OK. He concluded he liked the man, they shared an experience in common.

After a short pause, Adam resumed hitting the keypad and in a couple of hours or so, he was more or less done. He had a fair turn of speed typing, and two pieces, each over a thousand words long were soon ready to be read through and checked for mistakes before sending. Going through his material a second time he made a few changes and then as he customarily did with all his work, he read his scripts through a third time before signing them off. Then he had an idea. He went out into the foyer.

'Raqiyah,' he called. A door opened and there she was, anxiety written all over her face. She was holding an e-book reader, it's light shining against her colourful blue abaya.

'I can't concentrate. I'm reading the same thing over and over again. I keep wondering how he is. The worst is not having any news. I keep trying to comfort Mama, but she seems to handle it better, busying herself with endless chores. That's not me.' Then remembering herself added, 'Sorry, you called me.'

'Would you mind reading this through this for me? I've had to write two pieces, one for London, the other for the Embassy Media officer. There may be things I've missed or indeed things I ought to delete. Do you mind?'

'No, I'd love to. It'll be something useful to do.' After a hesitant glance in the direction of her mother, still busy in the kitchen, she walked across the foyer and joined him in the study.'

Once in there, she closed the door behind them, put her hand to the nape of Adam's neck and pulled him gently toward her. He turned his head and they kissed. It was a brief and stolen moment and they broke away almost immediately for fear of discovery.

When their eyes met a renewed look of love and intimacy flashed across the space between them. Like a switch that had been flicked, it released new energy, and lifted both their spirits. The kiss and look did more than any stilted, snatched conversation ever could.

Adam got up, pulled the chair away from the desk so that Raqiyah might sit down to read. He stood there, looking over her right shoulder to re-read the material again for himself. He ensured he was standing sufficiently far away from her so that if someone came in, they'd be reassured that no touching, no impropriety, was suggested.

It was just as well.

Almost immediately they'd begun work, the study door swung open and Maryam stood there, a dutiful chaperone, balancing two mint teas in one hand, whilst her other hand had silently turned the door handle.

'Oh thank you,' said Adam, turning and reaching across to take them from her. She passed the drinks over swiftly, and as quietly as she had arrived she left, this time leaving the study door wide open as they heard her departing footsteps cross the foyer back to the kitchen. It was then Adam called after her, he'd had another idea.

'Maryam, I've just asked Raqiyah to read through the news pieces I've written. When she's done, if I come over to the kitchen with them in a moment, could I discuss them with you before I submit them?' She looked confused, as if her opinion was not usually requested, then nodded a puzzled look of agreement, before disappearing once more into the kitchen, again leaving the door open.

'Thanks Adam,' Raqiyah murmured softly. 'I think you should ask her about what you want to say here about my Dad,' she said pointing a finger at the text. The rest is fine, it's thin on hard news, but it's the best you can do for the moment. Perhaps later today we'll learn more.'

Adam picked up the laptop in one hand and his mint tea in the other as Raqiyah led the way to the kitchen. He watched her body sway easily and smoothly ahead of him, his imagination taking hold. Then they were with Maryam and his mind returned to addressing the serious task in hand.

Maryam surprised Adam. Evidently a fount of knowledge, she had gleaned much useful information from her social world – mixing as she did with many other women in Muscat. She'd been with women who had the ear of the leading men, and she also held considered opinions of her own. She had clear ideas as to what forces and what power play might be at work and Adam was glad he'd included her and sought her reflections on the situation and on his articles.

He ended up making some significant additions which gave his writing a much more considered and balanced analysis.

Maryam was keen to add a religious dimension, which Adam had entirely missed – seeing the independence and strengths of the Omani Ibadi Muslim tradition as something that would see the people through this present crisis. Adam's reference to Abdul Aziz's detention remained in place – there had been no comment from her about it.

Finally, Adam downloaded his two pieces to a memory stick. By now it was time for a slow lunch with whatever food Maryam and Raqiyah had been able to find. They did surprisingly well. After lunch, time hung in the air as they waited for any news.

Late afternoon and Adam, after showering and smartening up, went to look for the family's driver. The two guards outside, now familiar with the routine were not going to argue with him, and after explaining to the soldiers where he was going, he set off back to the British Embassy and a second meeting with Mr Brian Merryweather.

Muscat's streets were no more busy than before. Nearly everyone was staying inside or being made to stay indoors, unless they had approval to move about. There was no-one to be seen on foot. Minutes later Adam noticed the soldiers on duty by the roundabout exit to the British Embassy driveway had increased in number from six to twelve and they bristled with enough armaments to conduct a small war. He sneaked a picture using his mobile phone. It would need cropping later, but he knew by instinct it would be good copy for London.

At the checkpoint there were the usual questions and answers, and once satisfied, the soldiers waved him through.

At the Embassy Reception counter there was a small queue, but this time Adam was recognised as he walked in and immediately waved to a side door and let into the inner sanctum. Bright late afternoon sunlight played dazzling reflective patterns across the room as the burning orange sun lay low on the bright blue Arabian Gulf outside. Adam recalled from his limited experience of British Embassies elsewhere, whoever built them had a penchant for choosing attractive locations. He was ushered into a small side room.

'Hello, Adam,' said Mr Merryweather, this time wearing a bow tie in blue, matching the frame of his glasses. It made him look slightly odd, definitely eccentric, to Adam's mind. He'd no doubt there was a sharp mind behind this quirky exterior and he determined to keep his wits about him.

'Good afternoon, Brian. I've a piece I'd like to send to London on here,' he said, waving his memory stick. 'Can we use a laptop or PC somewhere?'

'Oh sure, right here.' He pointed to a PC on a shelf in the corner, its blue screensaver showing a slowly spinning coloured cube imperceptibly gliding across the monitor; moving lethargically as if it too were tired at the end of a long, hot day. Brian brought the machine to life with a few taps and inserted Adam's memory stick.

'I've also got a picture on my phone. If I could Bluetooth it across then that can go off to London too, that OK?' Adam added nonchalantly.

'That's fine. No probs. Are you happy I see your piece first? I may be able to add something.' No, wasn't an option. Brian had taken his position in front of the screen and was waiting.

Leaning across, Adam carefully opened the one article he'd prepared for Brian's eyes only, and he proceeded to slowly read it through. This guy's either being very methodical or he's not a fast reader, thought Adam, but he said nothing, concluding the former the more likely.

'That looks a fine piece of work to me,' Brian concluded, lifting his head up from the screen. 'But, you might want to add a little piece about how much the late Sultan was adored by the people. How much they mourn his passing. That's the reality here, Adam. Genuinely! The man was much liked. I'd suggest you also add how much he was a friend of Britain and how close the two countries have become over the years. I think it would be appropriate to add something along the lines of… as we look to the future, the legacy of that special relationship is not in doubt. It could be inserted right there.' He jabbed a finger at the screen, held it there and waited until Adam had reached across and typed in the purportedly missing script.

Adam thought it prudent to accept most of the advice proffered, and whilst he appeared to be making all the required changes of him, in fact he only made the majority of them. But information gatekeeper Brian, other things on his mind, seemed happy enough and then left Adam alone as he took himself off for a comfort break.

Adam then opened the other file he'd not shared with Brian, made some changes of his own, downloaded the photo from his phone, and found his way to send the email material he really wanted London to have along with the photo.

Job done, as he waited, he wondered what system the Embassy were using to by-pass the communication shutdown outside, but all that was too technical for him. For personal security reasons, he then decided to delete the sent email and delete the deletion and then send the article Brian had seen and 'approved' to his parents' address, with a short covering note. He was confident the Embassy would be too busy to look further at his material, which is just what he wanted.

When Brian returned, Adam told him the job was done. Brian glanced briefly at the screen, made sure Adam had collected his memory stick, logged off, and then showed Adam back to reception. However, before leaving, Adam didn't want to part before asking Brian some questions.

'Where I'm staying, the head of the house, Abdul Aziz Nahari has been taken off by the security forces and we've heard nothing at all as to where he is. Can you help?' Brian considered this and then shrugged his shoulders.

'Sorry old chap. Unless he's one of ours… the answer's no. I'm afraid the dear chap, he's just one of many, swept up for security reasons. No doubt he'll be released, along with the others, in a few days.' Brian looked at his watch and turned. He was not going to answer any further questions.

'Until the same time tomorrow then?' said Adam. He got a quick affirmative nod and Brian Merryweather had gone.

Back in reception Adam decided he'd hang around a while and see what he could pick up. He'd been taught that a lot of journalism was done by just hanging around with intent, and it seemed like a good time to put his training to the test. He didn't have to wait long.

Two things happened of interest. He soon noticed that everyone who went to speak to the Receptionist spoke as if no-one else was listening to them, which was clearly not the case if one stopped to reflect for a minute. It was as if everyone was so preoccupied with their own story they were not thinking about others and their stories, and so Adam was listening, listening hard, to everyone else's story. Even the receptionist herself never lifted her eyes in his direction, maybe just thinking he was waiting for his driver to come and pick him up, or just waiting. He wasn't her problem.

There was one man, in particular, who had Adam's full attention. The receptionist was struggling to hear what he was saying, but not Adam. In a strong Indian accent he gave his name as Dilwar Patel, a British citizen. He said he'd arrived in Oman from Leeds six weeks ago, and he wanted to speak to someone senior.

'Why is that, Sir?' the receptionist asked politely.

'I've been here delivering a training programme for the Royal Oman Police.'

'And what would the training be for?'

'All about keeping the peace, maintaining public order, that kind of thing. I know now I was brought in because they knew this was going to happen. They've followed what I gave them to the letter. For more than a month they've had me thinking this was a training exercise, but no, it was for real. They've created all the holding areas just as I taught, they've identified the targets, they've taken them from their homes and off the streets, they've managed information. In fact, they've managed an information blackout so well, I think they've overdone it! Now do you see why I need to talk to someone senior? Just tell them it's Dilwar Patel, UK National Police Training College.'

The man was getting frustrated and the receptionist was being slow. Eventually, however, Adam sensed that she saw Dilwar Patel might need handling by someone else, not least because the queue waiting behind him had now grown to eight people, all anxiously waiting to be seen. She came to a decision.

'Please wait a moment Mr Patel, and I'll see what I can do,' she instructed politely, before turning and going out the door behind her. Adam took his chance and approached the man.

'Hello, I do hope you get to see someone soon,' offered Adam. 'What's it been like for you out there? I couldn't help but overhear, it sounded as if you've been in the middle of something you'd rather not have been.'

'Too true. I signed up to deliver a training programme. I thought it would be the usual thing with a good financial return, but I end up being the man brought in to help them manage their coup. This is way out of my league and I want out. Believe me, when I bribed someone to get me to the Embassy today, it was the best money I've ever spent! I want out on the first plane back to England. In the meantime, I want to be kept safe here. No knowing what will happen. I thought I'd be next…'

'You thought you'd be next for what?'

'Imprisonment. My British passport is the only thing that saved me. I've seen too many things.'

'What things?'
'You know, unlawful arrests, illegal use of torture against people, punishment beatings – it's all about someone taking power.'

'You mean one of the late Hamad's relatives?'

'No. The head of the army – the SAF, the Sultan of Oman's Armed Forces, that's who's calling the shots presently. My guess is there'll be a puppet leader in place any day now. It's the army who are running things – it's a coup by stealth. Them and the police, but the armed forces mainly. They literally call the shots – I've seen it.'

'Is that so?' said Adam all attention.

'The Ruling Family Council might be holding a second day of meetings to come up with a new Sultan's name, but it's all so much shop window dressing. From what I hear, they'll never agree – too much internal wrangling between family members. Everyone used to think one of Hamad's distant relatives will be chosen, but think about it. None have any long-standing history of politics and running things. Though one's been made Deputy Prime Minister recently, that doesn't mean a thing. The Family Council are meeting as ordered by the army who are guarding them and taking them to and from their meetings.'

'That so?' quizzed Adam.

'In the end my guess is they'll fail to agree and they'll have to open up Hamad's succession bequest envelopes – but ask yourself whose holding those? Who's looking after them and who's to say they haven't been replaced?'

'Who?'

'It's the Minister of Defence, a politician who's pulled a fast one, working alongside the head of the military – they're the ones to watch, you'll see. It's all a stitch up, by the two of them, a military coup in all but name. You wait. See if I'm not right!'

'What about Oman's powerful neighbours, Iran and Saudi? Don't you think they'll want a say in how things turn out?'

'Sure, but they're such opponents of each other, neither would want to see the other gain an advantage through all this. Besides, this country's tradition of Ibadi Islam will see off any attempt to impose Sunni or Shia ways.'

Adam recalled Maryam's words before he left the house. They resonated. After a slight pause for breath, Mr Dilwar Patel was in full flow once again.

'No, I'd ask myself why all these British agents and US personnel are hanging around here. These two Western powers are the real kingmakers. Forget Iran and Saudi. For years Oman's security forces have been massively strengthened – and who does the training, the leading, the influencing – we do, the Brits! People like me!'

'So what could they do?'

'You mean the Brits?' Adam nodded, observing the returning receptionist had a smartly suited man in attendance, no doubt to take on Adam's companion.

'Do you have a card? Can I ring you later? We weren't properly introduced. I'm Adam Taylor, also from the UK and want to learn more. I'll call you, and good luck… and maybe we could help each other?'

They were interrupted, the man hastily passing Adam his business card before being whisked into one of the interview rooms.

The second thing of interest was a smartly dressed Omani visitor who went up to the receptionist to ask whether the Ambassador was 'at home' and whether he would like to come to the Royal Palace early the next morning. Without further ado, he was immediately shown through and Adam saw a senior aide, bowing and scraping, as he escorted his Omani guest into the Embassy's hidden interior. In those few moments Adam instinctively knew Britain was engaged in whatever behind the scenes power struggle was currently going on.

With nothing else of interest to catch his attention, Adam made his way outside, found the white Mercedes, stepped inside and set off back to the Nahari house, his mind buzzing with the information he'd just picked up. As he glanced around watching the neighbourhoods flash by and seeing the green uniformed security forces dominating the light traffic on the road, he began to think his conversation with Dilwar Patel had given him the outline for the next article he had to write. He twirled Dilwar's business card in his fingers.

The problem was going to be how to make a call to him with all communication taken out? Only one solution offered itself, an early return to the Embassy. He'd make a call to him from there. He'd go first thing. The conversation with Dilwar had shown him things were looking much more unpredictable and unsettled than he'd imagined, dangerous even.

The Mercedes arrived back, the guards noting them as they glided to a halt. A cursory wave of the hand by one acknowledging their return seemed to suggest they considered him irrelevant. However, the other was talking into his radio, one eye on Adam.

Once inside he learned there was still no news of Abdul Aziz and the tension in the house had ratcheted up another notch. With good reason, thought Adam, but that thought he kept very much to himself.

30

It was the third day, he was sitting on the floor in a featureless grey concrete cell. At first light a tray of food was pushed into Abdul Aziz's cell – three slices of bread, and three dates. Perhaps he'd get four of each tomorrow, he mused.

It was the first food he'd seen since he'd arrived at the Army holding centre to the West of the city centre. He was now certain it was the army, not the police, running his country. In his solitary confinement he'd been provided with drinking water three times a day, so when the first food came, he devoured it quickly.

It wasn't the material losses of liberty and food that had most upset him, rather it was the lack of information and the sensory deprivation. He'd neither been interviewed for any knowledge they thought he might have, nor had he been told why he was being held, or indeed for how long. It was the endless uncertainty, tempered by fear, and the unaccounted for, unnerving noises by unseen people, that was so very wearing, so very sapping of his energy and morale. Used to long periods of travel, only having snatched moments of sleep, didn't bother him unduly.

An hour after he'd finished eating, his door was unlocked a second time, he thought so they could collect his tray or his soil bucket. But no, he was peremptorily told, 'stand up and follow'. This felt more unsafe still, but he quickly showed due deference and did what he was told, walked out, turned right, then left, and was led in through a door at the far end of a long rectangular office, decorated in more standard grey concrete finish.

Two men in khaki uniforms, one standing, one sitting, were at a desk at the far end of a long queue. The standing one with a cane under his arm was interrogating, the other writing everything down.

Abdul Aziz was told to join the end of the line of around thirty waiting men. It was then he thought he was actually just another detainee in a long line of detainees to be processed. He found comfort in thinking that, whether the reasoning was justified or not. If they'd thought he was important they wouldn't put him a line, they'd have singled him out, dragged him to the front. He'd have been seen earlier. Things looked more encouraging, feelings he kept well hidden, held down. The line looked orderly, civilised even. Perhaps he'd be let home, perhaps. The hope and the food he'd just eaten lifted his spirits.

When his turn came, he was waved forward by the man who was seated. The standing officer, holding a clip board leant over him. He was quickly scanning an information sheet, facts about him, of that he was certain. Abdul Aziz didn't dare try to appear as if he were looking, or reading the typed sheet upside down. He only glimpsed that it had his name at the top. Reading done, he could feel the standing man, watching, scrutinising him. He felt his eyes, his power over him.

The two men in front of him were a team. They were the decision makers here, and in the circumstances showing the right respect and attitude was the only sensible response open to him. He kept his eyes down. The officer spoke.

'Look at me.'

Abdul Aziz raised his head slowly and looked up. Their eyes met. Abdul Aziz thought they were not cruel eyes, but dark brown, soft eyes, but who was he to know how to read eyes?

'Abdul Aziz…?' he asked, knowing full well his name, but wanting to hear it said to his satisfaction.

'Nahari, Sir! Abdul Aziz Nahari.' He answered in as calm a voice as he could summon.

'Tell me about your business?' Abdul Aziz was thrown. Why that?

'I haven't all day.'

'Err. I work for Eastern Diplomatic Services. We facilitate business contracts for the good of Oman.'

'Who with? What countries? Name names.'

Abdul Aziz described the firms recent contracts, mainly with Iran, India and the UK. He chose not to mention Saudi or Israeli contacts. He knew they wouldn't go down well. The officer seemed satisfied and the standing man, now serving as a scribe worked hard to get it all down.

'And your home. Who lives there? Names.'

'Err, Maryam, my wife. My daughter Raqiyah. We have a visitor from the UK, a family friend Adam Taylor, and there are two domestic staff, a Bangladeshi driver and a Filipino housemaid. That's it.'

'Is Hassim Nahari your son?'

'Yes, but he has his own home. He's grown up.'

'We're holding him for now. You can go. Next…'

Before Abdul Aziz could say anything, ask anything, he was instructed to head for the door. His mind was spinning. They had Hassim, why?

Outside he joined a long line of other men waiting to have personal belongings returned and to be given reporting and other instructions before being allowed to leave for home. Men, once they'd been processed, left in batches of four at a time. Abdul Aziz assumed this was because a car was delivering them to their addresses.

As he waited his turn, Abdul Aziz was a troubled man. They were holding Hassim. He still couldn't work it out. Either Hassim was some kind of suspect or he was some kind of insurance to see that Abdul Aziz himself toed the line. There was, for now, simply no opportunity for him to find out more information. Of one thing he was sure, he'd been told quite deliberately. That in itself meant they wanted him to know they had power over him. It was a warning, to stay on side, to be very careful.

It was his turn at the front of another queue. He was handed a white plastic bag. He looked inside. All his personal items removed earlier from his pockets were there. The silver prayer box too. He signed for them. Then he was told he was to remain indoors at his home until further notice. Failure to do as instructed would be taken to be a treasonable offence. Abdul Aziz knew that meant he could be shot without question.

When his turn came to leave, he and three others were marched outside into the afternoon sun. Freedom felt good even when there was no shade. They stood and waited in the open, more than long enough for the sun's piercing rays to make them feel uncomfortably hot.

Finally, a white taxi appeared with its distinctive orange coloured wing panels. The taxi driver pulled up by them and without instruction they all climbed in, Abdul Aziz, the smartest dressed of the three in the front, the other three squashed in the back.

No one spoke, fear of criminal contamination over-ruling any desire for small talk. The driver asked them for the addresses he needed from them, and the voluntary code of silence continued – by now as if there was an unspoken no talking rule.

The taxi pulled away. Its radio was on. A few minutes of listening and Abdul Aziz concluded there was no news yet as to the new Sultan and still no-one was saying what was happening. This was worrying – it was the third day and not just because of his own incarceration, he believed his familiar Omani world was now an unsafe place.

Abdul Aziz was dropped off outside his front door mid-afternoon. He politely acknowledged the two soldiers, different ones to those posted before, and walked inside. The cool air was a welcome respite. He felt waves of relief, guilt and anxiety wash over him. He couldn't predict which would hit him next. Two strides into the hall and he had composed himself, for the sake of his household, whom he could hear approaching.

Maryam stood in the kitchen doorway impassively. She was quietly crying, her relief at seeing him alive uppermost in her mind. Raqiyah rushed over to her father and threw her arms round him, tears running down. Adam stepped out of the study, reassured but pensive, as he gazed across at Abdul Aziz's tired and strained face, wondering how the story went from here.

It took some minutes for some kind of order to settle and all adjourned to the large lounge with its flamboyant sofas. It was here they would hear all. The maid was called to bring tea. Adam's presence was wanted, and he was waved in to join them without hesitation, though he thought he detected in Maryam's face a hint of reluctance.

Abdul Aziz told what in sum amounted to not very much. Taken to the western army base, he'd been kept in solitary detention, and finally, after two days of solitary, he was asked a couple of questions about his job and suddenly released. Then he dropped the bombshell.

'They told me they have Hassim,' he said in a quiet measured tone. He let it sink in.

'I don't know why, but I think it's their way of letting me know they have a hold on me. They expect me to behave or else. But I've been thinking on the way back. I'm not sure it's just that. They could have used any means they like to keep me under control. For a start, they've told me I can't leave the house. So why? I'm afraid I think they must have another reason for holding Hassim that is nothing to do with me. They didn't pick up his brothers, so far as I know that is, it's everything to do with him, but I don't know what it might be. Are the phones still blocked – the internet down?'

''Fraid so,' said Adam, 'I just checked.'

'I'm no use here, nothing I can do, all we can do is wait it out. Rather frustrating,' said Abdul Aziz. He looked across at Maryam. She was looking at him accusingly.

'What are you thinking?' he asked her.

'Oh nothing, nothing.'

'Come on. You have something on your mind,' he persisted.

'Well, I'd rather not say. Hassim and you haven't exactly seen eye to eye and he may have stepped into dangerous areas – that is without a father to guide him,' she said. Adam and Raqiyah exchanged looks. They both knew they were about to be caught up in an unpleasant marital exchange of words.

'The only dangerous area I know I can think he's stepped into is… taking religion too seriously. Unless you know any different?' replied Abdul Aziz.

'Sometimes I think you're naive. Religion is dangerous in times like these. What a person believes shapes their path in the world. You might have thought it possible to step outside religion, it's not! Hassim has taken a noble path and that means he stands up for what he believes, but he's doing it without his father's guidance and it's your fault he's in custody now.'

'Now hold on a minute. Hassim's a grown man. He makes his own choices. When he left school he chose his own path. He took on that internship at the mosque. I tried my best to dissuade him from it. I admit our paths have drifted apart over the years since, but my door and my heart have never been shut to him. Have you, as his mother, any idea where his journey has taken him? Have you any idea at all why he might have been arrested?' Maryam fell silent.

'Mama, you must tell us,' broke in Raqiyah appealingly.

'I was going to tell you, when the time was right, but events have overtaken me. I've been keeping in contact with Hassim, seeing him sometimes,' said Maryam.

'Without my knowledge?' interrupted Abdul Aziz.

'Yes, he's my child too, but let me continue. You'd be proud to know he's been doing well and soon after his internship was over he gained a position at the mosque with a responsibility for social media. His job is to make the faith interesting for young people, the mosque were concerned that so many were falling to the wayside as Western education and values have taken over our land. He's shown himself to be very able and they've recently obtained sponsorship from friends in Saudi Arabia to promote the project and even pay for Hassim to have an assistant. I can't see any harm in that. Why on earth would they detain Hassim?'

'You really do meddle in things you don't understand! Of course he's in danger of arrest. Anyone who takes Saudi money for militant Islamic programmes will be thought to be a threat. Have you no idea…' Abdul Aziz was lost for words at Maryam's disclosure, and lifted his hands in despair.

'But we don't actually have any concrete news, do we?' interjected Adam. 'I wonder if we can come up with some way to learn more? If you can give me an address to call at,

I'll see if I can make a detour on the way back from the Embassy. It might be possible. Where does he live? Where else might I go?'

'There are bound to be soldiers outside his door too. It's too dangerous, it's not possible,' said Abdul Aziz, putting a restraining arm on Adam's.

'But, what if Maryam or Raqiyah came in the car with me? I need to get to the Embassy with today's pieces anyway. They know I'm coming, expecting me. We could simply say to the soldiers we need food, we're calling on friends to get some. A woman would be better able to do it, yes?' said Adam. Adam looked at Abdul Aziz. Maryam and Raqiyah looked at each other, and then all turned to Abdul Aziz for a decision who assented weakly with a nod.

Abdul Aziz sighed heavily. He'd have liked to let Raqiyah go, but Maryam was the more likely to achieve what was required, even though, in the light of what she had just shared, he wondered whether he could trust her to bring all or even any accurate information back. She'd gone behind his back, the gulf between them had been publicly exposed. He didn't want to put Raqiyah in danger.

'Just Maryam's to go with Adam,' he declared, without further explanation. Then it was settled.

'I need to make one or two changes to my draft piece and I'd like to include a photo of yourself, Abdul Aziz, as people back home will be interested to know you've been released,' said Adam, taking out his phone for the photo shot. Abdul Aziz agreed, but was unable to offer a smile. It was an appropriate image, thought Adam, conveying in his face the stress and seriousness of the wider situation.

All decided upon, each then turned to their separate activities. Adam to complete his articles, but only after spending some minutes questioning Abdul Aziz about his detention.

Raqiyah went back to her e-book and Maryam to put on the clothing she wore for going outside. By four-thirty it was time. Adam, with his memory stick in his pocket, Maryam with a shopping bag to complete her part. Maybe it was the fact she had regularly plied the soldiers outside the door with tea, but they didn't raise an eyebrow when she got in the back of the car with Adam sitting in the front. By five-o-clock the car was dropping Adam at the Embassy. This time though, the car didn't wait. Maryam was off to find out what she could about Hassim's situation. She had a particular address in mind.

As Adam walked into the now familiar British Embassy reception area, he hoped Maryam would have success. On his own for a moment, he thought it wasn't going to be easy to find a path for himself in the Nahari home, there were surprising minefields everywhere, a bit like the country itself, at present. He liked Abdul Aziz and found him good to talk to and he felt accepted. Maryam left him feeling ambivalent. Her personality seemed inaccessible to him somehow. In the car just now, they'd not exchanged a word. He couldn't work her out. Maybe she lived in a different world. And Raqiyah, they'd stolen one kiss and a look. They hadn't talked, they hadn't had fun, they hadn't been together, all because of how things worked in this place.

He sat down in reception and waited for Brian Merryweather to appear.

How, he wondered, was Raqiyah herself coping with the situation since they'd arrived back? Then he realised the two of them had hardly spoken together at all since they stepped off the plane in Oman merely forty-eight hours ago. It felt like a past aeon and he imagined that with each passing day a vast distance was opening up between them, something he was utterly powerless to prevent.

31

Raqiyah retreated to her room whilst her father went to find something to eat in the kitchen. She knew he'd be eating some of the dates left out on the marble worktop – easily digested and energy giving, and she was right. Then she heard him spitting out the stones, pinging and gonging as they hit the metal bin.

She was finding it strange being at home again. After three years at Exeter University she hadn't anticipated the culture shock in coming back. She didn't like her situation. Her Father had wanted to know how she felt, but there hadn't been a right moment to talk. How she felt seemed unimportant when real dangers and threats assailed the family. The fact she felt she had a double life was too dangerous to voice. Her secret life in Exeter had to be hidden deep down inside herself here in Oman.

After a few minutes she heard him cross the foyer making his way to his study and decided to go and be with him. There were things she wanted to ask. As head of the house he no doubt would keep much to himself, but she was no longer a little girl, though he sometimes seemed to forget that. He was always so over-protective of her. No doubt he had a lot to ponder right now and after two days in detention a backlog of outstanding work to catch up on. He had always seemed to find his work such a solace. However, the two needed to talk, well she did anyway, and she was resolved as she followed him to the study.

As she entered, his head turned and he smiled warmly but with tired, dark circles round his eyes. She could see in his face the stress of the past two days and could only imagine what he must have gone through. He got up and pulled a chair across from the far side of his study so that they could sit together – an encouraging sign.

'Daddy, these are difficult times. It's hard enough coming back home from life in the West, but to return to a national crisis and a family crisis is hard to bear. You remember when we were small you'd take us children out to the wilderness for the day, in a strange way, the past two days have reminded me of those times. Together, facing an inhospitable world.'

'I know, I know. I'm sorry you've come back to this. You're right – we're in the wilderness again. Anything might happen and life feels vulnerable. But, let's be optimistic. The Sultan left us a good legacy – I'd be surprised if the people choose to throw it away; and our family, well it's been through tough times before, we'll pull through. The next day or two of uncertainty must pass, then inshallah – God willing, things will get better, settle again.'

'I'd like to think you are right, but I don't think you're really saying that – "God willing", trust in Allah – I've always seen you as someone who thinks Allah's let's him down! I don't buy your effort at divine reassurance,' she voiced boldly.

'You know me too well, Raqiyah. I shouldn't have said that to you. It's what everyone wants to hear, and social convention shapes our lives like text written on stone. Maybe I don't think Allah will manage things like a puppeteer in response to the number of prayers from the righteous he receives today, but it may surprise you – I still believe, but not in the way your Mama does! Prayers are helpful, believe me, these past two days I've prayed, but when one's hands are reaching to heaven, one's feet also need to remain firmly planted on the ground.' He pulled out something from his pocket.

'I've never shown you this before. It's an old silver prayer box, with something written on parchment inside. Walood gave it me… a very long time ago, when I felt Allah had let me down… I was a young man. Since that day, I've found this silver box something of a comfort. Stroking it, carrying it everywhere. I've been around the world, it's been everywhere with me, and it's been the one point of contact I think I have with the divine. I argue with Allah, I defy him, I threaten him… but this delicately made artefact is my touchstone, my connection with the spiritual world, a reminder that we're more than what we think we are. I believe, but can't find a religious place to fit in. Culturally I'm a Muslim, so don't get me wrong, however I find little to discuss in common with your Mama when it comes to religion… This was taken from me whilst I was in my cell, it was a relief to get it back again. I realise how much I treasure it.'

'I know what you mean about belonging. I've spent so long in the West, three years a student in England. I feel I don't fit anywhere anymore, in Oman, in England, as a Muslim, as a human being, as a woman too. I'd forgotten how tied to the patterns of the past we in Oman are. Patriarchal society, the cultural life of the tribes, an unquestioning pleasing of the right people – it's still in our blood. Coming back, I feel I've stepped back into history. Everything here is working hard to try and shape me into the person I'm not, don't want to be. Am I making any sense?'

'Yes, I understand what you mean. Your Mama and I, we share our love for you all, and our desire you should all be happy…'

'But you, you… you are both so different from each other. It came out again earlier. She has a different take on Islam. She is pious, religious, almost needs to be.'

'That's true, and there's good reason for her to be, to live like she does. It serves her well. And you're right. I find I can live by arguing with Allah, and yes, I'll say it, Allah and I have got along fine by mutually giving each other space for long periods. That doesn't mean to say I don't know how to behave in public – to everyone's eyes I appear a good Muslim and have been blessed for it. But like a lot of people I share the private frustration at not being allowed the luxury of expressing how I feel in public and living, well carrying the guilt of being a hypocrite. In Oman, at least, we have the luxury of what happens in the family is something sacrosanct – and what goes on in the home stays in the home, and the State has no interest. Unlike elsewhere in the Middle East, we can actually have this conversation without being tried by a religious court!'

'But when you've lived in the West it feels really hard to come back here. It's as if the very walls of society and my home close in on me all the time. I can feel my mood sinking by the day and it's not just the political and family crisis we're in. You know Adam is a dear, dear, friend to me – but I worry for him and for me here, for the two of us. For all the wilderness in this country, there's no space for us. I wonder whether Adam also feels hemmed in here. I fear he'll want to leave – and the way things are going… it will remind him too much of what he went through before. He'll leave me.'

'Adam's not the person you once described him as. He seems an able, strong personality, who right now is being conscientious in his work. I haven't said this before, but I like him. He's a decent guy, a nice, good lad.'

A silence fell between them. Raqiyah felt a warm bond had been renewed through the honesty her father had expressed, and to have had his positive affirmation of Adam meant more than she could say. In spite of the lack of news of Hassim, and all the turmoil they were living under, the conversation had lifted her spirits.

Abdul Aziz for his part felt pain. He didn't know how to help his daughter find her way in the world. He could see her love for Adam, but her relationship with Adam was a puzzle without a solution. He realised how much he loved his daughter, and then he thought how strong she was and it allowed him to glimpse a little window of hope for her.

As he reflected, he stroked his silver prayer box.

32

Whilst waiting in the Embassy's Reception, Adam made a point of observing what he could, but unlike yesterday there was very little going on, very little to see. The place was as quiet as student halls in vacation – all life sucked out. The bored receptionist said the earlier queues of needy callers had all been dealt with, and Mr Brian Merryweather was obviously busy with something else for now. Adam glanced around, he was once again, he noted, just hanging around, loitering with intent.

There was just the receptionist and himself. He went up to the counter to talk to her again. She also had time on her hands and was finishing tidying up her work station. Some red nail polish was waiting to be applied. Her name plate read, "Karen".

'Hi there, Karen. How's your day? Am I mistaken or is it much quieter here today?' She looked up, a friendly face.

'Yes. Things have reached a waiting point. Those who needed immediate help have been and gone, most are waiting for flights out. Everyone else has hunkered down until the storm blows over and normal Omani service is resumed… whatever that means, and then they'll all come flooding back in here, you'll see. You're becoming quite a regular here, aren't you?'

'Seems like it. Do you think they might allow me to use your phone? One quick phone call, – it's just we can't where I'm staying, no-one can? The lines are still down.'

'Sure, only too happy to help, that's one of the easiest requests I've been asked.' She passed a handsfree desk phone to him, simply adding, 'you'll need to dial 9 for an outside line. Do you know the number you want?'

'Yes thanks.' Adam replied, pulling Dilwar Patel's card from his pocket and punching in the numbers. He didn't get through. He wasn't really surprised. He called across to Karen.

'Do you remember this guy?' He pushed the business card forward so she could read it. 'He was here yesterday. Asked me to call him. Asian man with a British passport, been giving training courses to the Royal Oman Police. You must remember. There was a queue building and you went to fetch someone to see him. He was a bit charged up, wanting to get out.'

'Oh yes, talked a lot that one.'

'How can I reach him – this number's not getting through?'

'Try it again. He should be back in the UK soon, most likely still on his way, probably in Dubai or Dofa. I can only suggest you try again and then hang on, you might get lucky.'

The advice was sound, and on his third attempt, Dilwar Patel with his strong Indian accent, picked up with a tired 'hello'.

'Hi, it's Adam Taylor here, phoning from the British Embassy in Muscat. You gave me your card yesterday and I promised I'd give you a call. So, you got out then?' asked Adam.

He heard Dilwar grunt in acknowledgement at the other end, slowly tuning in to whom he was speaking. Adam moved away from the reception counter, leaving Karen to concentrate on applying her high odour, red nail polish.

'We never had a chance to finish our conversation yesterday. I was wondering why you thought the British had a stake in who next holds the political reigns here? Sounded like you had a fair insight into the likely scenario.'

'You're one lucky guy Adam. I'm just now sitting in Dubai International Airport, waiting for my flight to London Heathrow and enjoying a G&T to celebrate. Yes, you're absolutely right. Britain's deeply involved in lining up the ducks in Oman. It's pay-off time. The Brits have been helping rich Omanis invest in the UK, educating their military, facilitating high level conversations, MI6 chiefs coming over with HRH Prince Charles. There's been so much British–Omani cooperation at a military and political level over a long period of time… its almost like the two are married to each other! You bet the two countries are in cahoots.'

'So, what? Who gets to be in charge?' pushed Adam.

'Whoever Britain most wants in charge.'

'Yes, and that's who?'

'Like I say – the military and security services. They're the only ones who, with Britain's constant help, can hold the country together. It won't matter what name the Ruling Family Council come up with today or what name the two succession bequest envelopes reveal. It'll be the armed forces in charge, I saw it on the ground with my own eyes. Think about it. Does Britain want an Islamic State, even a so-called tolerant Ibadi Muslim one? – No! Does Britain want to keep access for its forces to Oman's airfields and its Duqm naval base? – Yes, of course! The only ones they know can deliver what they want are the military. You'll see.'

Then the line suddenly went dead. Adam looked up and back at the Reception counter, a man standing next to Karen on her side of the counter screen, was looking straight at him, the phone cradle in his hand. Adam immediately knew, whoever this guy was, he'd ended the call he was making. The guy lifted his curled index finger. He was calling Adam across to him, offering the handset cradle for him to return the phone. It was an instruction not a request; the receptionist was looking as if she'd been reprimanded.

'Thank you,' said Adam cheerfully, 'though I think I lost the call. And you are?'

He never got an answer, for it was just then Brian Merryweather appeared and Adam was ushered away by him to his waiting PC. Minutes later he was lining up his double entry journalism style articles – one for Brian and a second for CNPI, London. This was already becoming a familiar routine.

'Brian, do you mind answering me a question?'

'I'll try, depends what it is.'

'Who's going to run this country next? If you're speculating, if you were a gambling man, just who would you put your money on? It can't be more than a five or six horse race.'

'Now that kind of question is way above my pay grade. You're the journalist... speculation, stories, that's your area. Have you got another piece you want to show me?'

Adam gave up and inserted his memory stick and opened the latest file and let Brian read it. Every now and then he would make slight noises as if he were registering something. When he'd finished reading he looked up.

'A well written piece, but what you haven't included is any speculation on your part as to what might happen today. Your editor in London will not only want to know about arrests and detentions but he will want to know whether there will be a smooth transition of power and who it might be to. You could give him a few possibilities to chew on, I think they'd like that. I'll leave you to it, I've things to do, copy me in to what you send to London – looks good to me, Adam, honestly.'

On his own once more, Adam decided to add what he'd learned from Dilwar to his private article, and then a more general scoping of possibilities to the piece he was letting Brian see. Then he copied his picture of Abdul Aziz over from his phone and pressed the 'send' button. He watched as the blue line tracked across, concluding with a satisfying 'ping' indicating job done, article safely delivered. Having retrieved his memory stick, he stood up. Ready to leave, he needed to be shown back to reception.

The man he'd seen earlier who'd ended his call to Dilwar was back. He was standing between Adam and his exit.

'I didn't get chance to introduce myself earlier. It's Rodney Smyth. We need to talk.'

'Thank you,' said Adam, realising from his earlier contact with Embassy and security staff that he was about to be sold a line.

'It's all very well your writing and sending articles off to London, we are, after all, champions of the freedom of the press. I'm all for it, but it takes a lot of experience and skill to get the reported message exactly right in the delicate time we're in now, and let's be frank… you're very new to this game.'

Adam wasn't liking his patronising, controlling manner, but he knew that he needed to discover what lay behind it and he played along with the charade.

'You're right on that point. I'm new, it's my first posting. I'm all at sea in a chaotic situation, so I need all the advice I can get. What did you want to tell me?'

'My advice would be to wait a few days before writing your next piece. I've just had a word with Brian. He thinks it would be a good idea, for your own safety too, if you were to remain indoors for a few more days, certainly until the situation becomes more stable… safe.' The words slid across as easily as a snake on the sand, with more than a hint of threat.

'Thank you for your concern for my well-being, but I'm here to do a job and I'd be letting my employer down if I didn't send him stuff – you understand. But it would helpful to hear from someone with your experience what you think the succession outcome will be. What do you think? How is it all going to play out?'

'I can't say.'

'Or won't say,' interjected Adam.

'Discretion, as they say, is the better part of valour,' he added firmly. 'Just be careful, Adam Taylor, be very careful. They say the pen is more powerful than the sword – you may discover the reverse is equally true.' With that he turned and disappeared into the building's interior.

Adam returned to Reception. He could be there some time, waiting for his driver to return. He wondered how Maryam was getting on enquiring after Hassim.

Looking around him, the Receptionist was now admiring her finished nails. She glanced at him, this time with a flirtatious smile, all in her eyes and mouth.

There might be more information to be gained by talking to her further, he thought, as he moved closer to engage and find out more. For a start who was Rodney Smyth? It would be good to tie a few comments in his next piece against the man's name. He just knew Rodney wouldn't like that!

33

It was only after dropping Adam at the Embassy, Maryam noticed she had never seen the capital looking so deserted. It rather unnerved her, all the empty streets, not a soul in sight.

Her plan, clear as crystal in her mind, from the moment she'd left the house, was to call on her friends who ran the corner shop near the mosque Hassim visited. The couple knew everything that went on in their neighbourhood, to the point of making it their business to know – and where better to start making enquiries? Everyone knew any visit to Ali and Sunita's was as much a social event, to catch up on gossip and news, as to buy groceries.

When the Mercedes pulled up outside the shop, she could see that the front door was closed for business. Shutters down over the windows, and a flip across plastic, "Closed" sign declared as much. She wondered how long it would be until normal life returned when she could shop, buy fresh bread, fruit and vegetables once again. Even after just a couple of days it felt a new and oppressive state of normality had asserted itself.

Maryam made her driver pull up right next to the shop front. She was certain her friends would be inside, either out at the storage area to the back of the shop or in their flat upstairs where they lived – they never both went out at once, one always minded things. A couple of times a day, Ali would go off in their white van to buy fresh supplies, sometimes with a lad to help him, but never with Sunita.

The thing is, she said to herself, how can I attract their attention? Casting a glance up and down the road, she could see the street was empty but for two policemen standing idly some way off at the far corner. They were looking her way, but hadn't moved. She assumed they wouldn't trouble her and mustering as much self-confidence as she could, she stepped out of the car, took two paces to the shop door and then banged it hard with the back of her hand, the rings on her fingers crashing loudly against the glass.

Almost immediately, Sunita appeared, with Ali right behind her. She waved a hand and they quickly opened up as she knew they would and beckoned her inside. In the sanctuary of the storage area at the back, they met standing behind the half empty shelves, the hum of refrigerators the only sound.

The absence of fresh items hadn't totally changed the air, for there was still the familiar smell of spices, ground coffee and groceries pervading the place. Ali went off to boil a pan and make tea, leaving the two women together. Sunita pulled across a couple of unopened boxes to improvise as seats. Once customary greetings had been exchanged, Maryam went straight to the point.

'Our Hassim has disappeared and we think he's being held by the security services. My Abdul Aziz was picked up two days ago, but Allah be praised, they've released him and let him come home, but mind, he's forbidden from leaving the house. What's worrying us is that we've heard nothing of Hassim, we're all very worried.' She looked down, realising she was clasping and wringing her hands.

'You poor thing. You took a risk coming out. How did you get away with it?'

'We've got young Adam from England staying with us at the moment and, because he needed to go to the British

Embassy, I took a ride with him, which allowed me out the house. We've got two soldiers at our front door. They watch our every move. Seeing Adam with me, our local security just nodded us through. But have you heard anything of Hassim? Anything at all of what's going on?'

'I don't want to alarm you Maryam, but there was a big security operation here two days ago. All the streets were cordoned off and raids were made on many houses in the area. Any young man who was attached to the mosque up the road was picked up and taken away in an army lorry. I've heard that around thirty were detained altogether and I'm pretty certain Hassim was amongst them.'

Maryam couldn't help letting out a low moan.

Sunita continued, 'We all think it's because the mosque has been inviting in radical speakers, some from Saudi, and was supportive of a social engagement programme inciting a new Arab Spring uprising. Well, that's what we heard, and I can see why the army wouldn't like that, especially at a time like this. Once we have a new Sultan they'll all be let go, you'll see. I wouldn't worry,' she said, as Ali returned with the tea. He'd overhead the gist of the conversation and ventured to join in.

'Sorry it's not the news you wanted to hear, Maryam,' he said. 'You're not the first anxious parent to come knocking on our door to find out what's happening. Five or maybe six families have done the same, most at dead of night, dodging the police and army patrols. Some, the soldiers at the corner stopped, wouldn't let them visit us. We could see everything from our window upstairs. With nothing to do, we've spent hours just observing what's happening out on the street. I'm sure there were others too, those who never made it as far as our street let alone our door.'

'Where have they taken the young men?'

'No-one seems to know. My guess it's to one of the army barracks out of the city, maybe the big one on the Nizwa road. I'm afraid there's no option but to wait it out, and as Sunita says, I'm sure they'll be released soon, once we get an announcement. Strange thing is, it's day three and the TV is still giving us no news. Everyone's just desperate to hear. In the excitement of having a new Sultan, releases are bound to follow, you'll see. It's what happens. He'll be home soon. He's a good lad, you'll see.'

The three then sat in an awkward silence drinking tea. What troubled Maryam was the extent to which the mosque group Hassim had linked up with was radical. As a woman, she never went to mosque, she'd relied on Hassim's accounts as to what it was like and what he'd been doing there. Until now she'd assumed it was an all too welcome resurgence of sincere faith. Now it sounded like it was more worrying, the use of the word, "radical" had further unsettled her, as too had the description of the detained being all young people. Abdul Aziz's fears, expressed so forcibly earlier, came back to haunt her.

'What do you make of the mosque being, well, "radical"?' she asked, 'that bit's news to me.'

'Oh, yes, we've been concerned about things there for several months,' said Ali. Some of our best customers have been worried for their sons. Many of the older men have stopped going or have been told to stop attending and most now go to the main road mosque instead. Some of the youngsters who've stayed have been withdrawing from their families, taking positions at the mosque, dropping out of promising careers – that is those who had jobs. Those without work have found a welcome there too. I think the youngsters have seen the mosque as a place to go, to kill time on their hands, not having jobs and all that. It's understandable. But you know what they say about who makes use of idle hands?'

'What do you know about the mosque?' asked Maryam, hungry to know more. 'Who are their trustees? Who sponsors their imam?'

'Well it's all been rather odd. When the old Imam died last year, the trustees did something irregular, they appointed a new man from outside the Ibadi tradition. When people kicked up a fuss, he claimed to see the light, he switched sides and everyone was happy again. I think it was the beauty of his Arabic, his leading of the liturgy, that meant people were ready to overlook theological niceties. They loved hearing him lead prayers. He's young and over time has proved himself reliable – never late, certainly never misses – that counts for a lot.'

Maryam had heard enough to know how things lay and turned the conversation to more normal chatter, asking after family and business, sharing news of friends, before she remembered Adam, who was by now probably waiting for her return. Finally, she looked at her watch and made her excuses to leave. Ali complained at how the situation was beginning to impact on his business. 'Have you noticed all the gaps on my shelves,' he said despairingly.

Maryam didn't want to be too long, and for some reason she wanted to return to the safety of her home, to her mind the world outside had begun to feel unsafe. A little creature called fear had crept inside her at some point since she'd left the house, it had grown and was shaking her, causing her to tremble. She couldn't pinpoint when exactly it had begun to trouble her, but she couldn't quieten it down or shake it off.

The door pushed firmly shut behind her, she was alone and back on the dusty street. Looking somewhat furtive as she glanced up and then down the street, she gave a hurried farewell wave to Ali and Sunita, in their "closed" shop. She heard more locks and bolts rasping and being slid in place behind the shop door and hurriedly stepped inside the back of the Mercedes.

The two headed back for the Embassy to collect Adam. Less than one block down the road, the police spotted them and flagged them down.

'Leave this to me,' said Maryam to her driver, 'I'll take care of these two.' She wound down her window and called out to them. 'We have to go to the British Embassy right away to collect someone, then we're returning to the house. We had permission to leave. I trust that's OK?'

'Just need to see your ID ma'am,' insisted the serious faced policeman nearest to them.

Maryam duly obliged. The officer took his time, glancing at her once, then twice more. She forced a smile; the officer didn't smile back. Then just as she was wondering what she might say next, her ID was passed back and she was waved on her way.

Ten minutes later they collected Adam. Twenty minutes, and they were pulling up back at the house. Maryam sitting quietly, feeling guilty. She should have realised the dangers

Hassim was getting himself into. She was wondering how she was going to tell Abdul Aziz and Raqiyah what she'd learnt from Ali and Sunita. This wasn't going to be easy.

34

Once safely back inside the house, everyone crowded into the kitchen to share news. Abdul Aziz said there had been nothing announced yet on the TV. He'd tried talking to the soldiers outside and got nowhere before being ordered, in no uncertain terms, to get back inside if he knew what was good for him.

Maryam's relief at having successfully made the journey to her friends and back was tempered by her newly gained knowledge of the seriousness of Hassim's situation. She reported back exactly what Sunita and Ali had told her, restraining herself from adding any personal gloss.

She realised, even as she spoke, she'd been duped by Hassim, she should at least have paid more attention to what he was doing and been better informed. Thankfully Abdul Aziz did not chide her for her folly. She guessed he could read what had happened and how she felt. They were an odd couple, she thought, a mixture of comfort and conflict in their relationship – it had been that way for a long time. Sometimes there was comfort, though it seemed to her to have given way to more conflict in recent times.

'So Hassim's in detention somewhere, probably at an army base, possibly for his association with a revolutionary mosque-based group of young people, led by someone from Saudi who's calling the shots. Doesn't sound too good,' summed up Adam. 'The security forces won't like it.'

'It might not be as bad as that, Adam. You make it sound worse than it is,' said Raqiyah.

'I'm afraid Adam might be right. It felt like that kind of place when I first went there several years ago. It was around the time Hassim left school. I've not been back since, it's no good for personal reprimands now, too late for that,' said Abdul Aziz, as much addressing Maryam as himself, before continuing.

'I reckoned Hassim wouldn't have appreciated or even allowed his father to crowd his space. When I was there that time, I was regarded with real suspicion. I was left in no doubt I was an unwanted, unwelcome outsider. I could very easily have been thrown out, well politely shown the door,' added Abdul Aziz, 'but I was only spared the indignity by spotting Hassim just in time.

'Whenever he's visited back home, he's never given us any cause to think he was with a radical group, that he might be in trouble,' said Maryam. 'I thought he was really doing well from what he said, setting up social media platforms, websites, blogs, chat rooms, that kind of thing. It's not me, I don't know about such things, but he seemed to be very committed, fulfilled, happy even. I never questioned him, never, not once.'

'You might as well know Adam, Hassim and I haven't really spoken since, just seen each other, you understand. I'm away a lot working. He doesn't want to cross paths with me. We both see the world very differently. I've rather let things drift, but now I think I should have done more to try and talk to him. He always seemed to come to the house when I was out, our paths hardly ever crossed.'

'He preferred it that way Abdul Aziz. He thought you'd disapprove, so he'd phone to see if you were at home before he'd show up. He'd only come if you weren't around. If he'd ended up meeting you here , I thought he might give up coming all together,' Maryam added, 'I'm sorry for that now.'

'You went behind my back,' said Abdul Aziz, feeling betrayed, but not bitter about it. Then regaining his composure added, 'but let's let bygones be bygones. We've got a situation to deal with. There can be little doubt Hassim is in real trouble. Do we just wait on events? We might have to.'

'I'm the only one with some freedom of movement here and access to communication channels. I'm not sure what I can do, but I'll try and have a conversation with someone at the Embassy tomorrow.'

The others looked at Adam, nodding their approval.

'I feel tomorrow's a critical day. It's three days, the Ruling Family Council's time will be up. My guess is we'll all hear something very soon, then we'll have something to go on. Also, they can't keep everyone cooped up in their homes much longer, they'll have to allow the markets and shops to re-open. They'll want to assure the watching world as to a degree of normality here – Oman being open for business, that kind of thing. In the meantime, I think we should see how things are in the morning before we do anything further.'

Adam decided it wasn't the time to speculate what kind of new national leadership might emerge, or indeed what part the British Embassy might play behind the scenes. He kept all that to himself.

'That sounds good to me,' said Abdul Aziz.

Maryam and Raqiyah nodded their assent and slowly people drifted off to their separate areas of the house. First, Abdul Aziz ambled slowly over to his study, then Maryam went to the kitchen. The sound of a tap running and vegetables being washed and scraped could be heard – the routine of kitchen-based therapy doing its work.

Adam and Raqiyah found themselves unexpectedly left alone in the central foyer, the one point in the house they'd accidentally discovered that both parents seemed to find an acceptable place for the two to meet – a sort of public area in the home, where there was always someone likely to pass through. The two stood facing each other, glad of the chance for a semi-private chat.

'This is crap,' whispered Adam under his breath, taking the opportunity to express his feelings with someone who would not be shocked and understood. Raqiyah adjusted the colourful veil, moving it a little further back from her face.

'I don't know about Hassim, but I feel so constricted living here I can hardly breathe. In effect we're all under house arrest. It's rubbish! We've been back here no more than a few days and we've hardly spoken to each other, and the strain here, understandable as it is, is getting to me too. Why did the Sultan have to fucking die? Sorry… that wasn't helpful. Just needed to say something…' said Adam, realising his now raised voice might be heard.

'I know. None of this was predictable. We arrived home to a time of national crisis. It's got to get better soon,' she replied without any inner confidence, not really believing it would.

'My visit here last summer kind of alerted me to the do's and don'ts of Omani society. No touching between sexes in public, or as I also soon discovered so far as we're concerned, in private too. There's rarely even the opportunity to find a private space for a proper conversation together, so much so I don't feel I know you when we're here. We kind of drifted apart as the plane landed. Can't we negotiate a better accommodation with your father than this?'

'Don't say that Adam, it's hurtful. And no, this is home, it's… it's Oman, there's absolutely no way we can be together as two single people. You know that I find it hard too. I feel like I'm living a lie. Can you imagine what that feels like?' Her voice was now the one being raised. There were tears in her eyes and Adam reached across the space and held her forearms. Words faltered.

'But don't you think, living like this is, well it's a throwback to another age, when patriarchy ruled, when women were supposed to be somewhere hidden in the house secretly doing home things – babies, food, washing, cooking and cleaning up? I've watched us. You've started doing that too, and I find I'm doing the work, doing the manly thing – like what Oman expects of me. I'm telling you, I don't like living like this. It's bad for me, for you, for us. My mind is already thinking about how we can get away.'

But even as he said it, Adam realised he'd gone way too far. He could see tears once more welling up in Raqiyah's eyes and he regretted his outburst the moment it escaped his lips. She hid more of her face, her hand clutching her veil. It was as if he'd, in that instant, created a fault line in their relationship and he wondered if it could be repaired.

'Sorry,' he said, still holding on to her, 'all that stuff rather came out stronger than I intended. We're all living under a lot of strain. I'm not going anywhere. You know that, don't you? We both know that. My place is by you. I need to start on my next piece. I didn't tell you. I got hold of that Dilwar Patel guy I told you about, phoned him in Dubai. He'd got out of Oman and was en route for London. He gave me some more insights. I best ought to get them down. Writing helps put things in their place. Love you Raq.' He reached across once more, their hands squeezed each other's arms and Adam planted a kiss on her lips.

'That's fine. I'll be in the kitchen,' she said softly, pulling away from him.

That was neither what Adam wanted to hear, nor what Raqiyah herself really wanted, but for now there was nothing further to be said on the matter. She was an Omani woman.

35

Maryam was up first for dawn prayers. Before she settled into the ritual, and whilst waiting for Raqiyah to join her, she woke everyone else to break the news.

'It's on TV now,' she cried out excitedly. 'They've sorted the succession question. Everything can return to normal again. The curfew's been lifted, shops and businesses can re-open, schools too. Isn't it great! Hassim will be home soon inshallah.'

'Let's not get carried away here,' said Abdul Aziz flatly, always slow to get going in the morning, trying his best to feel alert. 'Who's "they" and who's in charge of us all?'

'It's the Head of the Sultan's Special Armed Forces, Major General Sadiq bin Mahmut. He's already announced two deputies for the new Sultan, the last Sultan's Cousin from the Ministry of Defence and what's a surprise, a British Head of Armed Forces, Brigadier Martin Harper-Grimes, I think they called him. Apparently, the Ruling Family Council came up with the same solution, so there we are, we know at last,' concluded Maryam.

'It's a military coup,' said Adam bluntly.

'I agree,' said a poker faced Abdul Aziz, failing to match Maryam's excitement.

'You're right. Thinking about it, I don't like it. It's not what we were led to expect, is it?' said a concerned Raqiyah watching her mother's first excitement evaporate.

'Let's see if our two guardians are still outside the front door,' said Abdul Aziz striding across the foyer and swinging open the heavy wood door.

'No, the coast's clear. Perhaps we're free at last! Free at last!' he declared opening his arms wide and taking a deep intake of breath, as he stepped outside to take the morning air.

There was the sharp sound like that of a spade into soft earth, followed almost instantaneously by the sound of a gunshot breaking the calm of the early morning air. There was a scrape, a scuffle outside, as if from Abdul Aziz's shoe.

Adam knew the sound of a bullet when he heard one. 'Get down!' he yelled pulling out his mobile and punching on the video as he did so.

Everyone instinctively ducked down low and away from the open door. Adam had the clearest line of sight outside and saw Abdul Aziz first. He was lying on his back in the dust, a bullet hole in the front of his forehead, his eyes wide open in a startled expression, a pool of blood and other matter flowing out; spreading on the sand behind his resting head.

An army jeep was approaching. Two different soldiers this time. Adam watched and surmised neither was apparently carrying the kind of weapon needed to have shot Abdul Aziz. Adam got up from his crouched position and moved cautiously toward the door to wave to them, holding and flapping a white tissue he'd grabbed from the side, to indicate he was not armed, but even so he chose not to step beyond the door's threshold.

'He was told not to go out,' the senior man barked.

'So he was executed,' said Adam.

'I'd be careful what you say if I were you, Mr British Citizen,' the man said threateningly, glowering at Adam. 'Make yourself useful and drag the body inside. It makes our guard duty location look untidy. Now move,' he ordered, brandishing a pistol he'd just pulled out. It was no time to argue.

Adam tried his best. No one else in the house was moving and he had to do it alone. It was a terrible business. The back of Abdul Aziz's head was missing, and it was hard to separate tissue from the dusty ground in the mix. Adam felt sick as he looked, but steeled himself and did as instructed, the image of the waving pistol never far from his mind.

Red and white gore, flecked with tiny bits of skull, dripped a trail as Adam dragged Abdul Aziz inside. He quickly put his fingers to Abdul Aziz's warm eyelids to close them; the stare was too much. Inadvertently he'd wiped some of Abdul Aziz's own blood over the one eye. He let go and looked away.

'We'll send someone over to get him buried. Now shut the door and keep it shut.'

The door closed with a solid clunk and the lock snicker gently clicked shut. There was an all-pervading silence and shock was written on every face. Adam could see pale-faced trauma written across all their faces. Maryam begun muttering a prayer under her breath, rocking and clutching at her prayer beads. Raqiyah hadn't moved. She was as a tree, stationary, rooted to the grey tiled floor. Adam, though badly shaken himself, felt he had to take charge. He was looking at two casualties. They were both in shock.

'We need to get the driver and the maid here, tell them what's happening as best we can. Raqiyah, can you do that, can you rouse them, fetch them here.' He grabbed her two arms and shook her, had to do it again, then pulled her head round, his hand on her chin so she faced him and not the body; then he pushed her firmly toward the back of the house.'

I'll see to Abdul Aziz, I'll get a blanket. Maryam, you're right to say the prayers. Will you be OK a moment doing just that?' She nodded vacantly as if in a dream. Adam watched Raqiyah move silently toward the back of the house. At least she's responding, thought Adam. She's in shock, he thought. A few minutes later Maryam also moved off to her room, still muttering something quietly under breath.

Adam took a white linen sheet from the walk-in cupboard off the rear hallway and laid it over Abdul Aziz's body as carefully as he could. No sooner had he done so then patches of red blood soaked through from Abdul Aziz's face, the circular hole where the bullet had entered could be clearly identified. A surge of panic arose as he watched the blood spreading out; he hadn't anticipated this. It wasn't discreet enough, the sheet hadn't done the intended job, to hide the nastiness. Adam looked around him for what to do next.

He had an idea and went to reach for some clingfilm from the kitchen worktop before fetching a second white linen sheet to supplement the first. He pushed the cling film firmly down on top of the red stained sheet above Abdul Aziz's forehead, taking care to avoid having to touch anything of the body again, before laying the second white sheet on top of it. That did the trick. He waited and watched, it was fine. Nothing was soaking through, though the contours of his features looked strangely smoothed.

As he gazed down at the body he saw Abdul Aziz still didn't look right. Gently, he pushed Abdul Aziz's legs together with his right foot, the left more than the right, which straightened the alignment. Order and tidiness – little attempts to take control in a chaotic situation. It would have to do. He felt tainted and slightly nauseous by death.

He went to the bathroom to wash his hands and arms, then his face and for a reason he couldn't grasp, wiped his right shoe with a tissue which he then flushed away. He looked in the mirror. To his surprise he read a picture of shock in his own face, a face drained of all colour. He looked at his hands and held them out straight. There was noticeable tremor. He closed his eyes and concentrated hard, focussed down on breathing calmly and slowly, letting minutes pass.

On his return to the foyer he found the driver and maid had been told and were clearly distressed and fearful at the turn of events. Frightened and jittery, Adam told them as calmly as he could to go and get dressed. It was better to keep people's minds occupied with simple tasks, he thought. He was determined to keep control.

Raqiyah then reappeared. Her eyes were unwillingly drawn to the shrouded body of her father and she hesitated. Adam, forgetting decorum, took her arm and held her. She didn't move away. In the silent space, they both felt warmth and life flowing between them as they contemplated what had occurred.

As they heard Maryam's door open, the two drifted apart. Maryam, had veiled her face, only her tearful eyes showed. She was clutching a cloth for dabbing her eyes. All three stood silently over the body. A moment later they were disturbed by a firm knock at the front door.

'Wait, I'll get it,' said Adam, feeling a heady adrenaline mix of apprehension and fear as to what this next intrusion might be.

He opened the door cautiously, just a crack, adjusting his eyes to the fierce sunlight outside. There was a man in white. Then he opened the door wider.

'Hassim,' called out Raqiyah.

36

Raqiyah moved slowly past Adam and embraced her brother. Adam watched a white and orange taxi that had brought him making a hurried departure. The two soldiers were by the wall, feigning to show no interest. All inside, he pushed the front door firmly shut. Instinctively, he sensed the hand of controlling officialdom in the unfolding scene.

Hassim saw his father's body lying on the hall floor. He paused. His disbelieving eyes were looking up and down the shrouded form as if to comprehend what they were seeing. A long embrace between mother and son followed, both shaking with emotion. The first of Maryam's tears and wails began to flow as Hassim tried to comfort her. Her hollow wails grew ever louder, as if something alien, beast-like was tearing her apart from the inside. Eventually, Maryam, fighting to control her emotions quietened and wiped her tears from her now red eyes, before trying to speak.

'Are you all right?' she said, looking into Hassim's face, seeking some solace he was not in harm's way. He was still looking past her, staring at the shape on the floor.

'They let me go.' He paused, staring fixedly at the ground, 'telling me as they did so, there was a message waiting for me when I got home. It's Father, he's the message…' he said quietly as tears now welled in his eyes.

'Yes, they shot him, through the head, when he stepped outside the front door. Just now. Can't be half an hour ago. Hassim, what does this mean?' asked Adam.

'It's their way of telling me to toe the line, not cause them any trouble, that's why they let me out – the infidels.'

'He said, they told him, they were holding you, Hassim, just before they let him come home from detention,' said Adam.

Hassim stroked his beard and then looked at Adam warily. 'Are you the guy who's been hanging around my sister? News gets around.' As he spoke, he nodded toward Maryam, the information source.

'The name's Adam,' Adam said, offering his hand. A moment's hesitation, then Hassim reached out, took and grasped it firmly.

'Adam, you are our guest. I'm sorry, you are here at an unfortunate time.'

Adam thought the gesture gracious in the circumstances and given what he'd heard of Hassim. He thought Hassim could well blame him, being a Brit and a Westerner for being part of the problem with the world as he saw it. He could even be viewed as an accessory contributing to both his incarceration and his Father's death. Adam knew he was making assumptions, but he couldn't stop himself, and it left him feeling uncomfortable, even more unsure of his new and changed situation.

To Adam's mind, all the trappings of unquantified extremism were readily associated with Hassim. He raised too many echoes of his own past. Adam stayed quiet, he consciously stepped back from the leadership he'd hitherto been exercising.

The eldest son was back home, he'd be the one assuming his familial duty – it was Hassim's duty. Adam was the guest. On reflection, Adam thought Hassim's use of the word 'guest' was a hopeful, more promising tag tied to his presence in the house. It pulled him away from his more negative thoughts. The next question showed Adam that Hassim was indeed taking on the duties that went with being the eldest son.

'Tell me,' he said in a matter of fact tone. 'Are they going to let us get him buried today? What have they said?'

'They're sending someone over,' said Adam, 'but they didn't say when. We heard on the TV earlier that the succession question has been resolved and that people can go about their everyday business again. What have you seen? Do you know if it's true?'

'It's still too quiet for my liking, but it's early yet. I was dropped home by army arranged taxi. Brought me from the barracks on the Nizwa road, so I got to see a fair picture of the city on the way here – nothing much is happening, the roads are empty, soldiers still everywhere. Two military guys seemed to be leaving here as I arrived. They were collecting two others from down by the gate, one with a sniper rifle I think – is that how he was killed?'

'Yes, I guess so, almost certainly, though none of us saw it. We only heard the shot, sounded like only one,' said Adam. Raqiyah moved to be next to her mother.

'Asad, the house driver, and Jasmine, the family maid are both here' said Adam, seeking to introduce them. Hassim nodded to each in turn. He'd known them both as part of the family as long as he could remember.

'I think we'll take charge of the funeral arrangements ourselves. I don't want them coming in and treating Father's death as part of their tidying up – his body thrown in some anonymous pit somewhere. We might have disagreed on a few things, but he deserves a proper Islamic burial. We must arrange it out of respect for him. Given the current problems at the mosque where I say prayers, I think we'll use the Imam at the main road mosque. They at least knew Father. He has… had friends there. Asad, I want you to take me over there now. Happy with that?'

Asad, who seemed lost in his own thoughts, lifted his head on hearing his name, and nodded.

'I'm afraid we'll have to leave Father where he lies until I can get someone to pick him up. Adam, I leave you in charge of the women.' Adam nodded, feeling further affirmed, and now a lot less worried about his standing with Hassim.

With that, the two men, Hassim and Asad, walked cautiously out of the front door, headed straight for the car and left, bound for the mosque, a funeral to arrange. Custom required all should be done before sunset. The rest of the day was now spoken for and there was much to be done.

Adam once again took the initiative. He asked Maryam if she were up to sorting out some simple breakfast for everyone. She seemed to understand, nodded and went into the kitchen. Raqiyah said in an empty voice she'd like to see what was happening in the world outside and wanted to take a look at the TV news channel. As she spoke she glanced down to check her phone.

'Look! We have WiFi again. I'll begin by making some family calls – I need to let people know what's happened here and that there'll be a funeral later. I'll make a start before I have coffee – I shan't want anything else. I need to do something, it... it's true isn't it... Adam?'

'Yes, it's true, he's dead... I've got a signal too,' said Adam quietly. 'I need to ring my parents and one or two other people and look at what social media are saying about what's going on here in Oman. We need to know what's happening. I'll use the study. Sorry, but I'll also need to write a further news piece today, there can't be many foreign correspondents here in Oman yet.' Raqiyah nodded vacantly, showing she understood, then called the maid, Jasmine.

'Jasmine, can you go and help Mama in the kitchen, there's a huge amount to do.' No second bidding was needed. Everyone seemed to cope better with some task to occupy them.

Raqiyah knew that custom required the family ought to washing and prepare the body. She thought her mother would be mindful of this duty. She shook at the thought. Her guess was she didn't want to undertake it. As Raqiyah reflected on the task, she knew that on this occasion, in the light of the sudden trauma and violence to the body, it would be too difficult for any of them and resolved to ask her brother on his return to see that it was done by the mosque funeral team instead. They were the experts, they must see road traffic victims all the time, that's what they're used to seeing, she reasoned. They'd understand and know what to do. That much we can spare ourselves. We'll need to clean the floor when they've taken him, she thought. The horror of it. The mopping of blood with the foam tile cleaner and the white plastic bucket, she couldn't do it...

She also wondered about the blood and mess outside, already drying under the hot sun. That too would need to be dealt with, but she didn't know how. Perhaps when Asad returned he could see to it. The tiles inside were easier than the courtyard gravel. It would feel all wrong to walk on part of her Father every time people went in or out the front door. This thought felt somehow both distasteful and wholly inappropriate. Best to get some contractor in later – were there such people? The mosque team would know, she'd ask them later. Her thoughts were so ghoulish, so bizarre, like something from a scary movie, unreal.

She got up, forced down her emotions and steeled herself to the difficult task of telling the wider family what had happened. Muslim funeral practice didn't allow space before the funeral. In some ways this helped. Jobs had to be done, but then time would open up again – she couldn't bear the thought. Returning to the list of calls to be made, these could be more easily done in privacy. She went to her room. Before calling, she put her TV on, immediately pressing the mute, so she could both watch the images and read the news bulletin subtitle banner trailing across the screen whilst making her calls. She desperately wanted to view something reassuring, and normal. First, to call her brothers, Abbadi and Tariq, then her uncles…

Adam's phone pulsed into life as messages and mail spewed incessantly into his inbox – it was as if his mobile were some hungry insatiable beast demanding to be fed after too long going without. But the life in his phone meant he too was coming alive again, a connected person, and a free one.

Flicking through he found messages from London, family and employer. He ignored the bright world of Facebook, Instagram, WhatsApp and all his other apps. He sent a quick message home rather than make a call, it was after all still the middle of the night in London. He simply stated he was fine and safe, and promised to call later. That was enough.

His attention switched to his employer, CNPI. His editor, Keith Parker had written, twice. He'd used Adam's pieces and the photos, circulating them more widely and usefully earning good revenue from them. It was hard for a newspaper to survive these days, so Adam felt buoyed by such positive feedback.

In his latest missive, his editor Keith was asking Adam for more. He told Adam that there had been almost nothing coming out of the country for three days, so his pieces were, he said, like media gold dust. He was particularly interested in any British involvement, as the Foreign Office media machine were being rather coy about releasing anything.

Adam knew he had much more to tell but felt a certain apprehension in addressing the task. It all felt too raw, too personal, and no longer without risk to him or the Nahari family. His world had suddenly become very unsafe, unpredictable and dangerous. The soldiers earlier hard threat was still ringing in his ears.

The more he thought about it, the more worried he became. In an act of crude, cruel logic, he realised Abdul Aziz had been deliberately shot to make a point – to bring Hassim into line.

Adam couldn't think this would be just an isolated instance. Maybe there would be news later of others treated similarly. It wouldn't surprise him. The new regime was making an opening statement and it was already clear that it was in no wise comparable with the gentle rule of the former Sultan.

This was calculated and ruthless, a rule by fear approach, and his instincts were now warning him to be extremely careful. Summary execution had come right to his door. The thought and the body on the floor, just yards away, made him shudder.

There was a call from Jasmine, in the kitchen. It was time to assemble, have a drink, eat a little if possible, and reflect some more. He knew Hassim would most likely be gone for a while yet, funeral arrangements involved many people, and this may well not be the only pending funeral after three days of curfew. There would be a queue. Waiting for him to come back was only going to increase anxiety.

Raqiyah was the last to arrive in the kitchen and the first to speak. In a monotone, flat voice she updated everyone on the calls she'd made and the news she'd gained. 'It was strange,' she said, everyone she'd called seemed really nervous. She felt like she carried a plague. People were kindly offering condolences but were reluctant to say whether they'd be able to make it over later. Politeness meant they asked me to notify them of the time of the burial, but I felt they were all unusually wary. I wonder whether many, if any, will actually show up later.' The picture of life the calls mediated was, as Adam heard it, a scary one, that of a community under siege.

In part, all this was an understandable reaction to the past three days, but as Raqiyah told it, he felt sure it was more than that – as if others had a sense a Rubicon had been crossed. The gentle world of Sultan Hamad was no more and had been replaced by something severe, fearful, alien even.

When she'd had to say how her father had died, it was as if it had been expected. He was merely another one. Her eldest cousin said Abdul Aziz had always sailed close to the wind, adding, 'hadn't he been picked up by the security forces once before?'

Raqiyah had also heard of another arrest from a student friend she'd called. The friend's father had been picked up by the security forces and was still being held, his whereabouts unknown. Her call made her feel she'd added to that family's burden and she felt guilty for having made it. Her innocent call had removed their hope. Somehow, and against logic, she felt she had been tainted and made an unwilling accomplice in what the new leaders were doing.

Raqiyah and Adam took a mug of coffee each. Jasmine had squeezed the last of the oranges to make a jug of fresh juice which the others took. No-one was looking to eat the pale, watery rice pudding. Maryam was adding sugar to it and stirring with a vague faraway look on her face, until Jasmine took it from her. When Adam called her, Maryam finally came to the table and sat down. They were all now together as Adam made to speak first.

'I think we've all got to be very careful and take things extremely cautiously. My impression is, things are not yet safe out there. We now know there have been mass arrests and that the new regime is prepared to use state execution without trial, as a means of exercising control. I don't like it, and for the first time I'm thinking I've got to, for all our sakes, be careful what I send in my news piece to London today. I don't want it to cause problems here.'

'I agree,' said Raqiyah. 'My friend in Muttrah, her Father works for the Oman Telecom, he too has been detained. She was beside herself and my call was unfortunate to say the least. She took it very badly. It was as if I was a portend of doom. She called me an evil djinn – a demon spirit and hung up on me!'

'We will need to get food in today,' offered Maryam, 'it is expected with a funeral later. Jasmine, can you get things in if I prepare a list?'

'Sure. Asad will take me when he gets back. I think I ought to add something. My family called me this morning. They say the Philippine Foreign Ministry are reporting that Oman isn't safe. My family want me to come home until things get better. I told them I'm safe and that I'd decided I was staying on, for now.'

'Thank you, Jasmine. We are going to need your help,' said Raqiyah.

There was a knock at the door. All looked at each other. Once again, Adam felt it was up to him to see who it was.

Two different soldiers, one holding an upended stretcher stood outside.

'We're here for the body,' the one said.

'Not necessary,' said Adam, barring and blocking the door behind him.

'It's orders, Sir, we're to take it away.'

'Can't be done. I'm a British citizen and I have my orders too. There will be a British Embassy group attending a proper Muslim funeral for Mr Abdul Aziz Nahari. That'll be your orders carried out for you. It's all been taken care of. You haven't got to tackle an unpleasant job any more. It'll all be over in a few hours, sorry you've had a wasted journey, and thank you.'

The two soldiers looked at each other hesitatingly. They were unsure. The mention of the British Embassy was above their pay grade. They'd not been told a British citizen was handling things, or that Embassy representation would be at the funeral. A simple task had suddenly become all very irregular. They needed a way out. Fortunately for them, the young man at the door offered just that. Adam was ready to provide more assurances.

'I'm told that any minute now the Imam and funeral group from the main road mosque will be here. I'm sure they would be pleased to explain the due process and deal with any further questions you might have. They'll be arriving very shortly, they said. Would you like to wait inside? Won't take long.' He put his hand on the door knob as if to lead them inside. They hesitated. It felt like an age.

'That will be all, Sir. We may need to call back later. Our condolences to the family.'

'Thank you. I will make sure they receive them.'

With that the two were gone, and Adam breathed a mighty sigh of relief. As he pushed the front door open wider to go back in, he saw the others standing looking at him. He was shaking inside.

Raqiyah had tears running down her face. She was looking at him gratefully. He wanted to hold her, but he remembered it wasn't allowed.

Adam didn't know it, but his brave actions had in that decisive moment just endeared him to the family's heart in a way he could never have imagined. If he'd have looked, he'd have seen it too, in Maryam's wet eyes.

37

Adam retreated to write, Raqiyah to make more calls, Maryam and Jasmine to write shopping lists. All made themselves busy with their tasks. It took minds away from present pain and fears, it filled time, but only some of it; minds kept being drawn back to dark things, like clouds of hungry flies once shoed away soon return to a dead body.

The phone calls and emails started coming back into their mobiles and the home phone and the house became full of frenetic activity, like some over-busy call centre on Black Friday. With this and what had gone before, Adam found it almost impossible to settle and concentrate.

He'd managed to get through to the Embassy only once for a brief call, but thereafter had found all lines engaged. The successful call had told him nothing, other than that Brian Merryweather could only be reached after lunch. He'd guessed that they would be fully stretched in the Embassy today, catching up, dealing with the fallout.

He decided that with his personal communication channels restored, he no longer had to send his piece though the Embassy, nonetheless he felt it would be useful to him to keep his contacts there alive. Opening his laptop, he turned his attention to writing his third foreign correspondent piece.

Late morning they all took a break for a drink. Adam was hoping Hassim wouldn't be much longer, for he had a growing dread the two soldiers would have had second thoughts, come back and claim Abdul Aziz's body. Not having been exactly straight with them, they might even pick him up too for good measure.

It was as the glasses of water were poured, they heard sounds of a vehicle nearby, right outside. Adrenaline rushed. Everyone was on edge, panicky. It was followed by a silent pause, then the familiar clunk of the Mercedes car door shutting, a further pause, the crunch of footsteps on gravel, then relief as Hassim himself reappeared, leaving the front door wide open behind him.

The Mercedes had a white van pulling up behind it – no windows, no billboards, double doors open at the back, a refrigerator unit above the front cab – functional – it could only be the funeral company. Thankfully no soldiers in sight.

As the bearers followed Hassim inside, the women disappeared into the kitchen. The men all stood round looking at Abdul Aziz's prone form. It was the bearers who moved first and began attending to the difficult business of removing him from the floor.

Adam and Hassim watched. Having stepped backwards, they had their backs against the wall. Before them, without a word being spoken, there was a grim, ordered process being followed for the collection of a body.

They'd come equipped with stiff polythene sheeting and stainless steel accessories. Adam found the noises disturbing. Sticky sounds and random dripping noises created different splash tones in the silence of the house and these were followed by the flapping of plastic as it was laid and folded, wrapped and tied tight.

Why did they need to tie him up so tight to put him in the van? wondered Adam. It looked just like they'd trussed up and string-tied a carcass, like those that used to arrive on Wednesdays at the local butcher's shop back home in

Muswell Hill. The practical business of handling the body both captured his attention and repulsed him in equal measure.

There had been an extraordinary amount of blood and this had also been collected by the men in white. Much of it was placed in a sealed polythene container which was then placed in a shiny metal bucket. It was a mystery what would be done with it.

As if to signal, 'job done', blue disposable gloves were pulled off inside out, and bagged up with the many paper towel wipes they'd torn off a giant roll they obviously carried with them for the purpose. All were flung in a final act of perfunctory sanitary cleansing into a black bin liner. The team of two knew exactly what they were doing. There was a clinical efficient routine to it all, but to Adam's mind there was no effective way of sanitising the ugly process of tidying up a death. Seeing it all happen before his eyes, raw and gory, he felt life itself had been stripped of some of its very dignity.

Shocking and mesmerising as it was for him, Adam could tell it was just a job for them, and within minutes, with a final nod to Hassim, and to Adam's immense personal relief, they'd gone from the house, leaving only a smeared, darkening, bloodied stain on the tiled floor. It was the last remaining trace of where Abdul Aziz's body had so recently lain.

'I am so pleased to see you're back,' said Adam to Hassim.

'Soldiers came soon after you'd left to try and take him away,' he added.

'Adam stood up to them, Hassim. He sent them away,' said Maryam quietly, reappearing from the kitchen, a bucket of detergent in one hand and a floor mop in the other.

'Thank you, Adam,' said Hassim, this time offering his hand which Adam took. 'Come, let me tell you all what's to happen next.'

'First, Asad, I want you to take Jasmine to get some provisions for later. It's customary for family and friends to bring things round, but we should get something in too, OK?'

Asad nodded, reaching for a bottle of chilled water before heading back to the car. The day was already unrelentingly hot. Jasmine went and gathered her things and within minutes the two left for the short ride to the modern shopping Mall down the street, leaving the family and Adam gathered in the kitchen.

Adam asked if he should excuse himself as it was family business, but Hassim insisted he remain. Adam saw in Raqiyah's eyes how much this meant to her. Hassim wanted to brief everyone on what was to happen.

'It took some time to get things sorted for the burial, longer than I'd expected. There were so many different people to see, forms to be filled and fears to assuage. In the end it was all agreed, a negotiated contract, which included an extra cash bonus for the bearers and their supervisor, that finally settled things. The grave will be dug at the cemetery and the burial will take place fully in accord with the strict requirements of Ibadi Islam – in fact not so very different to Islam everywhere else,' Hassim added as an aside for Adam's benefit.

The only irregularity had been that Hassim had asked that prayers be said over Abdul Aziz whilst his body was in the funeral room of the mosque, and that they'd be said immediately after they'd prepared him for burial. It was just that with so many funerals today it wasn't going to be possible to find an Imam prepared to offer prayers at home. It had then taken him ages to find another Imam who was free to come and lead brief graveside prayers.

'By sunset it will all be over,' he finally told them.

Maryam got up and began using the bucket on the bloodied floor. One sweep across seemed about all she manage and Hassim reached and took it from her, settled her back in a chair and placed bucket and mop against the wall for use later.

Turning to Adam, he added, 'burials all happen very quickly here, on the same day. Unlike in the West, family and friends can then begin to move on, get back to their normal lives – so everyone hopes'.

No sooner had Hassim explained things, then there was a frightening loud knock on the front door, more a very sold metallic thud as if a gun butt had been used and they knew it could only be soldiers.

Hassim moved quickly to open the door, instructing everyone else to move into the kitchen before he did so. Adam, last to leave, left the kitchen door slightly ajar so they could hear what was happening.

Furtively, Adam's eyes searched for possible escape routes if the worst came to worst, his eye glancing first toward the back door, and then through the window at the five foot wall out the back. He might be able to make it. Raised voices could be heard.

'Where's the body of Abdul Aziz Nahari?' barked a voice.

'Taken to be buried,' answered Hassim calmly.

'Already! I don't believe you.'

'See for yourself. Look, this is where he was taken from.'

Adam could imagine Hassim pointing to the blood stained outline and smears on the foyer tiles, the pungent bucket of detergent and mop already red as Maryam had begun her cleaning up. There was a long pause.

'Who's the officiant? Which mosque?' barked the voice.

'Have no fears. Pity please this family in mourning. Inside his widow and family are grieving. Have pity,' he begged, avoiding their question.

More silence followed, then footsteps. Then the sound of the front door slamming shut and they heard Hassim walking back across the foyer toward them a they pushed open wide the kitchen door.

'There were more of them, six this time, a show of force,' he said. 'It's OK, they've gone, for now anyway. If it mattered more to them, they'd have been more thorough and persistent, they'd have gone to the mosque funeral area and collected the body. I don't think their heart is in it. I really don't think they'll be back again. Come, we need to talk through what still needs to be done. How's the calling round going Raqiyah? Who remains to be reached?'

Adam was surprised how calm and self-assured Hassim appeared.

Raqiyah, who'd been sitting quietly lost in her own thoughts, gave a synopsis of her calls so far. Close family were coming, but all kinds of apologies were being offered by the wider circle, the extended family and friends. Clearly there was still much unease in the air and people were feeling vulnerable, uncertain whether to poke their noses out of their front door, especially those who knew that Abdul Aziz had been shot following an earlier arrest and that Hassim had also been recently detained. For some it was adjudged too risky.

Adam knew the funeral itself was men only and he thought now was as good a time as any to raise the matter of his own attendance.

'Hassim, I want to ask a big favour, and I'll understand if you say "no", but I would like to be at your side, well, present at least when Abdul Aziz is laid to rest. Would that be OK?'

'No problem. It might be good if we dressed you up a bit, put a Dishdasha on you, might stave off a few questions from people who don't understand, if you're OK with that. There are lots of Muslim cemeteries across the city, but I've gone with one to the south where all our ancestors have been laid to rest. It seemed like what he'd have wanted and what the family expect.'

'A dishdasha. Fine by me. Abdul Aziz and I are about the same size and build, if that doesn't cause offence.'

'No problem, I'll pull one out for you later. I think it'll be good to have you along, just in case we need a British citizen to put our Omani soldiers in their place,' he added, grinning briefly.

Adam saw in that moment a first glimpse of some resemblance to the easy going style of Hassim's father, and some further welcome acceptance of his own presence.

'I need to tell Raqiyah the details of where and when, so she can let everyone know. There's so little time,' said Hassim, moving away.

With that he hurriedly disappeared into the back of the house, leaving Adam to his own thoughts, his gaze fixing upon the red stain on the floor; he began to realise that he was on the edge of this family, an outsider. This wasn't his land and, that at the end of the day, maybe blood would prove thicker than water – and what would happen to him then? Oman was starting to feel unsafe and alien. He had to rely on Hassim, a man he hardly knew, and the others, they were traumatised, in a state of shock. Everyone's safety seemed to be in the hands of soldiers, whose next action couldn't be predicted. Adam began to feel very vulnerable and he fought hard to overcome his rising anxiety levels.

38

The rest of the day passed in a frenzy of activity – phone calls, food preparation, and getting clothes ready. The funeral of Abdul Aziz was scheduled for five-o-clock. There really was so little time.

At four, there was a knock at the door, the white funeral parlour van had returned. Two different men to the two earlier, both way overweight for ones so young – and brothers by the look of their almost identical appearance, came to the door. Those who deal with the dead speak a universal language – they spoke to Hassim in hushed, reverential tones and then went back outside to the van. The rear doors were opened wide.

They'd brought Abdul Aziz back home, ready for his funeral, his visitors to be received. His roughly hewn wooden coffin was brought slowly and awkwardly inside the house, and placed centrally in the foyer on two purpose made stands also carried in from the van.

One of the men snatched away a square white cloth, like a freshly ironed handkerchief covering Abdul Aziz's pale face, exposing it from the forehead down. Adam's quick glance showed his dark moustache looked unnaturally waxed and combed. Abdul Aziz was ready and waiting for everyone to pay him their final respects.

As soon as the two bearers had left, Hassim went and stood quietly by his father's body, prayers being recited quietly under his breath. After a few minutes he'd done, then he turned, waved solemnly to Adam, beckoning him soundlessly to come and join him.

Adam and Hassim stood shoulder to shoulder, both men looking down. For his part, Adam could only recall some words of Psalm 23 from a funeral back home, so he recited them as best he could, 'The Lord is my shepherd. I shall not want. He makes me lie down in green pastures. He leads me beside still waters. He restores my soul… Though I walk through the valley of death, I will fear no evil, for you are with me.'

It surprised him he remembered as much as he did. He thought of his aunt Ruth, a vicar in north London. The words had felt strangely fitting and Hassim put his arm round his shoulder in an act of appreciation.

Abdul Aziz's eyes were closed, his expression peaceful, the bullet mark in his forehead, hardly visible. It had been neatly sewn and some whitish powder had been applied like filler but failed to fully hide the brutality of his sudden demise. The back of his head was entirely hidden, the visual impression given by his carefully arranged posture denying the impact of that exiting bullet.

As Adam gazed down his mind was strangely drawn to the mechanics of death. He thought the head must be propped up, stabilised and cushioned in some way; a white cloth strip had been tied under his jaw with a knot on top of his head. This had been employed presumably to keep his jaw tidily closed – a strange item of attire. To Adam's mind, the closed mouth was symbolic – the former diplomat's final words had been uttered, and though there was much left unsaid, equally there was nothing more that could be said.

As Adam's eyes moved downward, he noticed it was just possible to see Abdul Aziz had also had a change of clothes. He knew, like all Muslim dead, he would have been ritually washed, and the slightly forensic, soapy smell pervading the air confirmed this was the case.

Abdul Aziz was now wearing a new, freshly prepared kafn – a white linen shroud, just visible below his neck. Overall there was an air of sanitised, clean serenity about him. He was laid out straight, tidied up with new clothes for his final journey – brought to order, the cruel suddenness of his early morning death almost elided, almost but not quite, by the now peaceful scene of homely repose.

Feeling unsettled and nauseous, Adam lifted his gaze from the sight before him. He watched the funeral service attendants outside, who, having deposited their charge, were having a smoke in the shade at the side of their van. Seeing him, they put out their cigarettes in synchrony, leaning on the van, as if for support. Who'd want to do their job? wondered Adam. The sickly sweet smell of death in his own nostrils, he understood their need to smoke.

Family and friends started to arrive. The men stood around the foyer, the women disappeared into the kitchen or the back of the house. Raqiyah's other two brothers, Abbadi and Tariq, were the first to approach the body, looking confused and uncertain. Hassim quickly took the initiative, placing an arm over each of their shoulders. Adam politely acknowledged their presence, offered his condolences, before retreating a few steps back.

Then, a few minutes later, elderly male relatives arrived, who were much more at ease. They stood around in quiet conversational groups of twos and threes, lining the walls like sentinels. Each in turn came forward and paid their respects. By four-thirty there were around twenty to thirty men of varying ages, some standing outside the door in the hot late afternoon sun, rather than making an entrance.

Hassim more than once lamented the fact so few people had turned up. Usually a death in the family meant anything in excess of a hundred people would come to show support for the family. These were not normal times.

Throughout, Adam hung back, exercising discretion. Neither Maryam, Raqiyah or Jasmine were to be seen – as custom required. Unfolding events were entirely in the hands of the men. He knew the women were nearby, the occasional sound of food preparation emanating from the kitchen.

Then, as the last of the men paid their respects, Hassim went over to the kitchen to invite Maryam and the women to come to the coffin. Their subdued voices gave way to moans and soft crying as, unlike the men, the women filed past in a line. Raqiyah took her Mother's arm. The sight was almost unbearable, the two quivering and shaking in grief like dry flowers in a breeze. When the last of the women had come forward, Maryam and Raqiyah turned to leave proceedings once more to the men.

Adam went to change, reappearing in his borrowed white dishdasha. He stood and watched proceedings a little way off. Only once did he move, when Hassim asked him to get some water for a mourner.

Finally, the two bearers walked back in and spoke to Hassim.

'It's time. I take it your driver will be taking you. Follow us and we'll get you as near to the grave as we can. I've had a call from the Iman, he'll meet us at the graveside.' Hassim nodded in agreement.

It was a sombre, quiet atmosphere as everyone made their way outside to their vehicles. Hassim suddenly remembered Adam, and called him, beckoning him to join him in the Mercedes. With Asad, as ever behind the wheel, the two sat side by side in the back, Adam looking, to everyone's appearance as the cortege set off, as one more Omani mourner. Adam glanced around anxiously, mindful soldiers might make a further disruptive appearance – thankfully they were nowhere to be seen, they'd gone.

The white funeral van travelled sedately, neither slow nor fast, and with no traffic to slow its progress, it took exactly fifteen minutes to get to the cemetery.

As they left the road for the dirt trail, dust billowed up in great swirls as the convoy travelled the last few yards. Hassim told Adam there were literally scores of cemeteries around the city, but this one, on the south side, had a longer history than most, and he recalled his three earlier visits, occasions when other family members had died – grandparents, and an uncle.

Hassim told Adam what to expect – the burial would be quite brief, the Salut-ul-Janazah – the short funeral prayer, would be led by the Imam, brief words then offered in tribute by senior family members. Mohammed Mansoor, his work colleague and closest friend, had asked to say something. Some verses of the Qur'an would be read, then he would be laid in the sand in his simple wooden coffin, the grave filled in, the place marked, and then they would leave. Hassim thought that in all, the ceremony would last little more than fifteen minutes.

When they pulled up and got out of the cars, it was almost five-o-clock. A really hot wind had began to blow, stirring up the dust and hiding the sun. The surreal view was shortening by the minute, enclosing their graveyard world. Looking around them, the bearers were keen to get on with things. In fact haste now seemed paramount. Dust was in every mouth. In an apocalyptic scene, they carried him awkwardly over the mounds of sand and lifted him down to the sand, then wood bumping and jolting, lowered him down into the grave.

Prayers were largely lost on the rasping wind as Abdul Aziz was consigned to the mercy of Allah, his feet pointing toward Mecca. The gravediggers began completing their task, pushing the dry, swirling dirt into the grave – as much blowing up in their faces as falling into the hole.

When they were finally satisfied, a simple vertical wooden marker board was pushed into the ground with a handwritten black pen identifier, in Arabic script, upon its face. It served to mark the spot until the white headstone would be ready at some future, indeterminate date.

The mourners began to return to their vehicles, pulling their headscarves tight across their faces and shielding their eyes, the weather worsening by the minute. Hassim and Adam reached the sanctuary of the Mercedes – Asad immediately pulling away and cautiously nosing the car forward, overtaking the other cars when they picked up speed on the main road, in order to be home first – he'd need to welcome everyone, thank them, and listen to them.

The main reception room was laid out ready – a veritable buffet feast set out on a centrally placed table. Adam realised how hungry he was and joined the others, brushing and shaking off the dust, washing and then getting something to eat – lamb and rice, apricots and dates, with so much more.

Hassim had taken to the role expected of an eldest son and host with alacrity, directing and welcoming as necessary.

Once back and time began to stretch forward again, Adam began thinking of his next piece of writing for CNPI. It was still incomplete. Family events had taken precedent. This posed something of a dilemma for him. He couldn't be insensitive to the occasion, yet he needed to do some more work soon to create something of interest for his waiting editor.

The personal story of Abdul Aziz's funeral would have to be part of it. The compromise was that he could talk to some of those present and hopefully learn more from their insights, not only about the life of Abdul Aziz but also what had been happening across the capital and in the surrounding countryside these past three days, then he would seek some solitude and write.

Tariq, the youngest son was standing alone and Adam took his chance to speak with him. The two had only met once before and then only briefly, the previous summer, when Adam had been over in the long university vacation for what had amounted to very much a short sight-seeing holiday. Raqiyah had wanted him to meet her brothers, and Tariq, at the time, had just landed himself a job after qualifying as an accountant. He was tall and athletic looking, and held an orange fruit drink in his hand.

'Hello again. My condolences. So sorry about your Father,' said Adam, 'I liked him, a good man.'

'Indeed he was. I can't believe this has happened. Was it as they said? You were here. You saw? He went outside the door and, and was shot just outside. Did they warn him?'

‘It was like that, as you say. The door was ajar. We all knew the TV news had announced the end of the waiting, a new Sultan, a return to normality, an immediate lifting of restrictions. I guess he thought things were safe. It was a shock, totally unexpected. He fell back and mercifully never knew what had hit him. You can be sure he died instantly, even before he fell to the ground,’ said Adam.

‘But why? Was he a threat? Is there something we don’t know? What do you think?’

‘I’m guessing, but I think they let Hassim go with a warning. It was both to punish and warn him.’

‘Let me tell you, when Hassim left school he went seriously religious. I think the group he joined wanted to see a future Caliphate, one where the Imam and not the Sultan called the shots, a return to Sharia in a traditional sense. We argued, we fell out, then we stopped seeing each other, until today that is.’

‘What’s it like out there? We’ve been shut up here for three days and heard nothing,’ asked Adam.

‘It’s not good. No one’s sure what the succession means and there are reports of arrests and some deaths. The news media aren’t broadcasting anything much, but I know from my school friends of at least two other executions here in Muscat. Have you spoken to Abbadi?’

Adam shook his head. At that point Tariq had spotted a relative he wanted to speak to and excused himself. Adam helped himself to a plate, turned his attention to the generous buffet, and began spooning food.

Over the ensuing hour, he worked the crowd, moving from person to person, listening to their stories and gaining as he did so a better picture of recent events. The one person he really wanted to speak to, to offer some comfort maybe, he just couldn't get an opportunity to talk to. She was hidden in the kitchen.

He had no choice but to bide his time, and in the meantime getting something together for his editor seemed as good a way as any to keep himself usefully occupied.

39

Anxiety levels were rising. Throughout the early evening the funeral guests received calls from their concerned families at home and it became clear no one was wanting to stay out late.

Some popped out to go to the mosque for evening prayers, only a couple coming back to the Nahari residence afterwards. Then, before it was yet 9pm, and with much food remaining uneaten, Hassim, with a final 'thank you' and a shrug of his shoulders, saw the last of his visitors off and finally closed the front door.

Abdul Aziz was dead, buried, and his wake over, all within the space of twelve hours. Silence descended on the house and Adam took his chance.

'Hassim, have you a minute?'

'Yes, Adam. Is it about that piece you have still to write?'

'Yes, 'fraid so. Sorry, at a time like this… I was talking to those who came today, and I'm getting a better picture of what's happening here. I wondered whether you could fill in some of the missing pieces? Do you think the mosque you'd joined, were working for, were regarded as a threat?' asked Adam, going straight to the point.

'Of course! Of course! We tried to hold the late Sultan to account for his failings. We used to get regular infiltrations by security police. They were so obvious,' he laughed.

'How come?'

'They'd short hair, were security types… so, so, obvious! We chatted to them, and saw them off to their minders with what we wanted them to know. But then it got more serious about a month ago. We discovered our computers had been hacked and data messed with. We found our guests from Saudi were not being granted permission to visit. And, when the Sultan died almost all of us were taken to… to an army run concentration camp, made to sit under the hot sun in the open air in a barracks square, armed guards watching us. We all waited our turn to be seen. Each person was taken off individually for questioning – they didn't all come back to the square. We never knew what happened to them.'

'It must have been terrifying.'

'When it was my turn they used a mixture of water and electricity. I'm no hero and I saw no merit in hiding the truth from them. I told them what they wanted to know, but those bullies like to have their fun even if they get their answers – the bastards… I think I got off lightly. When they'd finished, two of them dragged me into a corridor, only sending me back into the square with the others when I could walk again. There I waited until they brought me here. Look…'

He then pushed up his sleeves and showed Adam the fierce red marks made by ties of some kind on his wrist. 'I won't show you the other marks,' he added, pointing toward his groin. 'Adam, don't tell the family, they've enough to worry about.'

'OK. But they cut a deal or made a threat before they let you go didn't they?' Adam gently pursued.

'Yes,' Hassim said, his head lowered. 'They told me they'd send me a warning message, one that would be waiting for me at home.'

'I thought it might be that,' said Adam.

'I've taken some calls during the day. The same message has been given to seven of us – we're all next if we don't behave ourselves. It's enough to make martyrs of us,' he laughed cynically. Adam, jolted by the use of the word, started to see a harder side to Hassim.

Adam's face betrayed his concern, causing Hassim to quickly add, 'but you know, I might have disagreed with my Father over many things, I might have let him down, failed him, but I'm no extreme Muslim, just a bit of an idealist, wanting to see a better world. Right now my priority is my responsibility to my family, you understand? I'm an Omani family man first,' he said, his voice lowered, 'I shall carry the pain of what I'm responsible for, for the rest of my life.'

'Thanks. For what it's worth, I thought you managed to handle today OK. It could have gone badly – the army might have taken Abdul Aziz's body, the funeral might not have been able to happen, and we could have been without any mourners. Even the weather looked set on a storm. He had as good a send off as you could have hoped for, given what's happening out there.'

'Thanks, Adam.'

'Would you excuse me for an hour. I'll catch up with you later.' With an affirming nod from Hassim, Adam disappeared into Abdul Aziz's study, opened his laptop, punched away at the keys, read his work through twice, and finally watched the blue thin 'send' line disappear as his latest piece left for London.

This time his piece left him uncertain of his own place in the world, too many ghosts of the past were clawing at him, and once again he felt himself to be a very long way from home. He turned his head, desperate now to spend time, seconds even with Raqiyah. How was she? But she and the other women were hidden away in the far area of the house – inaccessible. He began typing out some ideas that had arisen from his earlier conversations. They might come in useful, anything to keep busy, to avoid the pain.

40

Just before 10pm Hassim was back in the foyer. He called out loudly in the silent house, 'Maryam, Raqiyah, can you come into the kitchen.' He wanted to talk to them before they disappeared to their rooms for the night. Adam heard it from his room, but knew this time to stay put.

'I don't know exactly what's expected of me, but I wanted to say a few things to those of you in Father's home, your home.'

Maryam and Raqiyah were sitting next to each other at the kitchen table, pale-faced, staring straight ahead, the cold white marble surfaced top offering support to them – both were tired, not at all their earlier physical efforts and the clearing up, though both had worked hard, but at the emotional exhaustion they now felt. They were still reeling in shock at the events of the day, numbed by what had happened, feeling totally drained.

'I've decided to stay over tonight. My wife's family took herself and the kids off to her folks near Nizwa when I was picked up by the security forces. They thought it safer to be out of the capital and with them. She'll be fine there for the time being. I spoke to her earlier. She sends her condolences. Of course, she's worried… I told her what had happened here and that I was needed. She understands.'

'Are you sure, Hassim? We'll be alright if you want to get back home. There's nothing that can't wait. We're safe enough,' said Raqiyah, Maryam nodding in agreement.

'No, no, my mind's made up. My place is here tonight. There's some legal and other paperwork to be done, and it's my job to see to Father's affairs, sort things out, at least make a start. But apart from that, I need to have a conversation with Asad and Jasmine, to tell them not to worry about their own futures, just to continue performing their duties as before. I take it that is what you would want Mama.' Maryam nodded meekly, giving a dismissive wave of the hand.

'Thanks Hassim,' said Raqiyah, in a rare moment of spontaneity, reaching out and touching his arm.

'I hardly need tell you both, though I need to look at the accounts, Father was wealthy and prudent. He invested wisely. You won't go short. You won't need to move house or anything. I'll need to go to the bank tomorrow, just to tell them what's happened, and then there are a few bills to pay from today. We'll need some cash. I think I'll get Asad to run me round first thing.'

'You got close to some risky politics Hassim, and I'm worried they'll be back for you, I'm terrified you'll be next,' said Maryam, her eyes open wide.

'I know. I think if I'm careful, don't put my head above the parapet again, they'll leave me be. They gave me a warning. But who knows what the new regime will do? Don't worry, I'm no extremist, I only wanted our country to give Islam its rightful place in civil life. Maybe I also like to hold corrupt politicians to account! But I don't feel I'm in a position to call the shots any longer. Sorry I didn't mean to say it like that. Let's all take a day at a time, until things feel more settled again. I'll make a start now, going through things in Father's study. He was a stickler for routine. Don't suppose he changed any of his passwords?' he asked, looking enquiringly at the women.

'No, I think he'd have told me if he did,' said Maryam.

'Raqiyah, would you come and help me. There will be some emails to send and I could leave you with a list of things to be sorted over the coming days, if that's OK?'

'Yes, fine. I'm sure Adam would like to help out too, if there's anything he could do,' she added. 'He's come at such a terrible time.'

'We'll talk to him now. If he's not in his room, he's probably still at Father's desk,' Hassim added, rising from the table.

'I'm going to my room. I'll begin sorting through Abdul Aziz's clothes tomorrow,' a tired and bleary eyed Maryam offered, as they all made their way out of the kitchen. Raqiyah moved over to hug her broken mother and they held on to each other for a moment before Maryam pulled away and headed off for the night.

Adam had left the study door open and he was indeed, as they'd thought, still typing away at his laptop, sitting at Abdul Aziz's desk. Wearing the borrowed dishdasha he looked as if he was thoroughly at home. He heard them coming and looked round, getting up from his chair.

'Hi Adam, Hassim and I will need to deal with Father's affairs. He thought we ought to make a start,' said Raqiyah. Their eyes met, but no words came.

'Look, let me give you two a few minutes. I need to go and talk to Mama alone before she goes to bed,' said Hassim, excusing himself, leaving the two alone in the study.

They both sat down facing one another, looking into each other's faces, the only sound was Hassim's footsteps retreating across the foyer back to the kitchen. Adam was the first break the silence.

'That was thoughtful of him… how are you feeling?' he ventured.

'Oh, Adam, a huge sand dune of grief is blowing steadily my way and I fear it will drown me very soon. I'm numb, I don't believe the day we've just been through. I have to pinch myself to know I'm living through this, that it's not a nightmare – yet it is. I feel like a robot, going through programmed motions, not alive, not dead, a zombie. I… I don't know what I feel. Sorry,' she said. 'It seems to help if I'm doing things but I find it hard to know what to do, and I don't remember what I've done some of the time. Something has happened to time.'

'I can only say how sorry I am for what has happened, but I'd rather be here, near you, than anywhere else,' he said. Setting aside decorum, he put his hand comfortingly on her hand. Responding, she placed hers on top of his, and they were quiet again, sitting across the corner of the desk, holding warm hands, together. A sort of calm came slowly.

'I feel so bad you're caught up in all this, Adam. There's still a risk soldiers will come back – it scares me. I couldn't bear it if anything happened to you.'

'I know. It seems to help having a British Citizen in the house,' he added. 'Look on the bright side, Raqiyah. This has given my new job a flying start, an opportunity. Look at this email I've just had back from my editor in London. He's absolutely delighted with my material.'

'Every cloud, they say… but are you really OK here? No anxiety attacks?' said Raqiyah with concern, looking into his eyes. 'I know what you were like before.'

'So far so good. Nothing has been directed against me personally, and I've been OK. It's brought some memories back, a few flashbacks, but nothing I haven't been able to handle. I learned some good breathing, relaxation techniques over the past two years, used them to good effect a couple of times. I'm good, really. It's all the "what ifs" I'm finding difficult to deal with.'

'What do you mean?'

'I ask myself whether I could have saved Abdul Aziz, warned him against going outside first thing this morning. He'd been told not to go out.'

'You weren't to know. He thought it was safe, we all did. It was his decision. Others decided his fate,' said Raqiyah.

'Do you know what's happening outside? While you've been in here, have you seen, heard any news? Are things safe?' asked Adam.

'At one level, the new regime have made a big push to make everything seem normal. On TV they've been showing endlessly reassuring pictures of shopping malls being busy again, flights resuming, going in and out of the airport. You know the message – business as normal. But, behind the media spin, it can't really be like that.'

'So what do you think is happening?' he said.

'The rumour mill's running riot, from what I hear,' offered Raqiyah.

'Stories circulating abroad tell of competing factions in different parts of the country, the army no longer united, its leader having tried to seize power himself. His two deputies are called "mere stooges". There are reports in the foreign media of numerous summary executions of any suspected opponents and many people are still being detained in army camps up and down the country. It isn't a reassuring picture. What's on the Omani news channels is just window dressing,' offered Adam. 'You can see I've been talking to today's visitors and making full use of the restored WiFi.'

'So, Hassim could still be in danger?' asked Raqiyah.

'I don't know. We just have to await developments. Tonight he's free. I've learnt to take one day at a time when troubles come. It's served me well so far.'

They heard Hassim approaching and let go of each other.

'She's gone to bed. Some of her friends had called her. She's worried for me now. I think she'll be alright. I got her to take a sleeping tablet.'

'We're concerned for you too. Adam's heard from people. It doesn't sound safe outside.'

Adam shared with Hassim what he'd heard and what he'd told Raqiyah moments ago. Hassim sat pensively thinking.

'I think you ought to go and join your wife, where it's safer out of the city. The admin and other jobs can wait a few days. The most important thing is you stay safe,' suggested Raqiyah trying to sound persuasive.

'You could be right, but I'll make a start on things here tonight whilst I'm around. I also need to make a few more calls myself this evening, to see how my friends are, and to find out more.'

'I think I'll turn in then,' said Adam, standing up and making his way off to his room.

As he left, Hassim and Raqiyah began pulling box files from a shelf. He watched them for a moment before stepping into the foyer.

Adam had the distinct impression Hassim knew far more than he was letting on. He wondered if there was any truth in the tale a good journalist had a 'nose' for these things – maybe so. Something wasn't quite all it seemed, but he didn't yet know what it was. The media messages he'd been reading on line told him that the country really was divided, and the thought entered his mind that the mysterious Hassim was up to his neck in it, and much more than he was disclosing to him.

This left Adam just a short while later lying in bed looking at the ceiling not knowing whether he should try and leave Oman or stay. If he stayed life could be very dangerous, not just because the country was in turmoil, but he'd now landed up in a household with a dubious character in charge of things. Someone he didn't feel he could fully trust.

Then he thought of Raqiyah and Maryam. They'd been knocked for six by the day's events, could he really bring himself to leave them at a time like this?

41

At an uncertain time of the night everyone in the house was woken by a loud, splintering crash. This was immediately followed up by aggressive shouts – the soldiers were back!

As Adam grabbed his dressing gown, his bedroom door was suddenly flung open and unceremoniously he was bundled to the floor. He felt the impact of his right cheek hitting the hard, cold, tiles. A knee pressed into his spine and his arms were jerked back, he was pinioned, and he felt his hands being tied behind him. It was futile to think of resisting. Then he was fiercely pulled upright and perched on the edge of the bed, the metal barrel of an automatic weapon poking at his chest.

As Adam tried to control his breathing he slowly looked up. The face of the soldier before him was hidden by a black balaclava, otherwise he was wearing regular Oman Army fatigues. Adam heard shrieks of alarm coming from the other rooms. Everyone was being roused and ordered to comply. He was powerless and had little choice but to ignore the cries from around the house and sit quietly, to do as instructed, and hope, just hope. In his helplessness, the words, 'God help me,' escaped his lips. He felt his heart pounding in his chest and a pain beginning on his cheek just below his eye.

Then there was more crashing, the sound of hard boots on floors, as soldiers were clearly searching the house. Things were being pulled off shelves, turned over. What were they looking for? After maybe five minutes, the one who seemed to be in charge came into Adam's room with instructions to his minder.

'He's flown the nest. Let them go, we're out of here, pronto,' he ordered.

'Yes, Sir,' his minder replied.

Then Adam saw the knife. His adrenaline rushed, he was paralysed, couldn't move. A slash behind him, his arms falling down and forward. Relief as he realised it was nothing more than his restraining ties being cut.

Rubbing his pained wrists to stimulate the circulation, he could hear the soldiers moving one by one back into the foyer. Then his minder still holding the open knife turned, and before leaving placed the point of the blade under Adam's chin. Adam's pulse went into overdrive. As he lifted his chin ever upward, the point followed.

'You wouldn't know where he's gone, where we might find Hassim Nahari, now would you?' the soldier asked.

'I'm a British citizen visiting Oman. I know nothing at all,' answered Adam, struggling to keep his head stationary above the tip of the knife now resting against his skin.

The soldier hesitated, half turned, then before Adam could speak again there was a noise from outside. The man withdrew the blade, stepped away, strode off, his noisy army boots scraping as he strode across the foyer.

Adam heard feet retreating on the gravel outside, a vehicle starting up, more muffled voices, and then the sound of it driving away. Then there was quiet, only the silence of the Arabian night, then more deep breathing as Adam fought to take control of his racing heart and rising panic attack.

As soon as he had some control, Adam's mind turned to the others and he called out.

'Is everyone OK?' he said, trying to put confidence into his shaking voice. Rubbing his wrists some more to ease the pins and needles further, he moved into the foyer. In moments everyone was there – Maryam, Raqiyah, Asad and Jasmine. All looked shaken and dishevelled, but none had any complaints. Raqiyah looked at Adam in alarm.

'What happened to your face?'

Adam touched his cheek, then his chin. The cheek felt bruised and there was a little blood on it. 'They pulled me to the floor, it's nothing,' he said. Raqiyah grabbed a tissue and dabbed at it.

'And there,' she said, lifting his chin and seeing the cut the knife had made. Adam said nothing. She dabbed and cleaned it too.

Then Adam crossed the foyer and tried to push the front door shut. It wouldn't go, the timber was split all down the lock assembly side – it would need to be replaced.

'Where's Hassim?' enquired Adam. 'They wanted him, they were after him. Where is he?'

Maryam raised her palms.

'He's gone. He came to tell me he'd listened to what you said last night. After he'd called friends, he thought they'd come for him. He said it was too dangerous to stay any longer. Allah be praised! He was right! He's gone to join his wife and kids. I hope he's safe. Asad drove him,' said Maryam, looking fearful, shaking, clutching her robe tightly to her.

'Asad, you… you took him! How was the journey?' asked Raqiyah.

'No problems, a couple of road blocks, that was all. They only asked to see our identity papers and then let us pass. Outside of Muscat it was very quiet everywhere, nothing happening, except for lots of troop movements, soldiers being taken in lorries, mainly heading south. There's something big going on – things are not settled like they'd have us believe on TV. I got back here around 3am.'

'It's not yet 5am,' said Raqiyah. 'Do you think we should try and warn him what's happening? It's still so very early, will it be better to ring in an hour?'

'I'll call his mobile now. This is isn't something that can wait. He's in danger. I do hope he's alright. I need to know,' said Maryam beginning to show signs of agitation.

She waited a long time before her call was picked up.

'Hassim, are you in bed… are you safe?'

The others listened in to a one-sided conversation. Hassim was giving his Mother assurances and leading her to think he had safe houses he could use. She wasn't to worry. He thanked her for her warning and her call. He would call her again soon, he said, but it would not be on the number he was presently using. Then, he'd gone.

'I'll make us something to drink,' said Raqiyah. 'Then we need to get up. It will be dawn soon. No point going back to bed.' She looked over at Jasmine who had said nothing. 'Are you alright Jasmine, you're very quiet?'

Jasmine was almost the same age as Maryam. She'd been with the family since Hassim was a baby. Now she looked beaten, shaking, frightened and all of a sudden rather frail and old.

'I've come to a decision, I want to go home, back to Manilla,' she said under her breath. 'I can't cope with much more of this. It is too much to bear. I am worried for Hassim. I don't like the soldiers. I've decided I want to go home.'

'Jasmine, if that is what you want, then we can arrange that, then you can come back again when things are more settled. You're well overdue a break – now would be a good time. We'll look at flights for you and get you out. How about you Adam? You want to leave?' asked Maryam.

Adam thought for a moment. 'Give me time on that one,' he replied, thinking privately, he should have said, 'me too.'

'Asad, how about you? Are you sticking around?' asked Maryam.

'I've got nowhere else to go. No-one's going to worry about a Bangladeshi driver. I'm still needed here. How will you women cope?' said Asad, with a nonchalant shrug.

They moved from the foyer to the kitchen and sat down for their hot drinks which Raqiyah served. Sitting in the kitchen, and with things beginning to settle after the earlier raid, things were catching up with Adam.

He was beginning to read all the familiar signs of a coming anxiety attack and acting decisively, he began mentally withdrawing himself from those around him to try and head it off. The exercises he'd used in the past and had started using again were helpful and putting them into practice again he began calming himself with slow breaths and guided thoughts. His bouts of palpitations began to recede and a measure of calm gradually returned.

'You OK, Adam?' asked Raqiyah after watching him go through what she knew was a familiar routine, knowing what he was doing, seeing him ride the wave and then thankfully coming out the other side.

'Fine,' he lied, meaning he needed to put a brave face on things and didn't want to discuss it. A man would be needed around the house, and with the best will in the world, it wouldn't be Asad, he concluded. Asad just wasn't up to much other than driving, so Adam began believing he'd be sticking around a little longer.

'Let's meet up after breakfast, list what needs to be done, and take some control here,' he suggested to the others. 'I'll call my Embassy later, maybe call in there. They need to know what's happened here and I need to alert them I might need their help at some point. Besides, I might get a better picture of what's going on from them. In these circumstances the British usually advise against travel and suggest those caught up stay put where they are. It's not always the best advice. We'll need to think very carefully what we should do next.'

They all disappeared to get out of their night things and get ready for the day. Adam went first to the freezer to get some ice for his cheek, imagining he'd have a black eye to show later. Then, ice in a tea towel, and clutching it against his cheek he set off for his room.

As he wandered back across the foyer, dawn was breaking, sunlight outlining the shattered front door, illuminating the floor and far wall, piercing the splits in the wood, leaving jagged streaks of orange on the hall's grey tiles. Top of the list of jobs they needed to tackle was to ring for a handyman to come and see to that door. They should get hold of someone in an hour or so, then they may need to be persuaded to come out. If Adam had any say in the matter he'd make sure there was some metal reinforcement to the frame and a more substantial replacement door. Those soldiers had too easy an entrance.

After dressing, he gathered some things in his rucksack and returned to the kitchen.

With so much food left over from the previous evening's funeral meal, Jasmine who joined him, both found there was no shortage of things to choose for breakfast and they began to lay out a spread.

Adam's body was hungry and his mind was racing. As he pondered his situation he realised he was living out a contrary emotional mix – part paralysing terror, whilst at the same time having such an adrenaline rush he felt he felt he could walk on air.

Strangely, given the extreme highs and lows he was experiencing, nonetheless he felt unbelievably alive. He had a heightened sense of awareness, as if living out a comic book adventure. A life back in England would be dull by comparison, though on second thoughts he could do with a little more 'dull' right now. It wasn't to happen.

42

During and after breakfast later that morning, Adam, still felt fired up, wired even; he assembled a long list of things that would need attending to. Maryam and Raqiyah's phones came to life from time to time as friends and family enquired after events, some offering support, others wanting to extend condolences. After each call there would be another snippet of news and the building picture the Nahari household were getting was becoming, by the hour, ever more concerning.

Other people known to Abdul Aziz, friends of his for the most part, had also fallen foul of military searches and arrests. People were expressing a sense of fear for themselves and for the future, with no-one seeming to know the true big picture, what was really happening out there.

It was apparent the new regime had allowed some return to normality, but scratch the surface and things were far from normal. The road blocks, searches and troop movements, including snatch posses, were only the beginning of it. The latest news from a call to the mosque's undertakers indicated Abdul Aziz was one of many who had been killed and not all of the victims were so fortunate to have been shot cleanly.

They learned there had also been an armed security forces visit to Hassim's mosque, the message given to the mosque trustees was that talk was dangerous and they were warned to take care; so it had become hard to find out more.

Since yesterday's initial relief that the crisis was over and things would return to normal, today people were feeling increasingly ill at ease and afraid. Everyone was looking over their shoulders and asking, could they be next?

Meantime, whilst others were on their phones, Adam had been using his mobile to look at various online newsfeed channels and was getting a similar picture. What was particularly concerning him was the clamp down on news within Oman and the detention of in-country journalists. He began feeling very vulnerable, exposed. After all he too was a journalist and he had been sending messages out telling it how it is.

When he then read an email from his editor in London advising him to give priority to his own safety, he knew conditions must have considerably deteriorated within Oman. That personal message to him had, in particular, much alarmed him. There was no ambiguity, it had been marked as high priority and typed in upper case. After a few minutes thinking what he should do, Adam decided he had to get in touch with the British Embassy as a priority. Not wanting to burden the Nahari family further, he kept the news and his concerns to himself.

It felt like hours since the soldiers' raid, but it was still only 7am when a man appeared outside with a young teenager in tow, the lad wearing over-large blue overalls. They'd tapped on the window, the noise making an already jittery household jump.

They'd come to attend to the front door. The man grumbled that this was not his first job of the kind that morning. He was a miserable character, making a complaint with almost every sentence, his words accompanied by a sigh like a moan. However did he get any business, wondered Adam.

After showing him where the nearest power sockets were, the man complained at having to fetch another extension lead from his van. They left him to his task. Soon the sound of a slow electric drill could be heard as the two began to take down what was left of the door. A temporary panel would be fixed for today, 'providing there were no problems or other jobs taking priority. And use the rear door for the time being. Inshalla, hopefully, I'll be back later,' he instructed, waving to his young lad that it was time to go. The lad said nothing. He had a long and sullen face too. He was quickly learning his master's customer relations skills.

Through the gaping space where there once had been a door, the sun's early, yet piercing heat was now allowed full access and it invaded the normally cool interior. Adam stood there and watched as the old door, fractured in two long shards, was quickly removed, and loaded on the flat bed pick-up truck. The older man, shoulders bent, turned and yelled, 'We'll be back with the boarding shortly, subject to any delay at the timber yard.' Then with a puff of black diesel from the exhaust, they pulled off. Adam saw a house without a front door to be rather like being homeless, all the inside exposed to the elements, open to anyone who might have designs. The house had clearly been no fortress before, but now he felt as safe as a man on the street – not safe at all.

The house phone rang once again and Maryam went to take it. It was Hassim. Some kind of hurried exchange followed, before the brief call was terminated.

'Raqiyah, Adam, here a minute.' Raqiyah, reappeared from her room, mobile clutched in her hand.

'That was Hassim. He says he's heard news. He didn't say how – you are a target to be picked up.'

'And what about Hassim himself?' asked Adam.

'Hassim says he could be picked up again for further questioning too. The message he'd had was that it was all to do with people associated with his Father and irregularities in his Father's affairs. Hassim says he doesn't believe a word of it – it's all a pretext for silencing all possible opponents to the regime. Hassim has resolved to lie low, hide himself. He said it was just as well. Soon after he'd moved house a second time, one of the local police had called looking for him. The man had tried to pick him up, but had to go away empty handed.'

'The authorities are obviously worried things are not going as well as they say,' said Adam.

'Hassim's advice is that we should all move out of Muscat for a few days. Things are particularly hot here. He says there were plenty of safe places near him in Nizwa, and there would be no problem safely hiding out there until things settle down. He invited us all to join him, suggesting his, "in-the-interior" house address was a safe and hospitable temporary measure. He said that having us all nearby, under his roof, was a way for him to more easily exercise his family responsibilities.' Maryam fell silent.

She'd told them of the big risk they all now faced in staying put, but what should they do? She looked at the gaping hole where the front door should be, Adam could read the fear and vulnerability having no front door was adding to the situation.

Adam was in a quandary. He wanted to go to the Embassy, knowing he could ask to stay there, place himself in their care, but he'd seen how, at the onset of the present crisis, they'd simply moved people either quickly out of the country or into one of Muscat's hotels. It was unlikely they'd put him up, and he didn't want to wait in a soulless hotel, cooped up, waiting all alone for the dreaded knock on his room door.

A part of Adam didn't want to leave the country, not yet anyway. Part of him was glamourising the idea of his new journalism post. Wasn't he as a reporter supposed to be at the heart of the action, where everyone like him wanted to be? To be where the actions was – it had been the making of many a career. Wasn't this a chance to make his own name? There was a story to be had, but he knew he had to be really careful. More careful than he'd been up until now.

Then there was Raqiyah and Maryam to think about. They were vulnerable, shocked by recent events. How could he even contemplate running out on them? He looked at them and knew he couldn't leave, well not yet.

As if reading his mind, Raqiyah asked, 'what will you do Adam? Don't you think it's time for you to get out, until things calm down?'

Adam never had chance to answer his own question. There was the noise of a heavy vehicle approaching outside. No front door meant they heard the approach from afar. Adam rose, looked out, saw it was a military vehicle, and decided to make his exit. 'I'm not here,' he announced as he grabbed his rucksack and ran for the back door.

In a moment, he'd scaled the rear wall, grabbing the dishdasha outfit drying on the line as he went, the one he'd worn yesterday for the funeral, now washed and already dry. He stepped onto a garden chair and rolled himself over the five foot wall, dropped down the other side and walked stealthily toward the neighbour's house where he sat down in their carport behind a bin.

He knew the neighbours were away with relatives and he hunkered down hiding himself as best he could. He curled in a ball, tried to look small, putting even the noise of his breathing into short shallow breaths.

He guessed the security forces were looking for him or Hassim, or both of them. They'd probably look around the house, and once satisfied their prey had flown, would head off. He waited, hearing the occasional sounds of the soldiers going about their search. Then he heard the back door creak as it was pushed open, the sounds of boots in the backyard, then quiet. An age passed before the boots retreated back into the house, the back door slamming shut. He froze, unable to move.

Adam had guessed right. A quick search was exactly what they did, and after ten minutes, he heard a vehicle moving away. He got up and cautiously made his way back into the house, taking exactly the same route in reverse, this time spying out ahead at every turn to ensure the coast was clear, to be sure the soldiers weren't leaving one man behind, just in case. Seeing no soldiers, he rejoined the others gathered in the foyer.

'You can't stay, Adam,' said Raqiyah in a state of agitation. 'They wanted you. They weren't saying why, just had a long list of names on three or four sheets of paper as far as I could tell. But it clearly isn't safe here anymore. What will you do?'

'I don't think they'll come straight back, not right away, but you're right, I need to leave. Hassim was right. He warned us. Do you think we should do as he suggests, all of us make our way out, head out of the capital – head to Hassim's family house, his house in the country? I'd have thought we'd be safer there,' replied Adam.

'Maybe we should. I just don't know,' said Maryam wringing her hands, quite uncertain of herself, indecision writ large across her face.

Adam felt he should take some control in the situation. 'I think Asad should stay here and watch over the house – we've no front door! We also need someone to let us know what is happening here. Asad will be safe enough staying behind. I'm happy to drive us to Hassim's. We could take the chance. The drive there would be the most dangerous part. I'd be just as likely to be picked up, if not more so, if I tried to get to the Embassy. What do you say?'

'Are you sure Adam,' asked Raqiyah. 'We might get no further than the first road block. Why don't you go to the Embassy, try. Just ring them, get their advice. Talk to them.'

In his head, Adam felt torn, but in his heart he knew what he would do.

'We've got nothing to lose by going to Hassim's – you know the way there, you two, don't you?' Raqiyah and Maryam looked at each other before nodding in unison.

'I think you should both go and pack. I'll speak to Asad. We should aim to be on our way as soon as we can be ready. Should half an hour do it? We don't want to hang around any longer than we have to.' They nodded again. Raqiyah hesitated, a question maybe, then she spoke.

'I think it would be good to be with Hassim's family. Just to get away from here for a few days. I can't get Father's image out of my head. I walk round the edge of the foyer every time I cross it. I don't like being here. Mama, you must come. It will be good for you and the two of us should be together. Tell me Mama what should I do?'

But Maryam either didn't know or couldn't decide. Adam nodded at Raqiyah and suggested she help her mother with her packing. 'Let's get to it. I feel easier moving rather than waiting for the next round of unwelcome visitors. Time is of the essence. Those soldiers could be back.' They moved quickly.

Meanwhile the two handymen reappeared and with much loud hammering, accompanied by the whining of the drill, a board was secured in place, again shutting out the light, but securing the front door. It hadn't been the thickness the handyman had wanted, but 'would have to do.' In less than a quarter of an hour, the two men had gone.

Then the three assembled together by the back door with three cases, two large plastic bags and Adam's rucksack. Asad went outside and brought the car round, checking as he did so that the coast was clear. He'd been happy enough to stay when Adam asked him.

Then Asad placed all the baggage in the Mercedes' ample boot. Adam climbed into the driver's seat, Asad having left the keys in the ignition. He saw the fuel gauge showed full, giving a range of 800 kilometres – more than enough – one less thing to think about. It was time to depart.

'Asad, Asad,' Adam called out as he was about to disappear indoors. 'Can you tell us where the road blocks were when you dropped Hassim home? It would be good to know. We might be able to skirt round them. Soldiers don't tend to relocate them once they're in place.'

'Sure. I'll tell Maryam, she'll know the route best. It should be possible to work round them, just avoid the main road to the airport. Head out on the old road toward the university, turn left before you get there – the university has blocks all round it. Once you head out toward Samail and the north, the people out there seemed to be just going through the motions. It's here in Muscat you've got to be careful.'

Asad and Maryam began a conversation. When it was done, an anxious Adam, now wearing the white dishdasha once more, and with the two women in the back of the car, pulled the Mercedes away slowly, glancing every which way as he did so. The escape from Muscat to Nizwa had begun.

43

It was looking like another blistering day with temperatures approaching 50ºC. The heat made the grey road surface shimmer and shake, the longer view ahead was hidden in a heat haze. Adam had dark glasses on, and was well disguised in his borrowed Omani attire.

He was glad to be in the driver's seat, more in control of his own destiny. It felt a whole deal better than waiting, or hiding holed up somewhere, when there were soldiers with his name on their 'wanted' list. The sun was behind his back, which made looking in the rear view mirror tricky, and the driving on the right had taken him a few minutes of adjustment to get used to. But they were moving smoothly away from the Muscat home, the car itself lent a feeling of security, and that felt good, really good.

Whereas he was in white, Maryam and Raqiyah were wearing the most sombre, dark coloured outfits he'd seen on them. Both had chosen to wear veils, hiding all but a small window of their faces. Raqiyah explained that it was respectful to do so during the forty days of mourning, and besides, she added, 'it may help ease our passage through any hold ups. At a glance we look every part a respectable Omani family in mourning.'

Maryam directed Adam out of Muscat, taking a westerly direction. She knew her way and gave clear directions. There were a great many modern buildings lining the dual carriageway tarmac, some unfinished with high cranes marking the city's constant expansion into the surrounding desert. There was so much space in Oman, no-one bothered how much space they took up.

Maryam directed Adam on to al Jani al Akbar Street which, apart from a few roundabouts, was fast and straight. It was both surprising and reassuring that there was plenty of traffic on the road, cars as well as commercial vehicles. They were in a crowd, moving ever forward, and crowds always felt safer.

Skirting round and avoiding the main Muscat Express Road, they took al Ansab Street, knowing from Asad there were checkpoints to avoid at two of the roundabouts further to the west. Every roundabout passed, every junction reached was another goal achieved.

In a matter of minutes they could see the outskirts of the city and the Nizwa Road they needed lying straight ahead. An army truck heading in the opposite direction passed them at speed toward Muscat. They turned left, for the moment to the south, away from the sprawling conurbation, and into the dusty dry, rocky interior.

So far so good, the road was fast and the traffic busy, but already slightly quieter, though it would be difficult and inconvenient to stop anyone here on this fast dual-carriageway, thought Adam. The hiss of the car's air-con fan kept them chilled, their only conversation were the words of direction given by Maryam. The atmosphere in the car was very tense. Adam endlessly monitored the cars speed and performance – keep it going, normal, no speeding, do nothing to attract attention, he told himself.

Soon the mountain foothills of the Western Hajars rose sharp and brittle to meet them, a red-brown moonscape of inhospitable slopes. The surrounding land looked dry, empty, barren and sterile. Small, grey, ground-clinging scrub plants appeared from time to time, hanging on to life in the hope of future rain. There were hints of green in some of the deep clefts where underground water gave vegetation a perilous foothold. Everywhere else was dead.

The monotony of the tarmac and concrete surface of the dual carriageway, bounded sometimes by grey metal crash barriers, was lightened by the occasional blue road signs. Oman was not a country for road signs noted Adam. It made him anxiously check with Maryam they were still on course.

The road seemed to run ahead of them for ever. Adam became even more tense. Noticing how tightly his hands gripped the steering wheel he tried to relax. Seeing that there was now hardly any traffic at all, he wondered where it had gone. Its absence was unnerving. There was sweat on the palms of his hands, the steering wheel now slick to his grasp. Finally, what appeared to be a total absence of road signs did nothing to reassure, and he wasn't sure at all how far he still had to drive.

Adam didn't know where he was, had no idea of the road he was on, and therefore hadn't any idea how to make any escape off the road should one be needed. As he looked at the desolate landscape and hills around, he knew one turn off on to a dirt track and he could be very quickly completely lost in the surrounding desert wilderness. He told himself, death on or off the road – what was the difference? And he pressed on. The one reassuring thing was that Maryam remained confident of the route.

Mile after mile, the first hour seemingly interminable, the Highway 15 road took them ever higher into the interior. There were few settlements, just occasional signs of industry with heavy lorries throwing up clouds of dust as they made their way at right angles to and from the main road. Steep-sided gorges and occasional oasis with huddled date palms were welcome reminders that scarce water did exist, albeit it was hard to find.

Soon after the town of Imti, Maryam instructed Adam to take the car off the main road. This was unexpected, but Adam did as he was told, what else could he do?

They headed on, passing through Izki and Birka al Mouz, edging ever closer to the city of Nizwa, the mountains beginning to ease back to allow a barren plain to open out before them. Like a child going on holiday, Adam found himself asking time and again, 'are we nearly there?'

Raqiyah broke the silence to speak to Adam. 'Nizwa's small really. For all its historic status and reputation as one of Oman's leading cities, even with its surrounding suburban sprawl, it's still relatively small in size, less than 75,000 people. It's very spread out, so when we do get there Adam, you might be asking, "where is it?" – that's because there's so much space out here.'

'There's more date palms ahead, more buildings too, indicating the presence of water and settlement. I guess it can't be far now,' he replied, keenly anticipating an end to the interminable stress. At one point he'd felt relief at leaving the Nahari home, the car had seemed to offer anonymity and safety, but as they neared their destination Adam found himself wishing to get into a building again. He couldn't explain it, but he was feeling exposed.

Going into the mountains had brought the temperature down, so the car told him, by a heady 6ºC since leaving Muscat. Adam noted it was now only 44ºC outside. The clock told him they'd been on the road an hour and fifty minutes. So far so good.

Adam began to scan ahead for any sign of their destination, and occasionally glanced behind in his mirror at Maryam. She was saying nothing, her expression a blank, as if she were miles away. He pressed on, keeping the speed steady, not too fast, not too slow – keeping it unremarkable, staying constant, how it needed to be.

Soon they were definitely approaching Nizwa, coming in from the east. Maryam began talking again. They wound their way round the edge of the city to head out west. Progress was slower, speed limit signs to observe, but on the positive side, there was little sign of the army. In fact it looked like a normal day, businesses were closing, signalling the end of the morning and approaching midday prayers.

Maryam broke off from her normal left, right, straight on instructions, to point out the large round tower of a fort. Adam followed the line of her finger.

'That tower was bombed by your British RAF in the 1950s. The last, sorry I mean the Sultan two Sultan's ago, called for British help when local tribes people supported a coup to overthrow him. I don't think I ever told you Raqiyah, but your Father should have married a girl from round here, but she was killed by a land mine left at the end of that conflict. Her death always haunted our marriage.' No one picked up the remark, but both Adam and Raqiyah noted it as significant.

Maryam was saying no more and returned to giving road directions.

Hassim's family home they were going to belonged to his in-laws and was near the Bahla Fort, a little way west out of the city. With every minute they grew more confident in arriving – they might yet make it. Adam drove cautiously, always looking ahead, trying to anticipate any possible threats to their good progress. He felt their journey so far had been almost too good to be true.

Maryam said they were now leaving Nizwa, though it was a little difficult to see where it ended. Adam was the first to spot red tail lights indicating traffic slowing up ahead in the distance.

'What's there Maryam?' Adam asked urgently, scanning the side roads for an exit should he need it.

'A junction. Something must have happened. There's not usually any hold up here. Take the next left,' she urged confidently, pointing to nothing more than a dirt trail a few hundred years further up the road.

The car responded smoothly as Adam took it off the tarmac. Adam could see he was sending up clouds of dust which must have been visible to anyone looking in their direction, even those at the road block they'd so narrowly avoided. But then dirt roads and just another dust cloud were normal and unremarkable here he told himself. They might be OK.

'Where now?' asked Adam, having reduced his speed to little more than walking pace.

'Half a mile ahead, there's a right, take that, between those two buildings.'

Adam moved as directed, big guard dogs barking at the car's heels, but finding it too hot to bother giving chase.

He gave up checking in his rear mirror, the dust obscuring everything behind – he could see nothing. He anxiously scanned left and right for any sign of pursuing soldiers, but again saw none.

'Keep straight on, it bends and twists a bit. It's a farm track really, but quite passable. We cross straight over a busier tarmac road in a few minutes, then on to more dirt track. That will bring us out further up, ahead of whatever it was going on at that junction,' she said, her eyes glancing around. Adam was impressed at her anticipation and navigation skills. It felt reassuring that she so confidently knew their route, even on these dusty tracks.

Five minutes later and they were on the smooth tarmac of the Bahla Fort road. Soon the massive and domineering edifice of an ancient fort loomed up before them. On drawing near, its World Heritage Site credentials could be read on the roadside signs, not that there were any tourists around to read them. Adam hated the fact they seemed to be the only car on the road.

It was time to find Hassim. They'd made it. Adam realised that despite the best efforts of the car's dry aircon, he was now perspiring profusely. He wanted desperately to end the stress there had been in driving for two hours all the while never knowing whether at any moment they might be pulled over and arrested or worse.

His pent up anxiety levels were beginning to make themselves felt. He hadn't got much more to give. As they approached the towering walls of the fort he was near the end of his tether.

44

Maryam, perhaps accurately reading Adam's condition, continued to direct him forward in calm tones, until finally they swung to the right of the main entrance to the red-walled, multi-tiered Bahla Fort, its ancient battlements silhouetted against a fierce blue sky.

They almost immediately pulled up to a halt outside a tall, two-storey house, the Mercedes so close to it, Adam almost blocked the front door. They climbed out. All was quiet. It was midday, the sun's overhead heat was controlling and shutting down everything. It was no time to be outdoors. Even so, Adam glimpsed up at the building before them.

Above the entrance, was a central square tower with a pair of tall ground floor windows on the walls either side, marked out in red and white fantail-like patterning above. Bigger than many houses nearby, it made a statement. The lower windows were repeated above, making eight large windows on the front of the property in all. Glass bricks had been inserted above the front door in a vertical column to the top of the building, no doubt, thought Adam, illuminating a central stairwell. Above was a typical Omani house flat roof.

No modest property this, thought Adam. The surrounding, ochre coloured houses also had flat roofs, most with fort wall style edging balustrades, mimicking the huge fort in whose shadow they lay.

A surprising number of green trees, certainly irrigated, stood in their grounds, giving the area a long-settled, almost genteel feel. All was tranquil as they stood there. It struck Adam that something was odd about the building. He looked again – it wasn't square – it was oddly narrower at the front than the back. He was intrigued how it worked inside. How could someone build that way? They'd soon find out. The front door opened.

The three were beckoned straight inside by a hidden hand in the deep shade of the house. They left their luggage in the car's trunk.

A momentary quizzical look was shot at Adam as they stepped into the private space of Hassim's in-laws' home. It was a simpler home than where they'd been in Muscat, no ornaments, no wall decorations, fewer items of furniture, and nothing new.

They left their sandals in the entrance hall and moved further inside. More people appeared, two, another two, then three young children standing still in a line with serious faces, next a Filipino maid, then an elderly man with a thin grey beard and a short, stooped woman, the latter two standing side by side, the man leaning on his stick. But there was no Hassim.

The elderly man had let them in. He stepped forward, his voice rasping as if hoarse. It was a greeting of welcome. He asked after their journey, invited everyone through to a room to the rear, where coffee and dates, lemonade and fruit were laid out in readiness for their arrival. The Filipino maid moved swiftly behind the table, darting this way and that to start serving people. Maryam led the visiting trio in and warmly introduced Adam, the move breaking the ice. There was still no mention of Hassim.

Everyone took much needed drinks. Even limited exposure to the intense heat of the early afternoon sun having subdued and beaten everyone into submission. Adam began trying to have a conversation with the adults. He discovered the elderly couple, whose house it was, were, as he suspected, Hassim's in-laws. He met Hassim's wife, Tanvi, who, unlike her mother, had her face mainly hidden from view. Raqiyah then beckoned Adam over to the three children.

'Adam, these are my nephews and niece. I'd like you to meet them. Walood is eight, Dana, she's seven, and Faheem, he'll be five next birthday.'

'Hello, I'm Adam, from England,' he said in his best Arabic, which brought smiles to their faces. Children were the same everywhere, he thought.

Gradually, tensions eased, there were no unexpected surprises and a more relaxed atmosphere prevailed, the more so as the children began running around, chasing one another. Chastised by their mother, they turned to playing a hand clapping game with a chorus. This gave Adam an idea and he waved Walood, the eldest, over. The two younger ones, their curiosity aroused, followed closely in his wake.

'Do you know this one?' asked Adam, holding up his palms facing Walood. Walood held up his palms facing Adam's. Adam began reciting and clapping, teaching Walood the rhythm, something he recalled from his own childhood days.

> 'My mother said, I never should,
> play with strangers in the wood.
> If I did, she would say,
> naughty little boy to disobey,
> naughty little boy to disobey.'

As Adam chanted, the two clapped out the rhythm. Walood was mesmerised. The rhyme was repeated, this time Walood quickly picking up the simple actions and soon mastering them. Turning to his sister Dana, he had a go teaching her the game until she too had the hang of it.

'What's a wood, Adam?' asked Walood, puzzled.

'A group of trees, lots of trees together,' he explained.

Adam turned and spotted Raqiyah and Tanvi deep in conversation. Not certain of the protocol, he decided to keep his distance and wandered toward the rear window to look around. Seeing a secluded, neat, walled courtyard outside, he spied irrigation pipes providing precious water to feed the date palms, and keep the floral borders and the spectacular purple, pink, orange and white bougainvillieas alive. Hassim's father in law came over to him.

'You like our garden?' he said smiling.

'It's very beautiful, a sanctuary in this dry land,' said Adam. Then, on sensing the man's pride in his garden, he added, 'you've created a beautiful oasis here. Where does the water come from?'

'No problem with water here in the mountains. It comes out of the ground in the springs and up through the bore holes. You want to walk round the garden with me? You like? We'll stay in the shade,' he said, moving to unlock a rear door.

Stepping outside, Adam put his sunglasses back on. Though not standing in the direct sun because of the date fronds above, the heat from the white hot sun, was nonetheless scorching. To move other than very slowly was out of the question. The walls enclosing the garden were high, all of ten feet or more, painted like the house in a tired, faded terracotta wash over the flat surface. Good for defence, noted Adam.

He could feel the walls also radiated heat, leaving Adam feeling they were standing in some open air furnace. The wiry elderly man didn't appear to notice, he bent down and flicked a switch. Somewhere a hidden pump kicked in and a fountain started splashing water, a column rising several feet before splattering down into the small circular pool surrounding it below.

'Do you have a garden in England?' he asked.

'My parents do, in London, it's very green, with a small patio for sitting in – though unlike here, it is often not warm enough to sit outside.' He smiled to himself as he thought of the contrast.

'Do you have a fountain and a pool?'

'No, just a green lawn and flower beds, that kind of thing.'

'Come and sit down. Let me tell you something.' He led Adam slowly to the corner of the garden nearest the fountain and they sat down next to each other.

'Hassim spoke well of you. He said we were to trust you and keep you safe as our guest. I want to tell you how we might do this,' he said, pausing to stroke his beard looking thoughtful. Adam gave him rapt attention.

'Hassim has gone to his field house, a mile or so from here. We have family land, other smaller houses, a herd of goats and one of us has to go up there to see to them from time to time. Most of the year Hassim is in his place in Muscat, but he loves coming out here and we like to see him.'

'I trust he's still safe?' asked Adam.

'Yes, he'll be fine here. No-one will go looking for him. We haven't yet had soldiers banging on our door or indeed breaking it in – inshallah. It's not like the capital. This is a different place. We have our own rules and ways.'

'I'm glad to hear it,' said Adam.

'But who knows what the next few days will bring? I've asked the maid to bring all your luggage in and then I will ask her to put a dust cover over the car. It'll keep prying eyes off it – it would be unwise to leave such a car visible, it might lead to unwelcome questions, you know how nosy neighbours can be – Abdul Aziz was a wealthy man and his car a fine model, it stands out. He was a man from the capital. We are different out here.'

Adam couldn't help but notice he'd twice described this place as different. He felt he'd been alerted to something important, but let it pass for now.

'And it's a very nice car to drive too. I liked the automatic shift. It made the journey very easy coming here. We were lucky avoiding the road blocks,' said Adam.

'Hassim will join us this evening. Then at some point he will take you to stay at the field house. It will be entirely safe for you there. Come, I would like you to come upstairs, then you can see exactly where we are. If it comes to making your escape, you need to know the lie of the land – not that I think you'll need to do that,' he added hastily. 'Come, let me show you the views. Come! It'll be worth the effort.'

Adam tasted his dry mouth, but nevertheless followed the surprisingly sprightly elderly man back inside to the foot of the central stairwell by the front door. Then they climbed up, exiting three floors higher on a kind of turret above the house's flat roof.

The glare on stepping out was something else. Here there was no shade, and not even the whisper of a breeze. On the plus side, it provided a commanding 360° panoramic view. The only blind spot was to the north where just metres away the Fort's walls and towers rose to a much greater height than the house and totally blocked any view beyond in that direction.

'That Fort's really impressive,' said Adam, pointing to the forbidding walls and turrets.

'The south façade wall you are looking at is nearly one hundred and twenty metres long. Look further, and you can see Bahla itself is a walled city. Those old battlements defend us still, they're maybe five miles long. Most of the fort was built around six hundred years ago, designed by a woman they say – personally I don't believe that a bit. I never cease to marvel at it, it's a wonder.... You can be sure that no security forces will approach from that direction, or that,' his wiry arm waving first in the direction of the wall and then slightly right of it.

'The way you came off the main road is the only approach to this house. I'm not saying it's the only way out,' he added with a mischievous smile, his index finger knowingly touching the side of his nose. 'It's a safe spot, as you can see for yourself.' He was enjoying this, telling the story, having his guest's undivided attention.

'Look behind the house and to the right. You see all those old buildings?'

'Yes.'

'No-one cares for them anymore. They're just left to fall down. It's a derelict wilderness. Every year another one crumbles and falls. Some are many hundreds of years old. No-one cares for them. The young people want to live in modern homes today. All those buildings are excellent places for you to hide. Only one house,' he said, pointing out a building about a hundred metres to the rear, 'is still occupied, and of course, these two houses sharing our front square,' he said, swinging his skinny arm round 180º. 'And you don't need to worry about any of them, all lifetime friends, wouldn't tell on a neighbour's business. We Omanis respect the privacy of our homes and the state can go hang itself,' he murmured with a rasp, but loud enough for Adam to hear.

'Which direction is Hassim? Where is he?' asked Adam, gazing east.

'Over there, a mile or more, in the foothills of the Hajars. There!' He pointed more north-east, beyond the corner of the fort, where the sharp relief of the mountains ran down to the plain.

'Come, we'd best rejoin the others, they'll be wondering where we are,' he said quickly, as if he'd forgotten for a moment all sense of time. Adam was only too glad to move out of the sun.

Once back downstairs, Raqiyah and Adam met up, the old man disappearing, no doubt some chore to do in mind. It was a precious chance for the two to talk alone.

'Adam, there you are. I've had an interesting catch up with Tanvi. I'm feeling a lot happier about things. I think we'll be safe here. People have no sympathy for the security forces and they won't give us away. There's a tradition of fierce independence round here and apart from a half-hearted call from a policeman, they've seen nothing of Muscat's security forces locally.'

'So I've gathered, it's a different place…' Adam said. 'Oh, tell me, do they have WiFi in these parts?'

'Yes, and probably a lot faster broadband than in England! The late Sultan's modernisation programme saw to that. The password's on the back of the router over there, where we first came in, see? Feel free.'

'Right. Great!' They walked over to the router and Adam signed in.

'When you get a chance, take a look at the amazing views from here, go on the roof, it's worth the effort. Just been given the house tour,' he said cheerfully.

'You forget, this is my extended family. I may not have been here often, but I've visited my brother's family home a few times over the years, even though Hassim and Daddy kind of fell out. It won't surprise you to know everyone who visits here gets taken to see the view!'

She laughed, then cried, mindful again of her father, and grabbed Adam's arm in a moment of forgetfulness. For a brief second he glimpsed how they were, back in a different life, back in Exeter. Her cheek touched his cheek. Then aware of herself again, she moved away.

'We need to get some ice on that cheek again, Mr Taylor,' she said, giving him a pull toward the kitchen. In her smile and her eyes, he saw a momentary escape from the sadness and tension in her face. It lasted little more than seconds, but it was enough. In that brief spell, he knew he was in the right place.

45

Later in the afternoon Maryam insisted Raqiyah and Tanvi join her for prayers for Abdul Aziz. Adam could hear the recitations taking place somewhere upstairs. There would be many more days of these.

For his part, he got out his laptop intending to put together another article for his editor at CNPI in London. He moved into the entrance hall and connected his laptop to the WiFi, and watched everything download from the outside world.

It was weird the sense of connection the incoming mail gave him, as if he were no longer vulnerable in a distant alien place. There was no logic to it. He made a mental note of the power of social media – it plays with the mind!

Taking his laptop into the back room lounge, with the desperation of an addict needing his next fix, he began searching on the news streams to find out anything he could about what was happening in Oman. It was hard finding anything he could rely on.

Being in Nizwa felt very strange after the capital. To his thinking, Muscat, as well as being the hottest capital in the world, temperature wise, was also the hottest place for really knowing what was going on in the country. Though allegedly safer here in the interior, he felt strangely dislocated, transported to a backwater, away from what had to be the centre of the action.

Finally he found a Reuters article that carried a certain ring of truth. It came from a correspondent in Iran, who was saying that Oman was now under military rule, the question of succession as yet still unresolved.

It didn't surprise him. There had been nothing seen or heard from the last Sultan's cousin, nor for that matter of the two deputies – the cousin from the Ministry of Defence and the British Head of Armed Forces, Brigadier Martin Harper-Grimes. Any and all Omani press statements and TV broadcasts had so far only been released under the say so of the Head of the Sultan's Special Armed Forces, Major General Sadiq bin Mahmut. 'Nothing short of a military coup,' said Adam under his breath.

He looked at other sites and gained the same impression. Concerns were being expressed in the West on two fronts – the building number of reports of human rights abuses coming from bodies like Amnesty International, as numerous people had allegedly been summarily executed, and at the large numbers of people who had been rounded up and detained by Sadiq bin Mahmut's forces.

Then he read the Omani Ambassador in London had been summoned to the Foreign Office to explain these incidents and to seek assurances that British interests were being safeguarded. All the reports Adam looked at were thin on detail, but taken together he didn't like the direction things were taking. There were no big surprises. Things were on the slide – downhill.

The country's future was described as falling under military rule. Then he spotted two reports of opposition, one in the far south around the old capital Salafah where large numbers of troops were being sent, the city in a state of continuing curfew, and the second in the A'Dakhiliyah Governorate, which a spokesperson for the military leadership was discounting as nothing more than a rumour. Adam was giving this report all his attention. He knew he was actually in the A'Dakhiliyah Governorate, one of the few roadsigns he'd passed was a sign telling him as much on the drive here. The one thing about a land with few road signs is that when one came along those passing read and remembered it.

He knew Oman was divided up into administrative areas called Wilayats. The A'Dakhiliyah Governorate Wilayat, he next discovered, included Nizwa and all its surrounding towns and villages, including Bahla where they were staying.

The peaceful lack of military activity suddenly changed its meaning for Adam. He'd somehow crossed an invisible newly created internal frontier to find himself on the other side of a building civil conflict.

In his mind, he was now hearing a threatening silence, a calm before a storm, and he became fearful as to the full significance of what he was discovering. His fears started telling him he was now the best part of two hours from Muscat, the Embassy, the airport and his route of escape out of this hellish place – hadn't he made a foolish decision in coming here? He was in rebel held territory on the cusp of a civil war!

He resolved to speak to Hassim as soon as this proved possible, but then he began to wonder if Hassim was all he'd first seemed – no longer someone innocently swept up in the initial security sweeps? Nagging doubts and questions assailed him.

Had Hassim another side to him? Was he part of something political? Adam tried to write a piece, but found he couldn't concentrate. For the first time ever, he thought he was experiencing what was called writer's block. He just didn't know where to start, what to write, and in the end decided to send a quick email to his parents to say where he was and to reassure them as to his safety.

When he read through what he had written the message was both untruthful – he was not safe; and, ironic – it contained a humour and lightheartedness which was totally out of step with his reality. He sent it anyway. Reapplying himself to his next journalistic piece, he thought just typing something might help get him started – anything, he reasoned, as he stared at the keyboard.

In his struggle to marshall his thoughts, he heard Raqiyah call his name. He flipped shut his laptop and stepped back into the central hallway. She was alone clutching a bag of ice.

'The others have gone into the kitchen. They wanted to start preparing food for this evening. They said Hassim would be here by then. What have you been doing?'

Adam hesitated. His fears were clawing at his insides, but dare he share them? For now, he decided not.

'Nothing much, just catching up with emails, working on my next journalistic piece. Can't seem to get it down. One of those days. I also sent a message home. My folks will be anxious, knowing them.' As soon as he said it, he wished he hadn't used the word, "anxious".

'This is better for us. Being here gives Mama more support, it's not just down to me. After the prayers we talked about my father. He didn't deserve to die. For the first time I've felt angry Adam, really angry at what they've done. What right has anyone to kill him? It doesn't make sense. It's not right.' Her voice was full of passion. I hate our leaders. They could have prevented this.

'We're living in a time of a military coup and these things happen. I agree with you there is nothing he did I can think of that could be considered treasonable. And what it was, well, it was state execution. It defies all morality. I think I could write about that. Give me a few minutes, do you mind?'

'No, you go ahead, I ought to go and help in the kitchen. It's expected. Do you realise that since we left Exeter you've not cooked once?' she jibed. Another smile. 'Oh, and take the ice.' With that she turned for the kitchen.

Adam returned to his article, hitting the keys with a determination to bring the story of Abdul Aziz's life and death to a wider audience, and to use it to bring human rights on to the agenda. He was driven by Raqiyah's anger and reminded that a grave injustice had been done. Finally, article drafted, he went to find Raqiyah to check a few gaps and facts before sending.

She read and re-read his piece and then began to cry.

'What is it? What have I said?' asked Adam quietly. 'I didn't mean to upset you. What's wrong with it, tell me,' he said, putting an arm over her shoulder.

'No, you haven't upset me, you've made me so proud. Proud of you, but proud of my father too. Thank you, Adam. I do so love you.'

Custom required the two remain a respectful distance from each other, but both desperately needed the embrace that followed, awkward though it was, Adam still clutching his laptop in one hand.

'You've started a campaign for justice,' she said, 'and I want to join the fight.'

There was a sound behind them as if someone was inserting a key in the front door. Raqiyah pulled away. They looked at each other and waited anxiously to see who it was.

46

The door opened. It was Hassim. He was not alone. He had others, two young men, with him. To Adam's eye Hassim didn't look like he'd been out herding goats. He had the appearance of a trendy Omani professional, and there was little dust on his lower garment or feet. The striking thing was all three were carrying automatic weapons.

Their weapons were casually slung over their shoulders in a way that showed familiarity with their arms. The men's appearance confirmed all Adam's earlier worst fears of civil war and he glanced across at Raqiyah who was just happy to see Hassim and seemed totally oblivious to the real situation that Adam knew, beyond doubt, now faced them.

Adam had no time to voice his concerns. He was swept up in convivial greetings which he'd no alternative but to graciously reciprocate. By now the other members of the house had all reappeared and the air was one more of celebration than serious intent. Adam was puzzled as to what all this might mean. Waiting for the right moment to begin enquiring, Adam eventually caught up with Hassim.

'Hassim, the weapons – you surprise me.'

'Oh, don't be alarmed. Everyone round here has a gun. It's a proud Omani tradition. Haven't you seen how busy the gun shops are in the souks? We've a fine one here in Nizwa. I must show you it sometime. Maybe not this week, eh?' he said light-heartedly. His tone irritating Adam, who did his best to mask how he felt.

'But you're the first people I've seen openly wearing them' he added.

'Under the surface we're a tribal people, everyone feels it's their right to have a gun. Out here we feel the need to defend ourselves. Hey, chill out, you look like you've entered a war, instead of come for supper,' he jested, Adam sensing evasive irony. It unnerved Adam that Hassim's mood showed no regard for the bereavement and shock his family so preoccupying his family. Maybe the others hadn't noticed, but Adam most certainly had.

'Come Adam, I smell cooking. There must be something to eat. I'm famished. Come, sit with the men and meet my friends,' he said, sweeping Adam under his arm and pulling him over to be with his young friends.

Unable to speak to her, Adam nodded to Raqiyah, but couldn't read her expression. She disappeared into the kitchen to eat with the women and children.

Inwardly Adam resented Hassim's bravado, his explanation of the guns had been superficial. Instinctively, Adam had the feeling he was being deceived, even taken for a fool. Above all he felt wary and worried. It was as if all the alarm bells of the past began ringing in his head at once. He knew he was trapped, and had to be extremely careful. There was nothing he could say or do about it, just simply go with how things were, play along for now. The thought that his very life depended on it crossed his mind.

A few moments later, trays of food were brought in by the Filipino maid and laid out on the low table. The five men, Hassim, his two friends (whose guns had been left in the entrance), Hassim's father whose name Adam discovered was Hanif, and finally Adam himself. All sat or lounged around the table and tucked into the local meze – the first course. The smell of fresh bread from the oven filled the air.

Adam joined the others in eating, sweeping his folded bread into the homemade humus, which proved to taste every bit as good as the aroma had promised. Hassim acted the part of a master of ceremonies, with Hanif, being the senior male and in whose home they were, apparently quite happy with this and taking a subservient role. Adam, noted this too, logging it as something to ask Raqiyah about privately later.

'This is Said,' Hassim said, taking his friend's hand to place it in Adam's, 'and this, Jassim. They're both from Nizwa.'

The two young men, both sporting dark beards, looked at Adam uncertainly. Adam tried his best to give as relaxed a friendly greeting as he could muster, trying out his best Arabic as their command of English was rudimentary. During the course of the meal Adam was determined to find out what he could about them and as much as he could as to their real situation.

Deep within his robe, Adam's phone made a soft, brief burring sound indicating a message had been received. He took his mobile out. It was from his parents in London. His Dad had written. He opened the email. It was brief.

'We've had a call from the British Embassy in Oman to advise us you've gone missing. They ask if we have any news. What do we tell them? Please advise.'

Adam was startled. He'd been in regular, daily contact with his parents. They would surely believe he was safe and well. It had been only a day since he last phoned and spoke to

Brian Merryweather at the British Embassy in Muscat. So what had triggered this strange call about him being missing? He re-read it – it struck him as odd.

He could only imagine the anxiety the thought of him being 'missing' must be causing his parents, given what had happened to him when he was kidnapped and held hostage in the Middle East just two years ago. Certain the Embassy's real motive behind their call to his parents was to keep tabs on him, to find out exactly where he was, he asked himself – why the subterfuge? Why hadn't they simply called him? It was all a mystery.

Perhaps they thought he wouldn't tell them – or couldn't tell them where he was now. No, he hadn't told the Embassy he was off to Nizwa, and perhaps someone had been in touch with Asad at the Nahari home? His mind was rapidly filling with conspiracy theories.

The first thing he decided to do was to send a simple reply reassuring his parents he was absolutely safe and well, but for the moment he had a gut feeling to withhold giving any further information as to his precise whereabouts, that was until he felt more secure about what exactly was going on. Then he began to wonder if his association with Hassim was compromising his safety?

By now the second course was being brought in, a hot goat stew with rice, steam rising from the circular metal platters. Between glances at Adam on his mobile, Hassim had been chatting to his friends about the next Grand Prix, but once Adam had his attention, he seemed intent on bringing the conversation round to something else, as if he had an announcement he wanted to make.

'Adam here,' he said confidently, 'is an international journalist, who wants to write about what's happening in this country and send it to his newspaper in London. What we need to do is help him with his story, tell him something about what's really going on here and why things will change for the better as we move ahead.'

Adam was all ears. No longer was he thinking he could trust Hassim to be his guardian. Hassim's father in law who had appeared to be so welcoming, so proud of his garden and the views from his roof, had now become Hassim's co-conspirator, endorsing his words, his body language deferentially backing everything Hassim said.

'Shall I get my laptop, then I can write as you talk,' said Adam. Hassim nodded and Adam promptly retrieved his laptop, sat down and listened.

'One of the problems our country faces is how to be a true Islamic state when the secularists and the corrupt politicians of the old family order try to hold on to power with the army's connivance,' said Hassim. Adam began typing furiously.

'If you know anything of our country's history, Adam, you will know this – when the last Sultan came to power, the Imamate who used to run things from here was ruthlessly suppressed. Hanif here, lost both his older brothers to British backed, government forces. Though the Imamate had to give way, some people have always dreamed of the day when things might be restored to how they used to be.'

'Is that what you have been doing Hassim?' asked Adam gently.

'Spot on Adam! Exactly! You now understand why my father and I didn't see eye to eye. When I was at the point of leaving school I realised my future lay in strengthening the organisation of Muslim community life and I went to work for the one Muscat mosque with the closest affiliation with the Imamate's ideals and practice. I think you need to know a little history.'

'I'm all ears.'

'About the time the first World War came to an end this whole area was independent. The Sultan was not our ruler. Mohammed al-Khalili was elected our local Imam in 1920 and for thirty years guided our path. Half the population of this country, until recently that was the figure, lived here in the interior, and we had our own rule, our own politics and religion coming together, following our Ibadi tradition under the authority of our Islamic State.'

'I learned about this before I came out here,' said Adam, 'but after those heady, early days when the Sultan and yourselves lived in separate worlds by what was called the Seeb Agreement, it subsequently began to fall apart when Imam al-Khalili died, didn't it?'

Hassim nodded, much impressed at his guest's knowledge of Omani history. Adam hadn't quite finished.

'There was no effective succession, no international recognition. You still had to get passports from the Sultan's office in Muscat. It all fell into factions. It couldn't translate into the modern era. And when oil became a factor, that was the end of the Imamate. Well that's how I was taught it,' summarised Adam as best as he could recall.

'Not exactly. You forgot to mention, the Sultans have since then fallen under the influence of foreign powers and they have consistently sought to undermine traditional family and religious values. The way of life here in the interior has been subject to interference from outside ever since, and the stable order once enjoyed in this area has, over the past hundred years, been systematically undermined. Back in the late 1950s it was your British RAF bombers that attacked Nizwa and then the Sultan called in your ground troops. We didn't have the weaponry to compete with them. These past few years, we've watched the present Sultan grow old and ill, and I've been part of a group looking to restore some of the best of the old values, peacefully where possible of course, but if we have no choice then we have to resort to other tactics,' Hassim added, watching Adam type as he listened.

'How strong is your movement for the restoration of the Imamate?' asked Adam, seeking to occupy the professional foreign correspondent role required of him.

'Oh, you'll find, under the surface, everyone round here in the interior resents the sultanic ideal of a modern state. Family traditions and Ibadi ways have always come first in these parts.' Adam spotted he'd typed "satanic" for "sultanic". No doubt Hassim would have liked that slip.

'Is it anything like the Taliban in Afghanistan? – Just looking for a comparison,' interrupted Adam.

'I don't know about that,' said Hassim, suddenly unsure of himself. 'I only know my people, and that some of our folk do say they see support coming from many parts of the Muslim world – I'm not a spokesperson for foreign affairs. And to answer your earlier question further – Yes, we are strong. It's hearts and minds that will win this. The older people here say that you British taught us how to be strong – when the bombs fell, you fed our resentment and our determination, and that has stayed with us ever since. It took your SAS directing the Sultan's forces to subdue our men in the Hajar mountains, around our highest peak, Jebel Akhdar.'

'So how are things going today?' asked Adam, wanting to keep Hassim talking whilst he was clearly enjoying holding the floor.

'Everything's there to be played for. The current power vacuum is an opportunity for us. The popular support the last Sultan enjoyed isn't there to be had by anyone claiming to be a successor, so whoever comes forward is going to have to negotiate. The army can only hold the ring for a short while – no-one will want them to rule – they have no legitimacy.'

'So who, who will rule?' asked Adam. 'That's the key question, isn't it?'

Hassim left the question hanging unanswered in the air, much to Adam's frustration. Hassim was playing with him again – Hassim the puppet master, Adam, his puppet. As Adam looked at Hassim's face he saw a selfish person, but one who held power over Adam and he knew Hassim hadn't finished pulling the strings. Adam had to wait for what came next. He would not have to wait long.

47

Hassim didn't answer Adam's question as to the next ruler of Oman. Rather he deflected it saying, 'that should give you enough to be getting on with. My friends and I are staying here overnight. It's safe enough. We're going to the mosque shortly and when we return we'll get the bedrooms arranged. All the men are on the middle floor. Adam, you can use my room facing the back, overlooking the garden, the three of us will share the room at the front – it'll be fine. Anyway, we've things we need to discuss. You'll see the bigger picture in the morning, I've a surprise for you!'

Hassim left his enigmatic final remark just hanging, teasing Adam. There was that grin again. Adam felt frustrated, every time he tried, he couldn't quite connect with the guy. It wasn't so hard now to see why Abdul Aziz and Hassim hadn't got on.

Adam didn't know what to make of him. One minute he liked him, the next minute he could happily have thumped him – he was so, well, annoying. More seriously, a side of Hassim kept showing itself that Adam was deeply worried by. Just how involved in the interior's succession campaign was he? Why did he dangle juicy bits of information temptingly then not disclose anything more? He wasn't sure he like the idea of surprise in store in the morning.

For the rest of the meal, Hassim turned the conversation to football. In recent years, he said, Omanis had shown a keen interest in the game and had been successful in Gulf competitions. The conversation was every bit what any group of young men might chat about. Adam had heard it said that football had become so popular in the country because there were no pubs unlike in England. It was one of the few permitted activities where men could legitimately let off steam.Though not specially interested in the subject, Adam thought it prudent to join in, to establish some kind of rapport with the others. Even so, it felt strange Hassim never once mentioned his father.

When, some while later, they heard the Muezzin calling the faithful to prayer, the others rose and left for the nearby mosque. Their departure was a signal for the Filipino maid to come in and begin collecting up all the dirty plates and glasses. Raqiyah followed her into the kitchen, a few paces behind, and when the maid was occupied washing up with her arms deep in the sink, Adam took his chance to talk with her.

'We're not as safe here as I thought,' he voiced quietly.

'I was thinking the same, but I haven't been able to tell you. In England you say, out of the frying pan into the fire,' she said with a straight face.

'Exactly. I think there is a movement, a campaign running in these parts. Hassim's linked with it, wanting to see a resurgence of the old Imamate. Hassim says the Imamate has a legitimate claim on power, but I'm not sure to what extent these ideals are backed by real power. Have they got support were it counts – in the armed forces, the backing of friends overseas?'

'What do you think?'

'It could all be youthful enthusiasm, I don't know. Sometimes he's playing games, teasing me. Even so, he seems convinced that the people in these parts around

Nizwa have no time for corrupt politicians who disregard Ibadi Islamic tradition, and that there's a serious contender for power here. I feel he's egging me along, giving me snippets of information, arousing the journalist feeding instincts in me and has left me not knowing what to do with what I've been told. Does he ever annoy you?'

'Sometimes. He's my eldest brother. He could tease with the best of them, but most of the time he's fine… We had a chat along similar lines among the women in the kitchen. We were all trying to second guess what's going to happen next. They're fearful the Sultan's Army are simply biding their time, building their forces before they make a move, and then they'll come to Nizwa, crush any opposition and then punish the community.'

'Not good.'

'On the other hand, they might not do anything, might even discount the Nizwa scenario as of no consequence – adopt a softly, softly approach hoping things will just settle down to where they were. Who knows? Certainly not us. Truth is I got the impression the women really don't know what's coming – talking about it just made us all anxious… Though, come to think, Mama might know more than she's letting on. I know what she's like, just a feeling I've got, but there's always been a bit of a distance between us. I was always Daddy's girl, and she had her own ideas,' she said.

'Oh! I can't put my finger on it, but the same thought crossed my mind earlier, when she was directing us here. She seemed a different Maryam somehow. I just feel I don't know either Maryam or Hassim as well as I should.'

'But I will say this, the women talked as if Hassim was someone who really did know what was happening. He's definitely king pin in this house, and it's clear Hanif, his father-in-law, just goes along with everything he says. Hassim's the one we need to talk to, and he's definitely connected to stuff going on.'

'I don't think he'll say any more tonight. His final comment before going to the mosque was, "you'll see the bigger picture in the morning". He was swaggering, teasing me. I don't like it. I'm even wondering if we need to get back to Muscat.'

'Not tonight, Adam. Just send a piece off to your editor this evening. Maybe try to contact your friend at the Embassy, find out what you can. Doing something useful like that will help.'

Adam was wondering how to handle this advice, when the kitchen door opened and the maid appeared to finish clearing away and moved toward them. She looked at them knowingly, knowing they had feelings for each other, that they had been chatting earnestly, but she gave a friendly look which said, it was OK by her, the two chatting, which was nice. Raqiyah smiled back in acknowledgement. She disappeared, leaving the two alone in the kitchen.

'OK. I'll start on my piece now, but I can't afford to get it wrong. Maybe I'll just put a draft together and hold the sending until it firms up.'

They both walked across to the lounge. Adam was pleased that where he sat, Raqiyah, contrary to custom, chose to be there too, not next to him, but nearby on a wicker chair. As members of the household passed through, no-one voiced any criticism from within the house. Maryam looked in on them a number of times, discomfort or was it displeasure behind her eyes – but she too voiced no comment.

Adam had begun to realise this was a characteristically Omani way – when cultural lines were crossed Omanis remained respectfully silent, though they might personally feel ill at ease. Maryam continued over the next hour to manage her discomfort by making frequent visits, checking for herself that no greater impropriety was being committed. In the end she decided to bring a magazine into the room and sit quietly reading it whilst remaining in their presence.

Adam and Raqiyah boldly stole exchanges with each other whenever they could, often their twinkling eyes and their glances doing what words could not – keeping the small sparks rather than the flame of their relationship and deep feelings for each other alive in an increasingly dark place.

Both felt, with the end of their first week back in Oman still a couple of days away, they now lived compartmentalised lives, distanced from each other, and both were left wondering how long either could last the course.

Raqiyah found herself overwhelmed by waves of grief and tearfulness at unexpected moments and this compounded the pressures on her time with Adam. These matters neither could yet voice, and their feelings for each other became something that both of them pushed to the back of their minds as best they might, waiting and hoping for a brighter dawn. A great silence existed between them.

Around ten, there was still no sign of the returning men. Raqiyah and her mother said goodnight, going upstairs slowly together. Adam finished his writing alone. He was left deep in his own thoughts, and didn't hear the front door open as the men returned.

'Still up, I see,' said Hassim cheerfully. 'We all need to get to bed, ready to be up first thing. Set your alarm so you can be ready by six – you won't be disappointed! Goodnight, Adam.'

With that Hassim and his two friends disappeared upstairs like three jovial co-conspirators. Very soon the house and the neighbourhood was, to Adam's ears, unnervingly, and totally quiet.

He thought he could hear his own heart beating but wasn't certain. He tried to ascertain once more his true position. At least he'd escaped the army in Muscat – that had to be good, but had he landed himself in a more dangerous place? The worst of it was the not knowing. He snapped his laptop shut and made his way slowly upstairs; though he was tired, he doubted he'd sleep.

48

Dressed by 5.30am, Adam made his way downstairs to hear the noises of others already up. He joined them in the kitchen. Outside, through the window beyond the sink, the first hints of daylight were lifting the dark, like the pulling off of a grey veil.

Apart from Tanvi and the three children who were still upstairs sleeping, the rest of the household, were up and looked as if they had been so for some time. Four small rucksacks stood on the floor, their tops open ready to receive food and drink from the spread laid out on the kitchen worktop. Preparations were well in hand for an outing.

'Good morning,' offered Adam. 'Why the provisions?'

'All in good time, Adam. Grab something to eat. You're going to be busy. Here, have some coffee. The four of us are going out for the day, and we need to be off shortly. We've an appointment to keep,' he announced without further explanation. 'We'll be back before evening prayers. You might want to bring your laptop with you. That's your rucksack,' he said, pointing to a navy coloured one.

Adam quickly surmised Hassim meant the travelling group of four would comprise his two armed friends, Hassim and himself. Raqiyah and the maid were busy wrapping and loading rucksacks under Maryam's direction.

Adam did as he was instructed and decided to eat well, for he simply had no idea what the day ahead would bring. Thinking on his feet, Adam began to wonder whether the instruction to bring his laptop suggested his foreign correspondent role had a bearing on things, and he concluded it probably did. He wondered if the role might even offer him some protection. Having eaten, he got up and went to his room to retrieve the device.

A few minutes later, as they went out the front door, the outside air already warm on the face, Adam saw an anxious looking Raqiyah standing behind the others, blowing him a kiss. He returned it with a warm nod in her direction.

A Toyota 4x4 white Hilux that had seen better days was parked out the front. It was next to the Mercedes, now hidden under a dark tarpaulin. The four piled inside, rucksacks at their feet, Adam in the front passenger seat next to Hassim.

As they pulled away Adam noticed the first glints of sunlight were already hitting the tops of the adjacent fort making them glow a fiery orange as if it were some storybook fairy castle, a film set even. The bright sun's highlighting, promised yet another burnished sky, intolerable heat, and merciless heat. In Oman it was as if the one unbearable daily constant was the sapping temperature, drying the mouth, draining the energy and never giving any respite. Adam wondered what the day ahead held in store.

'This is my vehicle, it's useful for getting out to the goats,' Hassim explained. 'We've about a half hour drive. I promised you an explanation, so here we go. You ready for this?'

Adam nodded.

'We're headed for the last roadblock you diverted around yesterday,' Hassim said, turning to give Adam a smile and to notice the confused look he knew would cross his face.

'Sorry for the little ruse yesterday. I told Maryam to direct you on to the dirt road. You may recall the detour. It was easier to get her to divert you around all the army checkpoints, but you'd have been safe enough at the last one, the one we're now going to – take my word for it. It's one of ours!' He must have seen the alarm on Adam's face.

'Stay cool Adam. You'll see, contrary to what the world's news feeds know, the army in Oman is in reality utterly divided. That stooge in Muscat who claims to head up the army has in reality lost the loyalty of half his forces. Yes half, and possibly more. The entire interior, as you will soon discover, belongs to the Imamate. The capital now sits on its own. The clock's been turned back to how it was half a century ago. Don't you say, what goes around, comes around in your country?' He turned once more grinning smugly, just to see what was registering on Adam's face.

'Is that right?' asked Adam, 'I have to say this is all news to me. As I understood things, the Head of the Army, Major General Sadiq bin Mahmut is running things – he's in charge of the whole of Oman. To my knowledge nothing has been heard from the last Sultan's cousin who was expected to be running things after his death. What I'd heard was, another of the old Sultan's cousins was acting as a Deputy to Mahmut, and a British Army guy, by the name of Harper-Grimes, as the other Deputy. Those are the three running things, aren't they? Aren't they?'

'Nope, you've been sold a line. Propaganda! Or should I say, fake news!' he said, disarmingly.

‘So are you saying I’ve only picked up one half of the story here?’ queried Adam.

‘That’s the sum of it. Dressed up in that dishdasha, you do remind me of that Lawrence of Arabia character I learned about in school – the Englishman who came to this land to fight the Turks, who neither had the whole story about Arabian wishes nor a complete knowledge of his own British Government’s support. You’re just the same – an Englishman abroad! Come let me tell you how it really is, Adam. I don’t want you to have an incorrect story, and you need to be aware of some basics before we get to where we’re going, otherwise I wouldn’t be doing my job.’

‘OK – I’m listening. Oh, and at some point fill me in on what your job is exactly.’

Hassim looked straight ahead, pausing in thought before speaking.

‘Look, before this day is out, I’m hoping you’ll meet the head of the legitimate new government of Oman. This is some big interview you’re getting here. One you’ll write in big letters on your CV one day.’ He looked across to Adam with a look of earnest seriousness.

‘Today we find out which one of our two candidates for Imam gets to rule. One’s been living quietly in exile for many years in Saudi but has now returned home, the other is local to the area. Be assured both have the support of the whole interior of this country and those members of the former Sultan’s SAF, the Sultan’s Armed Forces, who have come across to us. A word of warning – the British are not popular here. Understand this about the British, they’ve thrown their lot in with the army coup leader and Mahmut’s forces in

Muscat. As in the past, we expect Britain to use covert force against us here in the interior – which is why you need to be careful how you express your loyalties. Understand me? You can't play games, Adam Taylor – it's too dangerous. The stakes are too high. Ah, we're nearly there, look, they are expecting us.'

Adam had been watching the approaching road block carefully. At first a line across the road in the distance, then orange and white traffic cones and several army figures beside them were just discernible. When they got nearer, he could see a well organised chicane of concrete blocks to slow and steer all traffic into an inspection zone. The nearest soldier was waving them to one side, he'd clearly recognised their vehicle and given it special attention. They were directed to a separate by-pass where there was a white canvas tent and a parking area. Even given Hassim's control in the situation the approaching sight of soldiers unnerved him.

'We're being met, then taken to Nizwa Army HQ. It's not far. It's location may surprise you!' Hassim said, a further knowing smile on his face.

Adam was beginning to find Hassim both a scary man to know and an extremely irritating one. It was, he decided, politic to keep his true feelings well hidden.

Adam had already had his fill of surprises, more than he'd been ready for, since his arrival in the Nizwa area the previous day. In fact all six days he'd now been in Oman had been unexpectedly eventful. His arrival at Muscat airport seemed to belong to distant history.

It looked like he could expect yet more surprises! However, he really wasn't looking forward to any more excitement. He wasn't sure he could handle it.

49

Moving at walking pace, the white Toyota eventually pulled up. Adam and Hassim were escorted out into the building heat of the new day, carrying their rucksacks with them. It was only a few yards to where they were directed, a waiting army four wheel drive parked up beside the white tent. It was larger than a car but smaller than a lorry.

The two were shown into the vehicle, and were shown to the two rear seats. Hassim's two companions went off to chat with one of the other soldiers, evidently on friendly terms. Adam watched them disappear out of the back of the white tent. What more surprises had Hassim in store?

Adam quickly noticed the army driver and Hassim were on more than nodding acquaintance, and with hardly a word exchanged, the driver with one other soldier in the front, set off. Adam had exchanged one vehicle of four men for another vehicle of four men. Their new vehicle turned round, and Adam noticed they were going back precisely the way they'd just come, past the chicane, then past the orange cones, and back on the same road in the direction of Bahla Fort.

'There's no other way to do this, 'said Hassim, continuing in his travel guide role. 'We have to go by military vehicle. They're so twitchy about car bombs and the like, and yes, before you ask, we're heading all the way back on the road along which we've just come.'

Hassim smiled, looking to Adam's eye, every bit a confident and relaxed man, fully at ease in his own environment, enjoying playing Adam along as if it were all some game.

Adam registered the fact that the reception they'd just had from the army fitted well with what Hassim had been saying all the way along, and Adam's thoughts once again turned to the likely use of himself as a sympathetic foreign correspondent conveniently found, suitable for no other purpose than to serve their political ends.

The more he thought about it, the more he realised the situation could become very tricky for him. For the first time, he entertained the thought that he'd put himself outside the reach and protection of the British Embassy, and that began to worry him.

Having little or no control of his situation, he could see himself walking helplessly step by step into a life of ever greater risk, currently as a coerced mouthpiece for a counter-government uprising.

Trying to tell himself to look on the bright side, he also knew that if he could pull this off, he was ideally placed to get the foreign correspondent scoop any other professional would die for.

Their travelling companions, the two soldiers, said nothing. One drove, the other watched. In less than twenty minutes they were back at the main entrance to the Bahla Fort and their vehicle swept off the main road and this time straight inside the Fort and up the narrow upwardly sloped entrance roadway.

Only when they stopped, unseen to Adam's eye earlier, he could now see the place was bristling with intense military activity. Just ahead, a row of traffic spikes, or tyre shredders lay across the roadway – the device, effective enough to bring any foolish driver trying to run past it to a hasty stop.

Adam also observed a carefully arranged security detail who had the entrance covered by heavy weaponry, and there were signs of artillery unit placements at various strategic points up ahead and to the sides to provide further fire power should it be required.

Very quickly it was evident at the very least, he was in a local military garrison. The choice of the United Nations World Heritage site fort was inspired. Not only would the British probably not chose to bomb it – they loved ancient heritage with the kind of passion Omanis had for football, but also the ancient fort clearly still offered amazing defensive features even to a modern force.

Their driver told Adam and Hassim to wait a moment whilst he checked in. Then, on his return, Hassim and Adam were instructed to leave their rucksacks against the wall in the shade and follow him. Before doing so, Adam remembered to retrieve his laptop.

As they walked, Adam couldn't help but notice the historic features of the old building. The mortar used for the walls had been mixed with stubble and it reminded him of traditional farm buildings and red mud walls back in Devon, England.

The man led the way further uphill, the gentle rise taking them toward the fort's interior heart. Adam was surprised at the scale of the place. In each direction walls and turrets rose in chaotic, yet magnificent profusion. Numerous buildings in the fort's interior suggested many secret places to hide. Swinging right between grey-red, sand coloured walls, and clinging to the cooler shaded areas where they could, they walked slowly through a series of ancient rooms until they came to a guarded end room which Adam guessed was their destination. From within he could hear voices deep in conversation.

The guard outside, opened the ancient wooden door to glance in. There was a pause in the conversation and he murmured something to those inside, unintelligible to Adam's ear but conveying the meaning 'they're here', before almost immediately throwing the door open wide so that the visitors could enter.

Four military figures, their uniform epaulettes indicating their senior rank, were seated round a trestle table. A large, high resolution map of the whole of Oman was pinned on the wall to their right, with a more detailed local map adjacent to it. A simple white flag was displayed on the wall behind the soldiers. Adam hadn't seen such a flag before. It had a bright red horizontal sword across the middle, above which there was Arabic text also in red. It looked to be a revolutionary flag. Now wasn't the time to ask.

The most senior figure, in rank and years, who sat centrally, stood up. He was a tall and imposing man with a distinguished moustache, but had tired dark rings round his eyes as if he hadn't slept. Two extra seats were pulled forward from against the wall for Hassim and Adam, as simultaneously and silently a man in a dishdasha brought in six glasses of mint tea on a silver tray, before leaving and pulling the door firmly shut behind him.

'Welcome to the Imamate of Oman, Mr Adam Taylor,' said the man with the moustache. Adam couldn't take his eyes off it, wondering how much wax and self-grooming was involved in keeping it looking so splendid. He thought of the dead Abdul Aziz.

'I am Major General Said Dibashi, Supreme Commander of the Imamate Armed Forces.' A hand was offered for Adam to shake.

'Adam Taylor, Foreign Correspondent, Central News Publishing International, London,' Adam replied confidently, taking the army man's hand.

'I'm grateful to Hassim here for facilitating your visit. Let me introduce my fellow officers.'

Adam, opened his laptop, and with a wave of the hand by the Major General, he typed down their names as each were introduced.

It was the Comms officer, seated furthest from him, who paid him most attention. Adam took an instant dislike to the man. He had a sneer of superiority on his face and was watching Adam like a hawk. For an uncomfortable moment the man reminded him of someone from his past he rather wished he could forget. Thankfully, his professional role kicked in as he quickly re-focussed and paid close attention to what the important man, in front of him, Major General Said Dibashi, had to say.

'Do you mind if I record this?' asked Adam.

'Not at all,' was the reply and Adam switched the laptop video app on, leaving it on the table, the army contingent nicely framed.

'The Imamate of Oman have restored stability in the interior of the country and seek peaceful relations with their friends in the capital and their friends overseas.' The Major General paused, and was handed a sheet of paper by his Comms officer before continuing, this time reading from a pre-prepared written script.

'You will see behind me the flag of the Imamate, abolished by the Sultan, but once again brought back into service.'

'Nasr min-illah wa fatih qarib," read Adam pointing to the script on the flag, 'which actually means, if my Arabic is correct, "Victory is from God and conquest is near." Is that not so?'

'It's good to talk to someone who clearly knows our language well,' said the Major General smiling approvingly.

'Is that how things are – is victory near?' asked Adam, seizing the initiative, as the man opposite was trying to re-engage with his script. The Major General stood up and held the corner of the flag.

'This is the flag of the Imamate of Oman. A hundred years ago it could be seen across the interior of this country. Today it is proudly flying again. We are a people whose loyalty is to Allah and the Prophet, and our Ibadi tradition. The flag tells our story. That is why our people are true and strong. That is why our country is now safe and secure as an Imamate, power once again restored where it should belong, political control safely and properly held under the authority of a religious Imam.'

'So, Major General, the Imamate has been restored. Tell me, who is the new Imam?' asked Adam.

'There will be an announcement shortly. It is important that all the votes are cast and the Imam has everyone's legitimate backing.'

‘And who are the contenders?’

‘Well, at this point in time, just two. The Imam from Nizwa mosque and the exiled Imam from Saudi who has returned to make his claim.’

‘And when will this process be finalised. Do you have a date for an announcement?’

‘You will appreciate in these troubled times that to gather the views of the leadership takes time. I think it will happen very shortly, maybe today – and you will be the first to know,’ he said, smiling.

‘And how will the choice of leadership be accepted in Muscat?’ asked Adam.

‘That is something you will have to ask them. We hope of course that they will accept the rightful rule of the historic Imamate, but if not, it won’t be the first time in our history that the people of the coast have gone their own way. Currently there is a quiet stand-off between us. I have to say, we are waiting for a reply to our statement issued to them the day after the late Sultan’s death.’

‘Can I see a copy of your statement.'

The Comms officer handed Adam a typed sheet he had ready for him.

'Do you envisage this being a peaceful transition of power?’

‘I don’t see why not. We have been most careful not to issue incendiary statements or to allow our forces to position themselves where they might inadvertently create a crisis. The way of Allah is one of peace and mercy.'

'And if conflict comes? How will you respond?'

'We are ready. We have made our preparations. Our soldiers believe the cause is right and are prepared to fight as warriors to the last man. I cannot think the army in Muscat has any heart for a fight. If they try, they will discover what they are up against. We have strength and plans ourselves, and we have friends ready to help us.'

'Who are the friends and how will they help?'

The Major General hesitated, ever so slightly, it was barely perceptible, but Adam immediately realised that this was sensitive territory.

'We have national governments backing us and we enjoy the support of all the loyal Muslim world who see the justice of our cause.'

'This will be news. Is one of the friends Saudi Arabia?' asked Adam.

'Certainly.' There was that pause again. 'And we see many other nations as our friends too.'

'Some of this country's closest allies have included the United States of America and the United Kingdom. Have you their support?'

The, 'we hope so,' sounded a less than convincing answer.

'What I would like to do is show you how things are progressing in the Imamate already. A short tour round some of the towns and settlements around Nizwa will more than persuade you that the model society based on tribal and traditional values is securely conceived and enjoying everyone's support. Hassim here has done much in recent months to work with young people, training and equipping them for the new civil society with a strengthened shariah basis, settling how we intend to live.'

At that, a nod was given to Hassim who stood up and silently indicated to Adam it was time to turn off the recording and leave. Adam flipped closed his laptop politely thanking his host for the unexpected press interview, wanting as much to safeguard his personal position through politeness as gain the next scoop.

'Come Adam, there are things you must see,' said Hassim, who gave a final conspiratorial nod in the direction of the Major General.

As they went outside Adam was thinking he was learning so much new information so quickly it was becoming difficult to know how he would process it. As Hassim led the way, he realised he wanted to ask many more questions than he had been given chance to – what he heard, where he went, it was all being orchestrated – he was being led by the hand.

On the one hand he must be the luckiest journalist out to have been brought in for this press briefing, but on the other hand he was a pawn in someone else's power game. He didn't like his situation one bit, it was getting far too dangerous.

50

It was a strange request. Adam thought they'd be leaving, but Hassim insisted that Adam first walk round the Bahla Fort with him.

'You really must start here, Adam. Look around you. What can you see?'

The first thing Adam noticed was another white flag fluttering in the breeze from the Fort's towering flagpole. How hadn't he noticed it on the way in?

'I see the flag,' said Adam pointing it out.

'You'll see many more in a moment,' replied Hassim.

On being out in the open, caught between radiating heat from the walls and a sun now burning the top of his head and sucking his energy, Adam knew he had to show some fortitude. He only kept his cool by virtue of the fact that he was getting precious material for his next piece to send to London.

Ignoring the heat, he waited, taking time to gaze around him, pulling on his sunglasses to cut the harsh glare, hoping he cut a confident figure. Annoyingly, his sunglasses caught his bruised cheek and the pain made him wince.

In every direction he gazed, the high grey walls and massive towers extended, enclosing a significant interior area with underground as well as overground defensively built areas. It would be like trying to attack a city to launch an attack on this place, he thought. For any invading force it would be like fighting house by house in an urban jungle.

'Look carefully, Adam. Start counting,' instructed Hassim. He began pointing one way and then another. Then Adam began to observe the soldiers and their heavy weapons, occupying every possible piece of cover. When he had counted sixty three, he stopped and looked at Hassim.

'You know, no one would attack this place, would they? A World Heritage Site. It's a good choice for a force to make a secure base. How many more bases are there?' Instead of answering, Hassim adopted his usual annoying tactic, and moved on in his own way.

'Come. I'll show you some of them near here. It really is important that you are persuaded the Imamate is strong and secure, that the army forces are truly all you've been told they are. Come! There's a lot to see. We'll start by going up to the top of the fort's towers – you'll be amazed what you can see of the surrounding area from up there. Those who built this place in the 13th century knew what they were doing. And the best thing is, you're absolutely right, who in the world would ever attack it?'

At a leisurely pace, Hassim led Adam in an anticlockwise tour of the fort, making in turn for the highest towers, some square, some circular. Stairways were precarious, often with no handrails – just open steps set in the side of a high wall. There were few rails, fences or walls to prevent falling. Steps and walkways were often uneven. It was still a fort and despite the inviting sign outside, not yet some tourist attraction with tea rooms, handrails and lifts for disabled and elderly visitors.

Innumerable mud brick walls formed a spread of rooms whose original purposes one could only guess at. As they walked, at every turn there was yet another armed soldier and inside every room at least two or three, often one of them acting as a look-out, eyes peering out through binoculars across the expansive landscape spread below.

At each viewpoint, Hassim paused. Given the lofty rocky platform on which the fort was built and the low-lying plains adjacent to it, the views were incredible and worth pausing to see. Every now and then Adam half thought he was a tourist being shown the sights, but the sight of the nearby military soon brought him back to reality.

Adam gazed at the dusty grey-greens of the many palm trees in the immediate vicinity. They occupied every walled garden and some of the irrigated fields and squares between the creamy-yellow, flat walled, flat roofed properties. Neglected crumbling areas of building dereliction were everywhere, mud bricks turning back into dust where they fell.

The surrounding landscape had a timeless quality, the towering Hajar Mountains, not far distant, providing a solid wall of shimmering grey defence beyond to the north and west. The bright light and heat haze gave them a heavy feel, placing them much nearer than they actually were.

As Adam gazed he saw more and more white flags, not one or two, but flying on almost all the buildings, some small, some large. In seeing them he lost any doubt in the reality of the Imamate.

'Be alright if I take a couple of pictures?' asked Adam, getting out his mobile. 'Just asking, because I don't want to be accused of spying or anything.'

'I suggest you only take pictures of what's outside the walls. You're right, people will get nervous if you point that thing at anyone inside here.'

After climbing to the top of the circular tower, Adam was breathing hard and sweat was pouring off him. He wasn't sure if he was up for much more of this and craved the comfort of air conditioning and a cold drink.

Once up high, on top of the tower, there were six men under a makeshift camouflage bivouac to keep the sun off. It looked like they'd drawn the short straw in terms of their posting. Apart from descending a level there was no respite for them. Adam and Hassim's presence was acknowledged, the soldiers touching their caps politely. One of them drew Adam to one side and lifted his arm to point to the distance. There was dust in the air and beneath it a long convoy of army vehicles out on the road a mile or so away. It wasn't possible to see which way they were moving.

'Some of ours,' Hassim explained.

Adam was offered some binoculars by one of the soldiers. Then he could see them more clearly, tank transporters and more than twenty vehicles moving away from Bahla, heading east toward the capital. Adam was holding his mobile at that moment taking a video shot of the scene and included the convoy. No one objected – they knew they were too far away to make meaningful pictures.

He passed the binoculars back with one hand, holding his mobile in the other. As he did so there was a crackle on the soldiers' radio, a message maybe, then anxious confused looks between the soldiers. Before they could move, a fighter jet zipped low overhead, heads instinctively ducked down, followed instantaneously by a deafening, shaking roar, and then it had gone. The soldiers' eyes and Adam's mobile camera following its path into invisibility.

'Come,' said Hassim, 'we need to go,' some new seriousness having crept into his expression. Perhaps the change in him was caused by the unexpected arrival of the plane.

Adam followed him down the hollow space of the four floors of the circular tower's irregular staircase, emerging in the bright light of the fort's dusty inner compound. Following Hassim's lead, the two walked briskly from there across to the exit gates.

Adam observed a new level of activity around the fort as soldiers conferred with each other in corners or spoke into radios. The jet had clearly shaken the place. The two picked up their waiting rucksacks and headed for the gate. There they had to wait.

'What do you think that was about?' asked Adam, stepping two paces back into a patch of shade.

'Looked like an RAF plane to me. I'm no expert, but I think it was a Tornado. They've been used widely across the Gulf, especially against ISIL. But that's odd to me,' said Hassim, a frown on his face.

'Why's it so odd?' asked Adam.

'What was it doing? If recognisance, well why not use a drone, as they usually do, or failing that, a recognisance plane. It didn't do anything except shake us all up.'

'Maybe that was the point, to let you know they were there. Like you shouldn't think the British aren't going to be interested, don't you think?'

'Could be right there, Adam. The British have lined themselves up with Muscat and the coast. They could be flexing their muscles, rattling their sabres. It was probably no more than that. Come on, look, they've given us permission to be on our way. We're off around the local bases, just a few mind, the one's they want you to see,' he chuckled. He was enjoying this. 'And we'll need to stop off at the mosque.'

'Why's that then?'

'I want to catch up on the latest news – who the new Imam will be. Most of the votes will be in. Everyone wants to know. Think of that as a story Adam, you being the journalist and the first to know.'

'I hadn't realised,' said Adam, 'that the country was so divided. The Sultan's death has led to a total split between interior and coast, Nizwa and Muscat, just like it used to be in the past.'

'Exactly. We've co-existed side by side before. If we can't agree, then it'll happen again, history repeating itself.'

Following their two military companions, they were soon once more outside the fort's main entrance. They climbed into the rear of the army vehicle, and were passed a welcome plastic bottle of chilled water each.

As they moved away, Adam just caught a glimpse of Hanif's house. He wondered how Raqiyah really was and the feeling returned that a gulf had opened up between them since leaving England. He knew he must try and get some quality time with her, but out here it felt almost impossible. The thought made his spirits drop, he was beginning to despair. With a lurch, the vehicle swung left and all view of the house was lost, and Adam's attention quickly drawn back to more immediate matters.

'Hassim, you've not really explained your role in things. Can you tell me? Just so I don't get it wrong. You're clearly not just my guide?'

'I guess I've come to realise I owe more to my father Abdul Aziz than I realised. He was quite the skilled diplomat. You could say I've got the same genes. My role has been in brokering support for the Imamate at home and abroad. It's been vital to have all the local tribal leaders, politicians, trustees of mosques, Imams, public servants, police, army, and you name it, anyone who cares about our country on our side. At the same time it has been vital that our young men have had good teaching and have been taught the basics of the faith and that they, and local women too, have a good understanding of sharia. The local walis have been key to our progress.'

'Walis, who are the walis?' asked Adam.

'For hundreds of years communities have had their autonomous leaders, their wise local community leaders whom everyone respects. It's our custom. The last Sultan tried to replace them with only walis loyal to the capital, but old traditions are hard to overcome. In reality, try as he might, he never stood a chance out here. Ask about and you'll find that next to the extended family, the mosque, and the sharia court, the wali still reigns supreme. It's the walis who people go to to support their causes, solve their disputes and find leadership.'

'But the last Sultan successfully created a new and popular national identity, centred around himself, didn't he?' said Adam, feeling the need to push harder on this. Are you trying to tell me that's all been undermined, done away with at a stroke?'

'Yes, I guess that's how it is… Out with the old, in with the new, don't you say?' smiled Hassim.

'Look, see all the white flags,' he continued, 'that tells you something in itself, and we're just approaching our first stop. We won't get out, but you'll be able to see one of the largest military bases in the area. Look! Just there!'

Hassim asked the driver to slow up, which he did. It was now clear to Adam that Hassim had the authority to tell even military men what to do.

'See, over the entrance to the base, our flag. In order for this to work it's been vital that we've the military and community leaders totally in step with each other. I don't mind telling you that has been the single most and biggest challenge we have had to meet – and all done covertly until now. To be frank, a number of military personnel had to be immediately relieved of their duties to ensure the Imamate's future wasn't compromised. Many in the military had been corrupted over the years by the old regime, looking to the West for leadership and forgetting their Muslim and Ibadi roots.'

Adam fell silent. It felt like Hassim had revealed a great deal in just a few minutes. What he was telling him now felt honest, with little if any of the masquerading of earlier. Adam knew that there must have been some power brokering and that it had to have been ugly, Hassim had intimated as much.

'What's happened to the military leadership who didn't see things your way?' asked Adam.

'I think you can guess the answer to that. They're being held in detention – some right where you're looking. You can give them a wave if you like!' he chirped.

Adam didn't respond. There was no denying that to hear the army and community were working together under the same Ibadi ideology sounded as though there was a coherent and viable opposition. Back in Muscat it had sounded increasingly like simply a case of the army seizing control. Since Hassim was enjoying telling more of his story, Adam decided to question him further.

'That sounds a secure basis for what you are hoping to achieve, but how does this sit internationally? We've just seen a British fighter plane overhead, where are your friends abroad? Saudi?'

'Spot on, Adam. When the Imamate was crushed back in the 70s by the Sultan, the old Imam fled to Saudi. Yes, the last Sultan did much to secure Oman's place in the world by clever diplomacy, but now he's gone, much of it will unravel – you'll see. How do you say – the chickens have come home to roost, yes?'

Adam was getting tired of his sayings.

'The reality is, everyone has their knives out for a piece of Oman – the USA, Britain, Iran and yes, Saudi too. But it's what the grassroots want that's important here. It's what the people want and Saudi understand that.' Hassim paused for a moment lost in his own thoughts.

'The people here have seen enough of oil greed and colonialism. That's what the West's only real interest has been. And as for Iran, the last Sultan made us all very wary by cozying up to Iran. He brought in so many Shia Iranians and courted so much Iranian business and money, he alienated those of us following a true Ibadi tradition. Don't you see, the only friends we really have are those under threat like us – the Saudis, the guardians of the truth, the only ones who've looked after our Imams and exiles all these long years of waiting. Now it's safe for the exiles to return, our Saudi friends have been backing them, and us, all the way. I myself have made many fruitful trips to Mecca…' and then Hassim fell quiet again.

Adam reckoned Hassim had realised his enthusiasm had run away with him and was having to think through whether he'd gone too far.

Adam for his own part, sensing this, decided to bide his time with any more sensitive questions. For the time being he'd ask the questions any sightseer in Oman's interior might, about the public buildings, the mosques, the big houses, and many sights of interest they were passing.

At this, Hassim soon came back to life, only too pleased to talk about his own community and its proud tradition. He was so passionate about it, Adam getting used to Hassim's company and way of thinking could feel the dividing lines, much as he once could at a football match he'd attended between local rivals, Exeter and Plymouth. Hassim had the world neatly divided, polarised between those on his side and those who were not. Such rigid views, to Adam's mind, could only lead to conflict.

51

Adam and Hassim pulled up in front of a large mosque near the centre of Nizwa. It wasn't clear how grand it was until they were right upon it, the mosque being hemmed in by other buildings.

To Adam's eye, as he looked this way and that, there was absolutely no outward indication that the country was in the midst of a succession crisis or a pending civil war. He could have been just one more tourist, except that, he reminded himself, he was the only foreigner he could see.

To endorse the illusion of normality further, Hassim had become a veritable tour guide, latterly expounding on the virtues of the nearby Nizwa Souk whose future as a market and centre of the community's life had begun to be undermined.

Apparently, the late Sultan's programme of permitting the indiscriminate development of large Western style, out of town shopping malls, meant the ancient souks were seeing the new malls swallowing up all their trade. Tourists had done much to sustain the old customs and the old souks, but they needed a helping hand said, Hassim. They reflect the old traditions and patterns of authority. They must be kept.

'Time to step out into the midday sun again, Adam. Isn't that what you English are supposed to like doing – you and mad dogs?' he jibed. 'We're going to the mosque. I'm going to sit you out the way at the back. You'll be fine. Dare say you've been in mosques a few times?'

At which Adam nodded and began getting out to follow Hassim who had spotted some friends. They left the two soldiers to wait for them in the army vehicle. Both soldiers immediately started talking into their mobile phones – probably to catch up on family or business interests.

Sandals left outside, Adam could hear the splashing of water, the washing of heads, hands and feet as ablutions were performed by the faithful. He gave that part a miss. It was almost time for midday prayers to start. It had been a while since Adam had last attended mosque prayers, that had been back in Devon as part of his university course, but even across continents, the practice was strangely familiar.

As if transported by time and place to a universal medium, he watched from the back of the prayer hall as the serried ranks of men stood shoulder to shoulder facing Mecca in a dignified silence. Soon the prayers proceeded in beautiful, almost poetically spoken Arabic, the congregation's responses being followed by an address given by the Imam.

It was brief and as far as Adam's Arabic permitted, he thought the Imam was leading a reflection on the Quranic message behind the Imamate's new flag. He was arguing that it was a prayer as well as a public statement of identity, and that the faithful should be asking, praying for victory from Allah, and that deliverance should be soon, that Allah's mercy may be felt. It was all very didactic, leaving no room for argument.

The imam concluded his thoughts by reminding the congregation that this was no new message, but an old and true message. The people were to be faithful to Allah and share in the personal corporate jihad that lay ahead. This sermon was, to Adam's mind, something quite different to what he'd expected. Normally in Oman, he'd been told, a centrally produced uniform address that came weekly from the old Sultan's ministry offices, was issued for compulsory reading at every mosque. Times had definitely changed, and today's radical independent message was received with rapt attention and in a respectful silence. There was little doubt as to the new order of things around here, thought Adam.

After prayers were over, and whilst he waited for Hassim to reappear, Adam was shown some warm hospitality. He was made welcome by several people who stopped to talk to him. People were genuinely interested in him as if he were an innocent visitor or tourist, but he felt inwardly insecure, vulnerable and guarded in what he in turn said to them. Fortunately no one pressed him and after just a few minutes, Hassim returned to gather him up into a small entourage he had around him. This was becoming something of a pattern with Hassim, Adam noted.

'Meet some of my friends,' he said, once more with a broad smile on his face. 'Until now, like many young men, they've been travelling up to Muscat to work in the week. Sundays, they leave their families here, stay in Muscat and around until Thursday night. Then they come back home for the weekend. That's all stopped.'

'Nice to meet you,' said Adam, shaking as many hands as space allowed.

'We're just going to speak with the mosque chairman before leaving, would you like to come with us please,' said Hassim. It was more an instruction than a request, and Adam complied following them out of the prayer hall.

In a back room, they waited their turn with the many others who also wanted time with an elderly imam who was sitting behind an ornately carved wooden desk, with a pile of green, leather bound, Arabic texts stacked on one side. Time didn't seem to be an issue to the Imam – he was quite unhurried, totally chilled, as one person after another wanted his time, his answers to their questions.

Eventually, it was Hassim's turn, and he and his friends moved forward. Adam held back a little, but they pushed him forward and introduced him. Hassim went straight to the point. With a twinkle in his intelligent eyes, the Imam's wrinkled face turned to take in his foreign visitor. A bony hand was offered to Adam to shake. Hassim spoke up.

'With respect, is there a consensus yet amongst the Imams and the mosques as to the succession question?'

'Everyone's asking me the same question today. There are, as you know Hassim, two names under consideration – Imam Azzan, my younger colleague from Nizwa mosque, and the newly returned from Saudi exile, Imam Faisal.' Hassim nodded. The old imam continued…

'All the mosques in the Imamate have submitted their decisions and the two candidates are presently here in town at the nearby, main Nizwa mosque, where an announcement and presentation of the victor will be made in less than an hour's time.' He peered closely to check his watch, the stretch silver wrist band allowing it to slide on his thin arm nearly to his elbow. 'All I know, my friends, is that a decision has been made. You may want to go over there, wait outside for the public announcement, it won't be long, though I think you will find it very crowded.'

Hassim bent and touched the old Imam's hand and thanked him, turning away with his friends, Adam following in their wake. Hassim began walking outside with them. No doubt they would all want to be going to the main mosque and this is what they agreed. They retrieved their footwear, and made their way back to their various vehicles.

As Adam and Hassim dashed across the road between moving cars, Hassim's mobile buzzed. He glanced at it, turned his head away from Adam and took the call. It was clearly important. It was brief.

'Adam, it would appear that not one, but a whole squadron of RAF Tornados flew across the interior this morning. It was a determined, low altitude flight, to try and cause consternation amongst the population. There are reports of up to six planes, all spotted at precisely the same time as the one we saw at Bahla Fort. It was nothing more than sabre rattling, shaking of windows and frightening of goats, and that's all they've done,' he reported dismissively, before adding, 'Something else for your next report piece, Adam. What its significance is, I leave to your journalistic imagination. Personally, I don't rate it as any more than bluster.'

Adam wasn't so sure. He began to see himself entering the preliminaries of a building conflict and once again began feeling exposed and vulnerable.

Adam had no time to dwell on his sober thoughts, the army vehicle saw them approach, swept them up, and following Hassim's instruction, headed off. It took but a few minutes to get to the Central Mosque by the old Nizwa Souk. It was hard to get near, such were the large crowds. Hassim made arrangements for the army guys to pick them up at an agreed spot when he called them. Given the size of the crowds here was no way they were going to get the vehicle within half a mile of their destination.

As Adam looked round, he noticed for the first time that almost without exception the men, all heading in the same direction, were shouldering weapons, though some of the weaponry looked old, fit only for a museum – the people had been mobilised, possibly for the purposes of celebration rather than armed conflict, but the latter thought was what stayed with him.

Hassim and himself joined the huge throng, the heat from the midday sun, and the pressing together of the surrounding bodies made it unbearably hot, as well as claustrophobic. Adam was feeling uncomfortable, a feeling made worse by his dislike of being in a pressing crowd. Time was passing too slowly. He did his best to stay close to Hassim. It was all very physical and from time to time the hard metal of a weapon bumped his shoulder or arm. He hid behind his dark glasses, hoping to stay anonymous. How, he wondered, did he get in this situation?

The pace of the crowd slowed, but the Mosque was still the far side of a packed car park, all of a hundred metres away. Soon the two men were stationary, going nowhere, the combined heat from sun and bodies unendurable. Hassim must have read his thoughts, his hand snaking across in Adam's direction offering a water bottle.

They waited twenty minutes, there was no alternative. So many men now pressed behind them there was no way out anyway. Even so, a building excitement was in the air, the atmosphere electric under the piercing blue sky. Suddenly a large white Imamate flag was draped by invisible hands from high above the mosque, at which there was a rousing cheer from the expectant crowd.

A couple of minutes later, Adam made out movement on the Mosque steps, a presentation party of dignitaries were coming out in a line, one man scurrying in front making ready a microphone on a stand.

There was a certain amount of shuffling as the line ordered itself. Sensing something of significance was imminently about to happen, Adam took out his mobile phone and began recording. No one minded, others were doing the same. A loudspeaker somewhere made some squeaks. One man stepped forward to offer some polite preliminaries.

Next moment, Adam found himself lying on the ground. He couldn't hear. Choking thick clouds of grey dust swirled about and above him. Turning his head, he could see Hassim beside him, also in the dust, trying to pull himself upright, looking wild-eyed in Adam's direction, then offering an outstretched arm, a hand toward him.

'Need to get to cover,' he thought he heard him shout as he took the hand. The two got up, leaning on one another, they tried to retreat, climbing over people lying on the ground, some hurt, bumping people, then being pushed and carried along in a rushing tide of people, they were with others like themselves trying desperately to move away. Then there was panic, a seething chaotic crowd, pushing, shoving to get away, mouthing shouts, eyes darting full of fear.

Suddenly they were out on the main road, Hassim still grasping Adam's hand, looking this way and that, using his phone in his other hand to text a message to the army vehicle to collect them.

Adam observed Hassim's appearance had changed, the smiling man was a deeply troubled man, shrouded in streaks of grey dust, black lines marked across his forehead, glancing this way and that, trying to get a handle on what had happened. All the while, Adam's hand, as if guided by some unknown professional instinct had kept his mobile filming.

Then they saw their lift, the army vehicle, speeding and swerving around fleeing reckless pedestrians as it made its way toward them.

They were scooped up, the vehicle swinging round and in moments heading away.

In the minutes following, Adam noticed his hearing return accompanied by a high pitched continuous whistle. He felt his whole body shaking, noted his breathing was rapid – and knew he needed to take control. Focussing hard, using the mindfulness, self-calming techniques he had worked on so hard over the past year, he gradually regained some poise.

He realised that since the explosion, for surely that was what it was, he'd not spoken a word. The army vehicle accelerated hard swaying as it surged back in the direction of the Bahla Fort.

52

Adam wanted to get back to Raqiyah. Hassim wanted to get somewhere else, but never really explained where or why, except that it was important. He appeared to Adam to be a driven man, preoccupied if not obsessed. After a couple of insistent protests that he wanted to get back, Adam got his way.

Hassim instructed the soldiers to drop Adam back at the house by Bahla Fort where he would be left. His would be the first stop.

As they headed back, they were passed by numerous army and emergency vehicles heading toward where they had just left. Adam began to realise there must have been many casualties and felt guilty at running away. He recalled those injured he and Hassim and pushed past, maybe trodden on. Something inside him had been violated. He didn't like what he'd become. Things were slipping downhill by the day.

In the vehicle there was tension in the air. No one yet knew what sense to make of what had happened. Even the army guys who were on their radios and mobiles as they travelled clearly had no grasp yet of the new realities. Hassim said he would find out what he could and call Adam later, finally agreeing with Adam it was best if they parted for now. By then they were back at the house.

Raqiyah was standing alone just outside the front door, leaning against the doorpost. Waiting pensively, her hands were raised holding her face, anxiety written across it. Something in her expression reminded him of a painting called, "The Scream". Adam knew she'd heard something.

Hearing, then seeing them approach, her eyes looked up, her head moving, scrutinising their vehicle to see if Adam and Hassim were safe inside. Adam jumped out first, dragging his small rucksack with him, dropped it, and ignoring convention, stepped forward and put his arms round her. They hugged and held on to one another. He felt he was holding her upright. Her tears ran.

The army vehicle reversed and quickly moved off as the two remained statuesque and silent in their embrace. It was Adam who moved first. The two went slowly inside.

Maryam was waiting for them to come in. She explained that news had come in there had been a big explosion outside Nizwa mosque and that there had been many casualties. All their attempts to reach Hassim and Adam by mobile phone had failed. Adam glanced down at his phone and saw that it was still in silent mode from when the two had gone to mosque prayers earlier. He explained events as best he could in short bursts, broken sentences.

As he looked again at his phone he recalled that he'd been filming when the explosion happened, and wondered what, if anything he'd recorded as he'd held his phone high, pointing toward the Nizwa mosque platform party. He asked Raqiyah and Maryam to give him a minute.

He found he'd shot over six minutes of recorded time. A quick scan and he knew he had something worthwhile. Before viewing the content properly, he pulled Raqiyah over to share what he had, to view it with him.

'There! Look! Hassim and I couldn't get any nearer, because of the crowds. The platform party, the two imamate candidates, were at the centre of the explosion. Oh my God!'

The video shot had captured a white flash before the blast wave had tilted the camera angle up and back at the moment of impact – a sky shot, for some seconds.

'I was thrown to the ground,' he explained. They watched the grey dust cloud sweeping across, misting out almost all the view. It began to clear – the camera jogging and shaking as Adam and other people were running in fog, no dust, bodies, screams. Adam watched trance like.

'Oh no!' exclaimed Raqiyah, her hand over her mouth as she watched, then, turning, realising that he'd stopped speaking and was just staring at his phone, rooted, eyes locked on, she grabbed his arm, pleading, 'Adam, say something to me.'

'Sorry,' he said, 'It… it was bad, really, really bad.'

Raqiyah again reached for him and led him toward the kitchen. Maryam, sensing the need to do something practical, produced some mint tea. She added sugar, which Adam never normally had, and handed it him as he sat at the kitchen table. Fatigue followed shock and began to take hold. He sagged down, feeling the chair take all his weight.

Raqiyah's phone rang. It was Hassim.

'My apologies Sis. I'd had my phone switched off for prayers and have only just seen the missed calls. We were lucky, such a crowd we weren't able to get near. Had we been… I don't like to think. Army say many deaths and casualties. Local hospital overwhelmed. I told Adam I'd ring when I'd found out more. Can you tell him.'

A few moments later and the call was over. Raqiyah looked across to Adam who was quietly sipping the hot tea which was working its magic.

'I need to put something together for London and try and make a few calls first. Need to check out a few things, see if social media feeds have anything to tell. It'll be therapy to put something together in writing, honestly. Give me an hour will you Raqiyah. OK? I'll be fine, really. I don't mind if you look in on me from time to time,' he added, which made her smile.

She nodded and filled Adam in on Hassim's call. Adam then got up to retrieve his laptop from his rucksack. As he did so he realised that his full day's expedition with Hassim had been unexpectedly curtailed, and the packed lunches had remained unopened. Plans had had to be changed because there was no safety even here in the interior.

He passed his lunch pack over to Raqiyah, leaving her in the kitchen as he went to the lounge, his mind already trying to appraise what to make of it all. As he sat, he realised he missed having his own desk, his own space. Would being a correspondent always be like this, snatching borrowed places somewhere, anywhere, to work. He felt like a refugee, with nowhere to call his own, possessing only what he carried, always using someone else's room. It was yet another reminder he was an alien in a foreign land.

In the quiet he called the British Embassy. He asked for Brian Merryweather, Media Services, and this time was put straight through.

'Hi Brian, Adam Taylor here. I was hoping for a catch up conversation.'

'Sure. As it happens now is good. I've just had a late lunch. It's usually quiet at this time – I call it my siesta time. I used to be in Madrid once, probably a legacy of those days in Spain. How's things with you? Where are you? Had lunch yet?'

'Nizwa.'

'Nizwa,' his voice immediately more alert. 'Good God! What are you doing there?'

'Visiting family,' Adam offered warily.

'Lovely,' said Brian, sounding more relaxed again.

'But it hasn't turned out exactly as planned.'

'Oh!'

'No, it's not been without incident. News may not have reached you yet of an explosion a short while ago outside the main Nizwa Mosque. You don't happen to know anything about it?'

There was a detectable pause at the other end. Adam could almost hear Brian Merryweather trying to collect his thoughts. In that moment he knew Brian knew exactly what he was referring to.

'Funny you should say that. I was hearing only just now, not officially confirmed mind, something along those very lines. Don't know what it was, an explosion you say, do you have any ideas, any information?' he said cagily.

'I was hoping my friendly Embassy contact might be able to offer one of its citizens a crumb of solace – how about it?' he said trying strike an affable tone.

'News of an explosion of some sort is coming in on the screen in front of me as I speak. Let me read, "First reports indicate many casualties, some deaths," I'm afraid. We don't usually get anything like this in Oman, so don't really know what to make of it. There must have been some reason for the target chosen. No one seems to have claimed responsibility – it's all early days. I expect we'll know more in an hour or two, maybe longer.'

'I was there,' Adam volunteered, hoping that being open with the information would lead to a reciprocal response from Brian and release any further information he might be holding back.

'You OK, Adam? You weren't too near when it happened were you?'

'Pretty near. It was an election results event, for a new Imam. Any news on the platform party itself?' Adam fished.

'Ah! Something coming in now. Nothing definite until identities are formally confirmed, but it says here, "the two candidates for top position in the old Imamate, were killed", also a couple of Imams and several local people, many injuries, but, reading down, no one's quite sure of the significance of what's taken place there. How did you read it?'

'I was just a passing tourist,' said Adam evasively. 'Couldn't see what was going on from where I was. I just got out as quick as I could.'

'Best thing. Sure you're OK? Are you staying in Nizwa for a while?'

'No firm plans. It's rather up to my hosts. How's the succession going in the capital? Are the army still running things?' quizzed Adam.

'Looks that way to me, but that's a lowly Media Officer's view. I would say one thing though, it's taking a little longer for things to settle down than everyone thought. Everything isn't yet running as smoothly as we're used to. A lot of people aren't reporting in for work, even some of the Embassy ancillary staff. Guess they're waiting until things completely settle, not that I mean it's unsettled. Look, nice to hear from you, Adam. Do keep in touch. Bye for now.' With that he had gone, leaving Adam to ponder on what he'd learned.

Clearly the Embassy were more aware of events than they were letting on. Brian knew that the two candidates to run the Imamate had been killed in the explosion. From early on Adam himself had realised it had been a deliberate, targeted attack, wholly intended to do what it did – strike and kill the opposition to the government in Muscat. Whoever had done it had succeeded, but who was it? It had to be forces sympathetic to the capital, but how had they got here, to strike such a deadly blow in Nizwa?

These things usually followed a pattern – attack then retaliation, he reasoned. He began trying to anticipate what might happen next. Shock is soon followed by anger. He didn't think there would be long to wait until something happened.

He wondered what Hassim was up to. He still hadn't given Adam any idea of what he was really doing, yet in less than a day he'd learned that Hassim held considerable authority, nothing less than a senior civil position in the Imamate. He wouldn't have had access to the military without it.

Everything he'd learned today signalled to him that very quickly Oman was sliding into a civil war, and things could get very nasty, dangerous for him, very quickly.

The death of the Sultan had created a power vacuum. He'd already seen evidence of foreign powers muscling in. A British RAF Tornado fighter squadron making its presence felt for the capital's forces, and the Saudi exile returnee, Imam Faisal, poised to contend for power in the interior until his sudden demise. Would Saudi now step in?

And then what about the Iranians. They had such a strong presence around the capital, money invested, many migrant workers... this could all boil over, and Oman become... another Yemen.

He wondered whether the direction his thoughts were taking was unduly pessimistic. Maybe so, he might have missed something. It could be that the people here in the interior might settle quietly down, and Muscat re-impose its control over the whole country with some practical British help. No, he couldn't see it – even if that was the eventual outcome, the present reality was that everything was uncertain, volatile, a heady, unstable, boiling crisis. That would be how he would pen his next piece. He needed to get it written and sent. If Hassim updated him later with more news he'd do some follow up, add it later to what he'd write.

Twenty minutes later he had a first draft, an hour from when he started writing he finally pressed the "send" button – job done, hungry London fed and hopefully satisfied. He'd heard Raqiyah open the door behind him twice, whisper, 'you OK?' and then left him to it each time. Her concern felt good.

Job done, he got up, washed his face and walked to the kitchen. He was feeling hungry, and rejoined Raqiyah sitting at the kitchen table. Cutting himself a hunk of bread, he looked for some humus and a cold drink and fell into a chair.

'What happens next?' he asked out loud. 'It doesn't look good, not good at all.' Raqiyah looked at him.

'Just what I was thinking. We can only wait, sit it out, hope for the best.'

Adam didn't like the idea of a passive response. It made him feel powerless, a victim. He wanted to do something, but what it was he didn't know.

53

Adam and Raqiyah went up on to the roof to see what they could discover from looking out from the highest point of the house. Leaving the house, to go off for a walk, seemed unwise, unsafe, and besides, far too hot to try. Nobody appeared to walk in Oman unless they were poor and had no choice. Walking would only attract unwarranted attention, and neither wanted to do that.

From the rooftop, the surrounding landscape looked just as tranquil as it had the first time Adam had viewed the scene the previous day. This time though, looking for them, he did notice the fluttering of many white and red flags. He pointed them out to Raqiyah. There was nothing else they could see, a heat haze was closing things down.

They came back downstairs, delaying briefly in the privacy of the stairwell to steal a kiss. Back in the kitchen they drank cold drinks, iced mint lemonade and freshly squeezed orange. In the heat it never seemed possible to take on enough fluid.

As if it were just a normal day, Hanif and Tanvi were sorting out a delivery of fruit and vegetables a neighbour had dropped round, whilst Maryam was sitting at the table glancing through a magazine, or was she simply staring at it, lost in her own thoughts? There seemed to Adam an odd disconnect between the ordinary homeliness of the scene and the events happening outside in the political world.

From time to time someone would try to start a conversation but it wouldn't go anywhere, everyone mindful they were waiting for more news. For Adam and Raqiyah time hung still on the air as they sat. A large black house fly moved in darting movements around the kitchen, dividing attention between finding crumbs and seeing to escape, it was the only action. Adam found waiting around difficult. The day dragged slowly from afternoon to evening.

Hassim didn't arrive back until after dark. He looked strained and greeted them roughly before going straight to his room. A few minutes later, washed and changed, he looked somewhat better and joined everyone in the kitchen, but still seemed preoccupied and spoke gruffly. Maybe, thought Adam, things wren't going well?

At this point Raqiyah was preparing some vegetables, slicing green beans. Once again Adam felt she'd been relegated to the domestic sphere since her return to Oman. It was extinguishing the light in her, dousing her spark slowly, like turning down a light by dimmer switch. He didn't much like it, but felt powerless to change anything.

'Day didn't turn out as planned,' Hassim ventured by way of summary.

'You can say that again,' said Adam.

'That plane overhead shook the house, made us all jump,' said Raqiyah.

'They've not been back though, have they,' he told her.

'Thankfully. It took us all by surprise, we didn't immediately know what it was. Everyone was shaken.'

Hassim, nodded. 'More significantly, I've just heard the preliminary death toll at the mosque. Funerals are already starting. Amongst the twenty eight dead there are six youngsters. Everyone knows somebody. I've been down there – awful. Wailing, body parts. They've a fire tender, hosing down, washing away the blood. The best estimate is that there were fifty eight people being treated in the hospital, some of whom have life changing injuries, some I'm pretty certain, won't survive the night.'

'Who's responsible?' asked Adam.

'No formal claims yet, but the local army experts have had a team take a preliminary look. They also wanted to make sure there were no other devices. It took over an hour for the area to be declared safe. Until then they wouldn't let anyone near. From the fragments they've found, they recognised familiar bits of equipment – it was all Omani stuff.'

'Omani forces,'said Adam.

'Yes. They can't conceive that it was anyone loyal to the Imamate, so it had to be a Muscat sympathiser. Since the bomb deliberately targeted and killed both candidates for the Imamate leadership position, fingers are all pointing one way – to Muscat.'

'Hassim, you're well informed and this morning you took me and showed me around. The planned trip was cut short, so I never had chance to ask you about your own role in things. What is it you precisely do? What's your role here?'

'Me, think of me as a mere civil servant. There's a civil authority body in each wilayat – each local authority area. The Nizwa Wilayat Imamate Partnership Group, like the others, was tasked with bringing in the new governance arrangements. My role's been to help make preparations for a smooth transition from the old regime to the new. We've been preparing for this moment for years.'

'That figures,' said Adam.

'Trouble is, after what's happened with this bomb, things might have been slowed, derailed even. The process of holding another election is going to take a while, it'll have to be re-run. Whoever did this, went straight for the jugular. With no leader at a time like this, the Imamate is exposed to grave risk.'

'It seems that way to me too,' said Adam.

'Tell me, are the Saudis giving you their active support?'

'That's insightful of you, Adam. Until now it has all been terribly hush, hush. Don't suppose there's any need for secrecy now. Yes, the Saudis have started issuing public statements this afternoon backing our position and saying that the deliberate targeting of the candidates in Nizwa, one of whom carried Saudi citizenship, was a brazen act of naked aggression. So, yes, they've been helping quietly for years. Looking ahead, after what's happened today, I think we can count on them helping less quietly, and more overtly.'

'Will there be an act of retaliation do you think?' asked Adam.

'I can't comment on that Adam. You know why,' he said.

In that moment Adam knew that his reply meant "yes".

The conflict was building, both locally and internationally. Things could only escalate. The stakes had been raised by the mosque explosion and other interests would no longer be content look on. What happened next, thought Adam, could only be bad.

54

Adam excused himself before evening meal to write a supplementary piece to send to London. Having a foreign correspondent role definitely lifted him, gave him a sense of added purpose, self-esteem, in his situation. Before compiling his next piece, he emailed his parents, feeling guilty for not having talked to them earlier.

They'd tried to reach him by mobile a couple of times over the past couple of days, but each time he hadn't picked up. He knew they'd fuss and be over-protective and he just couldn't face talking to them – he was having enough trouble trying to understand his personal situation and his own motives for himself, let alone trying to explain things to them. He knew he couldn't hold off the call home indefinitely so he resolved to call them in a day or two, once things were, well, more settled. An email would have to suffice for now.

As he thought about London, he began thinking about what he was doing staying any longer in Oman – the sensible thing his parents would tell him was to get out. To do so, he really needed to get his own thoughts straight, in order. He'd have to come up with a plan – he had none.

He wasn't sure whether his new employer in London had any call on what he should do and where he should go and when, or whether he himself decided such things. Being new in a job meant being inexperienced and he didn't know how to manage his new role after just one week in. Should he try and bale out or hang in there? Could they get him out? He didn't know. It felt like his employer had left him to hang out and dry when he really needed some support. His mind wasn't functioning as it should, he couldn't seem to think clearly. See couldn't yet fathom a way forward. He was stuck in hell.

Life felt chaotic, out of control. He felt like a speck of dust being blown by the wind through the desert. It was hard to focus down and the continuing uncertainty of his situation coupled with his increasingly stressed state of mind started to make him anxious. Anxiety also meant loss of ability, a downward spiral lay ahead.

All this in turn led him to desperately want to talk properly with Raqiyah – she was always such a personal help whenever things had got difficult in the past, yet here in Oman, at every turn when he'd wanted her at his side, she rarely was. It was as if being in this country had created an invisible concrete wall between them. They had but snatched brief encounters in a climate of many forbiddances. Belonging to two separate worlds their lives were policed by a myriad of boundary lines.

He realised it was still less than a week since they'd flown in from London, and as he pondered on all the recent tumultuous events, he realised they'd entered a world he could never have imagined. He cursed his misfortune to have landed in Oman at a time when, a hitherto bastion of stability in the Middle East, had suddenly and unexpectedly slipped from its pedestal and fallen into chaos.

Then he thought how fortuitous for his new career this had been. He felt no clarity, he was utterly confused. He wondered whether he was suffering some delayed reaction to the earlier explosion. The closest people he was with more often than not appeared to be caught up in a debilitating condition caused by shock and loss.

He recalled how from the very day of their arrival in Muscat, after the Sultan had died, they had found themselves caught up in Oman's political transition – unsettling, as yet unclear, from precisely what to what. That transition now seemed to be heading in a terrifying direction, the promise of peaceful change passing into a civil war with no sign of an end.

He thought of Abdul Aziz, Raqiyah's father – first a prisoner, then released, then murdered by a sniper's bullet. The memory made him shudder. His dead image, the executioners bullet hole in the forehead, all came to mind many times a day, and he wondered whether the shock of that too, like a delayed reaction, was something he was going to pay for in the coming days and weeks.

His own early visits to the British Embassy were remembered for the queues, where all sensible foreigners were trying to fly out – why hadn't he got the message to get out to, whilst he still could? Hadn't he been thinking straight? Had he in fact made a string of bad decisions? Was he destined to always make bad choices? Maybe this foreign correspondent lark was too much for him, might even make an end of him? Maybe he was born to fail?

Then the ambiguous Hassim had appeared, as if from nowhere – at one moment an apparently caring brother and family man, yet also a revolutionary leader. Hassim whose moods swung from disconcerting humour to zealous religious revolutionary. Once the rebellious son, now the grown man with a "wanted" sign over his head.

Had he been emotionally misled when he'd thrown in his lot with Raqiyah, and allowed himself to take a trip from the capital to the interior on her brother's suggestion? In making such a journey to Nizwa, hadn't he jumped out of the frying pan into the fire? Which side was destined to win? He had simply no idea, nor an idea how long the uncertainty would last, but neither side, capital nor interior, were likely to offer him a helping hand. He was in dire straits. There was only one conclusion to draw, he was on his own.

As he took stock, he counted up all the occasions, the moments when things that had turned steadily worse for him day by day – each day's events, he concluded, were only going in one direction – plunging downhill fast. Like being in a car without brakes, surely the wise thing to do was to get off now before it hurtled to self-destruction.

His and others' early expectations of a smooth succession to a new Sultan in power were becoming more remote by the day, with foreign powers flexing their military muscle and lining up to take part. It looked bad, and he had no escape plan. He thought he needed to come up with something, and soon. Once before in his life, when the odds were stacked against him, he'd made a bid for freedom, but he wasn't sure he'd cope with the stress a second time.

He was still desperate to talk to Raqiyah again, but no chance to do so yet presented itself. He seemed doomed to wait in his bedroom or pace the corridors. This was no life for them.

On a brighter note, he'd had to admit his foreign correspondent role had had a flying start. The pieces he'd just sent to London had been valued by his editor as if they were gold dust. Just now, by return email, had come a follow up response asking him to send the video clip he'd shot at the mosque. He was also asked if they could arrange a live interview with him, and he was to get back to them with a convenient time for this. As London were several hours behind Oman, he thought he might do something later after dark, after supper. He might also know more by then. Somehow being valued, being useful, helped.

Dusk fell quickly in the Middle East, but at this time of year there was so much heat from the searing sun stored in the sand, rocks and walls, the temperature didn't fall with the sun's disappearance. Being near the Arabian Gulf made the hot air unbearably humid, such that it was almost impossible to function. Life was a struggle.

Adam was hot, perspiring, finding it ever more difficult to concentrate, but he knew if he didn't strive to apply himself he'd lose it. He could feel his pulse pumping hot blood in his ears, still hissing quietly from the explosion. He wiped his wet brow on his white sleeve. Even the air conditioning in the house was losing the will. He had to press on.

Opening up his laptop, he switched on, and looked again at the video piece he'd taken earlier outside the mosque. Beads of sweat fell from his forehead onto the keyboard. He'd been apprehensive on seeing the images earlier for the first time, but knew he had to look now at them again through professional eyes. He had to check it prior to sending, assess whether it would be any good to London at all.

As he began to watch the image of the table party being introduced in the bright sun outside the Nizwa mosque, his raised arm holding the shot remarkably steady and in frame, he didn't anticipate the shock he'd feel as the image flashed white and the camera turned skyward from the blast. Then, several seconds of shaking trauma followed, so evidently the immediate aftermath of an explosion. Noises that his own deafened ears hadn't registered initially had been fully captured by the microphone and suddenly all the sounds of blast, mayhem and human agony screamed in his ears for the first time, bringing back the event afresh. He knew London needed material like this – it was good – it could be the making of him.

When he'd gathered himself together again, he labelled, then emailed the film clip to his editor, resolving he never wanted to see it again. Job done, his hands were still quivering.

Adam realised he'd been badly shaken up. He snapped the laptop shut and headed across to the kitchen for some company and another cold drink. Kitchens were usually good places for therapy, relaxed conversation, something to nibble, the place of the humdrum ordinary things of daily existence. He could hear conversation and pushed open the door.

'Perfect timing Adam,' said Hassim, 'Raqiyah was just saying we ought to help you get out of here. The problems of Oman are not yours and for your own safety and security she thinks we ought to get you to your Embassy. I know it's easier said than done, may take a bit of arranging given the hardening of lines between interior and capital, but what do you think? Worth a try?' he said ambivalently.

Adam looked round at the others. He didn't know what to say, he was lost for words. He glanced at Raqiyah who was looking down at the floor and wondered what she was really thinking. He was determined he would talk with her before answering Hassim's question, so he dodged it, for the present.

'I'm thirsty, hungry too. What do we all say about something to eat? No one can take decisions on an empty stomach,' he ventured as confidently as he could. Hassim threw up his hands in frustration, as if to say he'd tried his best and this was all the response he'd got, but he let the matter drop.

Everyone quickly agreed food was needed. It had been a difficult day and indeed everyone was very hungry, the enticing smells in the kitchen only serving to emphasise the point. With the gathering of plates, cutlery, glasses, serviettes and a mat on which to place hot food, the large old table was quickly prepared. A short while later, chairs were scraped across the marble floor as everyone settled down to eat, gathered round the common table.

This evening there was no separation of men and women. At this time of crisis people felt more comfortable being all together and wanted to talk, though convention was only partially set to one side – the three men sitting one side of the table, the three women on the other. Only Maryam raised an eyebrow at the thought all should eat like this, but chose not to remonstrate. She was still wearing sombre clothes as one in mourning and had called upon the other women to join her earlier as she'd led her daily mourning prayers for Abdul Aziz.

Tonight there was lamb, though Adam thought it was hard to tell it apart from goat. It was the smell of the fresh bread that made his mouth water. The green beans Raqiyah had been preparing were served with a spicy and very tasty tomato and onion side dish, like a salsa. Adam was not only hungry for food, but for information and to engage further with Hassim.

'While you were out, did you manage to get a clearer picture of the realities here? I mean, what's the word on the street?' he asked.

'There's a tense stand off between forces on the road between here and the capital – a kind of front line if you like. A few shots have been exchanged, but there's no news of any casualties. Tanks have been transported by lorry to positions just to the rear of that point, but so far taking only a defensive stance. We've had some Saudi special forces visit to advise, can't say more about that, and we've taken delivery of some additional defensive hardware from Saudi of our own. That's also something I can't say more about.'

'So on the military front tensions and preparations are escalating. Forces are, well… facing one another in an uneasy stand-off? That's so?'

'That's the sum of it, but I'm not a military man,' Hassim answered flatly.

'But what's happening politically? What are you hearing from the capital about the succession? Is there any talk more widely of negotiations or of a two nations outcome?' asked Adam.

'The head of the armed forces is definitely running things in Muscat. Him and the British military, that is. Which is one reason I think we ought to think of helping you leave, Adam. The swiftly changing realities are, that right now, the Interior and Saudi are facing off against the Capital and the British – you may soon find yourself a persona non grata here. Oh, and not to alarm you, but on both sides there are numerous stories of people being picked up by the security forces – I wouldn't want you to be one of them.'

Even if it did contain an offer of help, the light-hearted presentation of the situation went down badly with Adam. He blamed Hassim for getting him to the Interior in the first place – the man wanted a foreign correspondent to tell the Imamate story – end of. However, he needed to keep on side with Hassim and suppressed his rising anger with a shrug – his expression meaning, "you know best".

Adam desperately wanted his long overdue conversation with Raqiyah more than ever – to make a plan they both could agree to. Two minds had to be better than one. In a non-committal way he said to Hassim, 'You think it's as bad as that?'

'I'm afraid so. Trouble is I'm being theoretical about getting you out. I don't yet have a way of making it actually happen, so you'll have to bear with me on that one. You'll be with us as our guest a little longer, Adam. Don't worry we'll look after you,' he said with another grating smile.

The trouble was, Adam couldn't ever work out whether Hassim was being sincere or not. Any confidence he might have had in him prior to today evaporated in that moment. He looked across at Raqiyah, wondering how well she really knew her brother. Presently he just couldn't read her face either.

The rest of the meal passed with only small talk – who's getting the next day's shop? when would Hassim be in again? That kind of thing. Maryam seemed to be withdrawing in on herself more and more. Adam wondered if he was seeing signs of depression, but who was he to know? Maryam had shown little of herself. He wish he knew her better, but didn't know where to start.

'We need to have some kind of plan for tomorrow,' Adam stated, looking at everyone and nobody in particular at the same time. No one came up with anything.

The meal over, Hassim excused himself with calls to make and headed off upstairs, mobile in hand. This left Adam feeling frustrated as the women started t clear the table.

Adam, wanted to kick out against the fixed gender roles, and decided to show willing and begin helping to clear the crocks from the table, but the two older women tut-tutted so vociferously he was made to give in and reluctantly backed off. Their message – men need to know their place here. Adam tried another approach.

'Would it be alright if Raqiyah showed me the view from the roof?' Adam asked Maryam. He knew he was pushing it and expected a "No", but to his surprise she simply nodded her assent as she noisily scooped up another pile of crocks for the sink. Maybe his request was a battle she didn't want to have. It seemed that with Maryam you win a few, you lose a few. He acknowledged the generosity with a 'thank you.'

The two walked up to the roof. Sharply defined stars lit the dark night sky. Looking out over the moonlit landscape it was surprisingly quiet. It looked timeless, unchanging. Very occasionally the sound of a car or motorbike could be heard somewhere unseen, in the distance. Momentarily, it felt to Adam that he was in another world, a parallel universe to his own, and a very long way from home.

'So glad you did that Adam. I tried to be with you earlier, but she said "No" to me. Since Father died she's been up and down, a bit unpredictable, I just don't know how to read her.'

'Me neither. I was going to ask you about Hassim. I need to be honest with you. Just between us, I think I've been duped. Yes, a big part of me wanted to stay with you, but it was

Hassim who fixed it to get me here for his own political ends. All that touring round yesterday, it was to get the Imamate's story out into the world, through me, his available foreign correspondent! Now I don't know whether he really means he'll help me to get out or not, even if he can find a way. I just don't know him well enough. I wondered whether you knew how his mind worked?'

'I don't know either. What Mama and I can't dismiss is that he's lined himself up with the Imamate cause here, big time. I don't know whether he's told you what his role is, but just from things I've overheard, what Mama's said, he's quite senior, a bit like a civilian Chief Exec.'

'That was my impression too, but he's not letting on to me. He's trying to protect himself. Maybe he doesn't fully trust us either.'

'He's right to think that,' said Adam testily.

'But in the day we've been here we can be certain of one thing, we're now in the middle of an escalating and unstable political scenario. My instinct is that things could very rapidly change for the worse, and all the recent stability under the last Sultan is beginning to… will evaporate as quickly as, well... as rain in summer.'

'My sentiment exactly. I think we need to try and plan to get out – the two of us,' said Adam quietly, conscious that sound carried long distances in the still night air. Raqiyah looked at him. Adam could see she was thinking on his words.

'That would mean I'd cut myself off from my family.'

'I don't mean that to happen.'

'But we both know that's the reality. After three years at Exeter University, I feel I've been changed. They warned us about cultural disorientation and adjustment – I know exactly what they meant now. But my mind's made up. If you truly love me, Adam, I will come with you, but you have to know that I doubt if I'd see my family, possibly never again.'

'I haven't thought this through. We need time to think about us. We need time to come up with an escape plan too. All I can think is we have two options. We ask Hassim for help to get us out – but then we're entirely in his hands and I'm not sure he really would, and he definitely won't help you to get out. He sees you as his responsibility now Abdul Aziz is no longer with us. I think the only option is we make a secret dash for it in your Father's car. I could alert the Embassy.'

'I'm not sure that would do any good,' said Raqiyah, her two hands resting flat on the warm wall of the rooftop.

'Let's give it some thought. I'll quietly ring Brian Merryweather at the Embassy to seek his guidance. I'll see what he advises on current flights out of the country for us both, to get us back to England. My parents in London have room, they'd put us up, they always have. It'll give us time to plan what next. You OK with that?'

'Yes, Adam,' but her answer carried no conviction.

Silence fell between them.

It was then they heard the unmistakeable sound of someone out on the stairs, nearby. Had they heard their conversation? They were definitely coming their way. They took a step apart, to establish a respectable space from each other and gazed out over the landscape, looking into the distance, merging their silence with the silence of the starlit Arabian night. At any other time it would be described as romantic. The door to the roof patio swung open. They both turned. It was Maryam. She was clutching two glasses of steaming drinks.

'Dishes are all done. Thought you'd like this,' she said, handing them each a mint tea.

'Thank you, Mama,' said Raqiyah warmly.

'Yes, thanks…' added Adam.

Maryam moved closer and stood in the space between them, also gazing out across the quiet expanse, the stars even brighter now – she was back in her regular chaperone role. They'd had as much time alone as her conscience would permit. She was not going anywhere. Their time together was over. Nothing had been settled. Adam looked out at the silent starlit Arabian night and saw a fierce beauty in it.

Deciding on taking a gamble, he then asked, 'Maryam, what do you think I should do?'

It was a deliberately open question, but he hoped it also made her think her opinion was important to him. She was quiet for a moment before replying.

'I think you're in real danger. I think you should save your own life and go, get somewhere safe. You don't belong here. Come, let's all go downstairs, I think it's time to talk about it.'

She led the way down, Adam and Raqiyah following.

55

The three of them were back downstairs in the kitchen, sitting round what had become their impromptu conference table. They had the room to themselves.

'Adam, your safest course is to talk to your Embassy first,' said Raqiyah. 'They may be helping other Brits and have organised something, an escape route, you know.'

'Doubt it,' said Adam. 'From what I saw from my visits there, they wait for the needy to come banging on their door and then they don't exactly offer much help.'

'Ring them anyway, Adam, nothing to lose by making one call,' said Maryam. 'Raqiyah and I need to talk, go and do it, you should. We'll wait here, to hear what you can find out. It's got to be worth a try.'

Adam couldn't think of any good reason why not, he shrugged and obediently took himself off to the privacy of his bedroom to make his call. He'd also finally resolved to talk to his parents, give them a heads up that he was thinking of coming home, possibly with Raqiyah. But then he wasn't sure whether it was a good time to ring when things were so uncertain, and with Raqiyah's loyalties so torn. So he decided to put the call off again – he'd do it later. He'd make the call to Brian first. He was relieved when he got straight through.

'Hi Brian,' he said. 'I need to be thinking about how I can safely extricate myself from the Interior and get on my way back home to London. What do you advise? Oh, and Raqiyah Nahari will possibly be travelling with me,' he added, not certain whether, in the event, she would, but wanting to explore the option, just in case. There was a long pause at the other end.

'Let's talk abut you first. You'll need to make your own way here to the Embassy. We book group tickets each day on Oman Air for people wanting to leave, then our minibus takes everyone down directly to the airport and their allocated flight home. We had a few hiccups earlier in the week. One or two people were taken off the bus at check points, those not allowed to leave, but it's working better now.' He didn't elaborate further.

'Do you have any secure transport arrangements for people like myself, those who need to get from the Interior to the capital?' asked Adam.

'No, afraid not, not yet anyway. You'll have to negotiate your own way out of the Imamate. That could be tricky. I'd advise against taking the main road down, Highway 15, to here as there have been a few incidents, flare ups between the military forces facing one another. I can't say who starts these. It's been especially volatile since the explosion at Nizwa mosque. No one seems to be travelling from Nizwa to the capital currently, so I suspect that route out really is a no-no. Officially, our advice is that all civilians keep away from all check points until tensions ease.'

'No telling when that will be, I suppose?'

'No. Things are said to be quieter to the north, in the mountains, but I really don't know whether that's true, it's just what people are saying.'

'You mean the roads toward the Hajar mountains are safer?'

'Yes, possibly. If you went that route, you could get out via the Emirates. But Adam I'm not in any position to advise you one way or the other. You need to get some local intelligence.'

'OK, I'll look into it. And what about Raqiyah. Can she fly to London with me?'

'Ah. Now then… she'll be an Omani citizen won't she, and she'll need to apply for a visa from here first. That might be a problem. London's issued new instructions for foreign nationals wanting to leave Oman. She'll need to come to the Embassy in person during a working day, register, then complete and submit a visa application form. I'm sorry, but she'll then have to join the already long queue of Omani nationals waiting for answers. You know how it is, the UK government's very sensitive on immigration, asylum seekers, that kind of thing. The new Plymouth MP, Harry McNamara spoke in the House yesterday, and created quite a stir.' Adam was all too familiar with the politics of Harry McNamara and stifled an expletive.

'And assuming she managed to safely get to the Embassy, and she filled in the paperwork, how long will she have to wait there for her visa?'

'Oh, Adam, I don't think you understand. Staff here run checks on all visa applications and then when these have been done, they are sent back and forth to London, and then in the course of time, a decision is reached. We then send an email or message to the applicant as to the individual decision. Applicants then come and collect their visa. They then get added to the permission granted list and wait their turn for a flight place to come up.'

'Come on Brian, tell me how long it takes. It's not that she is a difficult applicant. She's just come back here after three years studying in Exeter. How many applicants have you had, and how many decisions made?'

'Sorry, but it is a bit more complicated than you realise,' he replied evasively. 'We have a problem in the UK with people overstaying after finishing UK courses, so we'd need to see evidence of the applicant's employment in the UK and financial evidence that they'd be able to support themselves. Both of these aspects need to be verified and given the unrest, people are finding it hard to get the information they need to support their application – you understand.'

'This sounds like a bureaucratic obstacle course. It sounds like beginning a race to be told there's no finishing line, yes?' said Adam finally venting his frustration.

'I hear what you are saying, yes, but we're all under a lot of pressure here with large numbers of applicants, new rules from London, and reduced resources in difficult times. It'll all take time…'

'To sum up then, my Embassy can't help us?'

'We can only do what we can, Adam. Maybe you could contact your employer in London. They might be able to advise you.'

'Certainly will Brian. Goodnight,' Adam offered as politely as he could manage, wanting only to close a deeply frustrating conversation.

Adam stared at his mobile in disbelief, still reeling from the call. The reality hit him hard like a blow beneath the belt, winding him. He paused and took some measured breaths, to get control. He realised he was doing this more and more often and wondered just how long he'd be able to hold back a full blown anxiety attack. If that happened he'd be no use to anyone, least of all himself.

He had to face it, the Embassy was no immediate use, they were trapped with no way out. Raqiyah was unlikely to be given a visa to travel any time soon, and realistically it just wasn't going to happen that she popped into Muscat in person to make her visa application and then called back at some indefinite future date to collect it, in the unlikely event one was ever issued. It would be such a long shot. He held his head in his hands and took two more slow breaths. Raqiyah would have to stay, so might he. The reality floored him.

Getting a grip on himself, he decided to take Brian's advice and call his editor at CNPI in London. This too was a less than helpful call. His editor told him, 'as you're the man on the ground, you're the one to know what's a sound plan after considering your options.' In his view, Adam should make the best plan he could to get out of Oman if things were as unsafe as they seemed to be. If there were any costs, then of course he should submit them with his expenses. The brief call was getting him no further forward.

Adam then asked about Raqiyah. It was a mistake.

'Your Omani girl friend, well that's your private affair. She's not the company's responsibility, surely Adam, you know that? She may have to stay behind. It's her country after all'.

Then his editor, perhaps realising how harsh his reply must have sounded and remembering Adam was a prize asset where he was, seemed to have a bright idea – and suggested that rather than leave the Middle East, he might consider going to nearby Dubai where there was a company flat he could use for the time being. He'd be able to work as a correspondent from there, and still be close to the action. Adam was to let him know what he decided on before leaving Nizwa.

Finally, after reviewing together the two lots of material and the video Adam had sent through to him earlier, Adam asked the editor a small favour – would he call his parents to reassure them he was OK? The editor agreed to this simple request and promised he'd see to it immediately. Adam gave him their number. At least that felt like a positive result.

Call over, Adam knew that at some stage he'd have to make his own call to his parents, but he'd put off the moment again for now. He made his way directly down to the kitchen where he assumed Maryam and Raqiyah would be. He was ready now to tell them that they needed to talk about an exit strategy.

Raqiyah and Maryam were talking in hushed tones, leaning over the kitchen table, heads almost touching, a certain solemnity to their conversation.

'Come and join us Adam,' said Maryam who heard him enter. Adam sat down.

'Mama thinks you should leave. She doesn't want you to. She's appreciated your presence. Having you around since Daddy died has been good. But, she's been trying to impress on me that she would be failing in her duty of hospitality, her care of you as the family guest, if anything were to happen and she feels that she can't be sure of guaranteeing your safety.' Raqiyah looked to her mother who nodded in agreement and seemed happy for her to say more.

'She's been telling me that Hassim is totally committed to the Imamate cause and because of this, you might find the government in Muscat might not deal kindly with you. We think because you have been the foreign corespondent mouthpiece for the Imamate regime since yesterday, that also changes things there for you. She's not entirely happy that Hassim has dragged you into our Omani domestic agenda. We've been talking about what options are left open.'

'Please, I wasn't forced to come to Nizwa and I wanted to follow up the story. I've only been doing what foreign correspondents do. Your thinking makes sense to me, it's time to get out. The Embassy's no help – I just called them – so forget them. The only suggestion they could make was that I take the road north by the Hajar Mountains. They think it's quieter, many safer out that way. Brian said the road to the capital was impossible, no one's getting through that way. Then I called my employer and he said I was the best person to judge whether to stay or leave. Taking the two calls together, both Embassy and my boss lead me to think I should try and head for the Emirates. There's a company flat in Dubai, just a half day's drive away if I take the direct road – that's Route 21. The flat in Dubai's free for me to use. I've just got to get there.'

'Go for it Adam. Please use Abdul Aziz's car. It's yours to take,' said Maryam.

'No... I couldn't,' said Adam realising this was extraordinarily generous.

'Yes, I insist,' she said, and so Adam agreed.

'Mama says she and the family are safe enough living here with Hassim's in-laws. They could soon move to another house, a field house, if they needed to, if things got bad, but they won't go back to Muscat, not until things are settled, and who knows when that will be?'

'But what about you, Raqiyah?' asked Adam. His tone betraying his feelings for her and he knew Maryam would know it too, but right now he didn't care. He'd done with always behaving correctly. She looked at him, with some sadness in her eyes.

'I finished at Exeter Uni, with a good degree, same as you, hoping to come back and find a future career for myself here in Oman. Inside of a week my world's come crashing down. I lost my Dad, my rock, who backed me from when I was a little girl. He made sure I had an education and supported me right through. Since we came back here I've had to flee my home like a refugee, all my things in one suitcase. And I see my wonderful country crashing out of the modern age, going back to ancient tribal feuds. An age of uncertainty is dawning which could go one of three ways.'

'How do you mean three ways?' asked Adam.

'First, we could end up living in a military state, one allied to Britain. We'd be using our oil wealth, or what's left of it, to fund attempts to re-establish our modern Oman, using the motto, "open for business as normal"; or second, it could flip the other way so we return to the old days of a conservative Imamate – I'd have to buy a new set of clothes to cover up more! That would only be the start of it. Or thirdly, we could end up living in something a lot worse – I've this sinking feeling we're going to be another Yemen, facing a disastrous civil war, with never an end in sight. Another proxy war for foreign powers to fight out their differences on Omani sand. That's the three!'

'You ought to be the foreign correspondent; I think you're spot on in your analysis, and I don't see any joy in any one of those options,' said Adam.

'Adam, I've decided on something for myself. I feel bad because I'm Mama's only daughter, and at this time of loss I ought to be at her side. I find it very hard to think straight right now. I don't sleep at night for the nightmares and I don't feel at home anywhere. Adam, while you're making your calls I told Mama I'm going to be leaving Oman. One option is I go to Uncle Abdul in Istanbul. I'd stay there until it was safe and get a job there in the meantime, in Turkey. I'm sure he'd help me. Turkey is still accessible to Omanis.'

'What's the other option?' asked Adam.

'I come with you to Dubai. That's more tricky. You know how it is in a Muslim country.' Raqiyah looked across at Maryam and Adam knew Maryam was against such an idea. 'Keeping a good public reputation would be impossible.'

'Then I think you should either stay with your Mother or head for Istanbul to your uncle's family,' said Adam. He didn't want to be the cause of any more distress or division in the Nahari household.

Both Maryam and Raqiyah appreciated the respect in Adam's reply.

'What about Hassim?' asked Adam. 'He'll have a big say in all of this won't he? He's the head of the house. We need to talk with him. It'll all be up to him.'

56

'We can't leave without Hassim's help,' said Raqiyah. 'Well if not his help, knowing he won't try and stop us. He's been up in his room for ages. He's still in, isn't he Mama?'

'I think so. He'd a lot of calls to make. I'd have known if he'd gone out. I'll give him a call.'

Maryam left the kitchen and called out upstairs, her shrill loud voice reaching up through the house's central stairwell. Whilst she was out of the room, Adam briefly clenched Raqiyah's hand. There was the noise of a door shutting upstairs, then Hassim's voice and the sound of his approaching footsteps could be heard as he made his way down. Hassim and Maryam came into the kitchen. It was getting late in the evening.

'Hassim, have you a few minutes, please,' asked Maryam.

'Sure. I've been somewhat preoccupied. It's been call after call. I'd lost track of the time.'

The four sat round the kitchen table as if the earlier conference had simply continued after a short break.

'Hassim. The time has come when we must help Adam to leave Oman,' said Maryam.

Hassim looked across at Adam, giving nothing away. Then he spoke.

'I've learned much this evening, and I can tell you this Adam, that I can't see things getting any easier in this country for some while, and as I said earlier, I too think you should leave. I'll be honest. I'd be quite happy to have a foreign corespondent here on the spot. I fear however, it won't be so easy to guarantee your safety in the coming days. I haven't forgotten your loyalty to this family, and I want to help you.'

'Thank you'.

'You need to know the main road from Nizwa to Muscat isn't passable. Earlier this evening there were pot shots being exchanged at regular intervals between the military on both sides. It's not stopping. It simply isn't safe to head that way. Besides you'd be apprehended before you got very far. I think if you did get away from the Interior, Sultanate forces would be waiting to arrest you. Sorry, but I'm just saying how it is.'

'So what do you suggest, Hassim?' asked Adam.

'I think you'd be safest getting out by the mountain road north, heading over the border toward El Ain and into the Emirates. It's a couple of hours drive to the border and then a straight road as far again to Dubai. I'm told you can still get out that way and there are no army checkpoints, either Imamate or anyone else.'

'I want to leave too,' ventured Raqiyah.

Hassim turned his head to face her. He clearly hadn't expected this.

'Out of the question,' he said. 'I need you here to look after Mama. Sorry Mama, but you're not yourself and I can't be the one to help you.'

'I'm happy with her going Hassim, I'll be fine. I've spent years being on my own whilst your father was working abroad,' said Maryam. 'I think she'd like to go to Uncle Abdul in Istanbul. This is no place for her now and I want her to be happy and safe. On this occasion Hassim, I must insist.'

Hassim fell silent. Maryam's intervention had also been unexpected. Adam could see Hassim's mind working behind the dark brown eyes. He was weighing everything up carefully. He stood up.

'OK. The first priority is your safety Adam. I think you should take Father's Mercedes tomorrow morning at first light. I will travel with you, drop you over the border at El Ain, it's a sizeable place, then I'll drive straight back. It's all the time I can give. Hopefully I'll be back for midday prayers. If you want to come along too Raqiyah, that's fine by me. But we drop Adam there and return. He can easily get transport the last 75 miles to the north from El Ain to Dubai. That's my final word on the matter. You'll be safe. Alright, Adam?'

'Yes, thank you,' he replied, quietly thinking he had little other choice open to him.'

Hassim turned to Raqiyah, his voice softening, 'I'm not saying you can't go to Uncle Abdul in Turkey, but your request isn't so urgent or so pressing. I'd like you to help out here for a little longer. There's sense in that. I promise I will contact Uncle Abdul later to see what can be arranged. It may take a little while, but I will help sort it. I give you my word. That's the end of the matter. I need to make more calls tonight, you understand. Adam, you will need to get your things together for the morning. I suggest we're ready to leave by 6am. Have you decided whether you're coming along for the ride Raqiyah?'

'Yes, Hassim, I want to,' was all she said. She wasn't going to argue further, she'd knew she'd won a significant concession. She held on to the promise of a window of opportunity opening for her, and it would not be in Oman. Hassim's promise to her allowed her to breathe again. She saw in her mind's eye the chance, however unformed as yet, that she might progress with her life, maybe take a post-graduate course, make something of herself.

The immediate and painful reality of parting from Adam was beginning to dawn on her too. After spending every day with each other prior to coming to Oman, this past week had been a slow process of being torn apart, the final act of which would be tomorrow morning when an unknown period of separation would begin.

First, physical closeness had gone, then even time together for conversation. The precious moments of intimate chatting, the humour, the fun, the teasing, had all but disappeared when they stepped off the plane at Muscat. It had been all of two years they'd been an item in Exeter. Those early days of risk and excitement as they'd became friends, the unthinkable recklessness with which she had taken up with Adam, then the two of them sharing a house together with Bilal and Sophie. How she missed Sophie too. She must call her, it had been too long. She resolved she would speak to her later. One chapter of her life was closing, like the drawing of a curtain across the stage at the end of a play. But maybe, it was only the interval and the curtains would part for her again.

At the thought of Adam's imminent parting, she wondered when, and indeed if, she would ever see him again. She recollected, perhaps nostalgically what she recalled were overwhelmingly happy times in England, and how much her happiness was built around being with Adam with all his foibles – his love of bikes that had first taken him to the Muslim world in his gap year. His post traumatic stress when he started Uni and her coming alongside him to help him, and look after him – she marvelled at how much better, how much stronger he was now from that vulnerable young boy she had first met. Indeed how handsome and manly he had become. Though after this week, even now she wondered how he really was, how he was managing his stress, and realised she hadn't been close enough to him to really know and it filled her heart with a deep sadness. She wanted to care for him like she had at the beginning. All this was another loss in a week of building losses.

Her thoughts turned to her Father. It had been true what she had told her Mama, that he had made her who she was. As she thought of him, she knew his legacy in her was that she should be an independently minded woman. Though she couldn't see how, she knew she would one day break free from the enclosed and now diminished world to which she had returned. She saw Maryam and herself as two quite different women and she did not know how long she could cope with being under the same roof as her Mother. To do so would mean more dumbing down of her true self, a slow death, and she was determined that shouldn't happen.

Turkey was now in her sights, somewhere she could envisage a new beginning. She owed it to her Father's memory, she owed it to herself. The thought kindled some flame of inner strength, almost a spiritual moment. It was enough to sustain her. She heard Adam's voice. She looked up. The others must have slipped out, there were only the two of them still in the kitchen.

'Raqiyah, Raqiyah,' he said softly repeating her name. 'It's just the two of us. Maryam said "goodnight" but I don't think you were listening. Hassim's gone, busy with his calls. I'm glad you said you would come along tomorrow. I'm only sorry you won't be coming with me all the way.'

'I was so happy to think you were coming to Oman, but neither of us foresaw what kind of place we were coming to,' she said.

'How could we? The world changed when we arrived. The process of succession will change this country for ever.'

'Our two countries are so very different. Scratch the skin here and what do you find – deep seated conservative religion and tribal loyalties, fierce patriarchy and old allegiances. A minute ago I came to a decision, in part to honour Daddy, but mainly to be true to myself. I'm going to leave Oman, make my own way in life, my uncle in Turkey will help me, I know he will. That's where I'll begin.'

'And we'll meet up again soon,' said Adam looking longingly at her, the tears welling in her eyes.

She nodded her yes.

They embraced, holding each other close for as long as they dared. Now there were tears in both their eyes.

57

The quietness of the night had been punctured by the sound of occasional distant gunfire. Gunfire was always unsettling.

Each time he heard it, Adam wondered if it was nearer or further away. Things were definitely getting worse. A couple of times there had been something flying overhead, a plane or more likely a drone. He didn't know it, but no one in the house slept soundly. The nearby noises in the night, even the silences, together with the lack of sleep, left everyone's nerves frayed.

All wondered whether the next night time noise would be closer. Periodic military activity could be heard from the adjacent Bahla Fort, a reminder of the many desert camouflaged, fatigue dressed troops stationed there.

To Adam's mind he just couldn't feel safe being near so many armed men. Unsurprisingly, even the local cats were unsettled, spats breaking out as they sorted out their own disputes. Thankfully, all remained safe in the Nizwa home, noises came and went, and eventually the long night passed, the dawn came. It was the beginning of a second week.

It was already hot as Adam showered and then pulled on his white dishdasha. Packing had taken but a moment, his few things once more stuffed inside his rucksack. He sent a final email to London telling his editor his plans and asking he be forwarded the details of the Dubai flat and how to access it. By return he was told his parents had been given his message. Adam reminded himself to ring them soon. He was ready leave.

He felt a certain apprehension. There was adrenaline already coursing through his body as he contemplated his escape from a building Omani succession conflict. He felt as wired as if he'd had a double expresso on an empty stomach.

Maybe a more experienced journalist would have decided to stay on and make the most of the situation, getting and sending front line news reports. He knew he wasn't yet that person, he just wasn't ready for that, he was no journalist with a death wish. It was definitely time to leave.

Hassim insisted on driving. He'd pulled off the car's blue tarpaulin one handedly, whilst already making his first mobile calls of the day. Adam insisted on sitting next to Raqiyah in the back. Hassim assented with a nod, his focus on his mobile call.

Maryam had provided food and drinks for them to consume as they travelled. She placed the supplies on the front passenger seat in a wicker basket with a napkin over and gazed at Adam and Raqiyah with an expression of what could only be described as maternal tenderness.

Adam noticed that Raqiyah had put some subtle make up around her eyes, softening her face. She'd done it for him, and he liked that. Sitting next to her he could smell her, the perfume she'd chosen to wear. As he became aware of the familiar clean scent of her hair, he felt an incredible sadness and an ache in the imminent period of separation, so much so, he found it difficult to speak.

As they moved off, the first light of a grey dawn was showing, then only minutes later, it was bright, the golden orb of the sun rising over on the right hand side horizon, goats could be seen already marching out across parched stones in their unending quest to find something to eat.

Adam felt nervous watching Hassim drive with only one hand on the wheel, his attention as much on the phone in his other hand and the decisions in his mind, as on the road ahead.

They hadn't got more than half a mile from Bahla Fort when a sudden loud roar overhead alerted them to low flying aircraft.

Turning their heads, this time, looking back, they could see, and then hear the sound of explosions.

'Oh no! I think they're bombing the army position at the Fort,' said Hassim now looking through his rear view mirror as well as holding his mobile and the steering wheel. 'We need to keep moving.' He ended the call he was on, to urgently pump in another number to follow up what was happening behind them. 'I must get back as soon as I can,' he said.

The car accelerated quickly on the quiet, tarmac highway and soon all that could be seen behind them were two pillars of white smoke swirling high in the morning sky. Adam thought of it as a sign of things to come, but chose to say nothing. His mind seemed to be programmed to one thing – it was time for him to get out.

'I'm calling Mama,' said Raqiyah, 'just to be sure they're OK.'

After trying several times she failed to get through and gave up, leaving her phone resting in her lap. She looked very worried.

Ending his call, Hassim held his phone over his shoulder, 'Try mine,' he said, 'it's satellite.'

To her evident relief, Raqiyah got through to Maryam and was reassured all was well at the house. She learned there had indeed been a bombing raid.

'It shook the house, and put cracks in the hall way wall. After the planes had gone, Hanif went up on the roof to take a look at the fort, to see what damage there was. He says it was a precision raid. All he could see was that the central tower of the fort had been targeted. The flag pole with the white flag of the Imamate is no longer visible. It wasn't possible to see more, but he could hear shouts and sirens. He thinks people would have been injured or worse. The thing is, everyone at home's now on edge, shaken up. This marks another escalation.'

'Can someone get a picture to me later,' asked Adam, thinking it would be good to be able to send something of interest to London later.

'I'll see what I can do,' said Hassim.

'When you and I visited Bahla Fort yesterday morning, the main tower was the centre of operations, like the command room and where the Battalion's HQ were located, soldiers on every floor. What's happened sounds like a surgical strike to disable the place. In which case it could be a serious incident for the local Imamate forces,' surmised Adam, 'what do you think?'

A call came into Hassim preventing a reply. Hassim could then be overheard taking a report from someone. There was an edginess in their conversation. It sounded like something serious was going on somewhere, but it wasn't possible to make out what, hearing just one side of a conversation. The call ended.

'You're right Adam. A serious setback. The force at Bahla Fort are having to regroup under new leadership. The air attack was by British Tornados, so yesterday's flypast looks like it was recognisance for today's bombing. It also means your country has firmly tied itself to the government forces in Muscat and you yourself will not be popular round here. I think we made the right decision to get you out,' he said grimly.

Half an hour later Hassim slowed the Mercedes as he saw what looked like a troop convoy moving slowly up ahead. The white Mercedes followed the end truck which was full of soldiers moving at a sedate pace. The heat was such the canvas sides offering shade had been rolled half way up to allow some ventilation for those inside.

'I was told we'd catch up with this lot,' said Hassim. 'It's safest for us to tack on the end of the line of vehicles rather than try to overtake. We've still an hour to the border. These troops are making their way into the Hajars. The mountains remain our stronghold.'

'That sounds like a retreat to me,' offered Adam, at the same time mentally noting Hassim was clearly very well informed. He could see his remark had irritated Hassim and thought he should have kept his last comment to himself.

'No, not even a strategic withdrawal. However, I'm not going to be drawn into revealing the Imamate's plans to you, Adam. You'll get to know what's happening soon enough,' he said testily.

The landscape was hot and bare, the early morning sun pushing the outside temperature up into the high 30s already. It was going to be another punishing day. The soldiers' heads were down. Was it the heat draining them or the task ahead of them? Occasionally they could be seen taking water.

Raqiyah was quiet, lost in her own thoughts. Adam didn't know what to say to her. The world had suddenly become a very uncertain place, the tension in the car tangible. She nudged him, taking his hand, opening it. Under her hand she placed something in his, something small and metallic. She squeezed his hand closed and wrapped his fingers around it. It could only be a gift. She let go.

Adam glanced between his fingers. It was Abdul Aziz's silver prayer box. He slid it in his pocket and he looked at Raqiyah, saying thank you with his eyes. It felt such a precious gift.

Hassim was on yet another call. How he could concentrate on the driving at the same time defeated Adam. It was probably only the steady pace of the convoy on a straight road that made his driving manageable.

The road was forever dusty grey, mounds of sandy greyness and flat dullness either side swept up to the edge of the tarmac, the sameness of road stretching forward mile after never ending mile. There were glimpses of the cruel looking sharp, high mountains of the Hajars in the distance, like something alien out of Tolkein, a haze already building and removing the early morning clarity of first thing. Everywhere the landscape looked harsh and utterly unforgiving. It was a place of struggle for any form of life.

'We'll be at the town of Ibri soon,' announced Hassim. 'This lot in front will almost certainly take a break and we'll get by. Another half hour further on and we'll have you safely over the border.' It was said in a voice that conveyed he too felt the tension. Hassim, it seemed would be as relieved as the rest of the party to see Adam safely delivered from harm's way.

Soon they were in the outskirts of Ibri. White, low, scattered buildings announced a change of scene. There was absolutely no one about. It wasn't just the heat, people were hunkered down in their own homes, as if waiting for a sudden heavy mountain storm to pass by.

Hassim was correct in his assumption. The convoy began to slow, before peeling off right on to a dirt road. Clouds of dust made all view to that side impossible.

Once on an empty road again, Adam felt easier, not having to stare at military realities the whole time. He could almost believe he was touring, but immediately dismissed the fanciful thought.

'Wouldn't like to be in the last truck with all that dust,' said Adam.

'I think we'll just press on rather than stop here, if that's OK with everyone,' Hassim said, ignoring the remark.

Once through Ibri, and heading out of town, the car picked up speed. It was now not so very far to the border. Adam looked over Hassim's shoulder at the empty road ahead.

'Is it normally so quiet – it's unnerving,' he said.

'You speak too soon! We've got company, a police car behind, it followed us out of town. I'm certain he'll pull us over. Leave the talking with me, and have your passport and IDs ready.'

Sure enough the police car followed for a mile, overtook, then flashed its blue top light a couple of times indicating they were to pull over. Pulse rates started to climb. It all seemed like it was happening in slow motion. It was half a mile before the two vehicles finally pulled to a halt.

Adam watched as both policemen in the car got out. The border once so near, now seemed impossibly far away. Both policemen were armed and both wary. Perhaps they'd already had some intelligence on the car as that belonging to the late Abdul Aziz. Perhaps not. They looked capable and professional. The one stayed back, standing on the far side of the driver's blue door. Adam noticed the police car was also a Mercedes S class, but their version was marked by distinctive blue doors front and rear.

The taller officer walked toward them with a casual swagger as Hassim wound down his driver's window.

'I'm sure I kept to the speed limit,' Hassim ventured in a good humoured tone. The officer said nothing. He stepped away and spoke into his radio.

'Something's up,' said Hassim quietly. They waited. With the engine off, it was getting hot in the car.

The officer, call over, walked purposefully back to talk to Hassim.

'You've just left Nizwa, yes?'

'That's right, at 6am.'

'Where are you heading?'

'The border. True to good Omani hospitality, I'm giving this Englishman, caught out by things here, a lift to the border so he can get home.'

'I'd like to see your papers – all of you,' the officer said, scrutinising the faces of each one of them in turn. Pockets were searched, the documents produced and passed to the waiting hand at the open window.

Passports, IDs and a driving licence in his hand, the policeman strolled back to his car to scrutinise them, no doubt with the aircon on full as he did so. Hurry was not his middle name. His colleague though, didn't move an inch – he just stood and watched them, scrutinising their every move.

Adam could make out the tall officer in the car was on his radio again. He didn't like this interminable delay. What could he be doing? Would they decide not to let him go? He could feel sweat beginning to run down his brow and into his collar. He looked across at Raqiyah who said very little. Hassim, for his part, began taking more mobile calls and this began to annoy Adam.

'Don't you think the police will consider your actions subversive, making calls while your supposed to be patiently waiting?'

'Look these calls may help us, so stay cool, Mr Adam Taylor, right,' he said in measured tones. 'Don't make me want to change my mind about seeing you leave us.' His jest was ill judged and shook his two passengers.

'Sorry,' said Adam, 'just, we're so nearly there.'

Then all of a sudden it was over. The officer got out of his car, strode back to Hassim, handed their papers back, changed his severity for a smile and saluted Hassim.

'Sorry to have detained you, Sir. You will understand we have to check. Have a safe journey. We'll escort you to the border. Follow us if you please.'

Documents went back into pockets. Engines started up and they moved away. The air con kicked in.

'What happened there?' asked Adam. 'How come you carry authority? You got to him didn't you?'

'Adam, you need to to know I am the civil head of the Imamate in Bahla Wilayat. What I say carries weight with the interim authority here. The police work for us not the Sultan. Once he'd checked who I was, he was only to happy to provide us with every assistance.'

'Hassim, forgive me for asking, but do you think Abdul Aziz died because of what you do?'

'Yes. It was a message to me. It's what will happen to me if I don't do what Muscat says. But time has moved on since those days. Their biggest mistake was to release me not knowing that the Imamate was a serious opposition and set to be the next legitimate government. They should never have let me go! They'll be regretting what they did,' he said laughing out loud.

Hassim kept the Mercedes about a car's length behind the police car, which was close, considering the high speed they were going. Adam thought they must look like royalty being given a police escort, but there was no one else on the road to observe them. It was all eerily quiet. The miles were speeding by. They were moving again.

'Nearly there Adam. I've driven this road many times. Another five minutes and you'll see the border. First you'll spot the Omani customs building, then beyond it the Abu Dhabi Emirates one, where you'll need to get yourself a visa for entry. Every government's making its tourists pay for entry visas these days – quite a money spinner. Here we sell visas as readily as bus tickets.'

Hassim kept picking up more mobile calls and the latest one was troubling him.

'There's some serious fighting just outside Muscat, Imamate and Muscat forces are fighting for control of the airport. We definitely made the right choice coming this way.'

Then, eyes on the road ahead he pointed to something. 'Look there's our destination.' His lifted hand waved toward some low buildings less than half a mile away.

Adam looked down to his rucksack by his feet, thinking he'd check his laptop was fully switched off, when suddenly he was aware something was very different and lifted his head. He was never sure afterwards whether it was a premonition or whether he'd heard it coming.

One minute they were following the police car, and beginning to slow down as they approached the border, the next there was an almighty roar as if they'd hit a dirt road at high speed, debris striking the car with violent force. Adam's instinct was they'd been attacked!

Then there was a lurch and their car fell downwards, nose down, they were falling and sliding, before mercifully coming to a sudden jolting halt.

It had stopped upended, at a steep forty five degree angle, still upright, but leaning slightly sideways, lying in a chasm, a huge and dusty crater.

The forward tilting position meant he and Raqiyah were pressed tightly into their restraining seat belts. Neither of them could easily move themselves. Adam had his rucksack strap in one hand, the other trapped in his pocket, clutching a silver box. It was hard to see outside for the dust. He looked across. Raqiyah looked stunned but otherwise alright. She returned his gaze. There was an acrid smell in the air, a smell of something burning.

Adam looked up, the front windscreen had gone, flames licked up from the front of the car. He… they must get out. He didn't want to be burned alive.

Hassim, who had not been wearing his seatbelt was hanging half out of his door with blood pouring from a gaping hole in his forehead. What was left of his serrated face was facing Adam, the one side of his head had collapsed in on itself. Hassim's remaining eye was mercifully closed. No one was at home. His mobile could be heard making plaintiff sounds as someone was calling out, 'what's happened? What's going on? Hassim, Hassim…'

With difficulty, all caught up in his dishdasha, Adam managed to lever himself backwards and unclip his seat belt.

Using the front seat to lean on, he reached for Hassim. Seeing the catastrophic head injury, Adam put his fingers to Hassim's neck to feel for a pulse. He waited, tried again, but there was no sign of life. All the while flames were licking ever higher.

Pushing Raqiyah back in her seat he managed to free her seat belt too. He pointed to Hassim and shook his head. He didn't need to say anything. She understood.

'We need to get out of the car. It's really important, the flames, I can smell fuel. Come on. We need to move, get somewhere safer. You OK? Ready?'

'I'm OK I think.'

'We need to get out. Whoever attacked the first time might have a second go, but we need to be careful don't we.'

Raqiyah looked at Adam for reassurance. Then with an effort she managed to push her heavy door outwards and the two scrambled out her side and upwards into the dusty, hot air. Both moving crab-like on all fours, Adam dragging his rucksack across the ground, Raqiyah her small, fabric handbag.

As Adam looked around him, he saw the police car, that was once in front of them had all but entirely disappeared. He spotted the larger part of what was left of it some fifty yards away to the right. It was a mangled wreck, both Mercedes now burning furiously. There was no sign of the policemen He turned to Raqiyah.

'Move Raqiyah, move. We'll head for those buildings. They must have seen what happened. If you hear any planes, we need to lie flat. I hadn't heard it earlier, but I can hear them now, circling somewhere, over there I think. Can you run?'

'I can try. Can you take my hand?'

Adam and Raqiyah got to the customs building ahead. It was deserted. Rucksack over one shoulder, Raqiyah's hand grasped firmly, both with lungs bursting, they ran on.

'Come on, that building's in the Emirates,' said Adam gripping and pulling her by the hand. 'Come with me. Look their customs officers are there. Come, run to freedom, run Raqiyah, run for your life!'

Afterword

My original vision was to write a contemporary trilogy with the themes of cultural diversity and political extremism to the fore. In giving a serious treatment of these together with several other societal themes set in the genre of thriller I believe these novels to be unique. As sometimes happens with authors, once embarked on a course, it becomes hard to stop and ideas for further books based around the characters familiar to author and reader are now in hand.

Beginning with the stories of Adam, Ali and Kaylah the reader is introduced in **Flashbacks** to what has sadly become a reality – terror on city streets. The book's climax is set in the centre of London on Armistice Day. Aspects of the storyline have been disturbingly prophetic.

Flashbacks was followed by **IStanbul**. It was a privilege for me to spend time in the beautiful historic city of Istanbul in the spring of 2016. Turkey is a country to watch. It lies in the borderlands of east and west and has seen recent political upheaval and religious revival replacing Ataturk's secular republic. **IStanbul** imagines a possible future scenario in which an attempt is made to destabilised the country. In the course of events a visiting England football supporter, Harry McNamara, makes an appearance.

Harry is central to **Harry's England**, a novel which considers the possibility of an extreme right wing candidate being elected to parliament in the South West of England. I found historian Todd Gray's well researched book, 'Blackshirts in Devon', looking at local right wing extremism in the 1930s fascinating and it inspired me to ask the question, could it happen today? Indeed what would happen if the populace became fearful through terrorist activity?

In the course of writing I have been fortunate to have bent the ear of so many people and to have gained from their support and encouragement. Writers in Ottery St Mary and in the Exeter Authors Association have energised and advised. Editors, amongst whom are Jeni Braund, Steve Chapman, Ruth Ward, Angela Harvey and Margaret Whitlock, all kindly advised on the text – the remaining errors are mine! Many other people answered my obscure questions, friends and former colleagues in the inter-faith, policing and Prevent worlds offered their insights – you know who you are and thank you!

Early in 2018 I was fortunate to make a visit to Oman in which the whole of this book is set. My reason for going there was to respond to an invitation offered me to visit when I helped host an Omani group in Leicester a few years ago. I had been impressed by what I heard from them about the Omani tradition of 'tolerance' and the Ibadi Muslim culture in that country. So I wanted to see the place for myself.

When I arrived I discovered an amazingly dramatic and challenging land and a welcoming people. When I learned of the political situation in the country and added a little imagination of my own, I found Oman promised to be a fabulous setting for **Domain**.

As the title suggests, a major theme is the person and their relationship with place. It operates in the novel on a number of levels. This is a universal theme and not a matter that solely concerns Oman and Omanis. Characters in the story also have their personal domain issues. Key characters from the earlier books, are Adam Taylor and Raqiyah Nahari. Raqiyah's family, in particular her father Abdul Aziz Nahari feature. There is a diversity theme, once again operating in **Domain** at a number of levels. Other characters who play significant roles are Raqiyah's mother, Maryam and her brother, Hassim. Rather differently from my earlier books, **Domain** covers a longer period of time, taking the reader back to stories that certainly, as the author, I found so fascinating.

One thing I must underline is that all my novels and their characters are fiction. There is no attempt to demonise anyone or besmirch reputations of countries or cities. Sadly though, the subjects of extremism, terrorism and political instability mean these stories deal with challenges that are deeply felt and reflect the reality that all too many people's lives are damaged by such events.

In writing my hope is that these books serve to prompt helpful discussion, safe places to air ideas and explore societal issues, but most of all to be a good read!

I am always willing to hear from readers and reply to any questions. Please contact me through my website:

<u>http://jehallauthor.com</u>

Suggested Book Group Questions

1. The Nahari family are at the centre of this novel. What kind of family are they?

2. Raqiyah Nahari's life is covered extensively and the reader now knows her better than ever. How would you describe the Raqiyah you see here? What future do you see for her?

3. Adam Taylor has moved on from student life to employment as a foreign correspondent. He is an outsider to Oman and the Nahari family. How well does he handle his new situation? Is it possible to cross cultures?

4. Abdul Aziz's story features at length in the earlier part of the story. What are the highs and lows for him? What were the main challenges he faces and how well did he cope with them? How does knowing his story help you understand Raqiyah's better?

5. In this novel, Adam Taylor and Raqiyah Nahari's relationship enters a new stage. What kind of relationship is possible for them ? Do you think they have a future?

6. The political scene in Oman sets a backcloth before which a drama plays out. Is this political scenario realistic? Is this what could happen if a formerly stable state collapses? What are the key factors, the critical indicators that lead things toward a civil war?

7. Hassim's story is also extensively told. What kind of character is he – a kind brother? a responsible family man? a

terrorist? a religious extremist? What positive as well as negative qualities did he have?

8. How did you feel the story line developed, and did the ending satisfy you? What do you think happens to Raqiyah and Adam next?

9. What does the reader take away from this book?

Flashbacks

J E Hall

This, the author's first novel, introduces the characters featured in subsequent books.

In Flashbacks, Adam Taylor from Muswell Hill, north London, goes on an adventurous solo cycle ride across Europe to the Middle East before going to University.

It ends unexpectedly. Is his life over?

Ali Muhammed is haunted by flashbacks since seeing his father shot before his eyes. He is subsequently trained by IS and is sent to London as a jihadist.

Kaylah Kone has Afro-Caribbean cultural roots. A business studies student in London, she finds her life becomes tangled up with Ali.

All three characters and those around them are drawn into a terrorist plot to attack an Armistice Day parade outside Parliament. Can Ali be stopped and tragedy averted?

'Controversially current, intense and compelling debut thriller, grappling with themes and issues pertinent for contemporary societies'

Dr Irene Pérez-Fernández
University of Oviedo
Spain

IStanbul

J E Hall

This novel is a sequel to Flashbacks.

Ali Muhammed's lone-wolf attack in London on Armistice Day is followed by plans for a new and ambitious terrorist initiative in Turkey. Forces are mobilised. Ali travels from Mosul to Istanbul, and with local help, he hopes IS can destabilise the country.

Adam Taylor, traumatised by the events of the previous year, begins a new life as a student. He is determined to understand Islam better. At the end of his first year he goes to Istanbul with three other students to explore and learn from this great city.

Kaylah Kone, in new circumstances, agrees to help the security services.

Unimaginable tension and life-changing events in Istanbul take the reader on a compelling adventure.

'In the context of our multi-faith world and with a mix of the familiar and unfamiliar this drama succeeds in both entertaining and challenging the reader.'

Rt Rev Dame Sarah Mullally
Bishop of London

Harry's England

J E Hall

Harry McNamara is from Plymouth in the South West of England. A young man with ideals, not ones you'd probably agree with, but he can be very persuasive.

When he declares his intention to stand as an extreme right wing candidate for his parliamentary seat, after a slow start, his campaign suddenly gains momentum.

There are unknown sinister forces at work behind the scenes and Harry is suddenly on a roll.

Terrorist attacks in Exeter and Plymouth unsettle the population. Might these turn things Harry's way?

Adam Taylor, Raqiyah Nahari and Clive Kone don't like Harry one bit, but what can they do?

In the background the police and security services have a job on their hands.

Will Harry get elected?

'A novel of our times with all the twists of an accomplished thriller'

Ann Widdecombe

What's Next?

J E Hall is currently working on his next novel.

It returns the action to north London and is due to be published in 2019.

See the author's website for further details, for reviews and anticipated date of publication:

http://jehallauthor.com